THE DEVIL INSIDE

By Stephen Coulter

THE DEVIL INSIDE

DAMNED SHALL BE DESIRE

THE LOVED ENEMY

THE DEVIL INSIDE

A novel of Dostoevsky's life

STEPHEN COULTER

DOUBLEDAY & COMPANY, INC.
GARDEN CITY, NEW YORK
1960

Library of Congress Catalog Card Number 60-13997

PART ONE

Chapter One

1

They were shouting and calling, their voices tiny across the great frozen river.

"Lash 'em up. Go on!"

"Matvey. Matv-e-e-y. We're gaining!"

The two sleighs flew over the ice of the Neva, the tingling crystal air snatching away the sound of the shouting voices, young lusty voices livened by French wines. They flashed past the Court Quay, past the line of the Tsars' classical palaces and the golden needle of the Admiralty spire. The lights were showing on the Troitsky Bridge and the sky over the city was black as steel. For a moment the sleigh that had moved up hung level with the other, the half-dozen army cadets in it waving arms, the harness bells jingling, and the horses straining forward with bolting eyes. Over the ice the runners skimmed with a fine high-singing note. Then, having saved its spurt for the end, the first sleigh drew slowly ahead. The cadets in the other beat the shoulders of their driver. "Idiot! Faster!"

A minute or two later both sleighs were curving to a halt at the steps up the granite quayside and the two groups clambering out, pulling up their greatcoat collars and intermingling with fresh laughter and vociferations.

Somebody said, "What? He's not still here, surely?"

"Yes, I am. I'm still here," Dostoevsky said; his face was horribly red. "I won't oblige you by crawling off, gentlemen; I'll even march in front to show I'm part of your vile stupidity!"

There was a derisive shout of laughter. He knew it was

a ridiculous thing to have said. He was utterly, overwhelmingly ashamed and had been longing for hours to clear off and never set eyes on them again.

"Oh, come, Fyodor Mikhailovich," Totleben, tallest of the cadets, said and took his arm with a perplexed look. "For heaven's sake, let's forget it."

"He's showing off his intelligence," somebody said.

"This is hardly the company for that," Dostoevsky retorted, but it was drowned in the fresh burst of laughter. They all went, still laughing and talking noisily, up the steps.

Petersburg lay white, calm, and muffled under the snow of December 1838. At the end of the Summer Garden, dark, snowbound, and deserted, the Engineers' Château loomed in the night sky. The faint light from the gas lamps magnified its enormous medieval mass, the moated walls, parapets, drawbridges, and obelisks. The mad Emperor Paul, who had built it, had been murdered in it. It was a wry joke among the cadets that, having been found "uninhabitable" thereafter, the château had been selected as their barracks and school.

A Finnish policeman stamped his feet, eying the group of young men passing, and retreated into his box. Dostoevsky walked on, listening to their chatter in spite of himself. He was a short, thickset young figure of seventeen with a round freckled face, big forehead, and deep-set eyes. His light brown hair was hidden under the fur cap.

He was furious and sickened at having spent the afternoon with them. Totleben and Grigorovich were all right. But the others were all he thought most poisonous in the school. He especially hated the leader, Arekin, a vulgar swaggerer who showed off touchily about his honor and dignity and before whom all but a few of the cadets groveled in a disgusting way. He hated Arekin's classically handsome face (he would gladly have had it instead of his own intelligent one); he hated the way he boasted of his conquests with women and his future duels. Among the rest there was

Glazov, a bully, and Zavulonsky, an impudent blockhead who thought he cut a great figure.

They had all been to see off Arekin's brother, a lieutenant in the hussars who had just left for a post in Vienna. It was the sort of occasion Dostoevsky shuddered at—yet for some reason he had positively thrust himself on them! He didn't know what had possessed him. He knew they despised him; they had never concealed their aversion for him and they had been exasperated at his pushing himself into the party. He had seen their contempt and of course it had made him all the more furious. He had been unable to restrain himself, behaved outrageously, and, at a moment they had all intended to be gallant, noble, and affecting, had simply got up from the table in the restaurant where they had gathered and begun walking idiotically up and down on the other side of the room. They went on drinking, paying no attention to him. They treated him like an insect. He had walked up and down for two hours in an agony of shame and humiliation, knowing that he would remember every one of those ludicrous hateful moments with loathing for years to come. Once when he had laughed scornfully at some snatch of conversation he had caught, they had turned around and stared at him walking up and down *taking no notice of them;* the next moment they had forgotten him again.

Except for Totleben and Grigorovich, he detested his fellow cadets and kept to himself. They jibed and laughed at him. He could not give in to them, adopt the servile attitude toward their leaders which they all had. Their coarseness revolted him and he was struck by the pettiness of their thoughts, the stupidity of their pursuits, games, and conversations. They had no real feeling for anything, took no interest in the great subjects, and accepted all that was most blatantly obvious. Success they bowed down to; they laughed with callous contumely at everything that was decent, honorable, but oppressed and of small worldly account. For them, rank meant intelligence and they were already, as cadets, talking about getting cozy berths in the service and creating havoc with the local beauties.

"Step out, you fellows," Totleben called out to the stragglers behind. "Karasov is on duty." The discipline of the Engineers' School included plenty of "healthy floggings," prescribed almost as an education in themselves by the Most High—His Imperial Majesty the Emperor Nicholas. One could get twenty strokes for a simple drill mistake or a bad plan of fortifications. Once there had been a battle between the cadets and some had gone for their guns. The commander had arrived in time and, lining them up, shouted, "Now you will be reconciled. Cadets! To the right, kiss! To the left, kiss!"

They crossed the bridge over the Moika Canal and climbed the icy, glistening ramp to the château's Resurrection Gate. As the sentry brought his rifle to the salute and gave the shout to the guardroom, the group behind began quarreling.

"And I say it's not! It can't be done," Glazov shouted.

"Very well, if you are all cowards, I'll do it." It was Arekin, who had naturally been drinking more than the rest. In their coarse way he and Glazov were rivals. Inside the château they all straggled up the once magnificent marble staircase, now chipped and scarred, and filed through the Orderly Room. The dispute was being continued in lower tones.

"Fyodor Mikhailovich, your honor." An orderly came forward. "Professor Plaksin would like——"

"Yes, yes, I know." Dostoevsky turned away impatiently. Professor Plaksin had given him three extra topographic exercises. He taught topography and literature—and called Gogol "an author of no talent." Dostoevsky hung his coat, collected his drawings, and took them to Plaksin's office at the other end of the château. When he returned he could hear the buzz of voices from the room next to the dormitory. He went in. There was a wall of uniformed backs.

"Don't be a fool, Arekin."

"Stop him. He'll kill himself."

The bare, high-ceilinged barracks room was noisy with voices and shuffling boots. The cadets crowded around a group in the middle. Dostoevsky edged around to one side and caught sight of Arekin. Arekin held a big curving army saber with its point slightly raised from the board floor. Nearby, standing in the inner circle, was Glazov, plump and thick-faced.

"Watch the door!" somebody called out. A few of the cadets near Dostoevsky bustled reluctantly, then one of Glazov's friends pushed his way in, carrying an icicle a foot long and as thick as two fingers, and handed it to Arekin. Dostoevsky guessed what was happening; it was the stupid trick they had been boasting about earlier in the evening. It was typical of Arekin and the others.

Arekin cracked the icicle sharply against his boot; the lower third broke off and he kicked it aside.

"Give him room." Glazov spread his arms for the others to fall back. The circle widened and the cadets became silent. Everybody was watching Arekin. He straddled his legs, tipped back his head, and, holding the icicle upright between his eyes, slowly raised the saber by the blade and put the point on the upper end. Quickly he removed the hand holding the icicle. The other still held the saber on the upturned end. For a moment he paused, getting the balance, then, releasing his grasp on the saber, he was about to take the other hand away when there was a tiny sound of the steel chipping off a splinter of ice. Arekin twisted violently away.

The cadets shouted. The saber was vibrating upright in the wooden floor alongside Arekin's leg.

"Get back!" Arekin let out a bellow. Glazov was smiling.

"Stop him—stop him," somebody called out, and there was a scuffle and bump as the objector was squashed.

"Get another one," Arekin said. He had pulled the saber out of the floor and was holding it again. He looked pale.

"Of course, if you take one as thick as your arm anybody

can do it," Glazov said, smirking and nudging his companions. Arekin said nothing. They waited while Zavulonsky, Glazov's follower and slave, returned from outside with another icicle. It was scarcely thicker. Arekin broke it at about the same length.

"Look here, Arekin, drop this." It was Patton, Arekin's friend, who had gone up and firmly taken his arm.

"No. Let me alone. Go away," Arekin said. Patton shrugged and fell back.

Now, with his head back, Arekin had the icicle on his chin, holding it upright with one hand. He raised the saber to shoulder height and brought it around, the hilt on high, so that the point was poised over the icicle. He kept the position, the heavy saber, grasped only by the extreme end, shaking slightly in the air. Everybody's eyes were on the point. Slowly it approached the icicle, and then in one movement Arekin had joined the two, saber and icicle, taken both hands away, and was balancing the curved length of steel on the ice above his face.

In the silence none of the cadets dared to move or look away. For about five seconds Arekin kept perfect balance. The hilt of the saber swayed slightly to one side and he moved under it, catching the balance again. He had actually, for an instant, brought his feet together in a sort of defiance when, taking a step backward, his boot slipped, the broken-off end of the icicle shot out from under it, and, trying to recover everything at once, he fell heavily on his back.

"Ahh!" Dostoevsky saw the glint of the saber in the light, the icicle splintered on the floor—and there was Patton standing lunged forward, grasping the blade of the saber, the point touching Arekin's tunic. Arekin sprang lightly up and flung his arms around Patton. The cadets were bellowing.

"My God, that was close!"

"Bravo, Arekin."

Glazov had turned and was shrugging to his group. And

a clear high voice called out from behind Dostoevsky, "Messieurs. If you please."

"Karasov. Look out!" They stiffened to attention. Major Karasov came jauntily through the door; Dostoevsky caught the almost imperceptible creak of his long glistening boots. He was thin, with a thin nose and a small mustache. He walked around the edge of the circle to Arekin and Patton and stood looking at them. He smiled.

"Excellent, Alexey Pavlovich. I congratulate you. You have invented a new trick for our leisure hours. It is quite Cossack." He paused. "You shall do that with a rifle and bayonet tomorrow or have twenty strokes. It is really excellent. Your father, General Arekin, would certainly not understand it if you split your brains out. On the other hand, he would not question it if you were flogged to ribbons in the Emperor's service."

2

The ten strokes of the clock vibrated in the cold air. Dostoevsky turned up his coat collar going out through the side gate. The corporal in the guardroom was tipped back in his chair, exercising the limitless Russian capacity for short naps. The night was clear and the snow crunched crisply underfoot.

He walked with quick steps down the Sadovaya toward the Nevsky Prospect, excited and on edge. There was a risk in leaving the château at this hour, but he had done it before and not been caught. And he must—he *must* see Shidlovsky. His fingers felt Shidlovsky's note in his pocket. "I am relying on our meeting. I have something of great importance to tell you. If your brother Mikhail is there, bring him." At the bottom of the page he had scribbled, "I am walking to Petersburg with a peasant who is coming to petition the Tsar. He is like Christ."

Shidlovsky! It was nearly a year since Dostoevsky had

heard from him, the impassioned youth who had been their first and great friend in Petersburg when he and Mikhail had arrived with their father from Moscow to become cadets. At the pension where they had struck up acquaintance, even their father had felt Shidlovsky's strange attraction. Once back in Moscow, Dr. Dostoevsky had written: "Give your friend Shidlovsky my compliments."

Yes, yes! Hurrying, muffled in his coat, Dostoevsky caught the image of Shidlovsky's thin, eager face, dried up as if he lived on nothing, his eyes burning as they had talked for hours, often all night, of Schiller, George Sand, Gogol, and of God and Russia. They had been full of ideals and dreams. And now how far back it seemed. The circle had long since broken up—Mikhail now remote at the Engineers' School at Reval and Shidlovsky, his clerk's post abandoned, wandering along the roads of Russia, preaching in villages and still seeking the answer to his doubts. At intervals there was a letter from him, always apparently written in a fever. The last time, Shidlovsky had asked him to come to the Kazan Cathedral and Dostoevsky had found him there under the colonnade, in rags, among the beggars, still with the same inner illumination, eager, smiling, and tormented.

He reached the long straight sweep of the Nevsky. It was full of life and movement. The snow sparkled under the gaslight, troikas swished past with figures muffled in furs. Light "egoist" sleighs carrying officers and girls, their knees buried in bearskins, weaved dashingly in and out. The lamp-posts squeaked and croaked with a thousand voices in the wind. In Sumarov's restaurant the red-shaded lamps glowed warmly against the plush, the chandeliers glinted beneath the columns of the Alexandrinsky Theater, and a line of droshkies waited in the square in front, the drivers talking loudly together and gesticulating.

Dostoevsky felt his excitement growing. He had been restless and unsettled ever since Shidlovsky's message and now he was in a great hurry to arrive. As he came into the

Karetnaya district the streets became darker and narrower, the slippery, dirty wooden sidewalk which had become full of holes disappeared altogether, and the low houses were interspersed with empty lots. There were only a few passers-by. Occasionally fires flamed in the snow at street corners and the sentry stamped his feet, keeping close to the ring of warmth. The address Shidlovsky had given was a lodging house, taller than the rest, propped erect outside with wooden beams.

"Third floor," said the porter, a man with a red birthmark on his face, eying Dostoevsky's uniform coat. Dostoevsky felt his way up the creaking stairs. The whole house slanted, all the doors on the landings jammed open. There was a sailor sewing cross-legged on a table in one room, a woman wearing a chemise with her hair down and two boys in another.

"Fedya!" Leaning over the banister at the top, holding a candle, was Shidlovsky. And at the same moment Dostoevsky realized the cause of his excitement—the question that Shidlovsky's letter had brought back to him; all these feelings of the last few days came from the question he was bursting to ask Shidlovsky.

"There you are, Ivan Nikolayevich!" They clasped each other with eager joy, asking one another a score of things and hardly waiting for the answers. "Let me look at you." Shidlovsky was thinner, his face with its boyish features had grown older, and his eyes looked dry and burning as though he were ill. He had on a worn old frock coat, a neck rag, and rusty trousers. He dragged Dostoevsky into the room.

"Sit down, sit down. It's safest just there. One night this place will fall into the street. Wait a minute, I'll ask Zredin for some tea." He ran out and in a moment came back with two glasses of tea. "Zredin is the sailor; I dare say you made his acquaintance coming up. He has a samovar."

There was a sagging bed in the room, a wooden box for a table, a chair, and a tin bowl by the window. "Do you realize?" Shidlovsky said. "An entire room to oneself! What luxury, eh? It belongs to Zredin's brother; I met him in Tula." He suddenly began talking animatedly of his travels. He had also been in Riazan and Penza. For several months he had stayed in a monastery, thinking the strict rules would help him in his "endeavor to believe"; but in the end the elder had advised him to go.

They talked on, reciting Schiller, hastily catching each other up at hesitations. At last Dostoevsky interrupted. "Listen, Ivan Nikolayevich. You said you had 'something of great importance' to tell me in your letter."

Shidlovsky jumped up and went quickly to a knapsack in the corner. He pulled out a bundle of papers. "Here it is. I am writing a history of the Russian Church. That's what it is. It is beginning to explain things to me."

"No, but wait—wait," Dostoevsky broke in. "Please tell me about that in a moment." He could not keep his question any longer. "Ivan Nikolayevich, this is what you must answer me now. I have been thinking of it ever since you wrote to me from somewhere or other, I forget where. But you must answer it. You said everything for Christianity depends on the atonement, that that was the central fact. But what if something else had happened? What if, when Christ was going to Calvary, someone had stopped and saved him, some Roman of influence, a good man? Mankind would have been damned! Tell me, is that the answer? Is it —is it?"

To his surprise Shidlovsky laughed. "I'll ask you a question in return. Why is it when two Russians come together they always talk of these things—of God, of humanity, the eternal things? Here we have not met for a year and we begin on such things at once!"

"No, but answer, Ivan Nikolayevich."

Shidlovsky stood with the sheets of paper in his hand, serious again. "It was Christ's mission to atone for all. It would have happened in another way." He suddenly turned away, pacing the room. "I cannot explain it. It must be so."

"But if we can't understand, if we can't explain those things to ourselves, can we be sinful?" Dostoevsky looked at him. He remembered again the other nights when they had wrestled with these questions, both of them trying to find conviction for themselves and failing.

"Then what if God doesn't exist?" Shidlovsky almost shouted. "What if it's only an idea invented by men? Then man is master of the world. That's a splendid idea! Only how is he going to be good without God? That's the question. Because whom is man going to love then? Whom is he to be thankful for and to whom sing the hymn of praise?"

"He will live for virtue, without believing in immortality," Dostoevsky said, giving him a burning look. "He will love freedom, equality, and fraternity."

"But if you destroy belief in immortality, love and every living force in the world dries up."

"No, no," Dostoevsky said excitedly. "It is love that has made men believe in immortality."

Shidlovsky turned back. "You can prove the existence of God by active love, if you strive to love your neighbor actively and untiringly. Listen, Fyodor Mikhailovich, as you advance in love you will grow surer of the reality of God and the immortality of your soul. At the monastery the elder told me, 'If you attain perfect self-forgetfulness in the love of your neighbor, then you will believe and no doubt can enter your soul.'"

"Yes, yes—if one could cling to that! But how can it be? There is no choice about doubt, is there? We must believe or we must doubt."

"What do you mean?" Shidlovsky stepped up to him, his face flushed.

Dostoevsky was agitated too. "It isn't a matter of will, believing in God. You can't stop your thoughts. You can't be honest about your thoughts and opinions and you can't be dishonest either. You can be dishonest afterward when you speak of them, but not about the thoughts themselves."

"No!" Shidlovsky seemed about to say something very difficult for him, then with effort to grasp at affirmation again. "Fyodor Mikhailovich, heaven lies within all of us. We are responsible to all for all, apart from our own sins. When men understand that, the kingdom of heaven will at once be a living reality."

"What? I don't understand that. How can I be responsible for all?"

"You don't understand it because the world has been believing otherwise for too long, because we expect others to tell the same lies we tell."

"But wait a minute, Ivan Nikolayevich," Dostoevsky said. "I have something to say that is most important of all. The suffering in the world—listen, I saw it yesterday, a peasant's horse had fallen down and he was whipping it over the eyes. People were looking on and shouting, 'Whip it—the eyes, whip the eyes!' Do you understand *why God allows that?* Do you? Why must the horse be tortured? Because we must suffer to pay for salvation? Is that why the horse must be whipped on the eyes—on its meek eyes? But it's too much! It's too much! Is it sacrifice again? Why should God, if He is kind and forgiving, why should God demand sacrifice of men? I—I——" He stopped, greatly worked up.

Shidlovsky sat on the bed staring at him. "Yes. I think of it. I think of it. Why has God left us in so much doubt when it was so easy for Him to make things clear?"

"Why did Christ fail to speak when he knew of the crimes that would be committed in His name? One word would have been enough. One word! And eternal life—he could have explained that in a few syllables!"

"But—but—Fyodor Mikhailovich, listen, I beg you. There are mysteries, there are these terrible mysteries." Shidlovsky seemed to be struggling with himself. He threw his arms out toward Dostoevsky. "Please try to understand me. Everyone tries to keep apart, to secure the fullest possible life for

himself. Mankind has split up into units, each one holds
aloof and hides what he has from the rest, heaps up riches
by himself and thinks he is strong and secure. He doesn't
understand that the more he accumulates the nearer he
approaches self-destruction. Because he is accustomed to
rely on himself alone, to cut himself off from the whole, he
has trained himself not to believe in the help of others, in
men and in humanity, and he only trembles for fear of losing
his money and the privileges that he has won for himself.
But his individualism must come to an end and everybody
will see how unnaturally they are separated from one another.
That will be the spirit of the time and then the sign of the
Son of Man will be seen in the heavens. But meantime we
must go on. Even if he is alone and seems mad, a man must
set an example and draw men's souls out of their isolation
and spur them to acts of brotherly love, that the great idea
may not die."

He stopped speaking. Dostoevsky went quickly over to
him. "Ivan Nikolayevich, forgive me. I did not want——
Forgive me."

"Of course, of course; there is nothing to forgive." Shidlovsky smiled at him gently. In a minute he said, "I am
going on a pilgrimage. To Kiev."

"Yes. There are answers, Ivan Nikolayevich. You will find
the answers!" They embraced each other.

3

There were always maneuvers in June. Dostoevsky tramped
alongside Grigorovich over the sodden plain, their boots
squelching in the mud. Other groups of cadets trudged in
front and behind. It was nearly eight o'clock in the evening.
They had been out in the rain since early morning; their
uniforms were soaked and the heavy regulation cape felt
like lead. Some of the officers who had been sitting on their
mounts all day looked drowned. But the Tsar was conduct-

ing the maneuvers in person and he delighted in dragging out suffused and elderly generals who were more at home in their snug offices than on a horse.

The army—forty thousand men of the Corps of Guard and the Cadets—was divided into two groups, one of twenty-five thousand commanded by the Tsar and the other by the Tsarevich, the Grand Duke Alexander. The Emperor's army was supposed to be in full retreat, closely pursued by the Grand Duke's; twelve of the "office generals" were judges and were expected to give their opinions on the quality of each movement. A few of the cavalry had charged through the light troops, the heavy guns of the pursued opened fire, and, still retreating, the Emperor's army did its best to hold up the attackers. Dostoevsky and the other cadets had been throwing up defenses where they could while the artillery thundered along the line, swarms of Cossacks hovered on each flank, and the Emperor shouted his orders. Nicholas, still incredibly full of vigor, had just galloped back to the village, leaving the generals and the rest of the staff to follow as they were able.

The cadets reached the line of gray tents. "My God, for some tea!" Grigorovich pulled back the tent flap and they went in. "I'm frozen."

"Arkady! Where's that orderly?" Dostoevsky poked his head out again. "Here—give me something dry."

Half a dozen other cadets who had arrived already were changing and sorting their kits in the tent.

"Five more days of this! I shall grow fins." It was a cadet named Tian-Chansky.

"Did you see Krebsky, the distinguished cadet?" another said. "The Most High actually spoke to him."

"H'm. Something richly paternal, I suppose." Tian-Chansky, who had a brilliant comic gift, imitated the Tsar's stance and expression. There was a splutter—quickly stifled; it was safer.

Dostoevsky changed into a dry tunic and trousers. The

boots would have to do; he hadn't another pair. He sat on the straw paillasse scraping the mud off. Arkady, the orderly whom he shared with Grigorovich, came in with some tea and poured it out steaming for Grigorovich. Grigorovich stood warming his hands on the glass, sipping the tea.

"Here, Arkady, make mine." Dostoevsky shivered, rummaging in his field knapsack, and brought out a paper packet; there were only a few crumbs in the bottom. He paused, hearing Grigorovich's grunts of pleasure, then threw the paper aside. "Never mind. It doesn't matter." He would have given anything for tea. Grigorovich, who had become a closer friend lately, would, he knew, share his; but he had been drinking Grigorovich's tea for too long. Besides, he owed Totleben and Tian-Chansky ten rubles for supplies. He couldn't borrow more.

He pulled the boots on and stood up. It was impossible! Weeks ago he had written to his father asking for money and explaining. If he had been left to himself he wouldn't have asked for a kopeck, he would have borne the last misery. But in the regiment how could he do otherwise than ask, make promises, swear he wasn't wasteful? His father didn't seem to understand a cadet's life at all, which was curious because he had been in the army himself. For this period in camp, for instance, one needed at least forty rubles. Even without tea or sugar he needed sixteen rubles for a pair of boots; the army-issue ones wore out in a few weeks. He had no box to keep his papers, books, and equipment in; and in camp the orderlies wouldn't do anything without payment. He had explained all that, and his father had sent fifteen rubles, of which he had three left, to last indefinitely. What a strange character, his father. Life seemed to have taught him nothing; he had the same views of things he had thirty years before.

The tent steamed. He looked around at the wet clothes spread out, the cadets cramped in the small space, some talking and smoking, some briskly toweling themselves, a couple wrestling. The need for tea became overpowering. How he detested maneuvers. He flung on his cape and went out; perhaps after all he could ask Totleben for a glass.

Two of the cadets glanced up. "What a fellow, that Photius!" It was their nickname for him. "In the usual state of excitement." They laughed. "They say his father was in the army."

"Yes—surgeon major. That's how he got nobility titles. He used to be in charge of the Marinsky Poor Hospital in Moscow, a martinet. They're supposed to have a small estate somewhere in Tula, at a place called Daravoye or something."

"It can't be very imposing. Photius is always hard up."

"Perhaps he spends it on those books he's always poking his nose into. You never saw such stuff; people called Carlyle, Hoffmann—and poetry!"

The other puffed his cigarette. "Don't make a mistake, Boris Ivanovich. He's gristle."

Twenty minutes later the bugles sounded for cadets' inspection. There was a scramble to put the tent in order. Dostoevsky hurried in, grabbed up his loose kit, and began stowing it; wet or fine, there was never enough discipline. Still, he felt warmer for Totleben's tea.

"They say the Most High is coming around in person," Tian-Chansky announced.

"Don't you believe it."

"What do you mean? He's capable of it."

"Shut up. If you want to see Siberia, we don't."

As it turned out, Major Karasov, not the Tsar, was taking the inspection. When it was over the major flexed his knees springily while his orderly sergeant bawled at them. "By command of His Imperial Majesty! The orders of the day for tomorrow are changed. Cadets will report with full campaign kit in rapid-march order at 4 A.M." There were inward groans along the ranks. Four A.M.! The "office generals" must have made a heavy misjudgment somewhere. "Cannon pro-

ceeding at 4:15 A.M. . . ." The sergeant bellowed on while
they stood there. At last they were dismissed; the rain had
begun to come down hard again.

It was before dawn next morning when the draft from
the opened tent flap wakened Dostoevsky. "Tent number
five, your honors," somebody at the entrance said, and a
lantern gleamed in. The recumbent bodies stirred. There
was a murmur of protest.

"Not us. Wrong tent!"

"It's only just three o'clock."

The lantern showed the face of a night duty guard, his
rifle slung behind him. "Cadet Dostoevsky, Fyodor Mikhailovich, your honor," he said. Several in the tent were awake
now.

"Present." Dostoevsky squinted up, raised on his elbow.
"What is it?"

"Cadet Dostoevsky. Report to Captain Rosen, your honor.
At once," the guard said.

"For God's sake, Photius, clear off and let us get some
sleep."

"Middle of the night!" The other cadets swore, turning
back to sleep. Dostoevsky crawled hurriedly out of his
blankets, understanding nothing; the guard had disappeared.
He managed to dress in the dark, took his cape, and stumbled out over the legs of his fellow cadets. The rain had
stopped; outside the close confinement of the tent the air
was fresh and sweet. The dim light glowed from the watch
tent. He hastened toward it, adjusting his uniform; he was
still under the effect of the sudden awakening and did not
try to interpret what the summons meant. He stopped before
the tent, gave his tunic a last jerk, and went in. Captain
Rosen was sitting on a camp chair under the lamp, trying
on a pair of boots, turning his foot this way and that,
admiring the cut and gleam of the leather. Dostoevsky
saluted; Rosen looked up and leisurely reached to the table.
"I am instructed that you are to have leave, Cadet," he said.

"You may go to—what the devil's the name of the place?"
He picked up a sheet of paper from the table. "Daravoye.
Fifteen days' leave."

"Daravoye?" The complete unexpectedness of the name
gave him a shock. "I—I don't understand, Captain. I haven't
applied for leave."

"Your father——" Rosen looked up reluctantly from the
boots. "Your father has had an accident."

"My father?"

"Evidently your presence is necessary. You had better go
there at once." Rosen let the smoke of his cigarette drift
past his eyes. He bent and squeezed a glistening toe in
finger and thumb.

"What sort of accident? Is it serious?"

Rosen shrugged. "Fifteen days' leave by consent of Major
Karasov," he said. "Not sixteen, Cadet. Is that clear?"

"Yes, Captain." Dostoevsky saluted and rushed out. An
accident. Hurrying through the lines of tents with the first
faint light showing in the sky, he had a feeling of disaster.

4

The coach was rocking and plunging in the ruts of the
country road. Sometimes to urge the horses on the driver
let out a howl like a man in pain and the next minute
followed this with a volley of blows and curses. But the road
was liquid mud and the ruts engulfed the wheels to the
axles so that with all the lurching they moved at a miserable pace.

Dostoevsky sat in one of the forward-facing seats looking
out onto the endless plain. He was in a fever to reach
Daravoye. For the three days by posting coach from Petersburg to Moscow he had slept only in snatches, but he
scarcely felt the fatigue. There had been no further information at the camp about his father than "an accident."
Yet he had sensed something mysterious and perhaps ter-

rible, which Captain Rosen knew of but had not communicated. And as the slow and weary versts succeeded one another, he was torn with anxiety, trying to repel the half-formulated fears which returned persistently to his mind. In Moscow he had not stopped to see Aunt Kumanina but hurried for the first coach in the direction of Tula. Now at last they were on the final stage but one for Daravoye.

The afternoon flies buzzed in the interior of the coach. The other occupant in front, a merchant with a fan beard, was asleep; his snores snuffled off at the deeper lurches of the wheels, then droned rhythmically again. Dostoevsky stared out of the window, recalling the other occasions when they had traveled along this same road, his mother, Mikhail, and the rest of his brothers and sisters, on their way during summer holidays to Daravoye. It was no great estate—two small poverty-stricken villages, Daravoye and Chermashnya, a wooden three-room house with thatched roof, and about a hundred souls in all. His father had bought it years before while he and Mikhail were still small children. But in those holiday summers they had been glad to escape to it, to leave the uncomfortable family quarters in Moscow's Marinsky Hospital and spend days in the fields or playing at the garden pond.

On those occasions his father had stayed behind at his hospital work and small private practice. And they had been glad of that escape too, release from the severity with which he ruled the household, the hours standing before him reciting lessons, of listening, motionless under the penalty of an outburst, to his readings from Karamzin's *History of the Russian State* and Pushkin's poetry, the early bed, rising at six, rigid punctuality, the sedate, accompanied walks while Father spoke improvingly of arithmetic and geometry. Dostoevsky could never remember having a kopeck of pocket money. Amusements were rare—occasional Sunday visits to the Marinsky Wood, once or twice an outing to the Kremlin churches. Father permitted no games except the mildest;

they had never been let out alone and friendships with other boys were discouraged. Only one schoolmate from Chermak's College, Vanya Umnov, had ever been allowed to visit them. Then, when he was fifteen, his mother had died; and after placing him and Mikhail in Kostomarov's Preparatory Academy for the Engineering Corps in Petersburg, his father had retired from the hospital and gone to live at Daravoye, taking with him the two younger children, Vera and Alexandra.

His father's face came before his eyes—a small face, small cheeks and side whiskers curving across them, curly lips, the high collar of his uniform lifting his chin. The death of his mother had seemed to remove a restraint on his feelings about his father, so that his still childish fear of him was mixed with resistance, desire for revenge, and a tinge of something like hatred.

The stagnation of Daravoye had worsened his father's temper, monstrously heightened his avarice. He was convinced that Fyodor and Mikhail were throwing their money away, though God knows he sent them little enough. And there had been odd rumors from Alyona Frolovna, the old family nurse who had accompanied him to Daravoye. She had heard him pacing up and down the rooms talking with his dead wife's ghost, mimicking her voice. He became embittered at the bad harvest and raged at the peasants.

Dostoevsky knew he was doing his best for them according to his understanding. And now, as the coach rolled on in the afternoon, underlying the fear and the affection mixed with repugnance, the thought of Father isolated there in Daravoye, ending his days in the dull little village where probably everything frustrated him and offended his sense of fitness, oppressed and tormented him. Should he try to persuade him to return to Moscow? He did not know.

The coach stopped abruptly at a great black and white beam across the road and in a minute the guards came to

look at the passports; then the driver howled at the horses
and they went on again. It was dark when they reached the
post station, a cabin of logs with stables behind. Dostoevsky
jumped down, stepped over the bodies of half a dozen
prostrate muzhiks sleeping on the steps, and went in. The
station keeper, a man with an immense quantity of hair on
his face, was arguing with an officer in buckskin breeches.

"But, Your Excellency." The station master bowed. "It is
impossible. There are no horses."

"You've seen this order." The officer shook a government
paper at him. "I am empowered to commandeer horses, on
urgent official business. Go on, you scoundrel! You had better
find some quick or it'll be hot for you." He had a black
mustache and small, very white teeth. "I'll give you ten
minutes."

"Aie." Shaking his head, the station master ran out. The
officer took two imperious strides up and down the room,
clanking his saber and ignoring everybody, then went out
after him. He was a government courier on his way to
Moscow and would probably take any change of team there
was, leaving the rest of the travelers held up indefinitely.
It was the sort of thing that happened all along the roads.
Twenty minutes later, as they waited in the smoky, ill-lit
room, there was a tinkling of bells, a driver's cry of "Now,
darlings"—and the side lamp of a carriage flashed past the
window. Dostoevsky had a glimpse of the seated officer being
borne away. There went their horses! Daravoye was still
thirty versts off; his father was probably in great need of
him, perhaps his life depending on a speedy arrival. And
now they were stranded here.

Two hours passed and the station master was still absent.

Another pair of travelers who had come in were already
lying wrapped in their coats next to some peasants, ready
to make a night of it. Dostoevsky jumped up and shook one
of the peasants.

"Look here, my good fellow, isn't there a carriage I can

hire, a cart, anything? I can pay at the other end. Only I must leave *now*."

The man shook his head. "Alexey Platonovich has the priest in. They are baptizing his daughter's child."

"What—at this time of night?"

"Well, the priest is trying to get his price. You know these things, sir. They have been at it for two days. It may be another before they strike a bargain."

"Where are they?" The man vaguely indicated the rear with his head. Dostoevsky rushed out. There was a shack by the stables with a light shining from the window. He banged on the door and entered. The hairy station master and the priest in his black robes were sitting at one side of the room, both drunk. In the far corner a young woman slept in bed with an infant beside her.

The station master took no notice of Dostoevsky and continued speaking to the priest. "Father, you would not let a child suffer eternal damnation for the sake of twenty-five rubles? An innocent babe of four days who does not know the sight or smell or the lecherous touch of sin?"

"Alexey Platonovich, what are an extra twenty-five rubles to you for our Holy Mother, the Church? A trifle."

"Ah, Father, it's true what the people say: the priest takes from the living and the dead. Here I've been giving you ten rubles' worth of vodka and the best food these last two days and you still stick to the same price."

"And how am I to live and bring up my family, Alexey Platonovich?" the priest said, swallowing the drink in his glass.

"That's all very well. But listen, Father, there was a priest in Vochinny who baptized a pet dog, a poodle, last month because the woman paid him enough. What is one to think of that?"

"Give me another nip of that pepper vodka, my good fellow. You know you will come to my price in the end, but if it gives you pleasure that I should keep you company in the meantime, I'll not deprive you."

They both swayed tipsily. It was an absurd spectacle, yet oddly warm and at all events inescapably Russian. Dostoevsky stepped up. "I must continue tonight. Will you kindly order the horses for the coach."

"Immediately, your honor." The station master waved a hand. "Immediately. They are coming." He took no account of what he had told the officer and turned back to the priest, who had refilled his glass. "Now, Father. I am willing to consider, in principle, conceding an extra two rubles. You understand: *two* rubles; not a kopeck more."

Dostoevsky made a baffled attempt to interrupt once more, then went out. They would be at it till morning. In the post station everybody was curled up asleep. What was he to do? There must be somebody in the neighborhood who had a cart. The thought of further delay was intolerable.

Then all at once Alexey Platonovich came unsteadily in and in half an hour, with horses and the merchant mysteriously produced from nowhere, they were seated again in the coach and plunging down the moonlit road.

It was eight o'clock in the morning when they reached Daravoye. Dostoevsky was the only one to alight. He took his bag and walked down the quiet, deserted side road toward the village.

5

The road led past three of the peasants' huts almost directly to the house. Everything was silent. He could see no one in the fields. The only disturbance of the stillness was the squelching of his boots in the mud. But it was as if he were expected.

He pushed at the gate in the picket fence and it fell open, broken at the top hinge. The garden in front was unkempt and he had a sudden temptation to call out, to run toward the house shouting loudly and cheerfully; a rustle to one side made him start—a cat darting out of sight through the undergrowth.

The door of the house creaked like a voice as he swung it slowly wide. The main room was empty. His footsteps resounded. There were two bedrooms, one at each end; they were empty too, one of the beds unmade and some bottles on the floor. Some clothes of his father's and a pair of boots were lying about. He went back to the main room and stood looking around. The dust on the table showed in the sunlight; a newspaper, open and crumpled, lay on the floor and there was a plate with a fork and a potato in congealed grease on the stove. His father's woolen coat hung from a nail. The clock had stopped. Standing there looking around, he had the impression that people in the village outside were watching him. He unlatched the string from the door of a cupboard and staggered back at a sudden terrifying noise as an avalanche of empty bottles clattered out, hitting his chest and knees, clanking together and rolling across the floor. He slithered backward, treading on them, raising his arms protectively. His heart was thudding.

"Father!" He stepped to the kitchen; the floor was covered with upright empty bottles with a narrow track through them. In a fright he ran outside, calling out, wanting to raise company.

"Grigory! Grigory!" The headman's house was across the yard; he pushed the door wide open. "Grigory Pavlovich, what's happened? Where—" A girl of about ten, one of the headman's children, looked up at him from the floor.

"He is working in the copse," she said sullenly.

"Go and fetch him. Be quick." The child rose, ducked under his arm, and disappeared, clearly not to do the errand but to escape. The strangeness of the atmosphere, the whole scene, increased his apprehension. Some of the servants at least must be about. There were chickens in the yard. He hurried across it past the dung heap and yellow puddles toward the stables and the servants' quarters. His father's carriage was in the coach house; one wheel slanted crazily. The horse was not there. "Savely Antonovich!" He called up at the straw-hung trap door with a ladder propped in it for the coachman. "Savely Antonovich!" No answer. Then, as he burst into the servants' house adjoining, there was Marya Semyenovna, the old cook of their childhood, and Catherine, a servant girl from the village.

"Mashka! Well—somebody at last." Catherine was already going out of the back door. "Where has everybody else gone? I've just arrived and the place is like the dead. What's the matter with Catherine? Where are Alyona Frolovna and my sisters?"

She edged up, her tiny brown eyes averted, kissed his hand in the old-fashioned way, and shuffled back. "The men are at Chermashnya."

"What for?" She shook her head, meaning to indicate that she was deaf—and brought him a sudden recollection of boyhood evenings when she had heard the cock crow after dark and hurried him out to the feather-smelling, rustling fowl house to find the cock on the perch and clasp its feet: if they were warm it meant news and if they were cold it meant a strange visitor. He raised his voice. "Are the children there too—Vera and Alexandra?"

"No. They have gone to Lenskoy." It was a village some distance off. The old woman's hands were twisting her apron. He was astonished at the news, then saw the possible explanation. There was a German steward at Lenskoy who did doctoring and surgical dressing.

"They've gone there with my father, you mean? What was the accident? Is he much hurt, Mashka?" He thought of the clothes in the house; evidently his father had been so badly hurt he had had to be undressed. She was giving him uneasy glances and looking quickly away again; all at once she turned, trying to shuffle off, but he caught her arm.

"What's the matter?" When she didn't reply he shouted at her ear, "Where is my father?"

He saw she had become stiff with fear; the wrinkled old lips were turned in and the cold smell of age came off her. "You must ask Grigory. I don't know anything about it."

"About what? Mashka, answer me." He was frightened and gripped her shoulders. "Why is the house left like that —open, dirty, all those bottles? Is he——is he——"

She gasped; her tiny eyes stared at him. Her jaw shut and fell spasmodically in her struggle to repress speech, then she said in a sort of breathless mumble, "They murdered him. They took an oath to kill him and they did."

"My God—what are you saying?"

She clutched his coat. "They wanted to make it seem an accident; they tried to hide it." Her voice sank into an intense urgent whisper that she breathed into his face, standing close to him. "They all tormented him. Ah—he was an angry man and troublesome, but they never left him alone and sometimes it suffocated him so that he couldn't speak. Then he was drunk for three weeks and they robbed him in every way they could. One day Fedote, who was mocking him, went by without taking his cap off. Mikhail Andreyevich flew into a fury and ordered Fedote to be given a flogging there and then. After that they formed a plot against him. All the men at Chermashnya were in it and some here at Daravoye also. They waited until two weeks ago. Then Mikhail Andreyevich called them all out in the morning to cart the manure. They had arranged everything. Vassily, who was the worst, and two others stayed away and when Grigory said they were ill Mikhail Andreyevich saw they were having a game with him.

"He ran into the house, took his stick with the spikes, and called out, 'I'll cure them with this.' As soon as they got to Chermashnya, there were the three of them as large as life strolling about the street. Mikhail Andreyevich said, 'Why aren't you at work?' Vassily said, 'We're too tired.'

But before Mikhail Andreyevich could hit them with the stick they ran into the yard nearby. He chased after them but Vassily jumped on him inside the yard and caught his arms. At first the others were too frightened and Vassily began to swear at them about the oath they had taken—and then they all rushed on Mikhail Andreyevich."

Dostoevsky freed himself from her grasp. He was on the point of stopping her but could not.

"They didn't hit him. Vassily kept saying, 'No blood! No blood! Don't spill his blood and there won't be any mark on him.' They were afraid of marks. They held him down, opened his teeth with a knife, and tipped a keg of raw spirit down his throat. He was arching his back and choking. His eyes stared so hard they looked as if they would roll out on his cheek. Then they pushed the leather seat from the carriage over his face; but he didn't die. Igor was going to kick him between the legs but Vassily swore and shoved him back because it would leave a mark. So Igor bent down and gripped Mikhail Andreyevich there. He wrung him with all his strength, kept on wringing and twisting Mikhail Andreyevich.

"They put him in the carriage, drove off, and threw him out under a tree. But they remembered he had not confessed to the priest, those cowards; and after two days some of them plucked up courage and sent for Father Yosif. He found Mikhail Andreyevich under the tree. There were crows perching on him. They had begun to tear the corners of his mouth, so that one side of it reached round to his jawbone. He was just breathing and he died in half an hour. Father Yosif asked the men what they had done to him; and Savely Antonovich said, 'It was just a congestion of the blood, Father. There was no hope for him.' They made up a story. But I know the truth. When Mikhail Andreyevich was buried, Alyona Frolovna took the children away." She stopped abruptly as a chain clanked in the yard outside. Dostoevsky's hands were over his face; he was filled with horror. "Here they are," Marya Semyenovna said in her frightened voice. He looked up. A cart with Grigory, the headman, Savely Antonovich, and four or five other peasants in it was lumbering into the yard. He glanced at the old woman, his mind in turmoil, hesitated, then ran outside. As he appeared, all the men stood still looking at him; then, quickly eying each other, they began to get down.

"Grigory, Savely Antonovich."

They all took their caps off and made him low bows. "Your honor," Grigory said. "We did not know which day you would come." He was nearly seven feet tall, with an underslung jaw, and could lift a cart with his hands; he was wearing a peasant's blouse and a belt.

"I had a message in Petersburg saying my father had had an accident."

Savely Antonovich glanced at Grigory; they both smelled of liquor. "Permit us, Fyodor Mikhailovich your honor, to express our sorrow," Savely Antonovich said, bowing again. "Our good master has been taken from us suddenly. It's God's doing. It's the Lord's will."

"Yes, it's the Lord's will—and who are we to stand against it?" Grigory said.

Dostoevsky shuddered. The mental picture of his father lying under the tree with his face turned up and the crows hopping closer was unbearable.

He was unable to control himself and rushed across the yard toward the house. The door hung open as he had left it. His foot struck the bottles on the floor and he started back. The muscles of his neck were tightening as if he were going to choke, and he flung himself into a chair, his head buried in his arms on the table. He was shaken by grief and pity. The tears poured out in his bitter pain, soaking the sleeve of his coat, dropping onto the dust on the table. Unsummoned images fused and fragmented in his mind: Karamzin's history book, the dusty path in the Moscow gardens, hands held in trust. His own impatience, the neglect he had shown his father in the past two years, recurred to him with terrible self-reproach. At moments he had hated his father—on the absurd Sunday walks, during the roaring adult rages, in the deathly stillness that had to be kept when Father was asleep, all the other occasions. He'd wished him dead at some moments. He shared the guilt; he had seen his father dead in thought. He was also guilty!

He stood up in a torment. And what was to become of his five brothers and sisters, most of them still small? There was no money; and he had to denounce the murderers.

A faint noise made him turn around. Grigory was in the doorway with Savely Antonovich behind him.

"What do you want?" Dostoevsky said. Then before they could reply he was shouting, "What happened to my father? You saw it. Speak up, do you hear?" The two exchanged looks; Savely Antonovich bowed and said in a crafty tone, "Hasn't your honor been told about it?"

"What do you mean?" Dostoevsky stared at him. Savely Antonovich was a short man with thick short legs and a wily face. They both came two steps into the room; Grigory shuffled. "Your honor, you see it was like this," he said. "Mikhail Andreyevich had an attack. It was out by the wood at Chermashnya and the Devil knows what blew the idea into his head that somebody had been cutting down the trees. He told the men last spring to make a passage across the gulley; the wood was cut for that but he had forgotten it. Some of them tried to remind him but he flew into a rage and wouldn't listen. It was a hot day. He ran about shouting that half the wood was cut down and wanted to run around to the far side too and everybody said, 'Barin, Barin, don't take on so.' But he started racing up the little hill and then he fell on his face. When they came up his face was growing black. They put him in the cart but he was dead as soon as the priest came."

"You're lying! You killed him. You tortured him—like savages!"

Their mouths were suddenly taut, their eyes gliding away from his. Savely Antonovich said, "The Almighty save us, your honor, but we've told the truth. It was congestion of the blood. How could we do him harm?"

"You were all at Chermashnya, the day for carting manure. Vassily held him, you poured spirit into him and tried to stifle him with the cushion. You see, I know everything!"

A vein like a thick worm winding down the center of Grigory's forehead was swelling up; his face slowly became red. His arms fell out somewhat in front of his body and he stepped forward in a threatening way. "Nobody can know, Fyodor Mikhailovich, what did not happen," he said. Suddenly he shouted in a fury, his great bass voice very loud, "A man can't support too much. Mikhail Andreyevich wanted to treat us worse than cattle. He gave beatings for anything. When the carpenter went to him and said, 'Mikhail Andreyevich, your worship, the roof of the barn needs mending and there are no planks,' Mikhail Andreyevich seized him by the throat and had him flogged so that he died. The harvest was bad and he ran about hitting everybody and saying they had robbed him. The Devil was with him. And how can one live without a crust? Nikifor Pavlovich took the cart to Lenskoy to beg crusts for his wife, who was ill, and Mikhail Andreyevich had him arrested. How can one starve and bear that too?"

"No, no. Go away," Dostoevsky said. "It's——No, I cannot."

Savely Antonovich, clasping his hands together, said obsequiously, "We came to tell your honor that the police sergeant has been in Chermashnya this morning. He is coming here directly."

"The police sergeant?" Silence. "What does he know?"

For a moment the two stood looking at him with intent and rather strange expressions, then Savely Antonovich said, "Mikhail Andreyevich died of congestion, your honor," they stepped back, bowing two or three times, and went out.

As soon as they had gone Dostoevsky was overcome by anxiety. What could he do? Evidently all the men in Chermashnya and many in Daravoye had been in the conspiracy. If he denounced them to the police sergeant they would surely be arrested and sent to Siberia. It would be the ruin of the property, the place almost valueless without serfs—the single inheritance he and his brothers and sisters would share. So there could be no retribution. The murderers were property! They had to let the men who murdered their father go unpunished.

He cast about the room as if he did not know what to do next, then crossed to the far bedroom and rummaged at his father's desk among the dirty crumpled papers, bits of rag, rubbish.

There was a bang on the door. He went halfway toward it and stopped. He would have given anything not to answer. Another bang; he opened. It was the police sergeant and his clerk.

"Fyodor Mikhailovich." The police sergeant gave him a cursory salutation; he had a puffed face, one red eye, and was a renowned drunkard. "I have just learned you were here. Allow me to offer my condolences."

"Thank you." Dostoevsky knew that his father had had a violent quarrel with the police sergeant and that ever after it they had been on terms of sustained hostility. The red eye went around the room. The hump-shouldered clerk, who looked like a fly, was installing himself at the table, getting pens and papers out of his box.

"I am taking depositions about the death of Mikhail Andreyevich," the police sergeant said. "What——" He let out a curse as his foot slid on a bottle, but managed to catch his balance. "Ah, that's it, eh?" He looked down at the bottles scattered over the floor. The next moment he was rubbing his hands and passing his tongue over his lips. "If there's a little drop in the house, young sir, it would come well. A drop, isn't there?"

"I'm sorry, I don't know. Is there any reason for taking depositions now?"

"Reason?" The sergeant was obviously annoyed at being rebuffed. "There may be further inquiries."

"But didn't you take down all the evidence the first time you saw the body? That's the usual thing, isn't it?"

The sergeant cleared his throat in a prolonged and offensive way. "I am not obliged to answer your questions. As a matter of fact there are suspicious points."

"Surely that's ridiculous. What is one to suspect?" Now Dostoevsky was certain he meant trouble.

The sergeant leered at him slyly. "How did your father die, Fyodor Mikhailovich?"

"I can only tell you what I've been told. I mean, I am convinced it is true because—because he had had those attacks before."

"Oh, had he?" the sergeant said in an artful tone. He seemed pleased at the lie. Very carefully and without adding anything, Dostoevsky told what Grigory had said, the version of his father becoming excited over the wood and collapsing. The sergeant was walking about the room examining things. As Dostoevsky ended he halted in a position behind Dostoevsky's back. "You say they took him home in the cart, eh?"

"Yes."

"H'm. That's what all of them say." He came around to face Dostoevsky. "When I saw Mikhail Andreyevich with Father Yosif his clothes were damp at the back. The damp was through to the inside; I felt it. And I found a little snail on his boot. He had been lying out in the open. How could that be, Fyodor Mikhailovich?"

The sergeant's eye was fixed on him unblinking. "I—— He got wet in the cart when they laid him there, that's only natural."

"I examined the cart. The weather was hot and the bottom of the cart had only dry mud." He walked away again, evidently very pleased with himself. Dostoevsky glanced at the sly clerk; he was writing on a sheet of paper with dirty thumb marks on the corners, putting down the questions and answers. The thought flashed through Dostoevsky's mind that all this was really only for the sergeant's vanity and that he knew the truth. The authorities might arrest the men at any time. In a panic he blurted out, "But he fell down in the wood; yes, that's it. I can't remember now who told me, but I recollect somebody saying he tripped and fell in some damp spot. It was before he was taken ill." It sounded terribly weak. In the silence the clerk's pen scratched across the paper.

The police sergeant waited a moment; then he said with assurance, "But, Fyodor Mikhailovich, there was the gash on his mouth too." Plainly he had already formed his own opinion. Dostoevsky felt everything was going; he went up to the sergeant and tried to sound confidential.

"Look here, perhaps they have not told you everything. That is natural because it is something they are not proud of, you know." The sergeant was standing still, looking at him sideways. "They were frightened when he became ill. They didn't know what to do so they ran away. Some of them only came back next morning and he had been lying there all night. There was a bird; it had torn his face." He could hardly continue. "That was how it was. You see there are no grounds for suspicion. None at all. If I thought there were, I should ask for an immediate investigation."

The police sergeant's face seemed to become puffier. His expression changed into one of irritation, as if he were saying to himself, "Yes, they were bound to be ready with some story like this. Now I'll be lucky to get anything more. And Fyodor Mikhailovich—well, the Devil knows how deep he is in it." He said aloud, "Excuse me. I must send in a report on my visit here."

"Naturally."

Ten minutes later, when the clerk had finished and they

were leaving, the sergeant said, "You will be staying here, Fyodor Mikhailovich?"

"No. I must be back in Petersburg soon."

"I see. Yes, I see." He was nodding, making it clear that he would be poking about in the family's absence. Dostoevsky watched them drive away. He turned back toward the house and stopped on the threshold. He felt a profound reluctance to enter, but went in and slammed the door.

6

The door of Aunt Kumanina's salon opened softly and Aunt Kumanina came in. She was small and plump and her fashionable Paris crinoline made her look vast. She came over to where Dostoevsky was standing and handed him a fold of gray fifty-ruble notes. "You must take this, *mon cher enfant*. It will help you to manage in the meantime."

"Thank you, Aunt Olga. It's—I——"

"Good, then stop spluttering. Sit down and listen to me." She was his mother's sister, married to a rich Muscovite somewhat older than herself. When Dostoevsky reached Moscow the evening before from Daravoye he had come straight to Aunt Kumanina's where, he found, Alyona Frolovna, the nurse, had brought his two sisters. All five younger children were now staying with her at the Kumaninas' other house in the Moscow suburbs.

Aunt Kumanina sat down on one of the silk-covered chairs. "I want to speak frankly to you, *mon cher enfant*. You are the eldest of the family here and you should be told. Since you children are still all minors you must have a guardian. Mikhail has been writing, saying he will give up everything with the army and settle at Daravoye and bring up the family. That's brave and impractical. The obvious person is my husband, but as you know he is much too often away. So I have thought of Alexander Karepin."

"Who?"

"Alexander Karepin. He is a well-off man in the government service here and he is the ideal match for your sister Varvara. He is serious, presentable, generous. You might almost call him rich. He met Varvara while she was here with us this winter and I can see he is interested in her. I'm sure that with a little management he can be brought around to make a proposal. Once they are married he'll be the natural guardian for the family."

Dostoevsky felt there was something unreal about this parental world of arranged marriages involving his young sister. He said, "Would a young man be approved of? I mean legally, a young man as guardian?"

"He is a widower. He is forty—a young forty."

He could hardly believe it. "But Varinka's only seventeen."

"*Mon cher enfant,* one's youth passes and one's marriage remains. It is an opportunity we could hardly have hoped for. I have arranged for Varvara to come here to live with us while my husband and I prepare things. So your guardian will be provided."

Dostoevsky was excited in a curious way. "Does Mikhail know?"

"I shall write to explain. He will understand at once."

He had a sudden desire to tell her about the police sergeant. "Aunt Olga, there's something I want to——"

"Yes, I'm sure." She rose; she was not going to listen to any objections about Varvara. "You must be going. Is your bag ready? I will tell Sozont. He will take you to the post station."

Chapter Two

1

A damp wind blew up the Nevsky Prospect from the river, making noses drip and everybody uncomfortable. It was early afternoon at the end of September. Heavy clouds were forming up over the sea beyond the city and the droshky horses at the curb stamped and jingled their harness as if they would also be glad when these miserable weeks were over and the first snow fell.

Dostoevsky walked quickly; he was feverish and on edge. As he passed the Anichkov Palace the two sentries by the striped boxes noticed his lieutenant's epaulets and clanked their rifles. He returned the salute, hurrying. It was still fifteen minutes' walk to the Drawing Office of the Engineering Corps where he had been posted since his graduation from the château and promotion. And he was late. Wretched place, the very essence of the pygmy life! How he detested it. Ah, to live in the wild romance of Schiller, the world of heroic figures like Don Carlos, Faust, Eugene Onegin, or of the fantastic tales of Hoffmann. To be a hero or grovel in the mud—there was nothing between!

A glass sign outside a tailor's shop flashed his reflection back: medium height, thick shoulders, short neck; his young face, with broad-set cheekbones and harmonious mouth, was pale and hungry-looking, the light brown hair rather well back from his forehead, eyes burning. Today he hated his face even more than usual. Yes! Out of his unbounded vanity and the high standard he set for himself, he looked at himself with furious discontent. Every day in the office he tried to behave unconcernedly, to put on a lofty expres-

sion, because at any rate his colleagues ought to recognize
that his face was expressive and above all *strikingly* intelligent. He alternated between despising his fellow clerks and
thinking them superior to himself. He knew he was morbidly
sensitive; all at once he would go through a phase of being
skeptical and indifferent, laugh at his intolerance and sensitiveness, and reproach himself with being romantic. There
were phases when he could not bear to speak to anybody
and at other times he positively ran to make up to the office
people, absolutely cringed, called on them at home, played
yarolash and drank vodka with them, and talked of how to
please His Excellency and things of that sort which were
really quite disgusting, and went home ill afterward at the
mere thought of it. And of course the friendship phase never
lasted and deadly hatred grew up between them.

His free time he spent mostly alone, reading or roaming
the Petersburg streets. He craved for incongruity and con-
trast and sought them. There was nowhere like the Nevsky
for working up tingling resentments! He used to walk down
it at the busiest time of the evening, slinking and wriggling
along and constantly stepping back to let officers, excellencies, or ladies go by, actually cringing. At these moments, as
he almost scraped his foot with gratuitous deference, he
felt a tingle and a contraction of his heart and was excruci-
atingly aware of his miserable clothes, his abjectness. Among
all the bright uniforms and dashing carriages, he felt he was
being looked on as an insect, a disgusting beetle that made
way for them, humiliated and disdained, though of course
he was more cultivated, intelligent, and gifted than any of
them. He didn't know why he tormented himself in this way;
it was simply compulsion.

He glanced down at his neglected uniform overcoat and
boots. Yes, there was actually a patch on the overcoat. But
how was he to afford a new one? God knew how he was
going to buy boots for the winter and another tunic as well;
for his old tunic simply would not last three months longer.

What was more, he had been feeling the stinging nervous desire for a cigarette since morning and he hadn't even the price of a packet of tobacco. Could he ask Karepin for another loan? He winced at the thought of the letter Karepin would write back. To begin with, after his marriage to Varvara and his appointment as legal guardian, Karepin had been generous with allowances. Now he was didactic and insufferable. "I sent you a thousand rubles last week. They cannot have gone already? . . . I am informed your orderly robs you right and left. Why don't you get rid of the fellow? . . . Dr. Reisenkampf has been telling me you neglect your health, don't eat, allow suspicious people to steal the money I send you, and have just lost six hundred rubles gambling." In one letter Karepin had even warned him against reading Shakespeare!

He turned into the Sadovaya and noticed two merchants a few paces in front of him. They had folds of fat cascading from under their beards and were coming out of Gruber's, the German pastry cook's shop. Their faces were red, polished, beaming, their fingers glittered with diamond rings, and they both carried enormous balloon bellies before them like bass drums. A file of Gruber's pastry cooks and assistants followed them out of the shop, carrying tray after tray of cream marzipan cakes and dainties which the merchants had evidently ordered for some celebration. There was a flamboyantly and gaily delightful touch about the procession.

All at once the leading pastry cook stumbled, lurched in panic, hovered and crashed down, his tray flew upward, and the two big tiered cakes on it thudded down over his chest among a shower of meringues. At the same moment the second pastry cook tripped over him and fell, sending cream puffs, jam tarts, and turnovers everywhere. The third, with a tray of ice cream, was looking aside and pitched forward over the second, the next one's foot skidded on a custard pie and he came down too. In a moment the tangled arms and legs were all mixed up with jellies, liquid cream, icing, enormous decorated pineapples, éclairs, chocolate layer cakes, and so forth.

The merchants were laughing. Their laughing shook their chests, their arms, and their great bellies like laughing jellies. Their diamond rings flashed, their polished red cheeks glistened merrily with their fat jelly chins shaking. Gruber rushed out of the shop, threw his arms in the air, and started barking, then Frau Gruber appeared shouting in Swabian. Some of the onlookers smiled; others had an air of consternation. The fat merchants went on laughing.

Dostoevsky looked on. There must be four hundred rubles' worth of cakes and delicacies squashed to waste there. The warm sugary pastry-cook smell floated out of Gruber's open door. Dostoevsky swallowed hungrily. For the last three weeks he had been living on bread. Occasionally he had managed to afford some milk, but mainly it had been bread.

He turned away and walked on down the street. And at that moment, without his taking any decision in the matter, it became quite unimportant that he was late for the Drawing Office. His mind ran on the merchants. He saw them each counting on his abacus, their houses with the awful furniture around the walls, the hideous pictures, the close and secretive society in which they and their families lived. And money! Their wives were covered with diamonds, tiaras, bracelets, brooches, splendid furs. Four hundred rubles' worth of pastry cooks' fancies in the gutter. Money, money. It was possible for those men. Yet here I am always drowning in debts, he thought.

He had a hundred projects, he was bursting with ideas. His mind burned them up. He began hurrying again just thinking of them. Nothing but the most ordinary luck was needed to launch Mikhail and him into the literary world. Of course it was a great nuisance that Mikhail was still in Reval; but he had explained the situation to him. There was a fortune in translating. New magazines and papers were springing up every week, all eager for translations from French and German writers. Look at that fellow Strugovchik; Strugovchik translated no better than either of them and he'd not only made a pile but become a literary celebrity! Then there was a fortune in publishing. He had persuaded Mikhail to start translating Schiller. The most brilliant success was just around the corner for them. For the moment it was eluding them. If only he had a little more time— time—time!

And ahead of him now was the Drawing Office. A lifetime of service in the Engineering Corps—he shuddered at the monumental boredom of it. Out of the corner of his eye he saw a figure going by raising his cap. It was Bashmirsky, a poor government clerk. He saluted but Bashmirsky hurried on. Ugh! Dostoevsky shuddered again. Bashmirsky symbolized all that was soul-destroying in the service; his nose looked frostbitten already. His humility was distressing.

To add to his discomfort, he suddenly thought of the wages he owed to Arkady, his orderly. How he hated that man! He had allowed himself to bicker with him disgracefully for years. There was no question that Arkady despised him beyond measure. For years it had made Dostoevsky wince simply to wake up in the morning and think of another day with him. The way he compressed his lips alone was enough to give anybody the shudders. Arkady was a plump, middle-aged man of majestic bearing and an air of the greatest profundity. He looked on himself as someone of consequence and had a vanity of the most extreme kind. He behaved like a despot, spoke very little in the course of his duties, and kept throwing out firm, ironical looks that drove Dostoevsky to fury. Plainly he regarded Dostoevsky as the biggest fool in Petersburg, yet hung onto him out of spite and because he need do almost no work at all. He absolutely declined, for instance, to clean shoes twice a day and Dostoevsky had to creep out into the passage and steal the blacking and brushes, taking the utmost care not to let Arkady notice for fear of his contempt.

At the Drawing Office the orderly sergeant said, "General Svetlov wishes to see you, Lieutenant. He said to tell you the minute you came in."

"Very well," Dostoevsky said, and thought: What a bore. Svetlov was going to haul him over the coals for returning late. He had a good mind to say frankly, "I have been writing a play about Boris Godunov, which, if you want to know, General, happens to be a masterpiece."

He turned through the outer rooms leading to the general's office. The general's ADC kept him waiting fifteen minutes while he studied a small pimple on his chin and tried to decide whether to squeeze it. At last he showed Dostoevsky in. General Svetlov was sitting reading at his table. He took no notice and went on reading as if Dostoevsky did not exist. It was a trick that the ADC had picked up from him as something "distinguished." Russians were always doing such things, Dostoevsky thought, even officers who ought to know better. When General Svetlov finally looked up his eyes traveled slowly from Dostoevsky's face to his boots.

"Your appearance, Lieutenant Dostoevsky, leaves a great deal to be desired," he said. "A great deal. The Most High has been graciously pleased to command far more strictness in this respect. You understand?"

"Yes, General."

General Svetlov tapped his foot under the table. "You will have an opportunity to set an example," he said. "I am transferring you to Krasnoy. Every officer should do service in the provinces." He began to leaf through a portfolio of papers.

Dostoevsky was horrified. The provinces! Life would be dull beyond endurance; he would be good for nothing without Petersburg. He said, "I'd rather not, General."

"Eh?" The general looked up; he had moist protruding

eyes like a Pekinese dog's and now they looked moister with astonishment. "Rather not? Did you say rather not? Do you understand I am giving you an order?"

"Then I resign my commission, General Svetlov. Please accept it as from now."

"You what?"

"I resign. At once." There was a silence.

The general stood up, looking scandalized. "You do not seem to realize, Lieutenant. Things must be done in the proper way. There are regulations. You must *crave* the Most High to consider releasing you from the service. You will submit your request in writing tomorrow."

"Thank you, General. I will." Dostoevsky saluted.

Outside the ADC was still staring into the glass and fingering his pimple. Dostoevsky went to his office and began collecting his instruments and books. Well, it was done. Perhaps it was rather a stab to think what a quick end it was to all these years of labor. Totleben, his companion from the Engineers' Château, who had also been appointed to the Drawing Office, came up. "I heard Svetlov was asking for you. What's up?"

"I've resigned."

"Yes, I know, and the Tsar has liberated the serfs," Totleben said, then with astonishment saw that Dostoevsky was not joking. "The devil you have! Isn't it—I say, Fyodor Mikhailovich, isn't it a bit rash? What are you going to do? You'd better go to see him again and say it was a mistake. Say that in a moment of unreflecting—"

"My dear Adolf Ivanovich, I'm tired of this dreary life. I thought it was bad enough pouring my brains into Dyadin's *Artillery Course*, Braschman's *Fortifications*, Ozemov's *Physics*, Bolotov's *Surveying;* but this is drying up my soul. So now I'm going to make a fortune."

"What? How?"

"My brother and I are publishing a complete edition of Schiller. I've worked it all out, down to the last ruble. It can't fail. Mikhail's translation of *Don Carlos* is a master-piece. I've corrected one or two things, improved the verses here and there. We are bound to get well paid for it. In the autumn we can publish the rest. A hundred copies will cover our expenses—and a hundred copies is nothing!"

"I always thought that sort of thing was pretty uncertain."

"*Mon cher,* the translation will make a tremendous stir. They'll all be after us like flies when they see what we can do with translations. I can tell you, the publishers will marvel! They'll soon be pestering us with other offers. Oh, don't worry, we won't let the work go for a song. The least success and the profits will be unheard of!"

"I see." Totleben looked at him.

"I'm also finishing a play. But it's a secret, do you under-stand? The jealousy of these literary gentlemen is hardly to be believed; and since my work is original they'd dearly like to get their hands on it. But I know them."

They shook hands and said good-by. In the street the wind struck colder. Winter was in the air.

"Bread, your honor," a voice croaked at his elbow. He shook his head at the poor fellow. And suddenly he remem-bered that Karepin was arriving in Petersburg in three days' time. What would he say? He was capable of cutting off money supplies altogether. If so—— Pah! He hurried forward.

2

His room was in an alley on the north side of the Neva. It smelled of cabbage. The smell pervaded the whole house, rising up the terrifying banisterless stairs, clinging to the scarred walls, and overlaying the intermediary smells of past cooking, bugs, bug powder, slops, and long-worn clothes. Opposite the window of his room there was a broken fence. It had posters on it for a menagerie, blue paper with a tiger's head. Menageries only came to poor districts.

He stood shaving in the room one morning two weeks
after the snow had fallen and covered the city. Karepin
after all, it had turned out, was occupied with some depart-
mental matter in Moscow and had not come. Dostoevsky's
dismay at being unable to raise money from him was
balanced by his relief at not having to listen to his sermon-
izing about resigning.

A letter from Mikhail, just opened, lay among the
books, strewn sheets of manuscript, notebooks on the table.
Mikhail was getting married. Karepin, he wrote, had disapproved, arguing that it would jeopardize his army career.
They had had a dispute by letter, with the result that
Karepin had stopped his allowance, which left him without
a kopeck. But he was ecstatically happy, Emily was adorable;
they must all meet without delay.

Snicking the last islet of lather from his upper lip,
Dostoevsky wondered for the tenth time how he could get
to Reval. The second-class fare there and back was fifteen
rubles; there would be his keep and hotel to pay for once
he was there. And somehow he would have to help Mikhail
with funds. Altogether he needed sixty rubles.

There was a sound at the door and Pogodin, occupant of
the next room, came in. He had a round face of a dark red
color and one eye, bigger than the other, fixed in a down-
ward ruminative expression. Pogodin had taken Dostoevsky
on night excursions to the poorest parts of Petersburg (it
was he who had introduced him to Bashmirsky, the government clerk) and was always turning up in the room with
some piece of news or scandal. Pogodin gave his usual low
bow and said, "What's for your worship's service this morning?" looking around with his mobile eye for tobacco,
fluttering his nostrils to smell if any had been smoked.
Dostoevsky was pleased to see him. Pogodin had become a
confidant and took his position very solemnly, never allowing
himself a misplaced expression; he had a strange gimletlike
penetration for some things and at moments, in a flash,

would have fully, profoundly, wonderfully grasped all one was trying to convey, the big fixed ruminative brown eye bent to the floor boards.

"Pogodin, I'm in an infernal situation," Dostoevsky said excitedly. "The last of that money I sold my instruments and army kit for is gone. I have eight hundred rubles' worth of debts. I've written to Moscow telling them it's fifteen hundred. You know what they are—they always send half. Karepin will go to Aunt Kumanina and say, 'He is exaggerating as usual,' and they will have a voluptuous discussion about their charges. Ha!"

He was pacing the room restlessly and snatched up his old army tunic from a chair. "Look at this! I haven't a kopeck to clothe myself. If those pigs in Moscow don't pay up, I'm done for. Mind you, my dear fellow, if I hadn't resigned already, I'd do so now. I regret nothing, absolutely nothing!"

Pogodin, who was seated on the one chair, laid a hunk of bread and two large onions on the table. He said, "What about the inheritance from your father, Fyodor Mikhailovich?"

"Do you know what I did? I wrote to Karepin offering to give up my share for five hundred rubles now and five hundred more payable at ten rubles a month. That's all I asked. Admit it, Pogodin, it's not much. Admit that I'm not swindling anybody."

Pogodin assented pugnaciously.

"And they refused! They won't have anything to do with it. Admit it, it's not up to me to make another offer. I'd even take seven hundred in all. But they've no confidence in me. They think I am going to trick them. I asked Mikhail to guarantee that I wouldn't ask more. Think of it!"

"Sit down, your honor." Pogodin's outstretched hand caught his forearm like a vise and he nodded toward the food. Dostoevsky sat on the bed and they both ate, Pogodin cutting the bread with his penknife like a peasant and listening to Dostoevsky's verbose, excited outpourings as if this were his role.

"Look at Pushkin and Gogol. They haven't written much, but they'll have statues put up to them. And do you know how much Gogol gets for a page of print, eh? A thousand rubles! For one page! And Pushkin got a gold piece for a poem. Ah, but they had years of misery and starvation, Gogol especially. A thousand rubles. For a thousand rubles we'd get the Schiller translation printed. Think of that, Pogodin. Well, who knows how much my novel will bring in?"

When Pogodin had gone he waited a moment, then put on his coat and went out. The cold stung; he hurried along with his neck sunk into his collar. Crossing the square by St. Vladimir's Church, the cold wind took his breath away; as he reached the far side somebody said, "Dostoevsky? Yes, it is," and stepped in front of him.

"Grigorovich!" It was his companion of the château days. They wrung each other's hands.

"What are you doing? Why aren't you in uniform?"

"Damn it, why aren't you? I've cleared out of the army."

"So have I. I'm a writer."

"So am I! And translator, editor, and publisher."

They embraced on the strength of it. "You are coming to my rooms at once," Grigorovich said, taking his arm. "And staying for lunch too. I have fifty things to talk to you about." He looked prosperous in his marten-trimmed coat, Dostoevsky thought, and well fed; he had a slit of a mouth and a cleft chin, a froggy sort of face. "Hey! Isvostchik!" Grigorovich hailed a droshky and they plunged into talk as they drove away. Dostoevsky told Grigorovich about Schiller and his hopes.

"Where is your work appearing?" Grigorovich asked.

"Well, it isn't anywhere yet. I'm preparing things which will strike them dumb with admiration."

"What?" Grigorovich looked at him. "Oh yes—that's the

spirit!" Grigorovich, it appeared, was already succeeding fairly well in the literary world. He had had a few pieces published in magazines, was beginning to gain a footing in one or two newspaper offices. He was loquacious and in great good humor.

His address on a narrow back street failed to come up to his look of prosperity. They climbed high up to two bare rooms with windows looking out over Petersburg: the smoking chimneys, the snow-covered buildings, squares, cupolas, the black lines made by the carriages. Grigorovich prepared tea and when the samovar wouldn't draw whipped off his leather knee boot, fixing it over the top and pumping, the old army camp trick. "You'll have to listen to my new story," he said. "I haven't cornered you for nothing." He took a manuscript from the table. "It's called 'The Barrel Organ Player.' I've just finished it."

He read with gusto and Dostoevsky was enthusiastic. The sky became grayer and snow began to fall again; they refilled the samovar, talking on emphatically, forgetting food, discussing the writers and critics of the day, casting some to eternal oblivion, raising others to immortality.

Grigorovich was full of a new idea. "I want to write stories about the peasants *from their point of view*. Do you see what I mean? It's never been done before."

Dostoevsky jumped up. "But it's extraordinary!"

"What do you mean? There's——"

"I'm doing the same sort of thing, in a novel I am finishing; only not with peasants."

"What? A novel?"

"By God, we have started the new tendency."

"We've begun the revolution."

They looked at each other for a moment of silent excitement. Grigorovich said, "We must join forces. There's no getting away from it. You'll have to come and live here; enough room for two."

"All right. I haven't a kopeck, but we'll soon be making a packet."

"But this novel, my dear fellow, speak up. I'm dying with curiosity about it."

"Well, it's about——" Dostoevsky stopped. "Look here, Dmitry Vassilyevich, it's not finished. I'd rather wait till it is, then you can read it."

"All right. And I'll get to work on my peasant story; it's going to be called 'The Village.' You can move in this week. The room next door is yours."

"Hail Grigorovich!" Dostoevsky raised his glass of tea.

"To the conquest of Petersburg!"

3

The stub of candle stuck in the bottle began to sputter. He looked up, took another stump, and, lighting it from the dying one, stuck it into the socket; the transparent grease welled out around the bottle mouth and hardened to gray. He resumed writing. After a few more phrases he numbered the page and took up a pile of others already crisscrossed with changes.

The candle flame swayed in a current of air. "Good God!" Grigorovich said, entering behind him. "Are you still at it?" He was in his overcoat and fur cap, the snow melting on his boots. "Do you know what time it is? It's dawn, *mon cher*. Look here." He twitched the curtain back from the window and the cold daylight came in.

Dostoevsky dropped the pen and stretched. "For God's sake, give me a pinch of tobacco, Dmitry Vassilyevich. I smoked my last an hour ago."

"Do you know you haven't been out for three days, my dear fellow? No, four!"

"I went out with you on Sunday because you insisted so much," Dostoevsky said.

"For ten minutes. And you ran back here because you

couldn't stand the fresh air." Grigorovich held out his tobacco pouch. The table was heaped up with books, ink-pots, oddments, newspapers, sheets of manuscript and had drifts of tobacco ash on it. He took up one of the manuscript sheets. "It's time you showed me some of this, you know."

"No, no." Dostoevsky took it from him. "Not yet. When it's done."

"But I thought you finished it long ago. You even finished rewriting the whole thing last month."

"Well, now I've cut it and rewritten a lot more. There are some things to add; it will be ready next week." He was in a state of exaltation. "Do you know, Dmitry Vassilyevich, if it doesn't succeed, I'll jump into the Neva. Yes, I've decided. I've decided!"

It had appeared at once that Grigorovich's income from his writing was tenuous and they were soon living on bread, cigarettes, and an abominable "coffee" made of cheap barley; there were occasional interludes of better fare when Karepin sent money or Grigorovich managed to earn a small sum. Late one afternoon in May, as Grigorovich lay on the sofa reading the *Journal de Petersbourg,* Dostoevsky came in from the other room.

"The censorship's becoming absurd," Grigorovich said. "There's never any damned news in these papers at all." He threw the paper down. "Do you know I was talking to Radetsky at the *Gazette* yesterday and he says they've been forbidden to use the word 'great' about the French Revolution!"

"I wonder how they'll deal with *Poor Folk,*" Dostoevsky said. "I'll read it to you if you like."

"Eh? My God—is that your novel? It's finished at last? Let's have it." He jumped up. "I say, Fyodor Mikhailovich, has it got a touch of Schiller? I know we said a new school, but you know I can't help suspecting it has, eh?"

"Rubbish. Not a bit!" Dostoevsky laughed excitedly.

"None of those heroics—or rather, heroics in a different world. It happens here in Petersburg, among those government clerks, poor devils. You remember Bashmirsky, that clerk Pogodin brought here a couple of times? Well, I've often been to his quarters. He lives in a corner behind a partition at the end of somebody's kitchen. You have to be strong-willed even to approach it, to get up those back stairs. They wind up, the steps all crumbled and the walls so greasy your hand sticks if you touch them. The landings are piled with boxes and straw, broken chairs, old cupboards with rags hanging out, and tubs of filth and dirt and eggshells and refuse of fish; the stench is appalling. They simply can't keep canaries in that place; the birds die off because the air is so foul. Bashmirsky's cubicle in the kitchen hasn't a window and of course the partition doesn't go to the ceiling. There are always old clothes hanging on a line in the kitchen and the tenants—there are two or three in every room—often fry fish or cook meat scraps. Besides, people start coming in very early in the morning and at night as well, splashing about, washing things and so forth. Well, do you see, there's my hero's home! He's called Dyevushkin and he falls in love with a young woman, Varenka, who lives opposite. She is poor too. They want to visit each other but they're afraid of gossip, so they write letters."

"Read it, read it! Come on, my dear fellow," cried Grigorovich, grasping his arm and pulling him toward the sofa. "I want to hear everything."

They installed themselves and Dostoevsky began. He knew every word of the story, he had worked over it so many times. But as he read it the couple came over irresistibly, living in front of them with an extraordinary intensity.

"But you must give it to me." Grigorovich jumped up well before he had finished. "I'll take it to Kolya Nekrasov. Yes, yes, it's just the thing."

"I was going to give it to a good monthly, say *Annals of the Fatherland.*"

"To Krayevsky? No, no. Let me take it to Nekrasov. Believe me, he's the rising man. I know he's looking for a good thing. My dear fellow, leave it with me for this evening. I'll go straight away. I'll fly there." He was reaching for his coat.

Dostoevsky laughed. He had heard of Nekrasov, a young poet who was beginning to make his way in the Petersburg literary world. "All right."

"Good." Grigorovich bundled the manuscript into the newspaper. Then, as if suddenly brought up by prudence: "Of course, I don't *know* what Nekrasov will say. But anyway, it won't do any harm to have his opinion."

Dostoevsky felt empty-handed that evening. It was the first time for months that he had not sat working on the manuscript of *Poor Folk.* He went down to the floor below where Hlastov, a student, lived and sat talking with him and a couple of others about Gogol. It was early morning when he climbed the stairs again. No sign of Grigorovich. Well, Nekrasov was supposed to have a taste for dissipation; the two of them were probably enjoying themselves.

He opened the window wide. It was one of the short nights of spring, strange, warm, and disturbing. He sat looking out—Petersburg like a dream city lay silent in the milky opaline twilight of the White Night. Everything was still. The footsteps of a solitary passer-by resounded from somewhere below. Only the gilded cross on the top of St. Isaac's, the great cathedral still building across the river, caught a ray of the hidden sun. Through a gap in the intervening roofs he could see the ghost of the Winter Palace, faintly yellow, and farther along the gas jets flaring on the bridge.

A clock, far away, struck four, the strokes widely spaced; then another closer in and immediately several at once. Behind him the door opened and Grigorovich, followed by a dark, thin-faced young man, burst in. Dostoevsky looked around at them, then Grigorovich was running up, smiling and excited, embracing him, seizing him by the arms and leading him to the other. "Tell him what you think of it, Nekrasov. Tell him."

Nekrasov said, "It's wonderful. My God, you've written a work of art. We couldn't stop reading it. We read it all night in turns. It's superb."

He was pumping Dostoevsky's hand; he had a mustache and his hair was well back from his forehead. "I'm proud to know you—proud. You have done something outstanding, *mon cher* Dostoevsky."

"We said, 'What if he's asleep? Never mind, we'll wake him up; this is superior to sleep,' " Grigorovich said. "We read it to the end."

"There's genius in the book," Nekrasov said. "I don't mind using that word. We both wept—yes, we did!"

"I—I— it's too generous," Dostoevsky stuttered, his face flushed with pleasure.

"I'm going to take the manuscript to Belinsky," Nekrasov said. "I'll take it to him today." Dostoevsky was wordless. Belinsky—the great critic, the oracle, the tiger of the Russian literary world. "You'll meet him, my dear fellow. You'll see for yourself what a man he is, what a giant!"

Grigorovich said, "It'll be published under Belinsky's auspices. Nekrasov swears it."

"I don't know what to say," Dostoevsky said. "How to thank you, my good friends . . . I'm afraid there's not even any tea to offer you, Nekrasov."

"I'm going to tell Belinsky we've found a new Gogol," Nekrasov said.

They flew into a discussion, understanding each other at the smallest hints; they talked about poetry, Gogol, "the present situation," Belinsky. When Nekrasov left, Grigorovich gave him a final overjoyed handclasp, then went to bed. Dostoevsky was farther from sleep than he had ever been in his life. He paced the room, thinking of Belinsky, Nekrasov's words, the bright promise of success. One feeling was precious to him above all the rest; some people gave praise or congratulated in a formal way; but Nekrasov and Grigorovich had run to him with tears at four o'clock in the morning to wake him up because it was superior to sleep.

He went downstairs and stood at the street corner and looked at the sky and the people passing and felt that a solemn moment had occurred in his life, changing it forever, that he had begun something entirely new.

Chapter Three

1

"A top hat! Bring a top hat, the best you have." Dostoevsky adjusted his tie in the glass.

"Oui, monsieur. Tout de suite." Monsieur Cornillon did a pirouette and clapped his hands. The assistants darted away—three of them, exclaiming in French. Everybody spoke French at Cornillon's. The sound of Russian was never heard there, from either the customers or the Russian staff. It would have been thought not quite in keeping; in fact, most of the Russian excellencies who bought their shirts, hats, and canes there, and the latest novelties direct from Paris, were more at home in French than they were in Russian. Even Cornillon's prices were French.

Dostoevsky hooked a thumb in the armhole of his waistcoat and turned toward a display of gloves. Monsieur Cornillon, light as a bank note, whipped up two or three models, pirouetted, and presented them to him. Dostoevsky consented to glance at them. "The choicest material, monsieur. They arrived from the Boulevard des Italiens yesterday."

"H'm. Send me three pairs. Size six and a half."

"Certainly, monsieur," the glove assistant said. "What name, please?" Just for an instant Monsieur Cornillon hesitated, just for long enough to show he had forgotten.

"Dostoevsky."

Cornillon was already fluttering expostulation at the assistant. Well, thought Dostoevsky, if they hadn't realized who he was yet, they soon would. They had only to hear from Belinsky.

Belinsky, the most vehement critic, the most exacting man

in Petersburg, had adopted him like a son, was praising him everywhere and introducing him to the great of Petersburg society. The writers were crowding around him. Besides Nekrasov there were Panayev, a rich man and joint editor with Nekrasov of the *Contemporary* magazine, Ivan Turgenev, one of the coming young men, people like Prince Vyazemsky, who had been a friend of Pushkin's, a host of others.

He was launched! Belinsky had left no doubt of it. When Nekrasov hurried him to Belinsky's that day, Belinsky had jumped up from the sofa waving the manuscript of *Poor Folk*. "So you're Dostoevsky! Do you know what you've written here? Eh? Do you simply *understand* what you have written? It is the truth, wonderfully done. Only you with your immediate sense as an artist could have written it. You have found the secret of high artistic value. Young man, remain faithful to your talent and you will be one of Russia's great writers!" Praise, praise, praise! He had acclaimed Dostoevsky's artistic instinct in a torrent of words. That was already two months ago; more of the Petersburg salons had been opening to him every week since. And his novel was not even published yet!

"*Voilà*, Excellency. *Voilà, voilà, voilà.*" Cornillon fluttered his hands as the assistants appeared, hurrying, with piles of white hatboxes. Dostoevsky stood striking attitudes before the long oval glass, trying the hats on. The magnificence of the shop, the dandified dress of Monsieur Cornillon and the assistants contrasted with his shabby swallow-tail coat and lumpy boots. He noticed it himself. It was simply that his success had scarcely left him time to order new clothes. A new coat was being delivered today—on credit like the rest. In a curious way credit had suddenly become the easiest thing in the world; it was simply a question of confidence!

"Not bad." He tilted a hat with a curly brim to one side in a style he always thought of as "sarcastic."

"Ouf! Here you are at last." Grigorovich hurried up,

perspiring and breathless. "I've searched half the Nevsky. My dear fellow, Count Wielhorsky is looking for you everywhere. He wants you to give a reading."

"A what?" Dostoevsky said, his eye on the reflection, adjusting the hat. "I can't spare the time. Who is he?"

"Count Wielhorsky?" Grigorovich swallowed and looked at Dostoevsky, impressed. "He's a *grand seigneur*. He writes, in a dilettante sort of way. He knows everybody and—well, he'd be extraordinarily useful to have as one's ally." Then, as if anxious for Dostoevsky not to miss so excellent an occasion, he added hurriedly, "But finish with your purchases first, Fyodor Mikhailovich. We'll discuss it in a minute."

"This is all I need this morning," Dostoevsky said. "Cornillon, you will send the things at once, without fail." Cornillon did an entrechat. The two went out and were ten paces up the Nevsky when Dostoevsky stopped and ran back.

"What is it? What is it?" Grigorovich cried, running after him.

Dostoevsky shoved open the door of Cornillon's, put his head in, and shouted, "Send *two* of those hats."

As they went along the Nevsky again Grigorovich kept up a fast chatter. "You are coming to Prince Odoyevsky's tonight, aren't you? You know who's going to be there? I've a list somewhere. I've just seen Sternberg—his cousin is one of the assistant chamberlains at court—and I told him *Poor Folk* was the greatest book since *Dead Souls*. He opened his eyes wide! You must try to find time for Count Wielhorsky. Oh yes, and Baron Chenkin sent an invitation to a reception on Thursday . . ."

"I wish you wouldn't go on," Dostoevsky said in sudden agitation. Success was, of course, his due; but secretly the receptions, the society world, terrified him. He was exalted, excited, and frightened at the same time. Entering some notable's salon, feeling all eyes on him, he was taken by panic, an acute self-conscious awkwardness. He gulped, stuttered, blurted out half phrases. He knew his clothes were wretched. He felt they were all waiting for him to say something brilliant and he could not find it. Yet it was true that when he did say something they murmured appreciatively. In fact he often managed to recover his self-assurance after a while and show them what a remarkable fellow he was. But his awkward timidity returned at the next occasion.

Grigorovich caught his breath. They were at the Kazansky Bridge. "I promised Count Wielhorsky an answer. I'll tell him you're considering it," and he flew off.

Dostoevsky reached his room and sat down to write to Mikhail. "I don't think my glory can ever reach another peak like this. Everybody has an unheard-of esteem for me; they all want to know about me. I meet crowds of the very best people. Prince Odoyevsky—he's a philosopher and historian—has begged me to honor him with a visit. Count Sollogub is tearing his hair with despair, running around everywhere asking, 'Where can I get hold of Dostoevsky?' That little aristocrat on stilts, thinking he's going to impress me with his favors! Everybody treats me as a marvel. I only have to open my mouth and the whole of Petersburg is saying, 'Dostoevsky thinks this, Dostoevsky says that.' Turgenev hangs around me so much Belinsky says he's in love with me. And really, Turgenev is an excellent fellow —an aristocrat, rich, full of talent, young and handsome. I haven't much money—debts as usual. *Poor Folk* is still with the censor. But I'm not complaining. The other night I dashed off a thing in a few hours and Nekrasov paid me a hundred and twenty-five rubles for it. Now I'm writing another short novel, something far better than *Poor Folk*. It's called *The Double*. It will be my masterpiece!"

2

Celebrity was exacting.

Poor Folk, published in January of the New Year, 1846, set off a discordant chorus of abuse and praise. There were more critics than supporters; but they argued at the tops of their voices. He was lying in bed smoking, at the new apartment he had moved to from Grigorovich's, when Pogodin came in. "There's a long article here about you by Prince Odoyevsky," Pogodin said, wrenching a squashed-up pulpy journal from his pocket.

"I know; I've read it. Did you ever see such flattery? Running after me, of course. You have no idea the praise I'm getting, Pogodin. Plenty of people detest the book—but they're reading it! They're working for my glory, the fools. I've thrown a bone to the public. Belinsky himself thinks I've far outdone Gogol. I'm more profound for one thing." He shifted in the bed and squeezed his eyelids in finger and thumb.

Pogodin's bloodshot glance missed nothing. "Shall I make you some tea, your honor?"

"Yes, do. And give me one of those pills." He sighed noisily. "Too much champagne last night. Can't be helped. It's all part of the tribute one has to pay to popularity. One isn't an idol for nothing, Pogodin, my poor fellow. Do you know I sometimes spend a thousand rubles a night now? It's terrible." Pogodin, busy at the samovar, turned his head, nodding. "But what does it matter? I have a thousand ideas —and they are all worth gold. The editors and publishers are falling over themselves after me. They realize the enormous value of my talent. There's Krayevsky, for instance— he's the editor of *Annals of the Fatherland*. Do you know, Pogodin, Krayevsky is positively *begging* me to take loans!"

"It's a marvel," Pogodin said. "And doesn't *The Double* come out today, your honor?"

"Yes."

"*Poor Folk* out last month, now *The Double*. Extraordinary!"

"Oh, they can't get enough of it." Dostoevsky waved a hand. He smiled. The story of *The Double*, which gave him excruciating secret joys and pain, came from his deepest self. The hero, Yakov Petrovich Golyadkin, was a confused, awkward government clerk in Petersburg, suffering because he was unable to make himself felt, to force the respect he considered he merited. A particularly humiliating experience convinced him that other people were persecuting him, mysteriously plotting his downfall, and at this point, an emotional crisis in his life, he met a man who was his double to look at and indeed had the same name. The man had obtained a post in the same office and gradually Mr. Golyadkin saw the Double develop all the attributes he thought he had and longed to assert. Where he himself was timid, pale, ineffectual and crushed, secretly rebellious and yearning for grandeur, the Double turned out to be masterful, elegant, resourceful, a man who was able to impress everybody. His anxiety to compensate for his insignificance had made him project himself outside himself! With horror and utter humiliation, Mr. Golyadkin looked on while the Double succeeded in everything he had failed in—capturing the esteem of all, the delighted notice of his superiors, general admiration and respect. The Double even went so far as to mock at him cynically. Mr. Golyadkin was overwhelmed, concluded that the Double was leading the conspiracy against him, struggled vainly, and finally worried himself into such a state of mental confusion and instability that the scornfully triumphant Double at last packed him off to the madhouse.

Ah, how well he knew both those sides, that duality! The Golyadkins were the men within himself. It was his deepest soul. He knew he had done the story with subtlety and insight.

One evening at the end of the month he arrived at Prince Odoyevsky's. The Odoyevskys lived in a great house on the English Quay. It was the Princess's name day and they were giving a ball. The windows of the house blazed with light and the sleds ran into the snowy courtyard one after the other. The sound of animated voices and laughter mingled with the music in the ballroom with its colonnade on each side. People were standing and sitting about, a great many generals in uniform, two or three governors with Alexander Nevsky ribbons, the women wearing dresses from Paris and, posted around the walls, some incredibly ancient creatures, relations of Odoyevsky's, one of whom was supposed to be the last surviving maid of honor of the Empress Catherine's court. Other guests were dancing.

Belinsky, seated in an alcove with two newspaper editors, was showing all his dislike of large social gatherings by fidgeting and throwing mistrustful glances over his shoulder. The locks of hair were falling over his forehead as usual, his emaciated face glowing with his furious sick energy. Belinsky was really extremely shy in such surroundings and did all he could to conceal it. He was bound to appear at a certain number of these functions by reason of his position, often went through agonies because of them, and was ill for days afterward. A man of his intelligence could not be happy in Petersburg. He was shackled by the autocracy, exasperated by the censorship. He said, "Nature intended me to bark like a dog and howl like a jackal, but circumstances compel me to mew like a cat and wave my tail like a fox." He was forced by need of money to work like a hack and was prostrated by the Baltic climate, the worst there was for a man in his condition. Yet frail, shy, dying of consumption, the articles he poured out with all his stinging ferocity were devastating. If an opponent at some social gathering attacked the ideas he believed in, he sprang on him with his cheek muscles quivering, slashed him to pieces with his wit, his intelligence, the extraordinary force of his arguments, held him up like an absurd, disarticulated doll—and then often was forced to stop speaking, his face the color of cardboard, blood on the handkerchief he held to his mouth, profoundly dismayed by his own frailty.

At this moment his disquiet and hardly contained disgust were being aroused by an officer of the secret police standing nearby whom Odoyevsky had had the bad taste to invite.

These evenings at Odoyevsky's often produced a queer mixture—foreign ambassadors who didn't understand a word of Russian, archimandrites, lecturers, half-literary men, and so forth. Odoyevsky's wife was unfailingly distressed, but bore it.

On the other side of the room Nekrasov was talking in his lively way with Turgenev. "My dear fellow," Nekrasov was saying. "You have no idea how narrow they are there." He had just returned from Moscow, home of the Slavophiles, the men who urged that Russia turn its back on the West and Western civilization, renounce the Petersburg period of Peter the Great and the introduction of Western ideas, and go back to the old Russian ways, the essential beliefs, customs, and national excellencies of the Russian people which had been corrupted by foreign thought. "You should see the costumes—caps, Hungarian jackets, I don't know what. It isn't merely a question of wearing shirts that button up at the side of the neck, having long hair, and tucking your trousers into your boots. Ivan Aksakov goes about in a dress that's so *national* the peasants in the street think he's a Persian!"

Turgenev laughed. He was a bulky, spectacled young man of twenty-seven with a striking large head, powerful nose, and melancholy-looking greenish-brown eyes. There was an unmistakable Russian stamp about him; he kept his brown hair rather long and had a mustache over his full lips; but when he spoke his general handsome attractiveness was marred by his squeaky voice. Turgenev had recently made a reputation as a poet and was a great crony of Belinsky's. Heir to a fortune, endowed with intelligence, exceptional talent as a writer, and the power to charm, he had become a favorite of fashionable Petersburg society. But as Belinsky had noticed, there was also malice in him, a humiliated bitterness, a satirical wit. In company, Turgenev posed, played for effect, was superciliously opinionated. Belinsky was often irritated by his frivolity but saw that this side of him was only a defense against the world, against the griefs and problems Turgenev carried in his heart, and that behind it there was immense reserve, generosity and sensitiveness. It was a phase which would pass as Turgenev matured. Turgenev still suffered from his mother, who ruled with ferocious cruelty over her estates in Orel. In addition he was experiencing the frustration of an unhappy love for the prima donna of the day, Pauline Viardot, who ignored him.

Nekrasov bowed to a worried-looking middle-aged man going by and at Turgenev's inquiring glance said, "It's Skobyevich. I must tell you about his nephew." With shining eyes he began telling how a group of friends had invaded his apartment on the eve of his departure for Moscow, dragging with them young Skobyevich (who had just inherited an enormous estate) and settled down to play cards, "just to liven the fellow up. They were still there when I got back—except Skobyevich," Nekrasov said. "I asked them how the enlivening process had turned out. 'Oh, that blackguard,' they said. 'He swindled us.' 'What?' I said. I was amazed. 'Yes—we guarded him night and day, but the scoundrel managed to give us the slip and went off and lost ten thousand rubles somewhere else!'"

They laughed again. Yes, Turgenev thought; that was the unscrupulous side of life Nekrasov delighted in. He was turning away when Nekrasov said, "Here's our local immortal." He indicated the door with his eyes.

Dostoevsky stood in the doorway reddening under the looks of curiosity, with an appalling sinking feeling in his stomach and weak knees. If only he need not move forward; if only there could be some incident and all of them turn and become absorbed in it, forget him. He had been in a nervous fever since he had begun to dress for the evening. The wing of his high collar felt as if it were going to fly open again at any second, as it had half a dozen times while he was fastening it. Now he was certain the new green swallow-tail coat he had on was too waisted, *far* too waisted.

The tailor had sworn it was in the latest style. They were all noticing how ridiculous it was. He was a laughingstock! And the frangipani scent from Monsieur Cornillon's. Cornillon himself had insisted it was *the* thing. My God! Why did one submit to such humiliation? After the first glance he could not wrench his eyes from the floor and he did not know what to do with his hands. He kept repeating desperately to himself that if he merely stood there they would soon think it quite natural, that he was merely engaged in a minute or two's reflection on some serious matter. He had a brief flash of fantasy—he was arriving after winning the battle of the Berezina, seeing them all lined up in two ranks bowing to him in awe and admiration, then from somewhere the crash of music, a flood of light, the Emperor . . . It crumbled in a moment. He felt the sweat pricking at the top of his head, managed to swallow, and, telling himself that nothing mattered at all, that he didn't care for any of these people, that it wouldn't matter if he never saw them again —he shot forward as if on a spring.

He shouldered a governor, kicked away the walking stick of one of the old creatures who was being led across the floor and made her stagger, did not stop, came face to face with one of the servants and dodged ridiculously first one way and then the other and back again trying to get past him, and, not knowing where he was going, caught sight of Turgenev and Nekrasov. He bolted toward them for haven. But halfway there an arm shot out before him. He faltered— and Prince Odoyevsky, grasping his sleeve, was turning him aside, saying, "*Cher ami*, you're in a great hurry. You must come and meet everybody . . ." and confronting him with the group of men and women he had been talking to.

Dostoevsky felt the chasm opening for the worst of all— the moment when he must speak. He suddenly burst out, greatly astonished and realizing too late that he hadn't let Odoyevsky finish the introductions. He was saying something with polite wishes in it. He felt that if he began to stumble with the words he would be lost and he immediately did stumble, strove to recover, became entangled, hopelessly entangled, and dried up.

There was silence from the group. His face flushed more furiously red. He could not speak a single word and saw with horrifying clarity the expressions on all their faces around him. He looked supplicatingly at Odoyevsky. Fortunately Odoyevsky said something—Dostoevsky did not hear what—and the group broke into conversation, most of them eying him with amusement. He dreaded some withering comment which would set them all off; but the next moment Nekrasov appeared beside him saying, "Fyodor Mikhailovich, how are you? I was dining with Botkin the other night and he was saying to me that . . ." Nekrasov talked on, voluble and lighthearted. Dostoevsky was rescued.

After a while he glanced around and gradually found confidence. A big-chested man of about thirty with a handsome, intelligent face was talking to Belinsky. Nekrasov said it was Alexander Herzen, one of the new young writers. Turgenev was chatting with Panayev, whom Dostoevsky thought an absurd dandy in his striped trousers and pointed beard. He wondered why *she* was not there, Madame Panayeva. And then his heart gave a bump as she came with the hostess through the guests. She was wearing a Paris dress which showed her breasts and shoulders, her dark hair was built up rather high, and she was smiling in her mocking way.

He felt an electric nervousness return as he watched her. He was in love with her. Yes, yes, yes! It was inescapable, frightening, wonderful, utterly hopeless. She seemed to know her intense sexual attraction for him and to flaunt it. Half the young bloods of the Petersburg literary world had been in love with her; she was Nekrasov's mistress. Yet there was something in the way she had behaved lately—was it promise? And why not? He *was* superior to the rest, infinitely more intelligent! It had seemed lately that, every time they met, she gave him more attention, showed him special favor.

She was surrounded by a group of Odoyevsky's friends. Nearby Turgenev was telling a story about a serf being sold with a cart. Dostoevsky felt absolutely at ease now. He eclipsed all these mediocrities here. He darted up to Turgenev's side and said in a loud voice, "I was going down the Galernaya yesterday and there was a peasant arguing with another man, some visitor he'd been told to drive around. 'No, no, you're mistaken, Kondraty Trifonovich, that can't be the state pawnshop,' said the visitor. 'Yes, it is,' the peasant said. 'I should know. I'm pawned there myself.'"

He caught Madame Panayeva's glance on him among the others and he added nonchalantly, "You know, Turgenev, that's worthy of a story. You may care to write it. I throw it off to you, *mon cher*."

There was a brief silence, followed by chuckles, in which he joined. Turgenev looked at him, then smiled too. Dostoevsky shot his cuffs; he had made the effect brilliantly and as the general talk resumed Madame Panayeva moved smilingly to his side. "You are startling everyone this evening, Fyodor Mikhailovich," she said. And now that she was so close, now that he was smelling her perfume and trying to keep his eyes from the pearish breasts so visible in her décolleté, he was overcome with confusion, reddened, bowed, forgot to take her hand, snatched it up so abruptly that he jerked her arm, and almost fainted at the touch of his lips on her skin. "You mustn't say such clever things," she said.

"I—er——" In spite of his efforts his glance hung on the pouting breasts again and she put her finger into the décolleté and hitched some intimate strap or support there in a provocative way. They strolled into one of the outer salons where supper was laid and the ice buckets for the wine were glistening on the white cloth. "Will you——" he began, but at that moment Meiendorf, the writer on history, ran up behind her.

"Avdotya Yakovlevna, they're beginning our waltz."

"Oh—yes." But as she took his arm she gave Dostoevsky a killing glance. He was transported.

For a moment he watched her dancing, then caught sight of Nekrasov standing by one of the columns with Panayev, young Danilevsky, Minayev the poet, and a couple of others. They were all laughing at something between themselves. He sauntered up, giving them a smile himself. "What's the joke?"

"Joke? Oh—er——"

"One of Nekrasov's stupid gambling stories," Panayev said. "I say, Nekrasov, come and find Belinsky with me, will you?"

"We'll come too," Minayev said. Dostoevsky watched them go. He sighed. It was a pity they were so envious of him; perhaps not Nekrasov, no—but the rest made it obvious they were. Well, it must have been the same with all great artists; he would bear his burden nobly.

For the next hour he was caught up first with Count Sollogub, whom he cleverly put in his place and then completely subjugated with a few telling criticisms; then with a group led by Nikitenko, the intelligent government censor. He felt superbly assured and allowed himself some remarks which dazzled them all. At last he escaped. A moment before, he thought he had glimpsed Avdotya Yakovlevna disappearing into one of the salons at the far end of the ballroom. He made his way there, couldn't see her, and wandered into the conservatory. The conservatory was Odoyevsky's showpiece; there were palm trees to the glass ceiling, thickets of camellias in bloom, tropical plantations, orange trees, lemon trees, creepers, exotic foliage, bulbous plants, a regular African forest, a collection as fine as the Tsar's.

"Dostoevsky, of course!" somebody said nearby and he turned as a chorus of laughter followed.

"What was the last verse again?" The voices were almost at his elbow, behind thick leaves.

> "Upon the nose of literature,
> Fyodor Mikhailovich,
> You blossom
> Like an overripe pimple."

"And Dostoevsky came up just as he finished it!" There was another burst of laughter. It was Panayev's voice.

"The pimple with delusions of grandeur!" somebody said.

"Do you know he's insisting on a special gold border around the next edition of *Poor Folk?*" Chuckles.

"*Mon cher*, you should read his new product, what's it called—*The Double*. Fearful rubbish, quite indigestible."

"Yes. Belinsky thinks it's trash. Dull and prolix, he calls it. Poor Belinsky, he is having to pretend he hasn't read it yet; the gifted author is constantly pursuing him for his opinion!"

"He admits he made a mistake in the first place, overpraising the fellow."

"Dostoevsky thinks Belinsky is going to sound a fanfare for this new horror. He'll slaughter it instead, you see."

They moved off. There was only the music, the clatter of talk from beyond. Dostoevsky stood there shaking; his neck was sunk into his shoulders and he was unable to step away. He was burning with shame and humiliation. That was what they had been laughing about when he had gone up. He felt ashamed at having stood there listening, as though he had been in hiding. And behind the smooth friendly faces there was that mockery—Nekrasov the ringleader, Nekrasov whose admiration had seemed so genuine! He lighted a cigarette and puffed at it nervously. They were furiously jealous. This was another of the stabs he would have to get used to, the price of superiority. But Belinsky! It was true he had been eluding giving an opinion on *The Double*. Dostoevsky could not bear another second's doubt. Where was Belinsky? He must settle it at once.

He threw the cigarette away, rushed out into the ball-room, and collided with Spansky, one of Belinsky's disciples. "Where is Vassarion Grigoryevich?" he blurted out, taking Spansky by the shoulders.

"What's the matter? Hold on, my dear fellow. He's playing cards, I think." Spansky stared. Dostoevsky shoul-dered his way through the guests and reached the cardroom. At first he could not see Belinsky. Groups of guests were standing around the tables watching the play. He pushed among them and at last caught sight of Belinsky's cadaverous face. There were protests as he shouldered his way to the front. His shame had given way to a blazing anger. Belinsky, intent on the cards, did not notice the commotion of his arrival. Standing close to him, Dostoevsky said in a loud voice, "How can anybody be so stupid as to play cards? What brains!"

There was a startled pause. The players stopped. The onlookers stared at Dostoevsky. Belinsky, who had been about to throw a card on the table, raised his eyes. For a few seconds the expression of astonishment remained, then it changed into intense irritation. Two points of color came into Belinsky's cheeks, his lips were compressed. The expres-sion made Dostoevsky even angrier; in a flash he was con-vinced that Belinsky had not discouraged the backbiting and disparagement. It was infamous! He shouted out, "I prefer dullness and prolixity to deceit!"

"Go away, will you?" It was a big bearded man among the spectators sticking out an arm. Dostoevsky wanted to say something crushing, to obliterate him and Belinsky together in one phrase. He felt the muscles of his neck tightening, his face redden and the choking feeling of moments of panic.

"Who are you?" he shouted to the beard. "The imperti-nence! You perhaps have no idea whom you are speaking to?"

"You are quite right. I have no idea. Quite right!"

The other bystanders also began to protest. "Is he drunk?"

"Send him off. Go on, off with you."

"You are not invited to disturb other guests."

Dostoevsky felt he was losing foothold. He was beside himself. He could not speak. He struggled to say anything, an insult—anything. The only word that would come to his lips was ridiculous, grotesque; he realized he was making himself utterly absurd to say it, yet he felt an irrepressible desire to do so. He gasped, "P-p-pimple! . . . Pimple!"

They stared back at him. "What is he saying?"

Belinsky half rose. At that moment Dostoevsky saw Turgenev's handsome face coming through the onlookers. Madame Panayeva and Annenkov, the critic, were with him. Turgenev reached his side and linked one arm with him, Madame Panayeva the other, as if they were taking no account of the incident. Before he could resist they were leading him away.

"*Mon cher*," Turgenev said. "We have been searching for you. You must come over here." The onlookers parted as they went through.

"It will be the encounter of the evening—beauty and genius," Madame Panayeva said with an oblique glance at him. Dostoevsky felt in an intensely strange state, absolutely confused. He had never conceived being at white anger in her presence. Her hand on his arm only confused him more.

"What? I don't understand. Wait a minute."

"You're in the devil's own luck, my dear fellow," Turgenev was saying. "La Senyavana's here. She insists on meeting you. We swore we'd find you and introduce you. She's waiting now."

"No—no!" He suddenly hung back on their arms. La Senyavana was the most fashionable beauty of Petersburg; even the Tsar, it was said, desired her and did not dare. "Not now, not now!" The effect on him was like ice on fire. His mood was utterly wrong. In his instability, in his furious temper, the idea of being presented to her was overwhelming.

"Nonsense. Here she is." They had reached a part of the

ballroom between the columns. And before him was the smiling, cool figure of a blonde, in a dress of turquoise blue, her head slightly to one side and her eyes examining his face with amusement. Everything was too much—the pimple verse, Belinsky, timidity and shame, all surged back with double force. He took a step forward, felt the chill on his forehead. The lights dimmed—and he barely had time to see La Senyavana's eyebrows lift in surprise before the floor curved upward and blacked everything out.

He came to, lying on his back looking at a painted ceiling. The painting was an allegory involving three naked women, some fish, and a wheel. He could not puzzle it out. Then Prince Odoyevsky's face interposed itself.

"How do you feel? Would you like some more water?"

"What—er——" How curious Odoyevsky's mustache looked.

"You fainted, my dear fellow. And La Senyavana swears she hadn't uttered a syllable!" There was a titter round about. Dostoevsky sat up on the sofa. The semicircle of onlookers was smiling. Turgenev stood next to Nekrasov and Panayev. Avdotya was looking at him from behind Nekrasov's shoulder; he could only see her amused eyes and as he caught them she ducked her head and seemed to splutter.

He rose unsteadily. He was overcome with shame. He had made a terrible fool of himself. "I—I apologize." He bowed to Odoyevsky and without stopping to button his collar rushed out.

3

He spent a tormented morning and at two o'clock hastened to Belinsky's. Belinsky was lying on a sofa looking ill. Trembling, Dostoevsky threw himself into the chair beside him, then jumped up. "Vissarion Grigoryevich, I—I don't know how to express myself. I would like to convey my excuses in a formal way—a formal way, if that is possible. I was upset, that is . . . I . . . What am I saying? You know, all this morning I have been certain I should never be able to approach you, that all that was finished—and here I am explaining to you in your own study! I mean, you have every right to refuse to listen, Vissarion Grigoryevich. Every right. I understand that. I approve of it. There's nothing more to say on that score! It is only that—you see, I overheard something and I allowed it to carry me away. Yes, that's it, I was utterly carried away. . . ."

"It was of no importance." Belinsky gestured, cutting short his apologies.

But when *The Double* appeared, Belinsky made it clear he did not care for it. And everywhere else there were cries of indignation at it. Aksakov, the Moscow critic, called it a blatant copy of Gogol, a theft down to tricks of style. The book failed.

Dostoevsky began work feverishly on new stories, set in the same milieu of pathetic and absurd Petersburg func-tionaries. He felt he was improving his construction and extending the range of the characters he portrayed. In one of the stories, "Mr. Prokharchin", another study of the abnormal, he had portrayed a half-mad old miser, a government clerk, who was pushed into insanity by the torment of his fellow boarders. The old clerk lived in misery, without socks, hand-kerchiefs, or sheets for his greasy mattress, pleaded poverty, and starved himself for twenty years to hoard twenty-five hundred rubles. The story was also the picture of a milieu— the terrible world of the Petersburg poor living half a dozen to a room and all, as one of them said, "having a hard time of it."

In *A Faint Heart* he explored the psychological country where obsession and an instinct for disaster were strangely intermingled. The hero, Vasya Shumkov, a highly nervous young man, was a copying clerk in the government service and became overwrought at the intense happiness in prospect when he became engaged to be married. He had an elusive feeling that this was too much for him and it made him magnify a fault he committed in neglecting some copying work for his office chief. Thereafter the sheer obsessive sense of being condemned which this stirred up and which somehow seemed bound up with his condition drove him out of his mind.

The story was in halftones; but it was brief and well built. Above all, Dostoevsky was pleased with the subtlety of the two main figures. He recognized that he had a definite compulsion to do meek, submissive characters, or at least to make those qualities enter into the duality. There was the old attraction of Gogol in that, as there still was for Gogol's style.

But once again the critics sneered, expostulated. "Of all the drearily stodgy stuff we have unhappily been obliged to read this season, 'Mr. Prokharchin' is the worst," one said. "There is not a syllable showing a more lively imagination than one could expect from a grocer. . . ."

And when summer came and Petersburg emptied he found himself alone. Everybody was away. He roamed the streets at night, agitated, hungry, his nerves on edge, reflecting that, having been lionized not long before, he was now abandoned. The one amiable figure left was Petrashevsky, an aristocrat of his own age whom he had met at literary evenings. When Dostoevsky ran into him, Petrashevsky said, "Come along to our little meetings—*chez moi*, every Friday. Lively discussion." And he laughed.

"Thanks, thanks—perhaps," Dostoevsky said, moving on.

But at last in September he stood in the rain on the quay as the boat from Reval pulled in. He had persuaded Mikhail to give up the army for a literary career in Petersburg—and Mikhail was at last arriving. The gangway was freed and they threw themselves into each other's arms. Mikhail was the taller of the two, thinner, with a longish jaw, narrow nose, and a debonair, slightly feminine handsome look; he was without the strength that Dostoevsky had in his face and shoulders.

"Good God," Dostoevsky exclaimed, "that mustache! It's a wonder. How do you do it?"

"But you're soaked. It's good to see you."

"The celebrated author, I observe, isn't very gallant," said somebody nearby. Dostoevsky swung around.

"Emily!" He embraced his sister-in-law. She was fair and oval-faced with a short upper lip. A servant girl held the twin babies. As they all hurried off amid the bustle and rain to see the luggage loaded onto a carriage, Mikhail said eagerly, "I've brought the Schiller."

"The what?" Dostoevsky wasn't paying attention, watching a pair of priests.

"The Schiller translations you kept writing about. I've even been working on some on the boat."

"Oh yes."

"You said if we had them ready we'd make a fortune, so I——"

"Things have suddenly changed, you know. It's one of those caprices of the literary market. Nobody's interested in taking more Schiller for the time being."

"I see." Mikhail looked overcome with doubt. Dostoevsky saw it and laughingly threw his arm over his brother's shoulder. "*Mon cher,* don't worry. Krayevsky is publishing my new novelette next month, you remember, the one I wrote to you about. It's called *The Landlady.* It's brilliant. They'll all be green with envy."

Soon the carriage was ready and they started off. Mikhail and his family were installing themselves in a couple of rooms: Mikhail had sold his furniture in Reval and had funds enough to last a brief space. The rooms, on Vassilyevsky Island, were rather miserable, and on the landing outside them was a kitchen which had to serve three families. Emily Fyodorovna looked around rather forlornly and Mikhail seemed to be trying to hide his disappointment.

"Never mind," Dostoevsky said. "We'll launch out when *The Landlady* brings in the money."

When *The Landlady* was printed he sent a copy to Belinsky and waited. A few mornings later Mikhail came into his room with a copy of the *Contemporary* magazine. "I say, have you seen Belinsky's review of *The Landlady?*"

"No. By the way, before I forget: I don't think that porter of yours realizes whose brother you are. Tell him and he'll be more respectful." He settled back in the chair and languorously let the smoke of his cigarette rise from his mouth. "Go on. Read it to me."

Mikhail found the place. " 'There is not a single simple or living word or expression in this whole story. Everything is farfetched, exaggerated, stilted, spurious and false. . . . It is incomprehensible . . . a monstrosity. . . .' " He stopped and looked at his brother. "There is more on the same lines. I have never seen anything so fierce. He has absolutely condemned it."

Dostoevsky's face was crimson. He sprang up, snatched the magazine, read the notice, and flung it across the room. "It's idiotic! He doesn't know what he is talking about. He's raving—completely unstable. One day he is worshiping something, the next spitting on it. He changes his opinions as he changes his shirts. He's a superficial fool. It's insufferable!"

"The others are already conforming. The *Journal de Petersbourg* has an attack on you."

Dostoevsky was pacing the room, furious. "It's jealousy again. It's beyond anything, the lengths they'll go to. Belinsky hates me for writing for Krayevsky. They all do—Nekrasov, Panayev, the lot of them. Belinsky would like me to give everything to their paper, the *Contemporary*."

"Then why not?" Mikhail said in a worried way. "Wouldn't it be more to your interest, Fedka? After all——"

"But I can't, I can't! You don't understand. Krayevsky has lent me too much money, given me too many advances. I'm sold out! A slave. I'm mortaged to him. And now Belinsky tries to destroy my reputation. It's miserably unjust. Ah, the rogues!"

Later in the day Grigorovich called in. He behaved in such a sheepish way that Dostoevsky shouted at him in a fury of irritation. "I suppose you've been seeing Belinsky too. Haven't you? Go on, admit it, damn you! I've seen his review."

"I—er—I did see him last night at Annenkov's."

"What did he say? *Go on!*"

"He said—well, he said everything you write is a fresh falling off. He said, 'We made a ridiculous mistake saying Dostoevsky had genius, I worst of all. I was a perfect ass. Dostoevsky thinks the entire human race envies him and persecutes him.' Fyodor Mikhailovich, I wouldn't take it seriously. I beg you to——"

"My God! Go away. Leave me alone, Dmitry Vassilyevich, I want to be alone." Grigorovich went out looking unhappy.

Dostoevsky threw himself on the sofa. He was furious, frustrated, bitterly wounded. The injustice of it was intolerable. His work was treated as trivial and things by fourth- and fifth-rate writers were given honors. He—*he* was immense! There was a knock at the door. He wanted to shout out, "Go to the devil!" But the next moment Ivan, the Panayevs' servant, put his head in. He had a note from Avdotya Yakovlevna. She wrote to remind him that he was expected that evening at her house; she did not want him to forget, she said, since the reception had been arranged some time before.

"Very well." He dismissed the man. All at once the note had dispelled his anger and renewed his confidence. After all, he told himself, Belinsky was a waning influence; he was terribly ill, dying, and since he was unsympathetic to the new movement because he did not truly understand it, he tried to dissimulate by being extreme. Nekrasov probably saw that. In reality Nekrasov was itching to have him write regularly for the *Contemporary*. The controversy over *The Landlady* would make it sell better. And Avdotya . . . She was waiting for a clear step from him. She had encouraged him all she could and now was afraid of his slipping away. The note proved it.

Leaning forward to the glass, he fingered his fair beard which he kept trimmed very short around the line of his jaw. It was a strong face, otherwise clean-shaven, with rather heavy eyelids and broad, rounded chin, dominated by the big forehead which his thinnish hair accentuated. He adjusted his tie. Yes, she was waiting—he laughed aloud.

On the walk to the Panayevs' he was tense and excited. Avdotya Yakovlevna greeted him with warmth and a pleasing suggestion of fear. The salon was crowded; he suffered terrors as usual but there were many people he knew, besides some others of consequence he did not. Nekrasov and Panayev were cordial; nevertheless, he was glad to see Belinsky had not come. Avdotya was occupied with the guests but when he caught her hand and began leading her aside she said, "Later," in a low voice, smiled, and escaped.

He drank two glasses of champagne rather quickly. And in the midst of a critical outburst by Panayev about Gogol's latest book, *Selected Passages from a Correspondence with Friends,* he couldn't resist butting in in an emphatic voice: "Let me tell you, you don't understand anything about genius. So stop expounding theories. The practice is quite different, I assure you." He walked away. A few minutes later—he did not know how it happened—he found himself beside Turgenev in the center of a large group. He had the impression he had been maneuvered there and then noticed that the circle was drawing away, leaving him conspicuously in the middle of the floor alongside Turgenev.

"Dostoevsky, I must tell you about the genius I met in Tver the other day. A terrible place, Tver." Turgenev caught him by the lapel of the coat and began jerking himself about in a strange way. "I was so bored waiting for the coach I went to Rolman's for dinner and I was hardly at the table before Rolman came up and said, 'Do you see that man over there, Ivan Sergeyevich, the one with the twitch?

Well, he thinks he's a genius and I'd like your opinion. I'll bring him over.'"

There was a titter from the onlooking circle. Dostoevsky saw that everybody had immediately caught on to the lampoon of him.

"He brought him up and I said to the fellow, 'So you are a genius; I'm greatly honored.' 'Pah,' says the fellow into my face, twitching like mad. 'I haven't shown even a fraction of my gifts yet; I've had no apprenticeship, no education, I was trained to be a coal miner. But you can take it from me, I'm incomparably greater than Pushkin or Goethe or anybody else you can think of. Incomparably!'"

Turgenev, handsome and dapper, was looking at him sardonically but keeping the grip on his coat and twitching his face now and then. Dostoevsky saw the ring of faces, all of them bright with amusement. Many were frankly laughing. He longed to move and could not.

"So I asked him why he hadn't had any training," Turgenev said with insistence; he gave the coat lapel he was gripping a sort of shake. "And I told him that the poorest German sausage maker had more talent than geniuses like him, let alone Goethe; only they didn't brag about it. Whereas our splendid fellow had only to scribble off some trashy story and at once you saw him with his hands in his pockets and a sneer of contempt on his lips. 'I'm a genius,' he says, 'a double genius.' Bah!"

Turgenev's hand released him. Dostoevsky stepped back, his face as white as death. He was trembling and his head was jerking about as he stared around the circle of laughing faces, seeing the nudges, the whispering; they were all delighted at Turgenev's lampooning him.

Turgenev's high voice was continuing. He scarcely heard. "What would you have said to the fellow, Dostoevsky? You're the only one here who knows these mysteries. . . ."

He was the center of ridicule. He felt he was falling over a precipice; he wanted to rush away, to be obliterated. The "pimple" verse occurred crushingly to him and he had the absurd, irrational, but overwhelming desire to scratch his nose. He felt his neck swelling in his collar and stood there utterly annihilated, as if he had been accused of some disgraceful piece of behavior in front of them all. And what was more, he wanted to insist on that aspect before them. He actually felt he was on the point of doing something outrageous.

The heat in the place was unbearable. He turned to rush away, to save himself. He floundered, almost swooned. The guests parted before him, he ran the wrong way into a small salon from which there was no outlet, and in utter humiliation and confusion had to push his way through the main room again. In the center he saw Avdotya Yakovlevna smilingly approach Turgenev, who was surrounded, and kiss him on the cheek. They caught sight of him, directed everybody else's attention to him with fresh laughter, and he reached the door in a bath of sweat. He was hardly conscious of anything.

The Panayevs' footman could not find his coat and he waited in the entrance in an agony at the thought of some of them coming out and discovering him still there. At last the man produced the coat and he rushed out. He scarcely knew where he was going. He was choking with shame and anger and revulsion. His mind repeated the same thoughts with grinding, exhausting, pitiless persistency. They had arranged the scene expressly. Their suave cordiality, their praises had been only pretense; they had been entertaining themselves with him all along and thought no more of him than Belinsky did. They were all with Belinsky. They had praised him extravagantly only so as to get more amusement out of his disaster. He could hear the comments behind his back, Nekrasov, Panayev sniggering. Turgenev, that sarcastic creature with the woman's voice and the aristocratic attitude of the *grand seigneur*—he detested him. He particularly loathed the way Turgenev lisped; his tongue must be a little too long because he continually lisped and seemed proud of it and clearly thought it added to his dignity. Dostoevsky writhed at the recollection of how Turgenev had made a fool of him with La Senyavana; that had been done purposely too! My God! This was the end of the association with any of them. And with exasperation he remembered that he owed Nekrasov a hundred and fifty rubles. He must repay it at once—at once. He would have to ask Krayevsky for the money; one more debt! Perhaps Krayevsky was at home now? He halted and looked around; he was on the Kazanskaya. But it would be better to write. Krayevsky could never resist written solicitations; it was his weakness.

He hurried home and took the stairs two by two. On the landing he was startled by a figure coming forward out of the half-light. "What—oh, it's you, Petrashevsky."

Petrashevsky gave his rich fatty chuckle. "I was just calling, *mon cher*. I would have missed you. I say, are you ill? You look like a ghost."

"It's nothing, nothing—a headache, a trifle. Come in." He felt shakier than ever. They entered and Dostoevsky lighted the lamp.

Petrashevsky had a touch of the Byronic; he was romantically flamboyant. He wore a broad-brimmed soft hat, a Spanish cloak, and carried a stick. He long oval face with a trimmed beard and mustache, a humorous mouth, had a pleasant expression. He fiddled eternally with a watch chain hanging from a pocket of his silk waistcoat.

"I must ask you to excuse me," Dostoevsky said in a nervous jerky way he could not quite control. "I'm not ill but I—I need to rest. I'm not fit for company tonight. I'm sure you understand, Mikhail Vassilyevich."

"I am only here for an instant, the space of a breath," Petrashevsky said. He kept his hat on and turned, fat, jaunty, and stately, examining the things in the room. He made the circuit, reached Dostoevsky again, and stopped. "Why don't you come to my house for a meeting or two, Fyodor

Mikhailovich? Pokrov Square. On Fridays. You will approve."

There was a pause.

Dostoevsky had heard rumors about Petrashevsky's meetings. They sounded dangerous. The experience of the evening had strung him up; his nerves were tingling, he felt in a state of extreme perception, as if every sense had been sharpened to an unbearable degree. And in this hypersensitive mood, with his mind revolting against the world he had just rushed from, the salons, the easy cynics who tormented and destroyed one as a pastime, he desired with passion to assert something else. Perhaps the opposite, the antithesis . . . like a Double?

"All right, I'll come."

"The day after tomorrow," Petrashevsky said. He laughed in his fat way. "Good night."

Chapter Four

1

Mikhail Vassilyevich Butashevich-Petrashevsky was a man who took risks.

In the Petersburg of Nicholas I, center of the web drawn by the Third Section of the Tsar's Chancellery—the secret police—all over the great Russian Empire, he seemed to live for the purpose of laughing at the paternal autocracy of the Most High. Any house porter might be a police spy; most were. So were priests, barbers, coach drivers, tutors, head-waiters, cavalry captains, editors, merchants with boxes at the Marinsky, a man with the Kulm Cross on his breast or the Order of St. Vladimir ribbon, people who were affable, inquisitive, timid, anyone at all—who could tell? The Third Section, perfected by Count Benckendorf, now directed by Count Orlov, saw into every village, town, and hamlet of Russia. It was enormously efficient. If a man began a timid conspiracy five thousand versts away from Petersburg, the Most High knew the facts rapidly, thoroughly, and concisely. The voice of an official in the boredom of some dead and alive provincial hole, expressing "dangerous opinions," carried promptly to the capital and he was arrested. People were sent to prison and exile for "disrespectful thoughts," an "unseemly attitude," an "irreligious tendency" as readily as for murder or mutiny. An independent word was an offense against social morality. Since hanging the five leaders of the great December army revolt of 1825, which had nearly tipped him off the throne before he had properly settled on it, and sending hundreds more to Siberia, the Tsar had detected conspiracy, disrespect, unseemliness, opposition everywhere. Students had been imprisoned, exiled, and left to die for singing songs about him at an evening's drinking. And where he himself did not suspect, the Most High was supplied with suspicion by others—the others fed by the army of informers and denouncers.

The sense of moral and intellectual oppression weighed heavily. It was driving Belinsky to an even earlier death. Herzen, twice exiled, had gone abroad. Men with great gifts looked about them and saw a wilderness, a level waste swept clear of hope by the drill-square Tsar and his servitors, who could not endure any thought that might question the imperial order. Nobody could protest and escape being crushed. For more than twenty years, since the Decembrists, Russia had been a silent country. The arrest of students and "disrespectful elements" scarcely brought any compensating inspiration to those remaining, since the Third Section managed them so cleverly that they drew no attention. Chadayev, one of those who had dared to raise a terrible cry of denunciation in an unsigned article in the *Telescope*, was ordered to be declared insane by the Tsar and certified afresh every week by a doctor and a police officer. "Other nations march toward emancipation," Chadayev said. "Russian history is the progress of serfdom and autocracy."

A man of originality like Petrashevsky needed the fantastical to express his contempt for all this; he needed it as another man needs a certain atmosphere to work well in. He could not protest in another way. He collected books banned by the government censors and lent them to people, sometimes to people he scarcely knew. His face expressed enormous suppressed amusement as he handed them out. Walking along the street, he lit fireworks under his cloak and dropped them; he became very dexterous at it and produced several alarming scenes among crowds at markets which rattled the imperial police. He drafted an address to the imperial government which he showed about freely, suggesting that all the monasteries in Russia be turned into charitable homes. In another he demonstrated that burning down Moscow on Napoleon's invasion in 1812 had been a piece of barbarism rather than a patriotic act; in a further address, he demanded public court hearings for all law-breakers.

Any of these was enough cause for the police to arrest him forthwith. But something seemed to protect Petrashevsky. He continued performing his government service undisturbed, translating in the Ministry of Foreign Affairs. One day when the elder of one of the villages he owned appeared in Petersburg and reported that the village had burned to a cinder, Petrashevsky leaped up shouting, "Splendid! I was waiting for this!" He threw himself into rebuilding the village—in the middle of a forest—as a phalanstery, a communal unit with common dormitories, stables, dining room, pig styes according to the best teachings of the French socialist visionary Fourier. It was magnificent. The thirty peasant families he gathered ready to move in were aghast. But Petrashevsky hastened to bring his friends from Petersburg for the inauguration. They arrived, Petrashevsky leading them like Alexander of Macedon—to find the phalanstery a smoking ruin and the peasants joyfully drunk.

Petrashevsky rarely stopped playing the fool and then only for the shortest interval, when he showed he was capable and eaten up with anger at the Tsar's crimes.

At eight o'clock on Friday evening Dostoevsky walked up the creaking, rickety stairs at Petrashevsky's. He felt restless and uncertain. A hempseed oil lamp was smoking on the landing, smelling badly and making the shadows look thicker. He could hear several voices above and, reaching the top, found he was looking into a room with only one candle burning on a table. It gave just enough light to show several people reclining on the sofa and in broken armchairs in the midst of a great deal of tobacco smoke.

"*Ah, voilà.* Come in, come in." Petrashevsky loomed up before him, blocking the light completely, grasping his arm, and leading him into the room. "Whom do you know?"

They all went on talking; there was one girl and ten or a dozen men.

"This is Sergey Durov," Petrashevsky said. "Fyodor Dostoevsky." A young man with a big bald forehead, seated in an armchair, was shaking his hand. Petrashevsky led on to the next. "This is Antonelli and that's Ivanov. Ivanov has just shaved off his beard." The two nodded at Dostoevsky and turned back to an argument with one of the others. Dostoevsky could see better. The room was big but uncomfortable. There was a battered piano in one corner. He smiled at the careful effect of romantic dilapidation. Petrashevsky was well off but he had a tremendous feeling for décor. Petrashevsky made the rest of the introductions, the last to a man called Speshnev. Petrashevsky said to him, "*Poor Folk*, you remember that?" Speshnev, the only one standing, gave Dostoevsky a slight bow. He was handsome in almost a French way, with level eyebrows, a straight nose, a mouth with full lips. He had an aristocratic touch and was carefully dressed with his hair hanging down to his velvet collar. But what struck Dostoevsky about him was his remarkable stillness. He looked like a man who would take decisions and carry them out no matter what the consequences were, even if they were decisions of fearful importance for his whole life, with the same impassive calm as if he were sitting at breakfast. The impression of self-control and strength was such that looking at his relaxed, easy, reserved attitude was like looking at the soft velvet calm of a panther. He would scarcely notice danger at a moment of crisis; and yet his mind would know all about it and be working on it without anything showing in his outward manner except energy. He was a man one could never be at home with.

"Speshnev's just back from abroad. He has been picking up ideas, eh, Nikolay Antonovich?" Petrashevsky laughed. Speshnev kept a level look on them without changing his expression.

"Here, do you want this?" Dostoevsky turned. It was the girl, whom Petrashevsky had introduced as Sophie Baranova; she was holding out tea in a chipped cup.

"Thank you."

"There's no sugar. Katenev doesn't believe in it," she said, turning away in an independent fashion.

Somebody called out, "What Katenev doesn't believe in is an entire policy! D'you believe in physical love, Katenev?"

Dostoevsky noticed the girl glance quickly at Katenev on the sofa. Petrashevsky pulled out a stool for him next to a stout fellow of about thirty, Alexey Milyukov. "Milyukov wrote that book on the history of Russian thought," he said. "Remarkable—remarkable."

They were suddenly all arguing at once, the subsidiary discussions breaking up to become general, as if somebody had just declared the purpose of the meeting.

"Have you heard they have just ordered the Koran to be expurgated?" Ivanov said.

"What—the Koran?"

"Absolutely. Councilor Gatkov of the Censorship Bureau has ordered thirteen verses to be expunged from all copies printed in Russia. He has decided the verses are 'objectionable.' "

"Yes, and they've just made another admission." This was a broad-faced young student with blue eyes, who kept his peaked cap on, called Philippov. "The censor in Kazan has forbidden the use of the word 'intelligentsia,' meaning the intelligent class."

"What's it coming to?" They seemed to have become more animated.

"I'm told Herzmann's book, *Life and Materialism,* has been banned."

"Wait!" Petrashevsky leaned to a bookshelf. "Here it is. I present it to you with the compliments of the European —free—intelligentsia." He handed the book, his laugh sounding above the rest.

"Are you still reading Fourier to those workmen you collected, Mikhail Vassilyevich?" Antonelli asked. He had a freckled, snub-nosed face with a bunch of curly ginger hair on top. Dostoevsky thought he looked curiously out of place in this setting; it was the sort of face one would see on a peasant lounging stupidly in a village street chewing sunflower seeds.

"Why, do you know how that turned out, *mon cher?*" Petrashevsky said. "I used to ask them if they'd understood what I had read. They said yes and I gave them twenty kopecks. That was only to make them come again, of course, to encourage them. After a while I thought we were making progress and I gave them five kopecks. They were furious! They said, 'Here we have been obliging you longer and you give us less money. It's not right.' So I gave up." He spread his hands comically, then jumped up. "But I've forgotten. I have an announcement. My dictionary is published. Allow me to quote you a definition or two." He took a volume, approached the candle, and read: " 'Christianity: the establishment of liberty and the abolition of private property.' "

"Good."

"That's it!" They all approved warmly.

Petrashevsky flicked the pages. " 'Optimism: The attempt to defend God against the crushing attacks of practical atheism inspired by life itself.' "

"Splendid."

"But wait a minute." It was a wild-haired young man name Jastrzembsky. "Do you mean to say the censor *passed* that?"

"Yes. He only read the book's title: *A Dictionary of Foreign Words Incorporated into the Russian Language.*" They all laughed delightedly. The next minute, with the shadows of heads and arms on the walls, a continual restless changing of places about the room, they plunged into discussion about the Church, the official system, socialism, the serfs, property, and the Tsar. It was what they had come for. Sometimes they spoke calmly, in mild terms, sometimes excitedly and angrily. Dostoevsky was caught up and responded.

"If you sympathize with the peasants the government automatically puts you down as subversive," Ivanov said.

"Yes. And what plunderers they are, our devoted administrators," Antonelli said. "When the peasants do manage to pay their taxes the officials quite likely embezzle the money and they have to pay a second time."

"There has been a scandalous case in the Samara Province," Durov said. "I heard it from my cousin who has just gone back there. A merchant named Yusevich, who had 'friends' in the governor's office, bought up an estate; everyone knows how they do it—falsely declaring to Petersburg that there are no peasants on the land. Yusevich paid two rubles a dessiatine for it and the morning the governor's office registered the sale Yusevich told the peasants they would have to pay him twelve rubles a dessiatine rent each year. The peasants panicked. They said they couldn't pay such a heavy ransom for their own land. *It was their own land!* Yusevich drove to the governor's office and the governor turned out the soldiers. They flogged ten people in the peasants' village to 'make an example of the criminals' —and all the peasants had to pay. Now they are working the estate of Yusevich, their new landlord, which was their own land, for nothing—exhausting themselves, scratching for their own provisions on the wretched cat's plot Yusevich consented to leave them. My God! That such things happen; it's terrible." Durov was pale with anger.

"It's true what the peasants say: 'The rain drips off your roof onto your neighbor's land.'"

Dostoevsky looked across at Sophie Baranova, sitting smoking a cigarette, and thought she was pretty with her dark eyes and the faint dark shading of hair on her upper lip. Like Speshnev, she would coolly take any risk for what she believed in. He wondered if she were Katenev's mistress.

Ivanov or a young man called Mombelli kept going to the piano and playing noisily and twice Mombelli sang. At the end of each item everybody applauded mechanically, continuing to talk. Catching Dostoevsky's wincing look of appeal, Mombelli said in an aside, "It's for the police," and broke into "Hail to the Most High."

The others were listening to Antonelli telling a savage story of Count Zaslubin, the great landowner of his birthplace in the south. "He is a terrible old man and a fierce drunkard," Antonelli said. "When there was glass-ice on the Volga he used to call out the serfs and make them dive off the high cliff. He sat astride a barrel of sweet wine, helping himself with a ladle, and shouting to them to dive headfirst and make holes in the ice or have a flogging. One day the serfs entreated him, 'Your high honor, it's too thick. Look at it, that's not glass-ice. We've thrown logs on it—look, there they are.' 'Bah, you're all cowards,' said the count, who was drunk and anyway as strong as a tiger. 'You could break that ice with a five-kopeck piece. Go on—dive! If you don't, I'll throw your children down there,' and he banged his boot with the wine ladle. They had to obey. The first two men fell full length on the ice. 'What stupidity!' cried the count. 'That's not the thing at all. Give them twenty strokes.' The next man hit the side of the cliff and hurt himself badly; and three men who dived through where the ice was thinner never came up again. The count was drinking the wine and shouting, 'What are they doing down there? Are they staying to feed the carp?' And he flew into a fury, screamed that he was going to flog the serfs to death, and ordered two beggars who had been passing through the village that day to make holes. One of them dived through the ice but he could not break through to the surface again either and drowned. This threw the count into drunken tears and he called out that it was more than his patience could bear; there was not one there who could make a hole properly.

'What's a man to do?' he sobbed. 'It was my favorite entertainment. Ah, you villains, you wretches! You want me to die of boredom,' and he called his coachman to drive him home. There were four men dead but the police did not trouble the count. Besides, three were his own serfs! Perhaps the governor heard about it, but if so he hushed it up. The count was his supplier of horseflesh."

There was a horrified silence. Then all joined in at once with expressions of indignation. All at once Speshnev said, "I didn't know you came from the south, Antonelli." He had not spoken a word all evening and the others stopped.

Antonelli said, "Yes. From Saratov." He lighted his pipe and in the brief silence turned to Sophie Baranova. "Sophie, is there any more tea?"

The next minute everybody was joining in a loud discussion about the revolutions in France, Naples, Tuscany, and Austria, which they hailed as the beginning of the new Europe. It was nearly two o'clock in the morning when they left. Durov accompanied Dostoevsky part of the way. As they crossed the Voznessensky Prospect, Durov said, "Petrashevsky is such an actor."

"How do you mean?"

"He'll land in trouble one day. Plenty of people in Petersburg know about these meetings. Too many."

2

He found there was an extraordinary compulsion about the meetings. He could not stay away. He committed himself to Petrashevsky's circle with all his soul. That was how he thought of it—he committed his soul. After the first few times he began to hate Speshnev; and yet he could not resist.

There were about twenty-two regular members of the circle, although others appeared at times and drifted off again. Besides the ones he had met on the first evening, he noticed four others—Grigoryev, Akcharumov, Evrapeus, and Pleshcheyev. Pleshcheyev was a poet he had met at literary evenings.

They often talked and argued until Petrashevsky's candle guttered in the dawn. With glowing faces they proclaimed that the future of happiness in socialism was just being born; these ideas would become the rule for mankind. They expressed their disgust for hereditary ownership. The most sainted institutions they declared immoral—religion, the family, the right of property. Dostoevsky was among the foremost. Sometimes, carried away, he would have run out onto the square with a red banner! They demanded the suppression of nationalities in the name of universal brotherhood and called ringingly for the notion of "country" to be cast aside because it was a brake to evolution. And for all of them these were sublime principles, the most elevated expression of man's hopes. At every meeting they read aloud articles which they had written or which, appearing under the censorship, illustrated their arguments; they declaimed from books smuggled in from abroad—Saint-Simon, Fourier, Cabet's famous utopian novel, *Voyage en Icarie*. And they castigated Palka—"the stick"—the derisive secret name for the Tsar Nicholas, laughing at Petrashevsky's savage jokes about him.

Dostoevsky worked feverishly on a series of new stories, delivering them to Krayevsky simply to catch up on the advances he had already received and spent. One of them, "Another Man's Wife, or The Husband under the Bed," was a departure from his usual field—a comic piece about a husband, a lover, and a wife who was deceiving both. The wife was a very resourceful woman and the two men's continued suspicion of her involved them in an absurd tangle culminating in their meeting under the bed of another woman, unknown to them both, as her husband turned up. He wrote most of it in dialogue. It was almost stage farce, especially the last scene when the husband under the bed strangled the unknown woman's lapdog. It came off, he thought.

Another was "White Nights," the story of a poor clerk who wandered the Petersburg streets at night indulging in heroic fantasies (it was he himself!) and met a young girl but lost her to a former lover.

He particularly enjoyed a short story he called "A Christmas Tree and a Wedding." It gave a glimpse of a well-fed, paunchy middle-aged man at a Christmas party trying, with red face and scarcely suppressed desire, to make up to a little girl of eleven—and then, five years later, of them both coming out of church after being married. He wrote it in the first person and there was an intense enjoyment for him in the situation.

In another story, "An Honest Thief," he explored the relationship of pity. It was a study of two wretched souls, one an old soldier who scraped a living as a servant or by a bit of tailoring, the other a drunken vagrant, utterly submissive, who stuck to him and followed him like a dog. The old soldier couldn't drive the meek, useless creature away, even when he stole a pair of breeches from him and got drunk on the proceeds. Dostoevsky thought Emelyanushka, the vagrant, one of the best "meek" figures he had done.

In June Belinsky died. Dostoevsky heard the news with a shock, though Belinsky's weakness had been so visible. The circle discussed him. "He was a revolutionary," Evrapeus said.

"They say he wrote a withering letter to Gogol about the Holy Russian Church," Pleshcheyev said. Dostoevsky was silent; they all knew of his break with Belinsky.

One evening they were jokingly egging on Sophie after she had spoken on the emancipation of women. She slept indiscriminately with three or four of the group and made no secret of it; she had just left Katenev for Mombelli.

"So free love is moral and to have free lovers is revolutionary doctrine, Sophie Petrovna?" Katenev said.

"A woman is subjugated through love," she said to him. "Every time she claims her freedom, therefore, it's only natural she should begin by claiming liberty in love."

"That's what I said—free love."

"Yes, but it's a petty right, you know, Pyotr Sozontovich. Free love for a woman usually means nothing more than freedom to choose her master. Our emancipation will go beyond that—to economic independence, access to higher education."

"Yes, yes—and men's professions," Petrashevsky said.

Sophie jumped up and went over to Katenev. "You're jealous, you can't believe what I say. I'll spend the night with you and show you it's true. Even in exercising a petty right one can rise above it." She sat down beside him.

"Excellent! Excellent!" They all applauded, laughing.

The rhythmic tramp of feet sounded outside as a squad of soldiers marched by. The conversation dropped to a whisper, all of them sitting still until the sound died in the distance. Dostoevsky looked at Speshnev, who was in his usual place smoking. There was something hideous and devilish in his face. Speshnev was a monster, he thought. He had the impression that Speshnev was preparing a decisive step, that he would not much longer be content with this talk. And he felt that he also was being drawn to him more closely, being drawn to a precipice. He felt a violent revulsion and stood up.

"What do you say, Dostoevsky?"

"What?" He was shaking. "I—er—I'm sorry, I didn't hear."

"Sit down." Ivanov pulled him down from behind onto the sofa again. Speshnev was watching him.

An argument was going on, one of the endless arguments about the revolutionary new order. Akcharumov, one of the older of the circle, said, "The Tsar can stay, provided he is kept in tight harness by the Constitution."

"Never, never! That's weakness," said Durov.

"Besides, autocrats like the Romanovs will never consent to be constitutional monarchs."

"The whole of Russia must be covered with phalansteries," Petrashevsky said. "You must follow Fourier."

"The first thing is to abolish serfdom and the censorship," said Grigoryev.

"But if there is no legal means of freeing the serfs, what then?" It was Antonelli. "What then, eh?"

"Direct action," Speshnev broke in. "We must form a purely political society working for the revolution."

"But with us a revolution like the one in Paris is going to be extremely difficult, Nikolay Antonovich," Evrapeus said. "The towns contain only a tenth of the population, and God knows how many of them are not much more than big villages. If you take the real towns, say the ones with fifteen thousand inhabitants, they total about three million people and they are all far apart. What can you do with that? The government can mobilize soldiers from everywhere—a million two hundred thousand soldiers—and turn the five or six big towns into military camps. They're that already!"

Speshnev said, "Did Pestel and Ryleyev think like that?" (They were the leaders of the Decembrist revolt against Nicholas.) "Our task is to spread socialism, atheism, terrorism, everything good in the world. I accept riot, shooting, political murder. I accept them as principles and for myself personally I will put them into action."

There was the silence that Speshnev nearly always induced; but this time the words "terrorism" and "political murder" seemed to spread out through the room. Speshnev took a paper from his pocket. "I suggest that all those ready to act take the following oath. 'I agree to arm myself with firearms and to join the uprisings and fighting when the Executive Committee orders the revolution to begin.'"

"What Executive Committee?" Antonelli said.

But Petrashevsky was at the piano thumping out a boisterous tune. Speshnev folded the paper and put it in his pocket. He drew on his cigarette, looking around from one to the other of them with a scornful expression. In the loud jangling of the piano the talk gradually resumed. A moment later Petrashevsky's servant came in with the usual trays of cold food and presently there was a general move to go. On an uncontrollable impulse, Dostoevsky stepped up to Speshnev.

"Nikolay Antonovich, will you lend me five hundred rubles?"

"Comment?" Speshnev said; there was a strange instant with the two of them simply facing each other. Then to Dostoevsky's horror and confusion, Speshnev threw his shoulders back stiffly and gave a short laugh. His teeth were small and pointed. "Of course," he said, and took out his wallet. "Here. I've only four hundred with me. I will send you the rest tomorrow."

"Thank you. I'm obliged." Dostoevsky could hardly get the words out. He turned and rushed away, seeing nothing. At the bottom of the stairs somebody caught his arm.

"Fyodor Mikhailovich, wait for me." He turned. It was Ivanov. They went out together. "My dear fellow, don't hurry on so," Ivanov said in the street. "I say, haven't you noticed that Antonelli never wants anybody to go home with him? He is always keen to go home with whomever he leaves the meeting with, though it is out of his way. Even if he leaves with two or three others he always accompanies them one after the other, then goes home alone."

Dostoevsky was not listening. He could never repay the money. And he knew, he knew that Speshnev would not accept repayment in money. Now he was *with* Speshnev. He was in Speshnev's power. Now he had Mephistopheles at his elbow.

Ivanov left him at the corner of Spassky Street. Dostoevsky walked on down the Sadovaya toward the Nevsky. He was tremendously worked up, his head throbbed, and he hurried along scarcely seeing anything. All at once he stopped and looked around in a feverish way. He was at the entrance to the Arcade. The lights flickered under the vaulted ceiling. There was a sort of night traffic there, a busy, dubious movement and wakefulness, an atmosphere of brutality. The Arcade was notorious. He went in.

Young men and boys and beggars came up.

"Your honor, a crust!"

"This way, I'll show you. Here!"

The noises echoed. Some of the passers-by hurried. Women came forward. They seemed to float up to him out of the shadow and put their faces close to his, speaking softly to him, opening their mouths and showing their tongues. They were there for customers going to the baths in the Arcade. Their lips were red and wet. He saw their white skin against the dark. A man was marching level with him on the other side of the Arcade. He walked on, trembling.

A woman touched him and he stopped and listened to her; he had an intense desire to behave without restraint. He ran his eyes up and down her as she spoke to him. "Five rubles . . . you'll like it. Five rubles." She was young, about eighteen, with a pleasant fresh face.

"What will you do?" he said.

"What you want. Come with me."

"Anything I want?" He extended a hand to touch her dress at the waist. She looked at him strangely. "Anything I want?" he said again.

"Yes."

"Say it then. Say what you'll do." His hand touched, the palm feeling the young taut muscle. He felt himself trembling more violently than ever and at that moment she laughed coarsely, showing an ugly gap in her front teeth. He turned and hurried away.

Torn sheets of paper scuttered in the wind along the

Arcade. A little farther on there was a child, a girl of about thirteen in a short frock, with a woman, under one of the arches. He lingered by them in absolute confusion.

"Look here, sir. Look for a moment," the woman's voice said. His face was burning. He felt a great temptation and stole glances at the child. He wanted to put himself to the test, to convince himself of his ability to endure the knowledge of it afterward. What made everything worse was that the woman with her positively had the respectable air of a governess; that made his heart beat sickeningly. All at once the man who had been marching alongside crossed the Arcade, gave a small jump, and landed in front of him.

"Why are you saying no to her? Your High Excellency!" He gave a low bow and burst out laughing. He was broad-shouldered, about twenty-five, with a small bony face, and was dressed in a greasy coat, leg wrappings, and a formless hat. The smell of the Russian drunkard came from him—the smell of vodka mingled with onion and clove to conceal it. At the same moment the child, urged by the woman's hand, came forward and stood at his side. Dostoevsky began to walk away, knowing quite well and with acute shamefulness that he was going to stop; and then did so.

"Give me some money," the man said, and held his hand out with peculiar authority. His whole bearing expressed great authority. Dostoevsky saw the child looking steadily at him; he hesitated, then, going back, pulled out five rubles and handed it over.

The man laughed again. "Good. We'll drink it. Come with me, Natasha—and you. Kulikov will look after you. Come on." He took Dostoevsky's arm and marched quickly along the Arcade. Dostoevsky did not attempt to resist. The child walked beside him (the woman had disappeared). He felt almost unsteady, more feverish than ever, as if something appalling were going to happen.

"I'm Kulikov," the man said as they went along. "You can say you've been with Kulikov." He nudged Dostoevsky with an elbow and nodded toward the child. "A little beauty, eh? Quite fresh, you know. Oh yes! She's the daughter of an employee who went blind. He was in a good position, a man liked by all, but he had an accident. The mother works at Zhukov's tallow factory on the Obvodny Canal, a regular hole, I can tell you; and there are five other children to feed. This one, she had a governess, you know. When the misfortune came the governess stayed on with the family because they were all very united and also because she had nowhere else to go. So now the governess—h'm—I persuaded the governess to bring her here." He looked sharply at Dostoevsky, said, "A respectable family. Yes!" and chuckled.

Suddenly Kulikov turned and led the way into a drinking den where a dozen drunken customers were arguing, talking, and singing gutter songs. Some others were playing billiards and quarreling over it. Dostoevsky couldn't help glancing at Natasha; she was looking at him and it seemed to him that she understood. He blushed furiously; there was no doubt she understood! Yet she was quite silent and modest and sat with them at the table as if she were doing all this in obedience to some injunction. The thought of that was extraordinarily exciting to him. He kept stealing glances at her and touched her leg with his.

"Champagne! Bring some champagne!" Kulikov bawled out, and threw the five rubles on the table and another blue note as well. He had no sooner done so than three women, apparently old friends of his, appeared and threw themselves on him, all talking at once, kissing him, putting their arms around his neck.

"Sonya, Tanya, and Grushenka," Kulikov shouted their names. Two were common creatures with dyed hair and puffy faces, the third younger and better-looking. Kulikov treated them with rough scorn and Dostoevsky noticed that individually the women seemed afraid of Kulikov. The whole incident, after the commitment to Speshnev, had keyed him up to an unbearable pitch. He actually found it difficult to speak.

A waiter brought a bottle, they all began drinking and joining in the singing and generally kicking up a row. After a while Dostoevsky saw Kulikov watching him with a peculiar expression. He said, "Why did you follow me in the Arcade?"

Kulikov said, "Perhaps I was going to kill you. If you had had more money. Or if you had refused Natasha!" He chuckled, then leaned over and put his mouth to Dostoevsky's ear. "I've murdered a runaway soldier. Here in this district. The police have found out, oh yes! They know it's me; they have been trying to find me for a week. That makes you live!" He leaned back again, his eyes blazing. Dostoevsky believed him without question; Kulikov was a wild beast.

"For money? Did you kill him for money?"

Kulikov bellowed with laughter. "There you are! Money at once. They'll all believe that; it's inevitable, yes, yes. They won't be able to imagine anything except self-interest, Kulikov's advantage. Let alone——"

"What? You killed him for a reason, I suppose?" The discussion seemed to accord with his overstrung state.

"Oh, but you're proving it all to me again!" Kulikov exclaimed. "I'm going to have a fine time with them. I'm going to ask them what advantage is. When they've caught me and given me some of their treatment—I recognize they're bound to in the end—I'll ask them to define with perfect accuracy what Kulikov's advantage consists of." He went off into another laugh. "Perhaps it was just to choose what I wanted. Merely to choose. Perhaps that was why I did it. Can you understand that?"

"Yes."

"You can?"

Dostoevsky trembled, looking at Kulikov. "To assert your own unfettered will. Yes, I do understand that."

"Explain it then. Go on!"

"They will think in terms of well-being and won't see that you wanted to go against well-being, they won't understand—what you said just now, for instance, about 'that makes you live.'"

Kulikov's fierce eyes were on him. "Yes. You see that. You see that it's suffering which is important too, as well as well-being."

"I don't hold for one or the other," Dostoevsky said. "It's only——"

"That's right! It's only the choice. That's what I intend to tell them. It's the fact of being able to *choose!* I was standing for the rationality of my caprice, because if that isn't rational, then we're all pawns, automata, we're——" He suddenly exploded angrily, picked up the empty champagne bottle, and hurled it across the room, cursing and bawling at the top of his voice for more. Dostoevsky glanced at the child; she was lying back against the wall asleep, her short frock, rumpled up, showing her legs. He touched her arm; she did not stir.

More people came to the table, there was even more noise; everybody shouted, drank, and sang. All at once Kulikov touched Dostoevsky's arm and made a signal and Dostoevsky followed him out. He was unprepared for the darkness of the night outside. Kulikov said, "This way," at his elbow and tugged at his coat. In a few moments he could make things out; they went down an alley and re-entered the Arcade at the far end. A short distance farther on they stopped at a door with a dim light inside. Dostoevsky looked up at the sign overhead. HYGIENIC BATHS.

"Go on," Kulikov said in a whisper. Dostoevsky saw his face close to in the surrounding darkness. With his heart bumping he pushed open the door of the baths and went in.

He hardly noticed the man who took the money from him and led him inside. There was the smell of hot brick and steam, a greeny light. He found himself alone in a private steam room, the steam turned off and a fresh bath pool on the far side. He undressed completely and sat on a stool.

He sat waiting; the room was warm, comfortable, and quiet. There was a shaded lamp on one wall and big towels hanging up. He sat facing the door without moving, his hands on his slightly spread knees, every fiber of him tense. He was perfectly prepared for everything and told himself he had even foreseen it all and yet there was something so awful in it that he was going to believe he would not do it, he was believing that now, while he was waiting for her; and yet that was certainly the very thing to carry him on.

The door opened and Natasha came in.

He tingled all over but did not move. She looked at him, her eyes fixed; her lips parted a little, she seemed unable to look away. Then she raised her eyes to his face for an instant, blushed crimson, and turned her head. He stood up, awkwardly, rampant, quickly pulled the door shut behind her and took her by the hand. She hung her head. He put his arm around her small waist, sat down on the stool again, and drew her onto his lap.

"You—you're——" He could hardly speak; his throat was shut. "You're Natasha, aren't you?"

She was fair, with a deep natural wave of hair on one side of her face that made a specially pretty effect, full lips, and blue eyes. A phrase kept occurring to him: "an unopened bud." That was almost worse than anything; and it kept beating in his mind. An unopened bud. It was exactly how he saw her. "You're the eldest, aren't you?" he said, and at once realized it was grotesque.

She did not answer and seemed to be trying to keep her eyes away without being successful. Her glance always returned. He held her on his lap. She made no attempt to move. Gently he kissed her cheek; he could feel himself fearfully flushed, perspiring, breathless. He kissed her again and suddenly, although she had scarcely looked into his eyes until then, she put both arms around his neck and began kissing him warmly and passionately. He almost fainted with the intensity of feeling. She left off a moment, her face red and glowing, and he actually saw tears glistening in her eyes. Then, leaving one arm around his neck, she resumed the kissing. He shuddered at her light, childish-timid clasping touch and pressed his lips to hers. The light brushing touch of the center of him was completely unnerving. He was overcome by her not saying a word; he could feel her shaking at the unfastening, gliding.

He lifted her down, stood, and went to the bath pool and slipped in without the usual steam preliminary of the bath. The water was tepid. He lay down and began soaping, very carefully, watching the short muslin frock fall, watching her approach, the dainty little feet coming nearer. She entered the water, her face flushing like a sunset—and began rubbing the soap into a lather, caressing the smoothness of the tablet, the lather smoothing and gliding into smoothest softest lather, the water rising and swaying gently over her firm youthfulness, smoothly riding, gliding and riding . . .

As he dressed afterward she stood with her hair wet, waiting for him, looking at him silently. He felt weak, pleasantly drowsy. He shrugged his coat on, grasped the door handle, then turned to her. "You've said hardly a word, Natasha. Your reproach is——I—listen, I'm——"

She said in her child's voice, "I do not reproach you, sir. Look." She kissed him with unnecessary violence on the lips. "If you could help me find Matrona Borisovna. Perhaps she is in the Arcade."

"Who?"

"My governess."

The woman was waiting at the Sadovaya end. He walked away quite calmly, the suppressed horror just under the surface, feeling isolated from all the thousands and tens of thousands of people around him; and in a strange way, because of that, stronger.

3

He went to the next meeting in a strange state. His hearing and touch seemed to develop extraordinary sensitivity, he was inexhaustible, all his faculties became more acute. Once or twice he had an impulse to shout out in the street; he wanted to call out anything—perhaps "We are going to bring in the new age of brotherhood with political murder!" Indoors occasionally he had a curious euphoria and the impression of a breeze blowing lightly across his face. There were sometimes attacks of giddiness afterward.

He gave three hundred of Speshnev's five hundred rubles to Mikhail, who was finding scarcely enough work to keep his family, and paid another hundred to his most troublesome creditors. He owed seven hundred more to Krayevsky—and to meet Krayevsky's constant pressure for material for the *Annals of the Fatherland* he had thrown himself into writing a new novel, *Netochka Nezvanovna*. If it succeeded . . . Yes—its success must be his reply to Turgenev and Nekrasov. But it was already too late. He was bound to Speshnev! And at moments when these thoughts were at conflict in his mind he became confused and ran out of the house, hurrying through the streets and coming back hours later, his nerves as much on edge as ever.

He found the circle at Petrashevsky's fidgety; there seemed to be a common feeling of uneasiness.

"Things are going badly in Europe," Evrapeus said.

"It seems all over in France and Austria," Ivanov said.

"It is not!" Jastrzembsky shouted in a furious voice. "The reaction can't crush them now, I won't believe it. All we know is third hand, fourth hand. Even now the revolutionary forces may be carrying the last fight."

"I agree," Durov said. "The censorship isn't going to encourage anybody to believe otherwise."

"We must prepare a list of people in Petersburg to be accused," Dostoevsky said. "I'll draw one up for the next meeting."

But somehow the talk did not run as easily as usual. After about an hour there was a move to go. Some were on the stairs where Petrashevsky was submerging them with floods of eloquence, absurdly defying anybody hostile who might be listening; others were standing about the room. Philippov came over to where Dostoevsky was standing with Durov; he was in an agitated state.

"It's intolerable. The revolution in Europe is fighting for its life and we talk—we talk!" He looked as if he were going to burst into tears out of intense anger.

"Well, they're mortally afraid of words too," Durov said.

Philippov took his arm excitedly. "We ought to set up a printing press." At the same moment Dostoevsky saw Speshnev had come up and was watching him steadily, with his hands in his pockets. He felt under an extraordinary compulsion, made several attempts to speak, and at last said, "We all heard what Nikolay Antonovich said just now. We have to form a circle of our own."

"Restricted to six or seven," Speshnev said. "There is already a spy here."

"My God—who?"

"How do you know?"

"Be quiet," Speshnev said, not moving. They could hear Petrashevsky's voice outside still pouring out words; one or two others were still hanging about the room. "Settle this quickly," Speshnev said.

Durov said, "We can meet at my rooms." Speshnev nodded. Philippov said, "We must have Ivanov. He's all right, I'll swear." They exchanged glances as Philippov went to where Ivanov was putting on his coat and brought him over.

"We are forming a group apart, Sergey Ivanovich. Are you with us?" Ivanov looked around their faces; he understood at once and nodded.

"Speshnev says there's a police spy here," Philippov said to him.

Durov leaned forward and said in a whisper, "Is it Jastrzembsky?"

"No. It can't be."

"Antonelli?"

Speshnev shrugged. Standing close together, they softly passed the names to each other, looking around at each other's faces.

"Evrapeus?"

"No."

"Katenev?" A pause. "But surely not. It's out of the question."

"Mombelli?"

"Never—never!"

"Ah, my God! This is vile," Philippov interrupted. "This is the depth they drag you to—spying on your friends."

"Yes, the influence of the Most High on his subjects," Durov said disgustedly. They were all revolted. Speshnev exhaled the smoke of his cigarette and said, "We'll have a printing press—as a beginning." He looked at them impassively.

4

Procuring and assembling a secret printing press in Petersburg was like handling a lightly fused bomb.

They worked at Durov's. They brought in two others from Petrashevsky's—Mombelli and Pleshcheyev. Petrashevsky himself, they agreed, was too dangerous.

"We shall have to continue going to Petrashevsky's Fridays for the time being," Speshnev said. "It's a risk we must take. Otherwise the break will be too obvious." They agreed.

The ideal was to buy parts for the press one by one, at intervals, in different parts of the city. But this enormously

complicated things. There was a horrifying incident at the
outset. Philippov, who had volunteered to get the treadle
and balance arm, one of the riskiest items, turned up nervous
and empty-handed. He had gone to an address he had heard
of with some rags for wrapping the arm in; the people became suspicious and while he waited sent for the police.
Philippov had actually struggled with the policeman getting
away. He sweated, telling them about it. There was bound to
be an inquiry and he wasn't sure if they could trace him
through the man who had originally suggested his going
there.

Nothing happened.

They had chosen the simplest sort of press, a frame and
two flat circular beds, one for the paper, one for the type,
which pressed together when the weighted treadle was
worked. Ivanov acquired an old iron frame minus two braces
and carried it up with Durov, past the porter at the street
door, in a mattress. A week later Mombelli reported that he
knew where there was an old broken press and from it they
managed to take the beds and weight. They were appalled
at the cumbrousness of the whole thing.

Durov lived in two rooms on the first floor of an apartment
house. There was a common staircase, a neighbor on the same
landing and others above and below, besides a communal
lavatory just outside the door. Moreover, Durov's rooms
were sparsely furnished and had nothing on the board floor.
It was difficult enough to hide the parts of the press. But
they found it so awkward to assemble them that unless they
worked slowly and with great care they made terrible clanks
and bumps.

They practiced fitting the press together without the missing parts. It was an unpleasant process. Durov was the most
adroit but had to be spared because he knew the sounds of
the house and kept his ear to the door while the others
worked. From time to time he said quietly, "Stop." They
would pause, heads up, eyes on him, the frame half erected,

enough evidence displayed in the room to condemn them all for life. Operating a printing press was as serious a crime as shooting a police official.

The steps would come up the stairs, reach the landing, and pause—then proceed up. They would still wait, not moving. It could be a trap. And Durov would suddenly nod, they would swallow and resume.

"God knows what the noise will be when it's working," Mombelli said.

"It'll wake the house."

Two evenings later there was an alarm. A friend of Durov's called unexpectedly and had to be kept waiting on the landing while they hastily put the press away. He kept calling jokingly through the door, "Well, what are you doing in there, eh?" until Durov quickly slipped out to him. Durov's friends knew he was "not in" on certain evenings: he had hinted at a girl, but this caller had not been told. As they sat, constrained and uneasy afterward, Dostoevsky said, "We shall never get this working more smoothly. It's the wrong technique. We need something lighter and less cumbersome."

Speshnev nodded. "We must get rid of this."

They filed the frame into smaller parts, smuggled them out at night, and dropped them through the ice which was forming on the Neva. At the end of the following week Ivanov came in, shook the snow from a bag, and tipped a small pile of type from it onto the table.

"Splendid! How did you do it?" They crowded around excitedly.

"It's poor stuff, and there's not enough for more than a few lines," Ivanov said.

"We'll get more," Speshnev said.

Now they kept the equipment to the bare necessities. Besides the type, there was a small cylinder of a kind of gelatinous substance like carpenter's glue, with a pleasant smell, a heavy cylinder, procured by Philippov, covered with cloth, which served as the press, and some blackened brushes and sponges kept in a pan. They could get only one jar of printing ink.

Pleshcheyev, who had friends in Moscow, thought he could get some more type there and went to try. The others timed themselves in getting out the press and hiding it away, dividing the tasks. Dostoevsky and Mombelli wrapped the cylinders and put them in Durov's chest of drawers. The cavity under the bottom drawer was used for hiding the type; Ivanov did this. Durov was at the door. Philippov concealed the brushes and pan in the wood by the stove (they would go inside the stove in summer). The jar of ink they tied to the far corner leg of the sofa where Durov slept. They practiced talking conversationally and laughing as they were going through this. They found they could clear everything away, wipe the table, examine the room for stray type, ink marks, or other signs, take seats, and pick up cards which were left ready, in six minutes. It seemed a long time. "And it's noisy," Speshnev said. "Anybody listening could tell you were putting something away in a hurry." But they could not improve it.

"What are we going to print first?" Mombelli said one evening.

"Everybody must write something the censors would refuse," Speshnev said. He added in a mocking way, "We should give the first honor to Fyodor Mikhailovich."

Dostoevsky went red in the face. He was hardly sleeping at all, his nerves worse than ever. There were debts everywhere. He owed Krayevsky an enormous sum—and the whole five hundred still to Speshnev. He ate at intervals of several days. The bouts of giddiness were more frequent. Yanovsky, a young doctor friend of Grigorovich's, had offered to lend him twenty rubles. Twenty rubles! He owed hundreds. He had shackled himself to *Netochka Nezvanovna* and delivered two parts of it; he had even offered to give Krayevsky everything he wrote for fifty rubles a month.

"It will be another opportunity to please the critics," Speshnev said with a smile.

"Will it?" Dostoevsky shouted out. "Will it?" He jumped up, trembling, furious, in great confusion. Speshnev revolted him. He wanted to break, to liberate himself, and at the same time he felt he must commit himself further, that there was another side, of darkness and crime, which continued his personality too. The thought of his father lying in the field came unbearably into his mind, and his wish for his father's death. He stiffened, making a great effort to calm himself. He must prove to Speshnev that he could confront anything calmly, with indifference—anything. That was what Speshnev was taunting him with too. He managed a smile; he was fumbling in his pocket. "I have something better for you—some Belinsky. Yes, the admired Vissarion Grigoryevich. I have his letter to Gogol. Pleshcheyev sent it to me from Moscow. Did you think it would be unpleasant for me to suggest printing Belinsky, Nikolay Antonovich? Did you? Well, I will read it to you. Aren't we always saying that the revolution eliminates personal feelings? Here it is; I'll read it."

He was unfolding the paper, his hands shaking. Some things in it he disliked, so he was all the more resolved on reading it entirely. He began the letter which the Tsar had thought so dangerous it must be banned, the letter of a dying man. Belinsky had only escaped a cell in the Peter and Paul Fortress by death. And as Dostoevsky read, the thin pale-haired ghost seemed to rise up, with burning eyes, accusing, quivering with indignation at the hypocrisy of the regime —tsars, priests and slaveowners, spies and police, destroyers of freedom and human dignity.

Russia—a country where there are no guarantees for individuality, nothing but vast corporations of official thieves and robbers! A landowner's peasants are his brethren in Christ. A brother cannot be a slave to his brother, so shouldn't he give them their freedom or allow them to enjoy the fruits of their labor? But the Orthodox Church has always served as the prop of the knout and been a lackey to despotism.

" 'Do you really mean to say you don't know that our clergy is held in universal contempt by Russian society and the Russian people? Doesn't the priest represent for all Russians the embodiment of gluttony, avarice, servility, and shamelessness? Take a closer look—and you'll see that Russians are a profoundly atheistic people. They are superstitious, not religious. And most of our clergy has always been distinguished for fat bellies, scholastic pedantry, and savage ignorance. . . . I leave it to your conscience to admire the divine beauty of autocracy. Continue to admire it from afar —at close quarters it is not so attractive or safe. But fresh forces are seething and struggling for expression in Russian society. They are weighted down by oppression and find no outlet.' "

"Ah, but they will, they will!" Speshnev said in a loud startling voice. They saw he was altogether carried away.

"Wait, here's the end," Dostoevsky said. " 'Russia already understands that the only people who seek Christ and Jerusalem are those who have never carried him in their breasts or who have lost him.

" 'He who is capable of suffering at the sight of other people's sufferings and who is pained at the sight of other people's oppression bears Christ within his bosom and has no need to make a pilgrimage to Jerusalem.' "

"Yes, that's what we mean!" They broke out in chorus. "It's splendid."

"We must copy it. We must print it and send it out."

"Yes, yes."

Their faces shone. Dostoevsky felt a harsh satisfaction and humiliation in the triumph of his old enemy. At the same time he, with all the others, felt how the room was filled with a rapturous brotherhood, as if everything good had come already, as if all this that they wished to express above love, sharing, human serenity, and the truth were understood universally, by everyone in the world, everyone.

Something tapped outside. They were suddenly silent. Durov crept to the door. They waited, hardly breathing. In a minute he straightened out. "It's nothing—the lodger from upstairs." They were quiet and avoided looking at each other.

5

He felt events accelerating. It was winter and he was almost completely without money. Yegelin, a rough tradesman whom he owed eighty rubles for food, was hounding him, waiting for him in the street, banging at his door and making a scandal. He managed to borrow thirty rubles and paid it to Yegelin. He went for weeks without tobacco. Starshevsky, the editor of the Readers' Library, offered him sixty rubles to correct proofs and write articles for an encyclopedic dictionary he was publishing. The work was worth three times that but Dostoevsky needed the money too badly to refuse. He was nervous, irritable, inexhaustibly restless. More than anything the meetings at Durov's intensified his feverishness. Speshnev was bringing them nearer direct action. It was like the attraction of approaching a chasm.

Half Ivanov's type had proved to be too worn to print clearly and they consumed themselves with impatience, laboriously and exasperatingly trying to work with what remained. At the end of January Mombelli obtained a small extra supply. They had all prepared texts. Philippov brought one he had written, "A Comment on the Ten Commandments," and in a moment was bawling it out: " 'The Tsar, the autocrat with powers not from God but from the Devil, the——' "

"Keep your voice down!" Speshnev said urgently. Slowly he leaned back on the sofa. "Save it for when your heels are kicking."

"Well—that will be an honor, to die like that! And *I* shall think of Ryleyev and Pestel!" Philippov's face was flushed with emotion. And to everybody's surprise Speshnev got up and crossed over to him and kissed him. Speshnev was almost like Ryleyev, he was stronger than any.

They were still in touch with Petrashevsky's Fridays, attending irregularly in ones and twos, gradually severing. Then one evening at Durov's when they had the press out and were trying to compose a page, Durov said, "Stop." They could hear nothing but Durov kept his hand raised as the sign that they should not resume. They took up the "card game"—standing still around the press, making exclamations, laughing, commenting, suddenly chorusing as if they were playing cards; it allowed intervals of silence for Durov to listen in and sounded natural at the same time.

It went on for ten minutes. They were all very tense. At last Durov relaxed, dropped his hand, and moved away from the door.

"What was it?"

"Is somebody out there, Durov?"

Durov said, "It's Ivashev, the man who lives on this landing. He's been talking to somebody I don't know. I couldn't hear what they said. I think they've gone."

"Could they hear us?" Dostoevsky said; it was what everybody was thinking.

"I don't know. I think Ivashev is all right, I mean he is not a spy." Durov looked uneasy.

"We know Ivashev," Speshnev said. "He keeps humming that tune of Glinka's, doesn't he?"

"What?"

Speshnev was softly humming the tune from *A Life for the Tsar.* They were all looking at him, suddenly realizing that they had all heard the faint humming from the next room at intervals during the last few evenings. There was a movement of consternation, then Dostoevsky went quickly for the door.

"Where are you going?" Speshnev's arm stopped him.

"To that room, to find out what you can hear."

"Very well. Ask him if he can lend us a pinch of tea. We will continue here."

Durov opened the door and he was outside. Ivashev's door was to the right. The oil lamp below gave just enough light. He stepped to the door and knocked; there was no answer. The muffled sound of voices came from Durov's room. He tried Ivashev's door; it was locked. There was no light from the keyhole or underneath; he took out his penknife and worked its small spike in the lock without much hope; the spike caught and as he wrenched it the door eased and with a click opened under his push. He went in, leaving the door open by a crack. The room smelled of cooking— fish. He struck a match; he was nervous and perspiring, hating the dirty, untidy room that came out of the darkness. He lighted Ivashev's candle and stood listening; very faintly he could hear the voices from Durov's room. Moving to put his ear to the wall, he knocked over a chair and at the same moment there was a loud voice from outside, somebody speaking to the porter as he came into the house.

In a panic, Dostoevsky blew out the light, almost sprawled over the chair, reached the door, and heard the man coming up the stairs humming Glinka's tune.

His fingers trembling felt the lock; the hasp was only half out since the penknife had not fully turned the mechanism. By pulling it out a little more he might wedge the door enough to give the illusion that it had remained locked. He held the door almost shut, trying not to pull the hasp too far, then realized that Ivashev was almost within sight of the landing. He dare not step outside. The humming approached. He stood in the darkness, his mind in complete confusion. Everything was lost! He felt a perverse satisfaction, almost a thrill of pleasure in his soul! He must run out, dash past Ivashev hiding his face as if he were a thief. He pulled the door open, caught a shadow moving from the direction of the stairs, and suddenly Speshnev's voice was saying loudly and in a curiously unusual tone, "Good evening, my dear Ivashev. I'm glad I caught you. You see I know who you are. I'll explain in a moment. Yes, it's a crisp night, eh? But fine. You see, there's something I want to discuss with you. Can you spare me a moment? I'd like your advice . . ."

The voice retreated. He was leading Ivashev downstairs. Dostoevsky stepped quickly out of the room, adjusted the hasp with his knife, and went back to Durov's. They all eyed him anxiously.

"That was a near thing," Mombelli said.

"Speshnev will settle him."

Speshnev came back twenty minutes later, having left Ivashev at his room. He said to Dostoevsky, "Did you knock that chair over?"

"Oh, my God, I forgot it! Did he notice?"

"Of course." To his astonishment Speshnev shrugged carelessly and lit a cigarette. "There is something more serious. The porter downstairs—I've just observed it. I'm not sure somebody hasn't been speaking to him."

"What do you mean, somebody?"

"There are certain inflections in his voice. They sound as if the police have been at him."

Dostoevsky said excitedly, "I've been noticing the municipal guard at the corner of the street; I thought perhaps I was wrong, but he's had more of a soldier's air lately, as if he'd had orders to watch the house."

Everyone fidgeted.

"Shall we move—meet somewhere else?"

"That would confirm it for them, if they do suspect," Durov said.

"My God, we must keep that porter out."

"On the contrary, we'll invite him," Speshnev said. "The best thing is to make him come here as often as possible. We shall have to hide the material more effectively."

"But we can't!" they protested.

Speshnev said, "If he's here often enough and sees both rooms completely, he'll report we're harmless."

There was an argument but eventually they agreed. With great care they removed some of the stuffing from two parts of the sofa and this new cache took everything except the box of type and one of the brushes. They had another argument over Speshnev's insistence that they hide these in the pile of wood by the stove. "He's handling wood all day," Speshnev said. "He'd never dream of it as a hiding place."

Next evening Durov began calling the porter up. The porter was a short man with a walrus mustache and a snub nose who wore an apron and a peaked cap. He had the pushing manner of the parasite class and they thought was exceedingly suspicious since he said nothing about payment for the extra services Durov now asked of him. Sitting at cards, they could see his eyes going around the room and knew he was listening to all they said. Once or twice he seemed to notice the smell of ink, pausing with his mustache fluffing. Dostoevsky felt ill when he had gone.

Suddenly all this was intensified. Pleshcheyev arrived one evening humping a big parcel of type. They managed to hide some in the sofa but found the risk increased by the time it took to extract and replace it with the necessary caution.

"Now we can print everything," Philippov said in great excitement.

"Yes. We must finish the porter off quickly," Speshnev said.

They began to summon the porter relentlessly, incessantly. On various pretexts they made him see the whole of the room six times, eight times an evening. They merely covered the printing material up. At a loss for a further reason they even told him there was a rat in the room and made him search thoroughly. It was so nerve-racking that Dostoevsky sometimes had to leave and return later. The porter started grumbling, gradually became furious, vituper-

ated them, returned to his former arrogance—and finally
refused to climb the stairs at all.

At this climax, at this instant of passing to direct action,
Dostoevsky had the overwhelming and absurd impulse to
visit Petrashevsky. It was the last Friday but one in April
1849. He found Petrashevsky playing the fool as usual and
consumed with a new idea for starting a newspaper.

"My dear Fyodor Mikhailovich, you are a shareholder.
Yes, you are appointed to the editorial board."

Pointlessly, Dostoevsky encouraged him to discuss it. He
felt keyed up and kept asking Petrashevsky questions.

He left with the last, accompanied Jastrzembsky and
another member of the circle, Palm, to the Blue Bridge and
turned home. A fine penetrating rain began to fall and he
was soon soaked. His room was chaotic with papers, books,
unwashed linen, clothes, everything lying about in disorder.
He stood looking at the latest manuscript page of *Netochka
Nezvanovna* on the table. There was still an enormous
amount to do on the book and what he had done, he felt,
was poor. His head throbbed. And yet the nervous energy
churning in him left him uncontrollably restless. He paced
the room in his wet clothes, then stopped, trying to calm
himself. His thoughts were flying, night thoughts torturing
the past and finding all the uncertainties of the future. He
became giddy, sat on the bed, and after a moment took his
clothes off. He blew out the candle and pulled the blanket
over him. He heard three o'clock strike outside.

He was awakened, startled, by a clumping. Somebody in
a military greatcoat stood at the open door. "What is it?
What is it?"

"Get up." A voice at his elbow made him jump. It was
a major of the gendarmerie in the light blue uniform, white
strap and silver epaulets, and a steel casque standing beside
the bed. Beyond, in the room, was the district police master
with a light and a gendarme by the door who clashed and
clanked his saber.

"Get dressed," the major said in a soft voice. "We will wait."

"But what for? Where are we going?"

"I have the count's instructions to bring you to the Third Section."

"This is the precipice!"

"What's that?" the major of gendarmes said quickly. "What are you saying?"

"Nothing—nothing," Dostoevsky said. One threw oneself over it with the joyful horror of a man leaping to death.

He began to dress, all at once feeling ashamed that the officer should see his big toes with the toenails uncut. He had been meaning to cut them for two weeks and now the right one was particularly long and horny. What a stupid thing to occur to one at this moment! He tried to hide the toes and felt even more awkward. Perhaps the officer would recount to his wife how he had seen particularly ugly, even repulsive toes that morning and she would exclaim in disgust.

Pah! Why such fuss? He wanted to shock the man. He was shaking and not in the least tired though he had scarcely slept. A corporal of gendarmes had brought more candles. The police master, who had grandiose side whiskers, was rummaging about among the papers, books, and linen. "H'm," he grunted, looking at one book, then muttered the title, *True Christianity According to Christ*.

"What's interesting you?" Putting on his shirt, Dostoevsky looked over the police master's shoulder. He felt an almost uncontrollable desire to chatter, though there was something disgusting in the idea of friendly exchanges with these creatures. "Oh—Cabet. Do you know it?" It was one of the banned books Petrashevsky had lent him. "It teaches that true Christianity demands a social commonwealth in which all share their goods."

"It's against official Christianity, is it?" the police master said in an unpleasant tone.

"*Official* Christianity. That's good!" Dostoevsky laughed nervously. "Even salvation must be official, eh? Well, never mind, I don't mean to insult you. I hope this business will not take long. I must say it's a miserable morning to go out so early; if one could go later . . ." He knew he was speaking from nervous necessity, just as out of self-defense one pretended an injury was not so bad as it was and precisely in this way acknowledged its badness.

The police master was collecting all the papers and books and laying them aside. The major paused before the fireplace, glancing around for some implement, then picked up Dostoevsky's pipe from the table and began to stir the ashes with the stem. Dostoevsky watched with peculiar fascination. There was something intensely insulting and humiliating in the delicate way the major held the pipe bowl and poked among the dirty ashes with the mouthpiece.

In a moment the corporal brought something over to the police master. It was a bent five-kopeck piece.

"Is it counterfeit?" Dostoevsky asked.

"We shall see," the police master said with a glare, putting it on the table.

"Come, are you ready?" the major said to Dostoevsky. They went out, the police master and the corporal carrying the bundled books, papers, and other items. At the bottom of the stairs Dostoevsky caught sight of the white faces of the porter and his wife; the two were standing back in a cringing attitude as if not to draw the attention of the gendarmes to themselves. The woman shook her white moon-face and clasped her hands with a pitiful expression, and Dostoevsky felt a pang. He had hardly noticed the couple since he had been at the lodging—and yet that was where feeling lay; they entered into his position now.

Outside there was a carriage with the folding hood up. In the gray light the street looked specially dirty. The thin rain was falling again. There was nobody about. As they came out a wretched-looking man with a head held lopsidedly, who was standing at the fence, said to the police master, "Can I go now, honored sir?"

"Yes, clear off," the police master said.

"Who was that?" Dostoevsky said, trying to catch a better glimpse of the man who had darted away. Was it a spy? He did not think it had been the porter from Durov's.

"It was the impartial witness," the police master said. He added bad-temperedly, "Evidently you don't know that the government protects the people, even criminals. We cannot enter a house without an impartial witness."

"But he was here outside. What is he supposed to be impartial about?" Dostoevsky asked.

"Kindly go on!" The major gave him a slight push on the elbow. They all got into the carriage. It moved off slowly down the empty street, lurching in the potholes.

Chapter Five

1

They drove along the Ekaterinovsky Canal, through the end of the Summer Garden to the Lenka Bridge, and came to the mansion that had been Count Kochubey's house and was now the headquarters of the Third Section. They entered by the back gate. Many of the people who went in this way vanished; or left again for Siberia or the Peter and Paul Fortress.

The carriage rumbled through several courtyards and at last stopped at a door with steps up to it. The major dismissed the police master, who went off with obsequious bows. Inside, a gendarme, also in the light blue uniform of the secret police, was sitting at a table. The major held out a paper. "Here is the document concerning the prisoner." The gendarme declined to take it in spite of the major's rank and called the superintendent. (Apparently everybody was afraid of something, Dostoevsky thought.) There was the sound of another coach arriving on the cobbles outside and he watched the door expectantly; but nobody entered.

The superintendent read laboriously through the document, moving his lips at every syllable, and wrote an acknowledgment of having received a prisoner. "Guard!" he called out and, when the guard of four soldiers stepped forward, led the way down the corridor. At the end was a double-leafed door with sentries with rifles and bayonets outside. The superintendent jerked his head. Dostoevsky went in. It was a big whitewashed hall, two windows high up, soldiers around the sides and two or three officers

standing about. At once Jastrzembsky, Durov, and Pleshcheyev rushed toward him.

"You too, you too!" They threw their arms around him.

He embraced them all. "Who betrayed us?"

"Yes, who is it? Did they give you any clue?"

"What happened to you? Tell us, tell us."

"Are the others——"

"Sshh! Be quiet," Durov said. Two of the officers were
moving up, listening.

"We are going to be questioned now, I suppose?" he said
to Durov.

"Yes, no doubt."

Two minutes later the door opened and Grigoryev
appeared. It was the same welcoming and questioning for
him. The secret police had not confined themselves to the
Durov group; they had arrested those from Petrashevsky's
also. Others kept coming in—Palm, Katenev, Ivanov,
Akcharumov. Once the door opened and they saw Speshnev
standing outside, pale with fury, and just behind him
Philippov; Speshnev gave a piercing glance into the hall
but apparently the superintendent had misread his orders,
for the door was pulled shut again and the steps continued
along the corridor.

Then Petrashevsky was shown in—in his most hilarious
mood, not at all cast down but mocking at the gendarmes.
He had put on his cloak and broad-brimmed hat and greeted
them all affectionately. "They reserved me such distinction!
I was arrested by Dubbelt himself, the second most important hyena in person!" Leonty Vassilyevich Dubbelt was the
notorious vice-chief of the Third Section under Count Orlov.
"I was reading when they came in clanking their phallic
symbols and their masculine spurs," Petrashevsky said. "I
saw it was Dubbelt at once. He stretched out his hand to
pick up the book I had put down, so I bellowed at him,
'Take care! Don't touch it.' The hyena jumped back looking
alarmed. 'Why not?' he said. 'It'll give you leprosy,' I said.

'It's banned by the censor.'" Petrashevsky threw his head back and roared with laughter and several of the others couldn't help joining in.

"After that the hyena went through everything with great care. I was delighted to see that he was outraged particularly by a little article I'd just written about the way Oldenburg, that distinguished cousin of the Most High, has been punishing his college students. I intended to read the article at our next Friday meeting. 'But how *civilized*, Leonty Vassilyevich,' I said to him, 'for Prince Oldenburg to punish a boy by taking away the pillow from his bed . . .' Ah, he didn't like the word 'civilized'!

"But the best was when the thickheaded captain he had brought with him went through my books. He was magnificent! He picked up the first volume of Thiers' *History of the French Revolution*, then the second, then the third. By the time he'd got to ten he couldn't contain himself any longer. 'My God! What criminals—the number of revolutionary books!' And an instant after he cried, 'And here's another'— and he handed the police captain Auerbach's *Remarks on the Revolution of the Globe!*" Petrashevsky shook with laughter again and Dostoevsky positively loved him.

At that moment the door opened again and Evrapeus came in—with a girl. The loud buzz of conversation dropped; they looked at her in astonishment. She was young, very pretty, with a slim figure and a touch of coarseness in her face. Her brown hair was rather disordered and she held a coat close around her. It was obvious that she had nothing on underneath. Evrapeus left her on a bench at the side of the room while he plunged in among the others, questioning and answering questions in his turn.

"It's ridiculous," he said when they asked about the girl. "She was in bed with me when the gendarmes came. As a matter of fact I didn't hear them come in at first because— well, she was on top of me and I wasn't thinking of police! They made her come here. They wouldn't listen. 'We have to bring everybody,' they said. Since she wouldn't dress in front of them—there she is."

"Mombelli!" It was the latest arrival.

Presently there was a loud command outside, a major came in holding a document. He stood consulting it for a moment with one of the other officers. Dostoevsky managed a glimpse at it. He could only see the heading but caught the words 'Nominal List,' then 'Agent in the case: Antonelli.' He looked around: no, Antonelli wasn't there. He was revolted, sickened, as if something sacred had been dirtied, remembering Antonelli sitting there at Petrashevsky's when everybody there also had been inspired and felt the communion between them and wanted to embrace the world in love and goodness. He went up to Petrashevsky. "It was Antonelli. It's marked on that sheet."

For a second Petrashevsky's comic mask dissolved. He took the shock of revelation, breathed deeply once, and nodded quietly to Dostoevsky. Ivanov had heard and was passing it on in a low voice.

It seemed as if they had been brought up to this moment of harsh knowledge and left to reflect on it. The hours passed, the light at the high windows faded. The lamps were lighted. Dostoevsky went up to one of the officers. "Surely the interrogation can begin, can't it?" The officer ignored him.

At last the major came back and called out, "Silence! Separate and face the door, all of you." The soldiers around the wall clanked to attention. There was a brief expectant pause, then as the officers by the door saluted, General Dubbelt sauntered in. The collar of his uniform was unbuttoned. The foxy look on his sunken face was heightened by his fair mustache; it was the subtle shrewd face of a beast of prey. Fatigue had lined his cheeks and there was something evasive, conceited, and intelligent about his whole expression.

Slowly he walked around in a semicircle, looking them up and down, looking from their faces to their heels. He reached the end and without pausing said, "Good!" in a peculiarly loud, biting tone, nodded to the major, and disappeared.

At once squads of soldiers with rifles marched into the hall and the major began calling out names. Dostoevsky was second after Petrashevsky. A soldier moved to each side of him, two behind, and a captain in front.

"March!"

He felt great relief. At last they were going to get the interrogation done with. Petrashevsky was already on his way to explain that the meetings had been simply discussions. And suddenly he realized that by some process of self-defense he had forgotten about the printing press.

They were marching down the corridor in the opposite direction from which he had entered. At the end they came to a courtyard. The night was fresh and the rain had stopped. They continued in the open, then passed through two bare barracklike rooms and were again in the open air. They halted, a carriage appeared, and they drove off. Dostoevsky scarcely noticed any of these surroundings; his mind was concentrating on the coming interrogation. He would have to be prepared for treacherous questions about Durov's. A man like Dubbelt had great dialectic ability. Yet if they had discovered the press why take Speshnev off separately? Why Philippov too and not himself, Durov, the others?

He noticed they were driving a long way and at one point there seemed to be a bridge under the horse's hoofs. The window of the carriage was partly painted over and he could not see out.

The captain lit a cigarette and the tang of tobacco made him long for a few puffs. He felt the humiliation there would be in asking the captain for a cigarette, sat forward, and said, "Will you give me a cigarette, Captain?" The captain looked at him with an unpleasant expression, held out a silver case, and waited until Dostoevsky said, "And a light, please? Thank you." He noticed one of the soldiers, a young fellow, looking at him with contempt. He made a point of blowing out the smoke as if he did not really want the cigarette, was not a heavy smoker, and had really only asked for one to put himself in that position. It gave him a strange feeling of liberation in his soul, and yet he could not stop thinking apprehensively of the coming questioning. Why had he asked for the cigarette? It had been an attempt to prove his superiority, his superiority to the debasing treatment they were inflicting on him. Perhaps such a thing was only possible with a captain of gendarmes!

Presently the carriage crossed another bridge, stopped, and at a nod from the captain one of the soldiers got out. Evidently he did not intend to let the door go but missed his footing as he alighted and the door swung wide. Dostoevsky bent forward and looked out. They were at a gate in stone ramparts—almost resembling St. Peter's Gate, the main entrance to the Peter and Paul Fortress. The captain swore and grabbed the door. Dostoevsky craned his neck, trying to see further. He caught a glimpse of a statue that looked like Tresini's statue of Mars which every Petersburger had seen outside the St. Peter's Gate, and the captain pulled the door shut with a bang. Slowly Dostoevsky sat back. Surely it wasn't possible? The Fortress was reserved for serious political criminals. It must be some barracks. "Where are we?" he asked; the captain did not answer. There were muffled thuds and clinkings of metal outside and the carriage moved on again.

Now the echoes and reverberations seemed to come from the sides and above. It was as if they were passing under vaulted arches and along narrow roads between walls. His mind was concentrated on the exterior, on trying to catch some indication of where they were. After a moment there was again the hollow rumble underneath as if they were passing over a bridge—the third since they had set out. At the end of it they stopped and the captain said, "Get out." They were under a stone archway with a lighted office on one side. The captain went in. All at once there was a peal of bells behind them. Dostoevsky turned sharply and looked back over the bridge they had just crossed. Massive walls stood against the night sky and rising above them was the slender spire of the Peter and Paul Cathedral. He was in the Fortress; and the bridge meant this was the Alexeyevsky Ravelin, the worst part.

"Prisoner forward!" the captain shouted. A soldier gave him a prod. He sprang toward the office door. "Where is the investigation? I wish to explain, Captain. I shall be glad if we can begin at once. Your superiors want to ask me questions, no doubt. Very well, then let it be done, let it be done——" He stopped.

He was facing an old man, tall, gaunt with a transparent waxen face. He had on a faded plum-colored army coat from another age, some period long gone. The old man stood regarding him as if he were absorbing something of Dostoevsky's personality, sucking it in forever. Then he turned away without a word and signed a paper on the table. At the same moment an officer in a uniform Dostoevsky did not recognize and four more soldiers came forward from the other side of the room and the old man in a gigantic baying voice spoke the single word "Eight."

"This way," the officer said. They went through a stone passage, down steps, and into a room with scarred dirty walls. A guard with a heavy wet mustache came out from a cubicle, scanned Dostoevsky, disappeared, and came back with a bundle. "Take your clothes off," he said. Dostoevsky undressed and noticed how all of them, at the moment he was naked, observed his genitals. "Mouth!" the guard said, stepping close to him, and before Dostoevsky had understood the guard's arm was behind him, fingers searching between his buttocks, probing.

"Ahh!" He cried out in horror and disgust, springing away. The soldiers clanked forward as the guard said loudly, "Open your mouth!" and, catching his arm, stood close again. Dostoevsky opened his mouth; the guard grasped his chin, wrenching his head sideways and backward, peering in. The repulsive smell from the wet mustache so close to him, the man's hairy nostrils dark with snuff, made him want to be sick. With his chin pushed up again, he shuddered back once more as the man's finger came up his nose. "Keep still, won't you," the guard said. The other nostril, then each ear, his hair, and finally the man's hand lifting, exploring, probing again. The guard stepped back and, indicating the bundle, said, "There; put them on." There were a coarse gray shirt and trousers, a long blue flaxen coat, woolen stockings, and a pair of felt slippers. He put them on. The stuff scratched his skin and he felt grotesque.

"Follow," the officer said. Outside they went down more steps into a dim vaulted passage and Dostoevsky noticed with vague fear that now suddenly they were walking quite noiselessly, absolutely soundlessly. He looked down at the officer's feet, the feet of the two soldiers before him, and around at those of the soldiers behind him; they all wore felt boots. Now that he had felt slippers there was no sound from the stone floor.

They passed two sentries in the passage and reached a guard in a small embrasure. The officer spoke some words with him quietly and they went two paces on and unlocked a door. The guard tipped his head to Dostoevsky. Dostoevsky went forward. There was blackness beyond the door. He could feel the damp chill coming from it. He turned, facing the officer in a state of great agitation. "What about the examination? Aren't you going to ask me any questions? I haven't answered one, I haven't explained. I——"

"Take this." The guard held out a stub of lighted candle, as short as four stacked coins.

He took it. The chill from the cell struck on his back. The door swung in on him; he stepped backward and it shut in front of his face with a heavy boom, swaying the candle flame violently. The bolts rattled and screeched and then all was still.

He did not move. His head vibrated under the tightened muscles pulling in his neck. The candle burned his finger. He let it burn. His mouth stretched at the corners, strained wide, his lower teeth coming forward in a grimace of emotion and pain and mental anguish. He stared. The fever of the past months and years, the nervous tension, all seemed to have accumulated into this moment.

The shock went deep into his personality. An uncontrollable animallike exhalation of breath escaped his lips. He remained there. At last he turned, touching the wall with his arm. There was a small niche cut in the stone. Slowly he put the candle in it. His finger was stiffened with the burn but he did not look at it.

He had needed this disaster. He had sought it. It had cauterized his other life, like the self-inflicted burn. He started. A slow peal of bells came from outside, muffled and ghostly. They were from the cathedral and played slowly the solemn Russian liturgy "Have Pity, O Lord." When they ended the silence was more profound than ever. He could scarcely see the rest of the cell. He made out a bed against the other wall, went to it, and fell on it full length. The darkness bore him. He was exhausted. The straw bolster stank. There was absolute silence. The candle wick eased forward in its last grease and went out. He lay in the dark. Blackness.

Suddenly the cathedral bells sounded again. The dark cell seemed buried beneath them. The bells struck midnight and slowly sounded the hymn "Glory, Glory Be to God in Zion." And then slowly, slowly the notes of "God Save the Tsar."

2

He started awake and sat upright.

The door was before him. The faint bluish light of day showed on the stone walls. All was quiet.

He put his feet on the floor and looked around. The cell was large, about ten paces long, with walls curving from halfway up to a vaulted cryptlike roof. One could stand full upright in the middle, not elsewhere. The window in a deep niche was protected by a heavy iron grate and the glass was chalked over except for a small pane at the top with an aperture for air. Near the bed, which was cemented in place, was an iron tablet fixed in the wall as a table. There was a metal bowl on the floor, a box with a lavatory pail in it, and a stove which was fed and lighted from the passage outside. The walls glistened with moisture.

His finger was blistered and very painful. He got up and began to pace up and down. The prison dress horrified him. He had the image of Petrashevsky, Speshnev in the same ugly, depraving dress. He wondered if they were in other cells nearby. It was impossible that any of them should be here for long. At the worst, if the police discovered the printing press, the facts were clear; it was all straightforward. They had not distributed anything. Everybody seemed to have been arrested and there were no delaying complications.

He began to feel better. Of course! The shock of arrest had depressed him. The whole case could scarcely take two or three weeks to settle. They could expect to be exiled, as punishment, to some provincial town for a period—an opportunity he would be glad of to settle down to his writing away from the haste and falsity of Petersburg. No—that was sickly submission, *l'échine trop courbée!*

The cathedral bells sounded the quarter hour. His eyes caught a faint shining track the length of the floor. He stopped; it was not the light. He felt vaguely uneasy and bent down and touched the floor. There was the slightest indentation in the stone, hardly noticeable, polished and faintly slippery. And he understood at once that it was a path worn by the pacing of feet. By somebody who had been in the cell before him—perhaps somebody who had paced up and down on his first morning telling himself his case would soon be cleared up!

He stood up, all at once overwhelmingly oppressed. The other man had paced hundreds, thousands, tens of thousands of times up and down! And the man before him. He seemed to feel all the suffering of years and years of pacing, decaying muscle and hope in the polished pathway under his slipper. Lifetimes of pacing! The old man in the guardroom when he had arrived occurred to him. Lilien Ankern, the Swede who had been commandant of the Alexeyevsky Ravelin at the time the Decembrists were put there, was supposed to be still alive—over a hundred years old.

Perhaps one of the Decembrists had been in this cell— Trubetskoy, Galitsine, Battenkov? Some of them like Ensign Dibov had been only lads in 1825. They could be still alive —a quarter of a century here! There had been talk in Petersburg two or three years ago that Battenkov's family had received a letter from him after twenty-one years. *Twenty-one years' solitary confinement!* One could not conceive it. It would need an unbelievable force of will to withstand.

He sat down on the bed appalled. There was no sound from anywhere around him. He found himself listening acutely. He was forgotten. The cathedral bells sounded the quarter and the solemn notes of "Have Pity, O Lord."

He shouted out, "Make some NOISE!" The sound was odd. He clasped his head. To cling to sanity itself would prolong the torment. One would desire *insanity*. His glance caught something at the door. He got up quickly, uncertain of what the slight movement had been—and then saw at a hole an eye observing him. For a moment he tried to return the gaze, but the bodyless eye was too deterring and he turned away. Almost at once a bolt was drawn and a guard's head appeared at an open hatch in the door. "No talking," he said quietly.

"What time is it? Perhaps—could you tell me when the investigation is beginning?" At first he was hesitant, then spoke eagerly, rapidly. "Can I have some writing paper? And a book—anything, a book, any book."

The guard looked at him in silence, shut the hatch, and bolted it. Was it refusal or was he going to get the paper? Instantly Dostoevsky flung away knowing the man would not bring him anything. My God, how one ran after fragments of hope already! In any event it would scarcely be possible to read in the permanent half-gloom of the cell. How soon did the fragments become an entire illusory universe?

He went toward the window, stopped, and threw himself on the bed. He regretted having spoken of the writing paper and book; communicating the need had made it sharper. Idleness was looming up like a shadow even at this stage. There would be a certain acquisitive period while he was absorbing information about this new existence. But after that? He dared not think of it. Without any preparatory signal the wicket opened again and a guard's arm came in holding a jug of steaming water, evidently meant for tea. Dostoevsky saw it was a different guard, a young Tartar.

"I haven't any tea," he said.

"It is forbidden to talk. Give the head guard your money when he comes; he'll buy your tea."

"But the——"

The guard slammed the hatch and bolted it.

Dostoevsky turned away. The slightly warmer air from the passage made him realize he had been chilly and he rubbed his hands, looking around at the walls. The film of moisture extended from the floor to about halfway up, the flags of the floor were marbled with it, and in the far corner there was a cluster of fungus growing. The air was heavy and saturated with damp. The cell must be at water level now; with the Neva running high it would be much worse. Princess Tarakanova had drowned in her cell here during a flood. He looked at the window grating. No, no, that had been long ago, an age of barbarism. Such things weren't possible any longer.

Suddenly he wanted to shout, to bellow like an animal. He inhaled, stiffening his arms, shaking with the effort to control himself. He managed not to make any noise; he let his breath out in small jerks. It was a minute or two before he could recover.

He stepped toward the window, turned at the wall, took nine paces, turned. He had to see the officer of the guard, the major; he looked a decent man. He would insist on going before the authorities, knowing the charges, the regime of imprisonment, obtaining his rights in self-defense. He felt confident. He took the nine paces back, turned, nine more paces, his felt slippers polishing the track from one end of the cell to the other.

At ten o'clock the door opened and a major, not the same one, came in followed by two guards. He was young and handsome with a narrow black mustache and a pleasant expression and at the first glance Dostoevsky wondered how he had gone into the prison service instead of cavalry.

"Major, I should be obliged for a word with you." He went up. One of the guards, also a man he hadn't seen before, stepped in front, barring his way. Dostoevsky paid no attention, moving to avoid him. "I must speak with you officially, Major. It is to the advantage of the inquiry and as a former officer of the Imperial Engineering Corps I——"

"Silence!" the guard croaked.

"Get out of my way." Dostoevsky angrily raised his arm,

pushing him aside. "I don't ask subordinates' permission to speak. I wish, Major, to——"

The other guard's rifle butt hit him in the adam's apple. The major did not shift, his gloved finger caressing the black mustache. Dostoevsky staggered back but kept his balance. His eyes were watering from the blow. The major's glance flicked at the cell, flicked at him; he touched the mustache again, smartly twitched his nose, turned on his heel, and went out. The guards were moving to follow. The one Dostoevsky had pushed looked back over his shoulder with heavy pugnaciousness.

"The tea," Dostoevsky said. "There are five kopecks in the pocket of my coat." The door thudded to.

A different man again brought the food at two o'clock, a wooden bowl of soup with a shred of meat in it, a lump of black bread like glutinous dark straw, and a wooden spoon to eat. Dostoevsky dipped his blistered finger in the warmish soup to ease it. The food was not good but he ate it hungrily and when he had finished leaned back on the bed feeling he would like to sleep. The prospect of oblivion drew him; he reclined full length. Suddenly he thought that if he slept now he would be sure to wake in the night! He rose quickly and resumed pacing.

He began to amble, then run; he was running with an intense urgency up and down the cell. If one exhausted oneself physically one's mind was quieter. But his muscles needed hardening; after a moment he had to stop and sat panting on the bed. The eye appeared at the judas in the door. He averted his face. When he looked again it had gone; there had not been a sound.

And in a flash he was persuaded that he was alone in the Ravelin. They could not change the guard so constantly if there were other prisoners. He picked up the metal bowl and tapped sharply on the wall next to the bed. He put his ear to the wall. No answer. He banged with the bowl, much louder, banging the wall several times.

The hatch bolt shot and the guard looked in. "What are you up to? No tapping!"—spoken in the odd undertone they all used.

The interval between two peals of bells seemed to stretch to eternity. Now he had admitted the thought of idleness to his mind, it pursued him. He made dinner, more bread and soup, last nearly half an hour.

The dark was coming on. He saw with horror that they were going to leave him without light. And in a rush he understood that they wanted the silence, the felt slippers, quiet speech, darkness, all of it, to intensify the sense of isolation, the sense of being abandoned, put away from the world, from all sympathy, and to induce the conviction and certainty that one was alone.

When the cell was black he lay down. Somehow one had to live through the night.

3

The first examination was held two weeks later. An officer and a picket of soldiers marched him to a room where there were lamps burning although it was daylight (a peculiar *police* touch, he thought) and five men were sitting at a table. Two or three were smoking cigars, sitting back talking easily, their army uniforms unbuttoned. This was the investigating committee. General Dubbelt was between Prince Gagarin and General Rostovtsev; the chairman was Adjutant General Nabokov, commander of the Fortress, and next to him was Prince Dolgoruky.

The soldiers went out and Dubbelt raised his chin and said to somebody behind, "Would you mind, Father?"—and a priest who had evidently been sitting somewhere ambled forward, blinking and moving his tongue around in his mouth as if he had been asleep. He looked horribly bored, skeptical, and uninterested, shuffled to the end of the table, gave another yawn, and started in a singsong voice, "My son, all of us here are gathered in the presence of the Lord, our holy Savior. The all-hearing ear of God is bent upon the words we speak and His all-merciful eye sees unto our very hearts. It is vain, my son, therefore, to conceal a particle of the truth from those who have been assigned by His Imperial Majesty, our sovereign anointed in the Lord, from whom all mercies flow"—a rather ambiguous reference, Dostoevsky thought—"for the holy scriptures to lay upon us the duty . . ."

It was all an admonition to tell everything he knew. At the end the priest rather vaguely waved a Bible and a silver cross as if there had been an oath and began fussing and looking at the committee. Dubbelt said, "Thank you, Father; you may leave."

Dostoevsky was bursting to speak. As soon as the door shut General Nabokov said to him with a surprisingly engaging paternalism, "You understand that was done out of consideration for you? You understand that? It is best for you to speak openly and sincerely. In any event it would be pointless for you to deny the truth."

Dostoevsky said, "I should very much like to make an observation——"

"Kindly stop." General Nabokov held up his hand. "For the moment you will answer the questions you are asked. Nothing more." He was a young man with a high voice and a good-natured-looking face.

Dostoevsky could not contain the overpowering urge to express himself loquaciously. "I understand that is the committee's procedure, which I don't intend to hinder, but all the same I feel obliged——"

"Questions are——" Nabokov began.

"I feel absolutely obliged, gentlemen, to point out that without being notified of any charge I have been kept in a cell for——"

Loudly Dubbelt interrupted. "Questions are to be answered in writing!"

"Very well, that is certainly so, but——"

"Will you be quiet! You are making your position much worse."

Dostoevsky stopped. He was twisting his hands behind his back in his nervous agitation and jerking his shoulders. How was one to bear it, after the cell, after the conspiracy by an entire corps of guards to subdue one? The members of the committee were conferring together in low voices and Dubbelt was sharpening a pen. They wrote down a number of questions and motioned him to a side table to answer them. He was astounded at their ingenuousness. But then he saw with a sort of sharp enjoyment that this was exactly what the rigidity, the blindness, the peculiar slavish obtuseness of the autocracy demanded. "Do you know of any secret society?" one question said. He put, "No; only a private informal circle." The next question was "Who are the members of the society?" He put, "Unknown." The next was "Which actions of the society are known to you?" He wrote, "None." And so on. In spite of his agitation he found the position simple; he concealed all he could, admitted what was necessary, and if anything very awkward came along— well, he would see how to deal with it.

He handed the sheet back. Nabokov looked through the answers and passed the sheet around. Dubbelt said, "I see you know nothing."

"Where were you ed-ed-ed"—General Rostovtsev wrenched past his stutter—"educated?"

"Chermak's College, Kostomarov's Academy, the Imperial Engineering School."

"W-w-what is your income?"

"I—well, I must admit I have no idea. I've scarcely thought of it lately in terms of income. What I could borrow has been my income. In any event, permit me to inquire the relationship between the question and——"

"That is all," General Rostovtsev said sharply.

Dubbelt looked at him in an annoyed way. "You are

acting against your own interests. I advise you that this unfortunate attitude can only result in damage to you."

That ended the first examination. Back in the cell he began pacing up and down, inexhaustibly restless again.

Next day he was awake and ready for the committee summons early. He waited, sitting on the bed, trying to contain his nervous agitation. The afternoon passed, it became quite dark; there was no summons. The day after he asked the guard if he wasn't expected by the committee; the man gave him the usual indifferent look and didn't answer.

After a week, through sheer mental exhaustion pursuing the subject, endlessly going over examinations in his mind, he had blunted the anxious anticipation. Yet the absolute idleness, which burned up at immense speed every distraction he could think of, kept him strung up. He began saving morsels of bread and modeling paste figures out of them. The guards came in and took them. "Begin that again and you'll go to the Sack," the senior guard said.

"What's that?"

The guard jerked his forefinger toward the ground, meaning the Sack was below, evidently well below water level.

What made him hypersensitive was that the solitude drew everything, the whole universe, inward toward himself. Self-interest was the entire basis of life. He could not think of other prisoners being in the Ravelin. One helped the distortion of one's personality.

He made frantic efforts against it, to relate himself to the outside world. He stood looking out through the small aperture of the window at the stone wall opposite. He pressed himself to the door and became appalled at the acuteness his hearing developed; sometimes he could hear the tread of the guard in the passage—like the tread of a hunter!

He sat on the bed with his back to the door and began to talk aloud to himself. Some fantasy produced Karepin before him and he was explaining Buchez's theories on social Christianity to him when the hatch opened. "Not allowed," the guard said. "Stop it."

For a time this completely unbalanced him. He felt he *must* speak. He resorted to whispered conversations with himself, marching up and down the cell whispering intensely and softly, trying even not to move his lips because of the eye at the judas. He whispered speeches, recited poetry, all the passages from books he could remember, gave imaginary lectures, invented stories. But it disturbed him as much as it helped. He was contributing to the sum of whispers in the Ravelin, made part of the conspiracy! After a while he began to lack energy for it, to lose interest—and that frightened him. And then, as he sat on the bed, his mind became a conscious blank, so that he agonizingly observed himself in a state of mental stupor and could not end it. During one of these spells there was suddenly a loud noise in the cell. He sat up and saw a big blue fly had got in and was buzzing about. He dared not move, watching it; then all at once its buzz was gone, it had found the window.

Three days after this he was called to the second examination. General Nabokov, Dubbelt, Rostovtsev, and Prince Gagarin all asked questions, this time about the subjects Petrashevsky's circle had discussed, with what aims, what views Dostoevsky had expressed, and so forth. They all seemed anxious also to make accusing statements about Dostoevsky and the Petrashevists "thinking in a way opposed to the spirit of the government" and having opinions "drawn from the pernicious doctrines of Fourier and Saint-Simon."

General Rostovtsev said, "It is no good de-de-denying that you made speeches. We know it. There is no point in your p-p-penalizing yourself. Your companions have ad-m-m-admitted everything."

Dostoevsky felt that was a lie. If those were the terms they met him on, then he could do the same. Nevertheless, it upset him. He said, "I don't deny it. I did. Even heated speeches, General. It's my character. It has nothing to do with the imperial government; I need to express myself, perhaps. And who doesn't, even the most phlegmatic man, when the discussion is strong and——"

"Very well, very well." Rostovtsev tapped impatiently. Dostoevsky had seen that his talkativeness was extremely distasteful to the general.

"But it was all part of a general denigration of the government, wasn't it?" Dubbelt said. "Why discuss the censorship?"

"Or what has been happening in western Europe?" Prince Gagarin put in. "That is where this fatal influence comes from. Do you imagine that we can encourage such a thing? We can't behave like those people do, wallowing in filth, screaming out all their hatreds. In Russia there is order; the imperial government is paternal. We try to do everything as quietly, privately, and smoothly as we can."

"But, Prince," Dostoevsky said. "To take only one of those countries, you will admit yourself—*vous devez reconnaître* —that Russia owes an enormous debt to France; a whole side of Russian culture has resulted from that. If a Russian discusses events in France—and they may, for all we know, be opening the way to a new and brighter era—if a Russian discusses those events he is only following a natural instinct."

"That has nothing to do with the censorship," Dubbelt said.

"But who *doesn't* talk about the censorship, Your Excellency? I am no different from anybody else in Petersburg in that respect."

"What rubbish," Prince Dolgoruky said. "Do you imagine we discuss nothing but the censorship in my drawing room?"

"If your drawing room were full of writers, Prince, you would. If the committee wishes to consider that I am entirely different from many other citizens in that respect, very well. I am a writer. It is impossible for a writer not to discuss the censorship. It is a subject which *has* to be discussed, since if there were no differences to discuss there would be no censorship; it would simply fade away."

Dubbelt, obviously anxious to keep the exchanges to specific lines, said, "The difference is that one may discuss the censorship in a helpful way, in accordance with the spirit of the government, and in another way, a different way, calculated to alarm public opinion."

Dostoevsky said, "They were private discussions, General. Besides, you asked me at my first examination what my education had been. Why should one be educated at all if one is not to have opinions?"

General Rostovtsev gasped with anger. "It was also, was it not, a question of Belinsky's opinions? It has come t-t-to our knowledge that you read out Be-Be-Belinsky's letter."

"Quite true; I did. I hope it has come to your knowledge as well, General, that I also read out Gogol's reply." That was true, if not in the sense he meant it. But suddenly Dostoevsky was tired of it. One had a moral right to say what one liked to such people. In that he knew he was Russian. They had even begun it! With an enemy sufficiently far away from one's views, one was not engaged morally at all, in no way. One was not on the same moral footing, so what could it matter what one said? They might take one's words to be surrender, even groveling. In fact, it would not touch one. What Russian didn't really know that aspect of it? Besides, he was not going to worsen things for his friends. He felt no moral guilt about being evasive.

He said, "Very well, it was wrong to read that letter. Does the committee know why I did? For one reason because it is a literary document of great interest, for another because I had quarreled with Belinsky. Belinsky was a remarkable man with admirable qualities. The committee may decide for itself if I would have held up the letter of a man whom I had quarreled with as an example for everybody to follow."

"The letter is full of pernicious ideas."

"Who, General, would not be guilty if he were accused on account of his most personal ideas, for what he said in a small, well-disposed circle of friends?"

"Is that how you explain your association with dangerous persons like Petrashevsky?"

"Petrashevsky dangerous?" He was greatly worked up.

General Rostovtsev said, "He has admitted himself that he was s-s-spreading the doctrines of Fourier!"

"Yes—love for humanity. That is the doctrine. With respect, General, the imperial government has nothing to fear from that. There is nothing in Fourier against property, religion, government, the family, patriotism."

"With what aim did you become a socialist?" Dubbelt said.

"I can't claim to have been a socialist," Dostoevsky said. "I have studied socialism because I am interested in these things. But I do not condemn socialism, either. Something harmonious and good may come of it."

General Nabokov coughed and leaned forward and the committee members conferred together in low tones. In a moment General Rostovtsev looked up and said, "We are authorized to inform you that His Imperial Majesty is ready to consider a pardon if you fully and frankly confess all details about the secret society."

Dostoevsky's hands were working behind his back. He could hardly stand still. "That is impossible, because there was none," he said.

"Can you suppose for one moment we believe you did not form a secret society?"

"We did not."

"Ah! I can't b-b-bear to look at such people any longer!" General Rostovtsev stood up, pushing his chair back with a loud clatter.

Nothing about the printing press, Dostoevsky thought. Were they reserving that?

General Nabokov said, "You will be required to make a written deposition. Writing materials will be brought to you. It will be best if you are quite frank. That is all."

Dostoevsky reached the cell and threw himself on the bed exhausted.

He began to wonder how long he could endure the isolation. The means of suicide were limited; but somehow one wanted to be prepared. It might be feasible to plait a cord with thread from the blanket, though the officer of the guard glanced at the bed each morning. He could smash his head against the wall. The most certain thing would be to strike an officer. The idea excited him. He watched the captain who came next morning. He came a regulation four paces into the cell, the soldiers keeping close to him; it was a question of whether they would use their bayonets or "spare" one to be tried and shot. He said nothing in the written deposition about the printing press, mainly repeating what he had already said.

At moments the stone floor seemed to be moving under him, swaying like a boat. It was not *certain* that they would not use torture. He spent two weeks trying to extract a nail from the door and broke every fingernail down to the quick.

And suddenly everything changed. The guards were replaced less often and two of them began to exchange a few words with him. He was given a candle at night and, when he asked, was, unbelievably, allowed pen and paper. A few days later the officer of the guard brought him a letter from Mikhail and told him he could reply. Holding the letter up to the window, he devoured the news. Mikhail and Andrey, his younger brother, had both been arrested and released! Otherwise all was well. The Karepins had not given a sign, though they must know. Dostoevsky replied, begging for reading material—he would be allowed a Bible —and a few rubles for tea. On the day these arrived the sergeant of the guard opened the door and said, "Outside!"

"What? Is there somebody——?"

"Exercise."

He could not believe it. They marched to a small garden in the Fortress. Dostoevsky was blinded by the light, the air smelled strong. The garden was surrounded by high walls with the chimney of the Imperial Mint just beyond and some shrunken, meager trees. Walking around, staggering, excited and overjoyed, he counted seventeen trees; one was a big lime.

"Slow down!" the sergeant of the guard called out. "Walk slower! Do you think I want to keep twisting my neck, following you around?" Dostoevsky smiled.

They went there for a few minutes every day. Two more letters came from Mikhail, and books. To get enough light to write he had to stand close under the window but he managed to finish a story; it gave him intense pleasure. As the weeks went by he watched the leaves of the trees turn color and fall.

And he began to lose his nervous restlessness and agitation. One of the guards, an elderly man called Bolubov, got him tobacco. Days passed in peaceful routine. For some reason letters were stopped and he was told not to write any more. But he slept better and found himself recovering a balance he had not had for a long time. He thought nothing of the future and yet was optimistic. He had discovered some sort of inner strength that turned him toward optimism, cheerfulness, good spirits. When the first snow fell he found it invigorating, though the cell was much colder.

In the midst of the reassurance he was suddenly nervous and uneasy; it was a sort of breakdown. The winter cold changed the tones of the cathedral bells so that each quarter of an hour there was a torturing cacophony of sound. The air in the garden became poisoned by the smoke from the Mint chimney; and when he went back he had the impression that all the air was being pumped out of the cell. He reached up at the window, gasping.

With an effort he threw off the fears that were looming up. It was past mid-December. On the twenty-first, Bolubov brought him his supper.

"Do you think I'll be out by Christmas, Bolubov?" he said.
"I don't know why, but I have a feeling it will come off."

"Well, God's mercy will save us all," Bolubov said.

Dostoevsky went to bed cheerful.

The light of a lantern on his face woke him. A major and two guards were in the cell and two sentries at the door.

"Get up, please," the major said, "and dress." One of the guards held out some clothes. Dostoevsky saw they were the clothes and cap in which he had arrived at the Fortress.

"Ah! So it's true." He could not repress the exclamation of joy and looked smiling at their faces. Curious how that instinct had been right. After all, he had survived eight months' solitary confinement. The thought of Battenkov's twenty-one years occurred to him. He noticed a strange glance from the major.

"Are we going out straight away?"

"Kindly finish dressing," the major said.

4

The air in the courtyard made him shiver. It was barely daylight. The snow was yellow under the lanterns. Officers and soldiers in greatcoats were moving about; there were some carriages drawn up, the horses snuffling out clouds of breath, clumping their hoofs.

He made out a figure beating his arms in the cold, and another—Ivanov and Mombelli. They fell on each other.

"My God, you were here!"

"How are you? How are you?"

"So it's going to be all right, you see, after all. Yes, yes." Mombelli was clasping his arm, smiling eagerly into his face. Dostoevsky saw two front teeth were missing: and Mombelli's face had become bony.

"We shall be yawning in Krementchug or some provincial hole shortly, but I shan't mind!" Ivanov was laughing hysterically.

"It'll be a delight." Dostoevsky began laughing too.

"Stand away there!" one of the officers shouted. Soldiers separated them and led them apart.

"One to each carriage," somebody ordered. At that moment Speshnev appeared from the other entrance to the courtyard, followed by Palm. Dostoevsky raised his arm in a signal.

"Get in," a captain said, and pushed him toward a carriage. Dostoevsky climbed in, a gendarme got in beside him and slammed the door. The windows were covered with frost. Dostoevsky let one down and, looking out, began scratching the frost off.

"Don't do that. I'll get a beating," the gendarme said. He was a lad with a long neck sticking out of his greatcoat collar and a simple kind face. Dostoevsky shut the window. He could barely see out. Other carriages were forming up; there seemed to be a good number. Presently a horse trooper came level on each side of the carriage; each had a drawn saber. There was a shout ahead and they all began to move off. They passed out under the archway where he had first seen he was in the Ravelin and across the bridge. Farther on they stopped, apparently for other carriages to join the cortege, then resumed.

"Where are we going?" he said to the gendarme.

"I'm not allowed to say." The lad looked down in an embarrassed way and shifted the rifle between his knees.

Well, they were leaving the Fortress anyway; he was sure of that. The cathedral bells sounded seven o'clock at a distance behind them. After another brief halt (presumably to open the gates) they crossed the second bridge, then the Troitsky across the Neva and, peering out, Dostoevsky recognized Tsaritsinskaya Street. It was a good sight! They jolted and crunched over the snow, apparently crossing the city. With no overcoat he was cold. At one point, looking out, he saw quite a number of people walking in the same direction.

At last they stopped, there was a shouted order, and they alighted. Dostoevsky shrank, the cold suddenly wrapping around him again. There was thick snow. They were in an immense square which extended away into the distance. He recognized it, the Semyenovsky, the Tsar's drill and parade ground, the greatest square in Petersburg. A bluish-gray mist stretched over it, blurring the outlines round about; there were the yellow façades of the barracks on three sides, the cupolas of the Trinity Cathedral beyond, and the smoke from chimneys going straight up into the still atmosphere of the early morning.

He saw the crowd. A close mass of men and women was standing right across the square behind a double row of Cossacks with lances. Here and there in front of the Cossacks were groups of officers and civilian officials with cocked hats, swords, and embroidered collars, standing about, stamping their feet in the cold and blowing into their hands. More officers on horseback were nearby. The crowd was not pressing up against the Cossacks. It stood a little back and was quiet.

Dostoevsky glanced to the right and caught Pleshcheyev's bright look; Mombelli and others were standing beyond. The carriages emptied. There must be about twenty of them there, he thought. "Petrashevsky!" They embraced.

"What's happening here?" Dostoevsky said.

"I don't know, *mon cher*." Petrashevsky was smiling, his old self. At the other end of the line Dostoevsky saw Speshnev, looking as disdainful and impassive as ever.

"Close up and form ranks! About turn!"

"Guard, advance!" There was a faint echo of the commands across the great square.

Behind them the carriages were moving away; the gendarme escort re-formed and trotted off. Dostoevsky closed up toward Pleshcheyev, they about-faced with the rest, and as the last of the carriages drew clear saw the platform in front of them. It was draped in black with a wooden handrail. Farther off on one side there were three stakes. Facing it was a square of troops and a regimental band. Dostoevsky caught the faint trickle of chatter breaking off down the line as the last carriage drew away like a curtain.

"What's that for?" Pleshcheyev said. He was frowning, his mouth slightly open. Dostoevsky was looking at the band; the bandsmen had on the lanyards that they wore for celebrations. There seemed to be complete silence in the square.

"Two ranks there! Two ranks!"

As they formed two ranks a red-faced priest came up twitching his black robes, glanced at Katenev and Evrapeus, who were the leading pair, and said, "This way, over here." They all followed, marching unevenly through the snow past the troops. The priest skipped up the steps of the platform; the planks creaked as they assembled on it in front of the squad of waiting gendarmes. A major of the Preobazhensky Regiment stepped forward with a paper and began calling their names in some mysteriously prearranged order and dividing them off to opposite sides. Petrashevsky, Grigoryev, and Mombelli were first, to the left, Durov, Dostoevsky, and Pleshcheyev next, to the right. There were eleven on the left, nine on the right, a gendarme stationed behind each. The groups of officers and civilian officials had moved up to the foot of the platform; several of the mounted generals were talking to each other imperiously, touching their mounts with a spur now and then to make them start and jaunter about and look particularly difficult beasts to control.

"I don't like this—I——" Pleshcheyev next to him was shivering.

Dostoevsky had an absurd and irresistible desire to tell him the story he had written in the Fortress. He recognized it was irrational and might make Pleshcheyev uncomfortable, simply by adding another incomprehensible touch to the scene, but he couldn't help it. "I say, Pleshcheyev, I've written a new story. It's called 'A Little Hero,' about a boy of eleven, a boy who is just waking up to life and sensuality, you know. He has romantic ideas about knights and heroines and so

forth, and all that is confused with feelings toward women
who——"

"Silence there. Stand to attention. Off caps!"

Pleshcheyev glanced at him. Nobody moved. Petrashevsky
and the others opposite were trying to keep still in the cold.

"Take off your c-c-c-caps!" a voice bellowed. "Prepare for
sen-sen-sentence!" Dostoevsky saw General Rostovtsev's suffused face among the mounted group beside another he
recognized, General Golovatshev. He obeyed with the rest;
the cold clasped his head at once.

And then in the middle of the platform, between the two
ranks, one of the civilian officials was reading out from a
document. His voice did not carry; Dostoevsky could only
hear an occasional phrase. He suddenly caught the words
". . . accordingly condemn the above-named Butashevich-
Petrashevsky, Mikhail Vassilyevich, to death, the execution
to be carried out by shooting."

There was scarcely a pause. The indistinct voice was continuing. The official was shortsighted and held the document
almost touching his nose. ". . . the above-named Grigoryev
. . . to death . . ." Dostoevsky could not attach a meaning
to the words. He strained to hear. His own name came out
of the mumble: ". . . the said Dostoevsky, Fyodor Mikhailovich . . . violation of Article 178 of the Imperial Penal Code
. . . Article 181, Articles 242, 249, 250, and 252, condemn
the said Dostoevsky, Fyodor Mikhailovich——" The official
reached the end of the page, thumbed the edge to turn over,
could not separate the sheets, shook with the cold, wet his
thumb, and turned. "——to death, execution to be carried out
by shooting. . . ."

He noticed people in the crowd crossing themselves. All
at once there was somebody at the side of the platform
speaking in French. It was General Golovatshev, who had
detached himself from the group of generals; as he walked
his horse by he said, "You will all be reprieved—all, all
of you!"

It was a well-known piece of deception. They had done the same thing with the Decembrists, letting them understand that there would be some last-minute messenger with a reprieve. "Don't be afraid," they had said, taking them to the gallows. "It is only a pretense." Besides, there was the priest; they would never dare to make the Holy Orthodox Church a party to a pretense. And so it was certain they were going to be shot now!

The official abruptly stopped reading. In a sort of fixity, Dostoevsky watched him carefully shuffle the sheets into place, fold them along the creases, put them in his pocket, pinch the cold lobe of his ear, and step down from the platform. At that second the sun came out, shining on the yellow façades of the barracks and on the gilded cupolas of the Trinity Cathedral.

"It's not possible," Dostoevsky said to Durov. "They can't mean to kill us." Durov jerked his head in an odd way toward a cart standing in the snow behind the platform. "Coffins." It was loaded with something covered over with matting. The priest had reappeared and begun to preach in a shaky voice, turning from one rank to the other. He repeated the text from St. Paul, "The wages of sin is death," and his expression suggested that all this was extremely painful to him and distasteful. He got it over hurriedly and came forward holding out the silver crucifix, passing from one to the next. Dostoevsky kissed the cross. The silver was like ice. The priest's light blue eyes were before him, furtive and embarrassed, the full lips muttering an invitation to confession.

Dostoevsky shook his head. He looked at his companions on either side of him, Durov and Pleshcheyev, at Petrashevsky, Grigoryev in the rank opposite, and Speshnev, Philippov shivering in the cold. They were all being purified by something else—by the injustice, by the enormity of the sentence. If there was a God, He would forgive them much because of it. He felt no remorse. The joking at Petrashevsky's, the easy talk, occasional boasting, shone as their holy cause. One man in the opposite rank dropped on his knees to confess; they looked on. It was Shaposhnikov, a workman who had been a newcomer at Petrashevsky's. The priest lingered, fussing, repeating prayers, "doing his duty."

"That's enough of it, Father. You've done all that's necessary," one of the mounted generals shouted out. "Kindly come down." At the same moment two men in bright red and green kaftans mounted the platform carrying a bundle of swords.

My God, Dostoevsky thought, they need ritual with it. As the beating of drums struck up, echoing from one side of the square to the other, the men passed along the line, breaking the swords over the heads of the prisoners who were of the nobility, the ceremonial token of destitution. The swords had been partly cut through beforehand but some would not break easily. Dostoevsky's did. Pleshcheyev fell under the blow. So did several in the opposite rank. Almost immediately other men were on the platform.

"What's this?" Durov said. "Won't they get it finished?"

"Off with your coats and trousers," the men said.

"In—in this cold?" Durov looked at Dostoevsky. The men were shaking out long white shirts; the same was happening opposite. Dostoevsky and the rest undressed and began putting the shirts on awkwardly. The man helping Dostoevsky fastened the shirt with straps at the neck, elbows, and ankles. Dostoevsky noticed his fingers were covered with red hairs. The shirt reached to the boards. And suddenly there was Petrashevsky's voice, loud and contemptuous: "What a rig-out they give you. Good for their circus!" Dostoevsky looked across at him. How he loved Petrashevsky at that moment. Then his heart gave a heave. Three of the men were fixing white bags over the heads of Petrashevsky, Grigoryev, and Mombelli, the first three in the opposite rank. Gendarmes stepped forward and led them off the platform, across the snow to the three stakes. The band struck up the lively

"Komarinskaya." The gendarmes seemed to take a long time fixing the three hooded men to the stakes. The firing squad stood facing them at fifteen paces, rifle butts in the snow.

Dostoevsky glanced at Durov. They would be next, with Pleshcheyev. The next three to be shot.

He had four or five minutes to live. Five minutes seemed to him an endless period, a huge wealth of time. He felt it offered so many lives, such richness, that he needn't think of the end, and he divided it up—two minutes for saying farewell to his companions, two more for reflecting on his own life and everything about himself, another minute for a last look around. He turned to Durov. "Well, we are next. Goodby, Sergey Fyodorovich." Durov's face was white and strained. They embraced. Next Pleshcheyev. Something made him say to Pleshcheyev, "It's curious they don't move the coaching station from this square. Surely it's an inconvenient district for people to get to?" It seemed extraordinarily important to make this observation on the practical side of Petersburg life!

Pleshcheyev said, "What? Oh, the army stores kick up a fuss, so they leave it." Dostoevsky listened with particular interest to the answer.

"Good-by, Pleshcheyev." They embraced too.

Now two minutes to look into himself, to look into his heart. He knew already what he was going to think about. The sunlight shining on the cathedral cupola caught his eyes and he stared fixedly at the spot. Here he was, a living and thinking man, and in three minutes he would be nothing, a carcass; or if he was something, then what? He told himself he had to decide that once and for all in these last three minutes. He looked stubbornly at the cupola and the sunlight and had the idea that it would be mingling with what he was going to become in three minutes. Everything would be light, silence, and calm and cold. He was going to dissolve into the unknown emptiness.

Less than three minutes. He felt how hard it was; there

was no escaping it and yet there was terrible uncertainty. And worst of all: supposing he did not die now. What would he do, what would he do? What an infinity of time he would have! How he would grudge every minute so as not to waste a single instant! All at once he remembered a picture he had once seen pinned up at Shidlovsky's room, showing Christ just taken down from the cross—nothing beautiful, but a mangled body covered with wounds and bruises, marks of violence, all this combined with the anguish of the crucifixion. And he could not avoid the thought—he tried to but he could not—that death was so terrible and powerful that even Christ, who overcame it in miracles during his lifetime, was conquered by it at the end. He who called to Lazarus, "Come forth," and Lazarus lived—even he was taken by death.

Ah, only to live! Even if it were somewhere at a terrible height, on a rock, on a narrow ledge that gave him only just room to crouch on, the sea around him, everlasting dark, solitude, storms—even if he had to remain standing on such a tiny square of space all his life, for a thousand years, forever, it would be better than dying now, in two minutes! Only to live—no matter how!

He looked at the crowd in front of him in the square, particularly noticing a young man with whiskers and clipped mustache who seemed to be watching him with a sort of frightened despair. Others, many of them women with kerchiefs over their heads, were crossing themselves and muttering prayers. And, looking at them, he could not understand why they should be so poor. How was it that all these people with so much life in them and before them did not become *rich*? He wanted to shout it out. RICH! And when he thought of Pogodin telling him of a poor wretch who had actually died of starvation, he was beside himself with anger. Look at those faces before him—anxious, worried-looking. Why were they so anxious? Why were they looking so overcome with cares? Whose fault was it that they were all miserable, that they didn't know how to live, though they had *fifty years* of life before them? *Sixty years!* For a man to die of hunger with sixty years of life unlived before him! He was gasping at the enormity of such a thing. And all these people complaining, holding up their rough hands, moaning their everlasting refrain, "Look at us, working like cattle all our lives, always hungry while others live idle and are fat and rich." The fools. He had no patience with them. Why couldn't they be Rothschilds? Whose fault was it that a man had not got millions like Rothschild? He had life! It must all be there for him to take if he had life. Everything was in his power. Whose fault was it that he did not know how to live his life?

He longed, he longed with all his soul to be taken from the platform and thrown onto the street of some strange town, alone, without lodging, without work, without a crust, without family or a single acquaintance, hungry, beaten if they liked, but in health. *Then* he would show them! He was twenty-eight years old. And he wanted to shout out that, in reality, in their deepest spring, these convictions had nothing to do with his sentence of death. He had lived with them all along. It was not discovering death that had brought them on. He would have liked to run forward to the front of the platform and call out to all the people, to General Rostovtsev and the officials, "Listen, if you think Columbus was happiest after he had discovered America, you are wrong—completely wrong! It was *before* he saw the New World with his eyes, when his sailors mutinied and wanted to go back. That was when he was happiest. What did the New World matter after all? In fact, Columbus did not know at all what he had discovered. The important thing is life—life and nothing else!"

He shook all over. The thought of Mikhail was infinitely painful. He wished they would shoot him at once. At that moment there was a shouted order. The soldiers clanked their rifles.

"Ready to fire." The firing squad leveled rifles. "Take aim!"

As the officer raised his saber in readiness for the signal "Fire," Petrashevsky, with one hand freed, wrenched the hood off his head. There was complete silence. The leveled rifles were steady. He was braced for the noise of the salvo. The pause became atrocious. Among all the motionless figures there was one moving, an officer cantering from one side of the square. There was something disorderly and disrespectful in his not staying still like the rest at such a moment. His moving in fact became insistent, held the eye. It was an aide-de-camp with a yellow collar. He was agitating a paper above his head like a small white flag.

"Ground arms!" The soldiers brought their rifles down. One of the two beside Petrashevsky sagged at the stake. The ADC rode up to General Rostovtsev and presented the paper with an extravagant salute. The general glanced at it, spurred his horse forward a few paces, and began to read.

"We, by the grace of God, Emperor and Autocrat of all the Russias, Moscow, K-K-Kiev, Vla-Vladimir, Novgorod, Tsar of Astrakhan——"

"Oh, my God, what does it mean?" Dostoevsky said aloud.

"—Tsar of P-P-P-Poland, Tsar of Siberia, Grand D-Duke of Smolensk, Lord of Pskov, Prince of Es-Estonia . . ." Rostovtsev wrenched at the words. "Grand Duke of Finland . . ."

"Please—please!" Dostoevsky muttered. It went on interminably. At last Rostovtsev came to the words "The aforesaid guilty persons having fully merited death by reason of the Articles of the Code enumerated above, We, in our infinite clemency, ordain that the sentence shall be remitted as hereunder stated. . . ."

Reprieved! Life! The moment was hardly bearable. The breath rasped from his chest. Everything on the scene stood out with the most dazzling clearness, every footprint in the snow, every figure, every face. His head was aching violently. The gendarmes were untying Petrashevsky and the others.

Grigoryev, the middle of the three, was looking around with a mad face and speaking in a rapid mumble. The sergeant of gendarmes was holding him.

". . . Penal exile to S-S-Siberia, the p-p-place assigned in the ordinance concerning him, for a period of t-t-twenty years . . ." His mind came back to General Rostovtsev reading the sentences. Petrashevsky exiled to Siberia for twenty years. Grigoryev and Mombelli both to fifteen years' penal exile.

"My God! It would have been better to shoot us," Durov said; he was shaking all over.

"D-D-Dostoevsky, Fyodor Mikhailovich, to penal exile in Siberia for four years and thereafter to service as a s-s-soldier. . . . Durov, penal exile for four years . . ."

Palm was on his knees, clasped hands raised. "Ah, the good Tsar. Heaven's blessing on our father, the Emperor." Palm was entirely pardoned, the only one. "Do you know, I'm certain it was all arranged," Pleshcheyev said, his face burning with color. "I am certain of it. It was a sham. They meant to frighten us. Ah, my God!" He covered his face with his hands, trying to control himself. Dostoevsky stared at him. He had the intimate and overwhelming conviction that Pleshcheyev was right.

"Stand over here!" Gendarmes were bustling them into groups. The platform was swarming with people. A gendarme thrust a sheepskin at Dostoevsky. He felt the piercing cold for the first time since he had put on the execution shirt. There was a clank of chain. Three guards fixing fetters to Petrashevsky's legs were in some difficulty. "Here, my good fellow, like this." Petrashevsky bent forward, helping them, able even in such a moment to make his persecutors feel small. In a moment Petrashevsky stood with the fetters riveted on, took a step, and staggered, half falling. "Stand back!" He roared the gendarmes away.

"Come, march him off," the officer said.

"Wait a minute, my police captain." Petrashevsky's face

glowed; he seemed to tower above the captain of gendarmes, great and terrible, an uncrushable spirit. "I still have one right that the Most High has not deprived me of—the right to say farewell to my friends." The gendarmes stood back. Petrashevsky lifted the chain of the fetters and hobbled awkwardly among them. He embraced them all. Dostoevsky kissed him on the lips. His eyes shone with tears.

"Adieu. Adieu. All of you. Regret nothing." They bundled him into a waiting sledge, a gendarme beside him. "Farewell. All of you." They drove off.

Some of the crowd still hung about the square. All the generals had left. Carriages were brought. They got in, one by one, as before, each with a gendarme escort, and drove through the snowy streets back to the Peter and Paul Fortress. Dostoevsky sat staring out through the frosted pane. In the cell he paced up and down, singing at the top of his voice. He shouted out in his heart joyfully. Life was everywhere. Life was in him. At the window he could see a faint glimmer of the sun. Life was a gift and good. Life! Life! Life!

5

At six o'clock in the evening, two days later, the bolts of the cell door rattled and the sergeant of the guard came in with two soldiers. "Come and get your tinklers, my beauty," the sergeant said. "Go on, don't dawdle." He shoved him toward the door.

The marched to the room where he had first been searched. He was horrified to see the same guard with the wet mustache. There were also two others squatting beside a small portable forge, a lap anvil, and lengths of chain. "Well, what are you waiting for?" the guard said, and jerked a thumb at some convicts' clothes on the bench. "There you are, as fine a fit as you'll get on the Nevsky any day." Dostoevsky undressed and put the clothes on: shirt and trousers of gray stuff, long gray coat with a yellow diamond-shaped patch sewn between the shoulders, and a gray tam-o'-shanter cap. Everything was too big. The guard was talking to another man with a sly face who had come in and was evidently named Petrovich.

"Over here." The rough-faced men were kicking the fetters and chains loose on the floor. He stood while they fastened the iron rings around his ankles. The fetters were made of four iron rods, as thick as a finger, joined together by three rings. A strap was fastened to the middle ring; the men showed him how to hitch this to his belt. He grasped the iron rods dangling between his legs; they were heavy and cumbersome. Trying to walk, he tripped and fell.

"Go on, Petrovich, get it done with," the sergeant said disagreeably, putting snuff up his black nose.

"Here's Petrovich. Ready, ready," the small man said. "Sit down here, cocky." He shoved Dostoevsky down onto the bench, putting a bowl and razor beside him. He produced a pair of scissors, lopped the hair off the right side of Dostoevsky's head in tufts, lathered perfunctorily over the same part, and began hacking with the razor. The razor was blunt and had nicks in the edge. Petrovich knew it and shaved with all the power of his forearm. The thumb and fingers of his other hand dug into Dostoevsky's temples. Soon blood began to trickle down under them. Petrovich swore and wrenched the razor. As he worked over the crown where the skin was thinnest on the bone he pressed the strokes hard.

"That's it." Petrovich wiped a rag over the shaven side of the head; Dostoevsky caught his breath with the pain. "On with your cap," Petrovich said.

"I'd like to wait a moment." He felt faint.

A captain of the guard came in and said something to the sergeant. "This way," the captain said to Dostoevsky. He hobbled awkwardly forward, holding the fetters up to prevent their knocking against his legs. The iron skinned his ankles after a few steps. They reached the guardroom at the entrance to the Ravelin. Inside the door he stopped, staring at the figure standing between four soldiers—a caricature of Durov. One side of the head was smooth, red and blue, the other untidy long hair; the gray costume looked unbelievably depressing and there was a fixed ghastly look in the eyes. Then he saw that Durov was staring at him; the moment was quickly over. They both understood at the same second and tried to hide the feelings they feared had just shown too plainly, tried to smile encouragingly to each other, looked away, and glanced quickly and obliquely again in horror.

They started out with the escort across the bridge and came to the rear of the house where the governor of the Fortress lived. Sentries were posted outside. The captain showed them into a large bare room with whitewashed walls and a single lamp burning on a table. Dostoevsky heard a gasp. Then "Fedya!" Mikhail came toward him with outstretched arms.

"What—Misha! How did you manage this?" They clasped hands.

"What have they done?" Mikhail was staring at him.

"Yes, I know. They change one's appearance a little," he said. "Don't be upset, old fellow. It's nothing."

Behind them Durov was greeting Milyukov, who had come with Mikhail. Dostoevsky wrung his hand too. It appeared that Milyukov had been arrested for three days. He turned back to Mikhail. "How is Emily Fyodorovna? And the children?"

"They're all right. Oh, this is terrible. What's to become of you? It's disaster." Mikhail's lips were trembling, his shoulders hunched forward as if he were afraid of a blow. He could not get over the half-shaven head and gray clothes and kept looking at the fetters.

"My dear fellow, don't worry about me. I'm all right."

"Are they ill-treating you?"

"Not for a minute. I haven't lost courage. Come, come,

do I have to persuade you? In four years I'll already be better off, I'll be a trooper in the army instead of a convict. The other morning we had death in front of us for three quarters of an hour; my last minute had come—and you see I'm still living!" He was trying to communicate the new force he felt in himself. But Mikhail could not receive it; he was utterly discomposed, tears ran down his cheeks and he looked afraid.

"Where are they taking you?"

"I don't know. Orenburg, perhaps. What does it matter? Everything is changing for me—and you see, Misha, I'm changing too. In the end it will be better. All my hope is in that; it's the consolation for everything."

"But the terrible life, Siberia?"

"What do privations matter? They can't hurt me. When I look back on the past and think how little I cared for *time*, how much of it I wasted in idleness, in mistakes, how many times I went against my deepest feelings—yes, *that* makes me suffer. But now, Misha—now, I've never felt such an abundance of spiritual life. I'm not afraid of anything—anything!"

"But, my poor Fedya, living among convicts for years."

"They are human beings." He looked calmly at his brother, disturbed in spite of everything by this weakness. "And you know, Misha, to remain a man whatever happens, not to become discouraged, not to fail—well, that's life and the real problem of life."

Durov and Milyukov were walking slowly up and down the room, speaking together in low tones. The captain of the guard was looking out of the window. "Take this." Mikhail pressed some money into his hand.

"Thank you, thank you. Listen, Misha, if anybody remembers ill of me, if you come across anybody who quarreled with me or anybody I left a bad impression with, will you ask them to forget it?"

"Yes, yes."

"Tell everybody good-by for me, everybody who remembers me; and those who've forgotten, remind them of me, will you? Kiss Andrey, Kolya, and all the family; write to Aunt and Uncle for me. And look after yourself and the family, eh? Be positive. Send me letters."

Mikhail nodded.

"Did you get a Christmas tree for the children?"

"Yes. Krayevsky has invited them to a Christmas party at his house with Emily."

The captain was coming toward them. "Well, good-by, Mikhail. Happy Christmas."

"Good-by." They embraced. The next moment he and Durov were outside the door.

Just before midnight the guard told him to get ready to leave. Outside the guardroom there were three open sleighs, each harnessed with three horses abreast in troika style, and a closed sleigh in front beside which an official courier, an elderly man, was talking to the driver. The bells of the cathedral sounded the hour and began a discordant "Have Pity, O Lord." The sound of other bells floated across the Neva. He noticed some of the gendarmes had their blanket rolls strapped over their left shoulders, then saw Durov standing by the last sleigh, and Jastrzembsky. He stumbled over to them.

"Are we going together?"

"It seems so."

"Where to?"

"Tobolsk first."

"My God. It's far off." The others' faces were showing the same thought. Across the Urals: thousands of versts.

"They send us farther on from there too," Jastrzembsky said.

An officer called out, "Get them in there! Get them in. Is this going to last all night? Off with you, go on!" The soldiers separated them, pushed them to the sleighs. Dosto-

evsky was in the middle one. A gendarme got in beside him
and wrapped his greatcoat around himself.

"Whaoo. Ya—a-a-a-va! Noooo-oo-oo!" The leading driver
cried to his horses. The harness bells jingled. The snow
crunched under the runners and they all moved forward.

It was a clear cold night. The stars sparkled in the black
sky. The church bells pealed out from all over the city. His
heart was full. Confused feelings struggled in him and
agitated him; then as the sleighs ran through the streets
he became calmer.

Adieu, Petersburg. He was leaving so much of his life
behind him. He watched the rare passers-by as if they were
all brothers, and followed by the lighted windows the
sparkle of Christmas lights here and there. They went past
Mikhail's and Krayevsky's. Bright lights shone from the
windows at Krayevsky's and between the curtains he caught
the glimpse of a Christmas tree with candles. Good-by.

On the edge of the town an old soldier in a helmet lifted
the barrier. A Ural Cossack with narrow little eyes and a
broad face sat on his little shaggy horse, which was covered
with little icicles. Good-by. The harness bells jingled again
and the sleighs flew on into the dark.

Chapter Six

1

They took the exile route across the steppe, southward, then east—Nizhny Novogorod, Makaryev, Kazan. At first Dostoevsky found the other two lively and loquacious during the stops at the post stations. But after a while Durov lapsed into odd vacancies and Jastrzembsky, who had always been full of Polish dash and wildness, was afraid of the future.

They passed through villages of gray log houses with the snow deep in the single street, traveling all day and night. The courier, whose name was Kuzma Prokofyevich Prokofyev, was an old man of great friendliness and kindness. He was over sixty, with gray curls on his forehead and an athletic frame. At the first stop beyond Petersburg he changed their open sleighs for closed ones; he gave them leg wrappings against the cold and showed them how to protect their ankles from the fetters with strips of leather.

They were allowed fifteen kopecks a day to buy food and, when the owner of some village inn or teahouse saw their fetters and tripled the price, Kuzma Prokofyevich protested and argued and often paid half the money from his own pocket. "It's hard enough as it is lads," he said several times but in a low voice as if he did not want them to pay attention.

It was a dark frosty evening when they reached Kazan and drove into the courtyard of the prison. Dimly they made out a big white three-story stuccoed building with narrow arched windows. The warders locked them in a ground-floor cell. The minute after, Dostoevsky saw that it was alive with black "Prussian" beetles racing toward the candlelight, falling from the ceiling to the floor in their haste. Since there were only three straw mattresses on the floor and no bedsteads, he got little rest. Durov snored and Jastrzembsky kept twisting and mumbling. Half an hour before dawn, as he dropped into a doze, the air burst with the blast of a bugle just under the window, sounding reveille.

The prison was a forwarding center for convicts. They were led out into the courtyard where eighty or a hundred convicts were standing about in the snow and the faint morning light. Some had spread coats and were sitting down; a line of others was standing disconsolately against the wall. They all wore the same gray convict clothes and the ugly tam-o'-shanters, were fettered, and were all waiting to be moved on elsewhere.

Dostoevsky sat down on a step to smoke a cigarette. One of the two men beside him, a convict with a brutal face, was talking to the next. "You can see for yourself, Kalinovich, that you're in the devil's own mess. We'll be on the road for weeks yet, and you've already lost your money, your overcoat, and your good boots. You had no dinner last night and there's nothing in sight today. It's all that cursed passion of yours for vodka, isn't it?"

"No, don't believe that, Ostanin. Somebody stole my money and the other things—that is, I lost them, I mean I mislaid them, I—— Oh dear, I don't know how it was." He was a timid submissive man like a subordinate clerk in some provincial office who was downtrodden enough by the simple facts of his existence but who expected to pass through life copying documents, to grow middle-aged and old with nothing more disagreeable to contend with than the scorn and disregard of the head clerk of the table and the occasional terrors of the higher officials.

"Well, I'm ready to restore your position," Ostanin said. "It's lucky you've fallen in with me, Kalinovich. I won't mention that vodka I gave you last night; that was simply friendship, though it did cost me a ruble and a half. But a man has to help another when his luck's out, so I'll give you two rubles, my warm shuba, and half a bottle of vodka, and all you have to do is to change names with me. Come, Kalinovich, it's a bargain, eh?"

"But, Ostanin—Anton Gavrilovich, it's not in order." Kalinovich gave him a worried look. "It's irregular."

"What are you bothering your head about? I've explained to you already. By favor of Petersburg I am going to the special division. That's not prison, you know. Or rather, it is prison but special, so it's better. It's the mines, and a man is always treated more leniently there, as you know. Things are bad with you, now. You're in serious trouble and you're going to a settlement."

Kalinovich cringed and looked more worried than ever. Ostanin, who was watching him with a sort of animal fixity, seemed to suspect that Kalinovich had heard something about him, perhaps that he was a double murderer who had been sentenced several times before. "Anyway, if you don't like it at the mines you won't have to stay for long," he said. "Give me time to reach the settlement and run away, then you tell the head man who you are, say you've been sent by mistake. He'll soon find out you're not me and send you back. Perhaps they'll even send you back to your home town, who can tell?"

"Do you think they would?" Kalinovich's face lighted up.

"It's been known before. You and I are not the first ones at this game. You see, I have your interest at heart. Here, it's a bargain."

Dostoevsky, appalled, saw he was holding out two silver rubles at which Kalinovich was staring in fear and desire. Kalinovich made a last effort at resistance. "But how is it possible, how can it be done? Forgive me, Ostanin, but I don't understand."

"Listen, we're changing convoy officers here. The old one who brought us here didn't memorize all our faces, you may be sure. The new one doesn't know them yet. So at roll call you'll answer Ostanin and I Kalinovich." He pushed a bundle toward Kalinovich. "There, it's settled, eh? I'll even throw this in"—and he held out a piece of bread also.

It was too much for Kalinovich. "Thank you, thank you, Anton Gavrilovich." Dostoevsky watched him tremblingly take everything, eagerly begin munching the bread while he put away the money, then examined the rolled-up coat and the secreted bottle of vodka, which was not half but only a third full.

At the same time Ostanin made a sign to another convict standing with a group at a short distance. The convict said something to two others and went off across the yard. The two approached. In a moment others had come from different parts and about a dozen convicts were standing around Ostanin and Kalinovich. Dostoevsky saw they were the most brutal-looking in the yard.

"Kalinovich agrees to exchange with me," Ostanin said to them with a grin. "I've paid him two rubles, my shuba, and some vodka."

Kalinovich was looking around the rough faces with a new expression of fear. "Do you exchange with Ostanin?" one of the group said.

"Y-yes, that is——"

"And Ostanin gave you what he said?"

Kalinovich nodded. "Then it's registered." The members of the group all looked at each other, noting the fact.

"But please—I mean," Kalinovich began, "I don't——" But he was too terrified to continue.

"See that you answer," the convict said roughly. They all dispersed. Kalinovich went slowly away, more humbled and downtrodden than before.

Dostoevsky was incredulous and horrified; it was surely impossible that even such a spiritless creature should actually exchange places with a man like Ostanin who was probably going to twenty years' hard labor in the mines. About fifteen minutes later soldiers marched into the yard and the convicts began forming up into ranks. Dostoevsky and half a dozen others were kept aside. An officer with papers jumped up into a cart and began calling names. Dostoevsky could see Kalinovich twitching nervously in the second rank. When the officer called out "Kalinovich," Ostanin stepped forward so quickly and bellowed, "Kalinovich present, your honor," that Kalinovich seemed seized with terror and confusion, advanced one foot as though going to step out too, opened his mouth and uttered some syllable, retreated, and stood shaking violently.

"Ostanin," the officer called. No answer. The officer and NCOs looked up sharply. "Ostanin!"

Kalinovich seemed to be fixed to the spot; he clutched the bundled coat which he was likely to pay for with twenty years' hard labor. One of the savage-looking gang who had "registered" the bargain turned a quiet look on him.

Dostoevsky could not bear it any longer. In a moment more it would be too late; he must shout out. He stumbled forward and raised his hand to attract attention, the shout in his throat. He was roughly pulled backward, somebody said in a fierce, low voice, "Keep quiet! What are you doing?" and he was looking into the angry intelligent face of a young convict.

"Let go. They're playing a trick on that poor Kalinovich."

"What's it to you? Keep quiet—they'll kill you if you breathe a word." He kept his grip on Dostoevsky's arm.

"Ostanin! Where's Ostanin?" A sergeant was bawling out furiously, while the NCOs went along the ranks of the convicts.

"Os-tanin pr-present, your high nobility," Kalinovich said in a weak voice, stepping out at last with a cringing look.

"Why can't you answer promptly?" the sergeant shouted in his face, giving him a vicious shove.

"So that's you, Ostanin," the officer said. "You're bashful, eh? Well, we'll give you the right treatment."

Dostoevsky turned away, sickened and angry, hobbling as quickly as the fetters allowed. The young convict caught him up. "I don't recommend your repeating that," he said with the same irritated expression.

"Who are those men, that gang who 'registered' it?"

The other looked him up and down. "You're new in this uniform, aren't you? That's the artel. In other words, the convicts' elected union. What they say is law and the Tsar himself can't help it."

As the convicts were marched away Kuzma Prokofyevich appeared and in half an hour Dostoevsky and the other two were driving in the sleighs again across the snow eastward.

They headed toward Perm and the Ural Mountains. The weather became very cold. Sitting immobile for hours in the sleigh was torment. Dostoevsky broke icicles from his face. The horses whitened with frost, the snow squeaked under the runners with a sharp metallic sound. Smoke stood in high unwavering columns over the houses they passed, the endless white plain lay on both sides, and presently they could see the distant Urals like a blue opalescent haze on the horizon.

At night the throbbing beat of a night watchman's rattle, like a big pebble shaken in a box, came from the villages, the sound carrying a long way through the still air. Sometimes it was a slow "ting . . . ting . . ." on a triangle, sweet and melancholy. In places the drivers veered the sleighs off the road into the deep snowdrifts at the side to avoid the convoys of freight sleighs that charged by, high as houses with pyramids of baled goods for the Irbit fair, driven by narrow-eyed grinning men covered with frost.

Then there were great ice waves, rising vertically the height of a man from trough to crest, made by the pounding freight sleighs and storms. Dostoevsky felt every bone shaken as they drove relentlessly up one side, banged and

jolted down into the hollow, swished up the next wave—
for hours on end.

One evening in the mountains they were overtaken by a
snowstorm that soon hid the road altogether. They could
see no fences and sank constantly into deep drifts. Kuzma
Prokofyevich trudged back from the lead in the falling dusk.
"How are we, lads? Lend a hand here, pull her out." They
floundered in the snow, the links of their fetters frozen,
helping to heave the sleighs clear, to turn the plunging
horses onto some firmer footing. After dark they lost the
way completely, pitched into fresh drifts with no guiding
mark anywhere. The horses would scarcely move. "They
know they're off the road," Dostoevsky's Votyak driver
yelled. Kuzma Prokofyevich sent him to find the way; after
an interminable time he came back with two peasants; they
reached the road again with a struggle and traveled on.

Every day they passed the dirty yellow-painted stockades
of spiked logs of the exile étapes—the station houses for
marching exile parties. There was something sinister and
terrible about them and they were glad to leave them behind.

At Perm, two of the horses were harnessed side by side
with the third in front. Dostoevsky noticed the change with
a pang—farewell to the Russian troika. They made for
Ekaterinburg. The cold became even worse. Vapor rose
from the horses in clouds. They drank tea at every other
post station to try to warm themselves. When they opened
the door a volume of vapor rushed in before them and there
was white frost on the window joints inside the heated room.
They ran through endless forests. It was bright moonlight.
The tree trunks ran past the sleigh like soldiers. Dostoevsky
fell asleep. When he woke up the regiments of pines would
still be marching quickly by. The drivers stopped to change
horses, the bells tinkled, and on they went again, the blue
light of the moon on the snow, pines, and once more the
great white plain.

On the evening after they had left Ekaterinburg they

were overtaken by two fast sleighs that whirled by carrying officials wrapped up in furs. At the next post station there was a picket of soldiers and an officer who took Kuzma Prokofyevich aside. Dostoevsky and the others waited. Kuzma Prokofyevich came back shaking his head.

"His Excellency Anton Ardalinovich is in a terrible temper. They are having all sorts of trouble with some bandits in the district. His Excellency Anton Ardalinovich is the new governor, on a visit, finding everything wrong. Everybody must go forward on foot. There's no help for it, lads. You will have to go on with the next marching party."

Dusk was coming on. They walked to the stockade of the étape, a short distance away. Kuzma Prokofyevich said that in forty-eight hours or so, when His Excellency Anton Ardalinovich had left the district, he would catch them up with the sleighs again. Soldiers with shouldered rifles were pacing slowly along the sides of the stockade from the zigzag painted sentry boxes at each corner. Faintly from inside they caught the jingling of chains. They looked at each other.

The high gates were opened, they entered and saw three or four long narrow log huts. The étape guards prodded them with rifles. "Over there. Hut number one." They walked to the biggest hut, from which the jingling and other noise came; a soldier unlocked the door, pushed them in, and, as the smell and heat swam over them, slammed the door in their backs.

Dostoevsky stood still with the others. He wanted to vomit from the stench filling his throat and nose, to run from the scene in front of him. The hut was filled with a dense throng of men, women, and children lying packed on the two rows of narrow, sloping plank beds without blankets or pillows, standing over every inch of floor space, even clinging to the roof beams. They couldn't breathe, they couldn't move without kicking, knocking each other; some hadn't space to stand, others tried to ease their cramped aching limbs. They were all encumbered by piles of bundles, gray convict bags, kettles, pots, obstructing the gangways and getting in everybody's way, causing quarrels and adding to the chaos and misery.

They were kicking up an unending clatter and clamor, talking, complaining, trying to relieve their wretchedness, some laughing strangely. Children were crying; fetters kept up a continual clashing. It was suffocatingly hot and the floor was slippery with filth. Dirty rags dripped from the beams. An old man was excreting into a great open tub against which sat a woman with a small child on her lap and two or three convicts. In one corner a huge man with a hanging apelike face was pressing a girl against the wall, holding her arms while he jerked his hips. Next to them a woman was dipping a morsel of bread into water and giving it to a sickly-looking young man whose head she was holding. One group of crouching convicts with bulletheads and squashed features was noisily gambling. Near the door stood an old couple, the man in fetters, with a gray beard, a dignified face with a broad nose, the woman thinner.

Dostoevsky couldn't move. And these women and children had committed no crime but were voluntarily suffering these horrors to show their love and devotion to the husbands or fathers or brothers, going into exile with them.

"My God," Dostoevsky said. "My God."

2

They spent a night without rest, squatting in the only free space—next to the *parashka*, the excrement tub, which was in constant use. When the doors were opened at dawn they gasped, scarcely able to breathe with the sudden plunge from the steam heat into the cold.

The men and women poured out into the snow. The air was filled with the clinking of fetters like the jingling of innumerable bunches of keys. Everybody busily began to do odd jobs—to rearrange bundles, adjust leg wrappings, preparing for the day's march. Presently some carts crunched up across the compound and the convoy commander, a captain, appeared twisting the ends of his mustache.

"Form up!" an NCO called out. Dostoevsky found himself next to a small crafty-looking nimble man with a bullethead.

"Very well—ready," the captain said. One by one the exiles went forward, shouting their names to an NCO with the muster roll. The blacksmith looked at their fetters to see that they were fast and the links could not be slipped over the heel, and they crossed to a second NCO with a bag of copper coins who handed each of them eleven kopecks to buy food between the étapes. Dostoevsky shivered with cold. At that moment a gigantic exile with a beard advanced and called out, "Arkady Dontremember." As the NCO checked this off as a "name," the nimble man gave Dostoevsky a nudge.

"You say the same, eh? Go on, go on." His toothless gums gaped.

"What?" Dostoevsky said, puzzled. "He doesn't remember his name?"

"Oh no! Oh no, he doesn't! If you gave him a beating till he was black, he couldn't remember." He laughed as if it were a great joke, having plainly seen Dostoevsky's ignorance from the beginning and enjoying it. "He's a brodyaga like me, brother. He has heard General Cuckoo call six times. I've heard him ten. No wonder we don't remember our names, eh?" His cheeks quivered with silent laughter.

"Next!" the NCO called. The small brodyaga sprang forward and shouted, "Osip Ivanovich Dontremember." When Dostoevsky reached the far rank the brodyaga darted up again, attaching himself in the curious protective way of some criminals. "You stay with me, brother. You'll be well off, you'll see. The road's hard enough if you don't know how to manage. Osip Ivanovich Dontremember's a man of experience, eh?" He showed his gums again. There was a quick sly animal intelligence in his face. Brodyagi, he said, were convicts who escaped from exile stations, settlements, or marching parties; nearly all of them were recaptured or forced sooner or later by cold and hunger to give themselves up. They could not resist the cuckoo calling in spring, announcing the fine weather when they could live in the forest. "You'll see, brother—you'll see it too. We have to go and join General Cuckoo's army. Yes, the Tsar's cow pasture is large but you can't get out of it. They catch you in the end, if you're not dead. Sometimes when a brodyaga comes out of the forest he has to cut somebody's throat to get a crust of bread. So when the police captain asks him his name— well, he joins the Dontremember brigade." He nudged Dostoevsky and winked in a grotesque way. Every Dontremember caught was sent back for five years.

"Do you mean you have walked to Siberia ten times?" Dostoevsky said incredulously.

"That's right, brother." The brodyaga grinned at him. "I know the road."

The compound was filled with the voices of the exiles. There were about a hundred and fifty men in the gray costumes and about a hundred women and children. Some older men threw themselves on the snow to wait. Now and then children called out. The captain and NCOs were sorting out the sick and other applicants for places in the carts. Four or five old men and a pale, ill-looking girl had been lifted in; others had been allowed to climb up. Women were pleading with the captain to let the children ride. "Captain, for pity, let my little Vanya ride," one woman said, wringing her hands. "He's only eight and he can't keep up, I swear it."

"There's no more room," the NCO said, shoving her away. "Go on, mother, it's no good."

"Form ranks! Form ranks!" The buzz of talk stopped at once; those lying on the snow struggled up. "Here, take this." The brodyaga gave Dostoevsky a rag and showed him how to wrap it around his head and ears. All the exiles were doing likewise. A squad of Cossacks in their long dark green overcoats took up position at the head of the column; others stationed themselves at intervals on each side. There was a rear guard of half a dozen more, then the carts. The high gates of the stockade were open.

It was the moment of starting. The captain took off his cap, crossed himself, and bowed toward a wooden cross at the end of the compound. The soldiers and the exiles did the same. "Well, lads, we'll start. *S'Bogom.* God go with you," the captain said.

Nearly all had cumbersome bundles under their arms or tied to them with string. One man with a proud handsome face was carrying a woman on his back. Dostoevsky stared at another who held a small black dog; there was something terrible and touching in the sight. They all began to move in a broken and disorderly throng through the snow. Dostoevsky found it heavy going; the uneven snow made his steps lurch and the fetters banged constantly against his legs. After a few versts they came to the village of Markova. There was a cattle fence on each side of the road and an old man came out of a little half-buried shelter beside the gate and gazed at them with red eyes, crossing himself. On the other side of the village a square cemented brick pillar rose out of the snow, marking the boundary of Europe and Asia.

As they came up to it the Cossack soldiers halted. On one side of the boundary pillar were the arms of the Province of Perm and on the other the arms of Tobolsk. "Well, brother," the brodyaga said. "You can say good-by to home." They had stopped for a last good-by to Europe. It was a heartbreaking scene. Many of the exiles wept unrestrainedly, bowed down, and wrung their hands. Some dug away the snow and pressed their faces to the earth beneath or tried to scratch up a little to take with them into Siberia. Others flung their arms around the pillar as if they were once more embracing somebody from whom they were now separated by great distances. Most of them prayed. One elderly woman knelt touching the snow with her forehead. Next to her was a peasant lad who stood silently looking back across the plain with love and grief. The brutish-looking thieves and murderers snatched off their caps and crossed themselves. The brodyaga Osip Ivanovich was standing with bowed head. Another man was scratching an inscription among those covering the pillar: "Good-by, Masha." Dostoevsky wept.

"Form ranks!" the NCO called out. The exiles shuffled into loose order. "March!" In one united movement all crossed themselves—soldiers, NCOs, and exiles together—and with the irons jingling they trudged slowly forward into Siberia.

3

The brodyaga talked incessantly. He had a sort of slavish, Pogodin-like devotion and at the same time showed his savageness with a pleased simplicity. He knew every stretch of the road, every étape. "Bah, it'll be all right later on," he said. "Once we're past Tyumen the captain will let you bang the ankle band." By banging the ankle band of the fetters to an ellipse with a stone, he explained, Dostoevsky would be able to slip it over his heel. It was a matter to be negotiated between the captain and the marching party's artel.

Dostoevsky looked at him quickly. "Is there an artel here, among us?"

"For sure there is." He indicated the giant bearded brodyaga who had called himself Arkady. "He's the head man. We're all in it." All six brodyagi in the party were members of the artel, along with four other convicts. From Osip Ivanovich, Dostoevsky began to learn of the half-acknowledged, half-secret life of the artel within each marching party. It raised funds, bought and sold tea, bread, sugar, cards, vodka, bribed and tricked officers and escort;

it could bribe floggers to lay on lightly; it "registered" all bargains between exiles and saw they were enforced, and it was a terrorist organization. The artel had its own code of honor, recognized two crimes, betrayal and disobedience, and imposed a single penalty for them: death. A traitor to the artel, even if he betrayed secrets under a flogging, condemned himself. "Siberia isn't big enough, brother." The brodyaga grinned at him with raw gums. "They'll find him." Osip Ivanovich was only longing to reach his place of exile to escape once more. "I tell you, brother, you can't stand it when General Kukushka calls. You tie a kettle to your belt, take your ax, and walk into the forest. You have to go."

"Aren't they after you quickly?" Dostoevsky said.

"Eh?" Osip Ivanovich started quivering with laughter as if this were another great joke. "You're in the forest, but the prison commandant has you on his roll. He likes to go on getting your rations and clothing items, to sell for himself. So he doesn't tell anybody you've gone to General Kukushka's army and he keeps you down on the books. Why, at Ust Kara, Major Ofonkin kept a cell block of dead men and brodyagi on his roll for seven years and when he retired he lived like a landowner."

Early in the afternoon they bought food from some peasant women by the roadside, halted briefly for lunch, then marched on. It began to snow. As they came in sight of a village the brodyaga nudged him and pointed to the artel leader, Arkady, who had fallen back and was walking alongside the rear cart, speaking to the captain. "It's the *miloserdnaya*—the charity song," Osip Ivanovich said eagerly. "He's asking the captain if we can sing it." Evidently the captain agreed since Arkady returned along the line telling off various prisoners; they would collect money from the villagers.

The column reached the first few log huts of the village sunk in the whiteness of the vast plain. And marching with slow dragging steps along the single street with the snow falling, the exiled men and women began quaveringly and confusedly to sing and chant the *miloserdnaya*. The fetters clanked, voices chanted discordantly, words jarred and intermingled.

> "Have pity on us, O our fathers,
> Forget not the unwilling travelers,
> Forget not the long imprisoned.
> Feed us, O our fathers—help us.
> Have compassion, O our fathers.

> "We are held in close confinement,
> Behind walls of stone and gratings,
> Behind oaken doors and padlocks,
> Behind bars and locks of iron.
> For the sake of Christ have mercy.

> "We have parted from our fathers,
> Left behind our mothers, sweethearts,
> We are prisoners.
> Pity us, O our fathers."

All the grief, despair, lamentation, and longing of endless columns of Russian exiles were in the song; perhaps all the despair and agony of Russia. Dostoevsky was overcome. The alms collectors went along the street and children and women came to the doors of the huts, putting food and money into their caps. Beyond the village the column stopped and under the soldiers' supervision they shared out what they had been given. Dostoevsky received a lump of bread and two kopecks.

The snow fell steadily. It was toward evening when they came in sight of the étape stockade. Dostoevsky was wet to the skin and bitterly cold. A place on one leg was raw from the irons and he was so exhausted he could hardly put one foot before the other. The NCOs halted the column in front of the stockade gate, the exiles formed two ranks, and the captain counted them to make sure none were missing. He kept making mistakes, cursing and beginning again, reddening in the face from the hard work of counting. At last he was satisfied. Osip Ivanovich said to Dostoevsky excitedly, "Keep up now, brother. Look out that you keep up with me. Only a minute now." The other brodyagi and rough-looking convicts of the artel were bunched together with clenched fists as if they were going to attack something.

"Open!" the captain shouted. The stockade gates were swung open. "All right, lads—in you go."

Dostoevsky felt the brodyaga viciously jerk his arm, he was thudded in the back and swept forward amid screams and shouts, wails, the furious clanking of fetters as the throng of men and women wrenched up their last energy and made a mad wild rush into the étape, fighting through the doorway into the evil-smelling bare hut, striking each other, pushing to get places on the plank bed, underneath it, a corner, a space to rest for a few hours.

"This way—here!" The brodyaga pulled him so that he nearly fell. The convicts savagely thrust others aside. Inside the hut there was tumult. A big convict punched him in the chest and he fell backward, banging his head, into a space under the bed. His hands landed in thick slime, he struggled in disgust to rise and was dragged out by the brodyaga, who pushed him up onto the long plank bed and wrestled into place beside him. They had to cling on with all their strength, keeping others off with hands and feet.

Dostoevsky was shaking and sickened. The sight of the men and women, who had had a pitiful dignity as they marched through the village singing their half-articulate song, being forced to shed their last scrap of self-respect, to scramble and fight against each other for places in the hut, was appalling. Ah, but he clung to them in their suffering. He covered his face with his hands. In spite of his exhaustion and the terrible place, he felt his heart overflowing. Oh, God, have pity. Oh, God, if You exist have pity on Russia.

The noise, scuffling, shouting, and cries of children gradually died down, although there was incessant movement. Osip Ivanovich was twisting about on the *nari*, the plank bed. "The post office, brother. We mustn't forget it; perhaps there's a message for you."

"What? A message?"

"From your friends, eh?" He slid down, gave a nod to Arkady and two artel men on the nari to guard the places, and began closely examining the wooden uprights, the spaces between the occupants, whom he roughly thrust aside, then the walls. Dostoevsky followed. Could there be some word from Petrashevsky, the others? He saw that the sleeping platform and the walls were covered with messages, inscriptions, names, scratched by exiles for comrades following. He read simple pathetic greetings: "Hello, Sasha. I.N."; convict obituary notices: "Vassily Semyonovich Federenko died January 1847"; messages in code, sometimes lists of names conveying a world of information for an unknown reader, warnings, hints for brodyagi dreaming of escape, letters like one of two lines: "Dear Vanka, Good night. I have just eaten supper. I am thinking of Nastenka and you. Kostya."

No—there could be nothing for him. As he turned away the sentries slammed the door of the hut and bolted it for the night. At the far end he saw Jastrzembsky and struggled over to him. He did not care about the place on the bed.

"Are you all right?"

"Yes. And you?" They spoke a few words to each other. Nearby on the floor was a girl of about eighteen looking very ill; a middle-aged woman was tending her.

"What's the matter with her?" Dostoevsky said.

"She's bad. I don't know what will become of her, poor child," the woman said.

"I noticed her this morning," Jastrzembsky said. "It's typhus fever. She'll die unless she is treated."

"Can't they get a doctor to her?" Dostoevsky said to the woman. She gave him a curious glance. "The nearest doctor is at the lazaret at Tyumen. It's six days' march away. We have been carrying her in the cart for a week. The snow today was bad."

"Aren't there any medicines here?"

"Oh no. Nothing."

"But there's a medical orderly with the troop, surely?" The woman didn't reply. "Is she alone?"

"Yes."

"Why is she being exiled?"

"Oh, you see, she wasn't charged with anything," the woman said. "She is an administrative exile. Her brother was arrested a year ago on suspicion of having talked about a sentry at the Red Bridge in Petersburg who killed and robbed a man at night."

"I remember that. It was true. Plenty of people were talking about it," Dostoevsky said.

"Well, they pitched onto him for it and banished him. They said he was criticizing the government by repeating the story. A little while later they arrested her and told her that she would be sent into exile because she might be tempted to talk about it too; and if she did it might, for all anyone could tell, turn out to be prejudicial to public tranquillity."

"Because it might?"

"So they had to exile her, they said."

"And now she is dying of typhus here," Jastrzembsky said in a choking voice. "Not for anything she did but for something she might do—perhaps. Ah!" He bent down and kissed the girl and lifted the irons on his legs and kissed them too.

4

Kuzma Prokofyevich and the sleighs overtook them at the next étape. They were called out from the marching party, which was shut up in the hut for its rest day. At the last minute Osip Ivanovich, the brodyaga, insisted on giving Dostoevsky a stream of tips about "joining General Kukushka's army" in the spring.

They drove on in fine cold weather, the snow sparkling under the sun. From far off they saw Tobolsk—a long line of board roofs and here and there the white stuccoed walls of government buildings, the green-domed towers of a church. Kuzma Prokofyevich said good-by to them in the guardroom of the forwarding prison. They wrung his hand. "Thank you, thank you for all you did."

"One day we'll see you again, when we're free."

"Our love to Petersburg, Kuzma Prokofyevich."

They waited interminably after he had gone and at last were led off by a lieutenant and four Mongol soldiers. Tobolsk forwarding prison was the great center where convicts, political prisoners, exiles of all sorts were gathered before being sent on to various remoter parts of Siberia. From the yard it looked like an enlarged étape, the gray log huts bigger and more numerous. As they reached the middle one Dostoevsky saw it was standing in a ditch full of urine and rotting garbage. The lieutenant unlocked a small door and stood away. Dostoevsky, who was leading, faltered at the stench, a soldier gave him a prod, and they had hardly entered when Dostoevsky slid on the floor and fell slithering full length. He rose covered with slime. At the end of the passage past a further door they were pushed through into a long dark room the length of the hut and the door bolted quickly after them.

Dostoevsky felt as though filthy hands were thrust over his face. The air was unbelievably foul—damp with the acrid, slightly ammoniacal stench from unwashed bodies, warm, smelling of excrement, so polluted it was hardly breathable. And even after experiencing the étape he staggered at the scene of misery in the hut.

Hundreds of men and women and complaining children were cramped in every imaginable posture on the floor and the long plank beds. The floor boards were slippery with a thick spongy accumulation. In one place there was an evil-smelling pool where an overflowing excrement tub on the floor above was dripping through the ceiling; three men and two women were trying to sleep on the floor there. Nearby a woman held a year-old infant in her arms; at other spots there were dark holes full of slops and rubbish where the decayed boards had collapsed.

Durov's hand was on his arm. He saw Durov was going to faint from the polluted air. There was scarcely any space to move in. They held him up and when he vomited help-lessly there were loud complaints, swearing, and protests from those who were soiled and their arrival was cursed.

They spent six days in the hut. A group of the roughest convicts, who terrorized many of the prisoners, questioned them about whom they had met on the way from Petersburg. When Dostoevsky mentioned Osip Ivanovich, the brodyaga, three of them eyed each other, laughing and nodding. "Yes, that's him. You've described him well. That's Osip Ivano-vich." Dostoevsky found the acquaintance gave him a standing with the convicts. They all had a great belief in luck, would do anything for it, and thought it alone would settle the prisons they were to be sent to. One of the worst, they said, was Omsk. "Ah, it'll be bad luck if we're sent there. That Major Krivtsov there—well, we'd rather avoid that brute."

"Eight-eyes Krivtsov. He'll flog you for a bold look."

One morning at the end of a week a captain and the lieutenant came in; the captain was grimacing at the smell and spitting. "Durov! Dostoevsky! Fall out. Get your bundles." As they reached for their coats, Jastrzembsky struggled over to them.

"Good-by, dear friends. Good-by."

They embraced him. Three sleighs were waiting outside in the yard. While the blacksmith was examining their irons the captain gave instructions to a Cossack sergeant evidently in charge of their escort. "And no nonsense, my good fellow. They're to be treated with no indulgence. His Excellency's orders, d'you understand?"

They drove off. The road left the town on the far side and crossed the Irtysh. Dostoevsky felt oppressed and uneasy. A few versts beyond the last houses the sergeant's sleigh ahead slowed down and they all stopped. Two women were standing at the roadside. As the sergeant got out, Dostoevsky heard him say to them gruffly, "Be quick!" He motioned the soldiers to stand clear.

The women approached. They were thin, bony, dressed in threadbare coats, but they smiled and a fine serenity showed in their faces. Dostoevsky stumbled out into the snow. Durov was beside him. "This is Madame Frantsev," the taller woman said. "I am Madame Von Vizen. We wanted to bring you blessings from Madame Muravyev, Madame Annenkov, Madame Ivanov, and ourselves and to wish you Godspeed." The wives of Decembrists! They were figures from another age, the heroic women who had followed their husbands to Siberia after the great revolt twenty-five years before and had shared the same torment with them all that time. Dostoevsky's lips trembled with emotion. Somehow the women had bribed the Cossacks to stop at this spot.

"Will you take this?" She handed Dostoevsky a Bible. Madame Frantsev gave one to Durov.

"Thank you. Thank you." Dostoevsky took Madame Von Vizen's hand and was going to kiss it but she leaned forward and kissed him on the cheek.

"Get in now. That'll do," the sergeant said impatiently. The soldiers separated them, pushed Dostoevsky and Durov back to the sleighs.

"God be with you."

The horses strained forward. Dostoevsky sat looking back at the two lonely figures waving their hands and becoming smaller and smaller in the white plain. At last they had gone.

The soldier beside him shrugged himself deeper into his coat collar. "Where are we going?" Dostoevsky said.

"To Omsk."

It meant the prison under military command, incomparably harsher than the mines, worse than anything else, except the Article, in Siberia. And there was Major Krivtsov.

Chapter Seven

1

The two halves of the gate in the high spiked wooden palisade shut behind them like a mouth. Across the yard Dostoevsky saw the log huts of the convict barracks. It was late afternoon, growing dark.

The guards marched them to the administration hut and they stood in the entry waiting for the major. In a minute he came out. He had a spiteful purple face with pimples and bunches of red veins like bloodworms and looked half drunk. His spectacles, greasy forage cap with the orange band on it, and his dirty silver epaulets increased the viciousness of his appearance.

"What's your name?" he said sharply.

"Durov."

"And yours?"

"Dostoevsky."

"You filthy imbeciles—both of you! I know about you!" Krivtsov's mean eyes squeezed up behind the spectacles and he began walking around them, looking them up and down. "Where did you get those coats? H'm. It must be a new style from Petersburg. Sergeant! Take 'em off. Shave their heads. Take away everything they've got and sell it! Money for the prison funds. Convicts own nothing." He confronted them again, thrusting his face out. "Careful you behave yourself. Don't let me hear a whisper about you. Or it's cor-por-al pun-ish-ment. D'you hear? One whisper, the very first one—and you'll have it!" He turned on his heel and the guards grabbed their elbows.

They were separated. Dostoevsky was shaved in the guard-

room, given new brown and gray convict clothes, and led
out to a long low barrack hut like the one at Tobolsk. It
was dimly lit by tallow candles, with the same rotting woodwork, the floor slippery with filth, melting snow dripping
through the ceiling, and a heavy stifling smell. There were
about thirty men in it. They had just been locked in for the
night and were making an uproar, laughing, swearing, croak-
ing like animals, clanking fetters. Dostoevsky braced himself against the savagery of the scene—the grime, shaven
heads, branded and scarred faces, the terrible hut. This was
where he must live for four years.

"There's your place." The NCO jerked his head to a space
on the wooden sleeping platform and went out locking the
door. Dostoevsky felt that all the prisoners in the hut had
already slyly observed him while continuing what they were
doing. The space on the platform was three planks wide. He
lay down on it. Nobody spoke to him. He flicked away some
insect that kept returning and running over his neck, then up
his trouser leg. Presently the racket in the hut changed tone
and he saw that most of the men were working at something,
cobbling, sewing, making things. Next to him a tall, lean,
dull-witted man was precisely and methodically making a
sort of colored Chinese lantern. Beyond there were three
Tartars and an old man with a long thin hooked brigand's
nose. Many men were also smoking. The way they worked
and smoked made it seem certain that such things were forbidden but that, at the smallest signal, the men would snatch
everything out of sight with the greatest dexterity.

All at once one of the Tartars, a gigantic creature with a
bald head and dangling arms, came up. He stood squinting
at Dostoevsky with his little pig eyes. "What are you doin'
here, iron beak? We can smell nobles ten versts away. Eh,
iron beak?" He put out a hand and jerked Dostoevsky's fetters, almost pulling him off the platform. "Tearing the flesh
of the poor! You pecked us to death, you tortured us when
you was a gentleman, didn't you, eh? And now here you are,

as low as us." The clatter in the hut had fallen; all the men
were watching motionless and silent. "And now you're like
us, I said, iron beak. Eh?" He gave another vicious wrench at
Dostoevsky's fetters. Dostoevsky climbed down. The Tartar
lurched forward and at that moment a small skinny figure
skipped up, dug the Tartar's belly with an elbow as he passed
between them, and called out, "Have some tea, Gazin! Have
some tea." The Tartar took no notice; he was grasping
Dostoevsky's neck with one hand when the skinny man
danced up again, kicked his legs, and cackled, "The major
wants you, Gazin. He enjoys Tartars. Bend over, Gazin!"
He skipped around the Tartar, giving him ankle taps and
digs. Gazin released his grip on Dostoevsky and turned
slowly like a bear at an annoying fly. "Hey, Jew—I'll give
you a smashing."

"One blow and I'll give you ten," the little man cried out,
laughing, skipping, and dancing about with surprising agility
in spite of his irons. He was a thin, feeble, puny man of about
fifty with a wrinkled white body like a plucked chicken's
and terrible scars on his cheeks and forehead where he had
been branded as a murderer.

Somebody called out, "Go on, Izay Fomich! He won't
touch you."

"You dirty itching Solomon-scab!" Gazin flipped a long
arm but missed.

"I may itch but I'm rich," Izay Fomich cackled. "I've got
money, Gazin."

Gazin made a lunge and missed again. His neck was red.
Dostoevsky saw that he was furious at the little man intervening to draw off his attention. Gazin let out a string of
filth, sprang to the stove, snatched up a log, and in the same
movement accidentally tripped Izay Fomich. He raised the
log high in the air, flung it down with terrific force to smash
the Jew's head. There was a thick crump as it hit—and Izay
Formich was dancing away on his heels, untouched, the log
on the floor.

There was a delighted roar from the other prisoners. They began calling out encouragement to Izay Fomich, twitting him with pleasure, to which he joyfully responded, continually in movement.

"You sold Christ, you Jew!"

"What do I care if I did?"

"You'll get the whip and Siberia, Izay."

"Ain't this Siberia?"

"Oh, they'll send you up north."

"Well, if the Lord God's there and there's money, I'll be fine."

"Bravo, Izay Fomich!"

The tension was gone. Gazin was back in his place as if nothing had happened and Izay Fomich ran to the far side. The noise in the hut resumed.

Dostoevsky stood by the sleeping platform. He could feel the lice in his "fresh" clothes; he kept jerking away from the groups of cockroaches running along the platform; they were nearly as big as his thumb, great fat bodies with long twitching whiskers. Some prisoners nearby had scratched two circles on the woodwork, torn legs off some cockroaches, and were betting on which one first crawled across the outer ring; another group had an incredibly greasy pack of cards and was ferociously playing Three Leaves.

Gradually the atmosphere thickened. Yet the hut was full of drafts and damp; the stove gave out an acrid smoke and heated so feebly that the inside of the windows was coated with ice. The open excrement bucket stank insupportably. For a long time Dostoevsky stood unable to move. At last he climbed onto the platform. His body tautened as the cockroaches scuttered over him, into his clothes. He had no pillow, drew his short sheepskin over his knees and managed to lie still.

The hut was quieter. One by one the men snuffed out their candles and went to sleep. In the end only the card players were crouched around their candle, slapping the cards down; then they finished the game and the hut was in darkness. He was utterly worn out but could not sleep. This was a new life just beginning. Somehow he must survive. Suddenly, with no preliminary warning, the door bolts rattled, the icy night air rushed in, there were lights, and Major Krivtsov with several solders stamped in. Dostoevsky sat up. With astonishment he saw that none of the recumbent prisoners was stirring, all of them sleeping or pretending to. He had time to see Major Krivtsov reel drunkenly, then threw himself quickly down, imitating the rest.

Major Krivtsov, followed by the soldiers and NCOs, stumped down the side of the sleeping bench, swearing, apparently trying to find something to punish. All at once he stopped and let out a bellow: "What! You son of shit! Haven't I told you to sleep on the right side?" They were only two paces away. Krivtsov began to lash at the man with his stick, shouting, "The right side! Defying the regulations! Sergeant—take him. Twenty lashes!" The soldiers seized the man and dragged him off. Krivtsov half ran along the row of unmoving prisoners. "And another! Twenty lashes. I'll teach you cowsons. You sleep on the *right!* On the *right!*"

In a few minutes they had gone. The hut was again in darkness and the door bolted. The men barely stirred. One or two muttered together. There were the sounds of snoring, the clink of irons as men shifted their legs, the scuttering of the cockroaches. Dostoevsky wondered how long it would be before he was flogged and how he would stand it.

The dark was heavy. Perhaps he was beginning to doze. A terrifying scream burst into his ear. He sat upright, clasping at the darkness around him. The man next door was calling in a high straining voice, "Hold him, hold him. Saw off his head, his head!"

"Oh, my God." He was tense with horror. The man was dreaming, reliving some terrible crime he had committed.

"His head! Hold—saw it off!"

There were some grunts nearby, a clink of fetters as a

neighbor kicked the man, and the shouts stopped. Dostoevsky lay staring into the dark.

2

He saw that to survive he must not make any approach to
the convicts. He had to be friendly if they wanted, but at
the same time keep his independence. Gazin and the rest
expected him to be overbearing, insulting, and—since it was
their idea of how a man showed his class superiority—they
were ready in their Russian way to respect him for it while
abusing him. They profoundly mistrusted him. And he saw
that if he tried to make up to them they would treat him
savagely as a coward.

The compulsory work outside brought trouble at once. He
was led out with others to break up old government barges
on the Irtysh River, to shovel snow, to pound alabaster. The
convicts cursed at him, obstructed him, and whenever he
tried to do something shoved him off roughly.

"Get out of it, iron beak."

"Poke your claws in somewhere else. Clear off!"

They cleared their throats spectacularly and spat at him.
As soon as he stood aside they jibed in chorus and abused
him.

"Look at him for a workman!"

"Won't soil your hands, eh? Not you. What can you get
done with parasites like that?"

He said nothing and did what work he could. When most
of them tired of that sort of hostility, some still showed
individual hatred. But after a while a few spoke to him
normally. Since the days were short they were back in the
prison hut early. Akim Akimovich, the convict next to him
on the sleeping platform, who was a brodyaga, a "Dontremember," chatted prosaically about the hut's organization.
There were five men in the artel, including Gazin. They let
out the maidan, the secret "shop" of the hut, where the

convicts could buy tea, sugar, tobacco, and other things and hire cards. The maidan had just changed hands. The new holder was a small, shifty-eyed, avaricious prisoner named Alfonsky who was always gnawing the ends of his fingers and watching someone slyly. He had not been in the prison long and nobody knew exactly what crime he had committed. Some prisoners did work on their own account, getting orders from the town and earning a little money. There were cabinetmakers, wood carvers, shoemakers, tailors. Izay Fomich even managed to do business as a jeweler and pawnbroker. All that was forbidden, the work, money, tools, tobacco, and cards liable to be seized at Major Krivtsov's next raid.

There were constant fights; all the convicts had knives. Every night, once they were locked in, the gambling and drinking began. The specialists smuggled in vodka past the guards and sentries in lengths of ox gut and passed it on to the "publican" convict they worked for. The "publican," having poured the vodka into a wooden bucket and tasted it, always yelled, "That Petrovich!" or "That Kusikov, the thief! He's watered it"—and at once began watering it down himself to at least double volume. With the European Russians and Poles there were Kalmuks, Tartars, Cheremisses, Lezghians—parricides, bandits, lust murderers, pederasts, men who were insane. He learned about them gradually. Gazin, one of the biggest traders in vodka, was a monstrous creature. He had lured several small children away and, after frightening them and enjoying their terror, taken his knife and slowly murdered them for his pleasure. Petrov, a short, strongly built man of about forty, struck him particularly; he was agile, restless, and pale, with high cheekbones and fine white close-set teeth. Akim Akimovich said he was the most dangerous, determined, and fearless of all the convicts and would murder a man for a bottle of vodka absolutely without hesitating and then on another occasion let a man with ten thousand rubles pass by unharmed. Petrov was well behaved, courteous, and talked remarkably little. Nobody knew Akim Akimovich's real name, or his crime. There was Baklushin, a tall, good-natured fellow of thirty, full of capers and jokes, whose girl had jilted him for a German. Baklushin had put a pistol to the German's head in front of them all and, when the German said he dared not fire, Baklushin had blown his brains out. One of the parricides, a Georgian named Rukhadzey, talked about "my parent"—his murdered father. The police had found the body in a ditch covered with planks. Rukhadzey had sawed off the gray head, put a pillow under it, and laid it in place on the shoulders. Some of the prisoners who had never shed blood were more horrifying than those guilty of six murders—men like Alexandrov, a repulsive, depraved, and predatory convict, always practicing sodomy, a bag of flesh with protruding teeth and a little hairy paunch.

One morning at the end of the first month the drumbeat sounded as usual at daybreak outside. Dostoevsky and the others began shifting on the sleeping platform and getting up. They were all shivering, yawning, stretching, some crossing themselves, others already quarreling. The duty sergeant unlocked the door and the rush of fresh cold air filled the hut with clouds of steam. The *parashnik*—the convicts' slopman and janitor—brought in pails of water and in a few minutes the prisoners were fighting for the one dipper that had to do for all of them, snatching it, filling their mouths with water, sluicing their heads, shoving around the buckets, snarling at each other.

"More water, Petrovich."

"Who are you shoving, you dirty hole?"

"That's mine! Snot-rag, get out of it."

All at once, near Dostoevsky, there was pause. Baklushin, Akim Akimovich, and others were glancing at a convict who was still sleeping on the platform. Akim Akimovich gave him a prod. "Out of it, Zalit. The drum's gone."

Zalit slid a little, his sheepskin shifted, and a tangle of intestine fell out. An excited scrambling mass of cockroaches moved out, clotted together. Zalit's dead face looked as if he were going to cry.

"Sergeant. Zalit's had a bad dream," Baklushin called out, and they all moved a few paces away, turning their backs, having nothing to do with the murder. As the guards came up, Dostoevsky's eye caught the face of Alfonsky, the maidan man, at the farthest bucket. He shuddered. He must get a knife.

In the summer the drumbeat sounded at 4 A.M. They walked ten versts to the brick field and from there Dostoevsky carried loads of bricks to the Irtysh. He could only just get through the set stint. But slowly he found he was becoming stronger and could carry twelve, fifteen big bricks at a time.

Every evening there was a wild fight for dinner in the kitchen. Afterward the convicts stood about in the prison yard waiting to be locked up. There were groups around one or two of the men playing homemade balalaikas and singing. Dostoevsky noticed one of the convicts who bent down as he moved from one spot to another, extended his arms, trundled along something invisible, and at the other end straightened up.

"Is he mad?" he said to Akim Akimovich.

"That's Ignatyev. He tried to escape from prison at Tobolsk, so they riveted a wheelbarrow to him for eight years. He can't forget it; he got the habit, you see." Akim Akimovich laughed. Dostoevsky watched the man bend, still talking to another, take up the shafts of the invisible wheelbarrow, wheel it off across the yard, put it down, and fold his arms.

Golostchekin, the prison executioner, went across the far end of the yard with his guard. He was an ex-convict who had escaped sentence by accepting his official position as executioner, lived apart, kept house on his own, and was always guarded. The convicts looked on him with hatred and suspicious terror; he was rich from bribes. Almost every prisoner sentenced to flogging bargained with him to lay on lightly and all gave him something beforehand, even if it were their last kopeck.

"He can kill a man with one blow," Baklushin said.

"That's surely not true," Dostoevsky said.

"What? Golostchekin told me himself. He gives the blow a swing. He knows how to do it so there isn't the smallest bruise—and you don't feel any pain. You'll see how hard he can tap, brother, one of these days! But even if you give him everything you've got, he still has the first blow for himself. That's his affair, that one, and he gives it to you with all his might. He gave me fifty last year, so I can tell. He shouts out at you, 'Ready now, I'll burn you!' He gets all excited beforehand, Golostchekin does."

"They're all the same," Akim Akimovich said. "They enjoy it." He spat, disgusted.

"Is it painful, Baklushin?" Dostoevsky said.

"For Christ, it hurts! It's like fire. You feel they're cutting your back open and pouring coals of flame on."

"How much can a man stand?"

"Oh, it's not like 'the sticks,'" Akim Akimovich said. "The sticks" or "Green Street" meant that a prisoner was stripped to the waist and with his wrists tied to the butts of rifles was dragged by two sergeants between ranks of soldiers, each with a stick, who hit him with all their force as he went by. It was the common punishment.

"I had four thousand blows down Green Street for my German," Baklushin said. "It tingled all right."

"Yes, and with the birch you'd have been dead at five hundred," Akim Akimovich said.

Baklushin nodded agreement. "Give a man five hundred with the birch, brother, and you're almost certain to kill him."

The winter passed and the thaw set in. Outdoors all was

hazy and damp and there were oceans of mud in the compound, on the roads, a thick caking of it on the floor boards of the prison huts. Early one morning in April of the New Year, 1851, they were led out to dismantle a barge on the Irtysh. The orders were to retrieve the best timbers whole. The foreman told Dostoevsky off with two other convicts, Rozhnovsky and Zen, to work forward. The task went fairly quickly; the men unscrewed the wooden bolts, chopped away the woodwork at the extremities of the crossbeams, worked posts of willow underneath them, and levered them free. The barge was slippery with rain and mud. All at once, clearing a beam end, Zen slipped slideways, lurched, and, throwing his arms out to save himself, flung his ax into the water. The river gray and turgid, was running fast. Zen looked over the side, shrugged, and turned back. A guard came up. "Now you can go and get it. I saw you throw it in. Go on!"

"I didn't throw it. Anyway, how can I go in there? Look at it."

"I tell you to get it!"

Zen, a small stringy man with red hair, began hitching his fetters up with a woeful expression, taking his tobacco out of his pocket so as not to get it wet. He was muttering to himself, cursing and rolling his eyes, then looking gingerly over the high side of the barge into the water. It would reach at least to his chest.

"Hurry up!" the soldier said, giving him a dig with the rifle. Zen took off his coat. Dostoevsky went up. If Zen went in with the river flowing at that pace—and with his irons—he'd be done for.

"Wait a minute. Take this." He snatched up a length of rope and passed it around Zen's chest under the armpits; the soldier looked on with a sullen expression but did not object. "Take hold, Rozhnovsky. All right, Zen. Go on."

They let him down the side; the water swirled around him and it was all he could do to keep his feet. He ducked his head under to look for the ax, the line tightened in their hands, they heaved, and he came up gasping. "It's more this way," Rozhnovsky called out. Zen shoved against the current. He ducked down searching again, rising and clutching at the rope; he paused for breath, moved away from the barge, ducked again.

"What's this? What are you doing here?" They turned. Major Krivtsov was glaring at them, tapping his boot with his cane and swaying with drink. "Guard!" The soldier, already stiff with fear at the major's unexpected appearance, gave a confused shuffle with his feet. "Guard, who gave these prisoners permission to stop work? Did you?"

"No, sir. I——"

"Drop that rope!" Krivtsov shouted at Dostoevsky, although he had plainly seen what was going on.

"He's obeying the guard's orders," Dostoevsky said. "If we let go he'll drown."

"What! Did I ask you to speak, you brute? You heard what I said. Drop that rope and get back to work."

Dostoevsky looked into the flash of the major's spectacles. He felt a nervous trembling in himself, his head quavered slightly as he turned it away. He held onto the rope.

Major Krivtsov sprang in front of him. His mouth was working. "Drop it!"

Dostoevsky braced himself, keeping a firm grip on the rope; Rozhnovsky, encouraged, held on too. Krivtsov's mauve face seemed to swell, to puff up. He choked; he could not speak with fury. At last a hoarse bellow came out."Aah—— Arrest—arrest him. The two of them! Sergeant!" As the major jumped away, calling to the sergeant, Dostoevsky said to Rozhnovsky, "Quick, pull him up." They had just time to haul Zen dripping onto the deck before the soldiers seized them.

"I'll give you the birch, by God." Krivtsov was dancing and gasping with rage. "You'll get a flogging you've never heard the like of. Take 'em to the cells."

A squad of soldiers marched them back to the prison. Dostoevsky felt the excitement and tension rising in him. His thoughts seemed to fly and an intense anxiety overcame him. The guards threw open the door of the dark cell and began to chain him to the wall. The stench in the place caught him by the throat. All at once a breeze floated over his face. Everything became light. He felt an extreme consciousness of himself, more life than at other times. The moment seemed to be one of the highest beauty and harmony, overflowing with unbounded joy and rapture, ecstatic devotion, and the completest life. Then he heard an animal cry, small and far in the distance; it came nearer, louder. He was in dread of the instant it would reach him, he felt himself sweating—and then he heard the cry screaming up on him and screaming out of his own throat. He had time to glimpse the startled look on the guards' faces and a red curtain fell heavily, stifling everything out.

3

The ward was a long narrow room with rows of beds along each wall, the sort of green-painted wooden beds cherished by all the bugs in Russia. He lay with a blinding headache for twenty-four hours, then rapidly recovered and, apart from some shakiness, felt scarcely the worse. He remembered nothing and could not understand what had happened. When he asked Dr. Troitzky, the doctor said, "You've had that sort of attack before, haven't you?"

"Never. What was it?"

The doctor looked at him intently. "Well, you are epileptic. You had a fit, evidently your first. It's saved you a flogging. You must try to look after yourself."

Epilepsy! It was a deep shock. He caught a miniature of himself reflected in the metal bowl the doctor had put down. His clean-shaven face was still full, not sunken like some of the convicts'; the flesh above his eyes had become a little puffier and his hair was receding at the left-hand parting.

"Are the attacks going to recur?"

"You will know when you are going to have one. We will try to make things a little easier for you here—a little." Dr. Troitzky was the ward doctor, chesty, with a big chin and a good-humored expression: "too soft," the convicts said. Dostoevsky thought he was an admirable figure in his devotion to his task.

There were twenty-one other patients in the ward, all fettered. Patients died with their fetters on. The air was suffocatingly foul with the smells of festers, medicines, dirty bedclothes. Since Dostoevsky was allowed up he could seek the slightly less vitiated air in the corridor, slippering about in the hospital shirt, long stockings, nightcap, and thick dark brown dressing gown. The dressing gown was lined with something like sticking plaster and he soon realized that it smelled more and more strongly of ointments, discharges, pus, and sweat from the countless patients who had worn it before him; the warmth of his body was bringing out all that it was impregnated with. It also harbored a breed of fat lice, a specialty of the ward which the convicts delighted in squashing with a pop under their thumbnails. At night the stinking tub was placed in the ward and none of the prisoners allowed outside; only the guard came around. A sentry with his loaded Berdan rifle stood at the door and another ten paces off at the door of the next ward. Dr. Troitzky had his own method of easing the prisoners' lot. He had invented a malingerer's ailment, "febris catarrhalis," for the convicts who came for a rest from work or to have a few days in a warm room instead of the damp prison hut. If they stayed too long he said to them in a shy way, "Well, I'm glad you're almost well. Somebody else will be glad to move in." He rarely had to hint twice.

Every evening there was a horrifying operation on one of the convicts. It was Korochenko, a surly, suspicious young man who had stabbed a sentry and been sentenced to three thousand blows with the sticks. He had developed a mysterious eye disease and, in the hospital, had been seen one night rubbing plaster from the wall into his eyes to escape or at least defer the flogging.

"I tell you that's lies, Doctor," he said when they accused him of it. "How can I touch sores like this with my fingers?"

The senior doctor looked at him, now knowing he was inducing the ailment; he said to the orderlies, "Give him a seton until he stops." The orderlies came back twenty minutes later, stripped off Korochenko's shirt, and held him. One gripped the skin on the back of his neck, wrenched it out, and held it. The second orderly pushed a knife into the skin, piercing it through, sawing, and making a long, gaping double wound. The blood squirted. Korochenko did not utter a sound. The orderly dropped the knife, took a strip of coarse linen tape four fingers wide, thrust it into the wound, under the flap of skin, and left it hanging. After that they came in each evening, went to Korochenko sitting up in bed, took the ends of the tape, and jerked it with all their might. As the flap of skin tore away and the wound opened, Korochenko gave a heave, then subsided.

They came at the same hour every evening. Korochenko used to sweat before they appeared. They never spoke a word to him, folded his shirt back, and tore the wound open again. After five days Korochenko could not stand it any more. He said, "Tell the doctor it's all right about my eyes." They gave him twenty-four hours' rest, then took him down to the cell to wait for his three thousand blows.

He was assailed by thoughts of Mikhail and once more tried to find reasons why he did not write; why nobody had written all this time—Andrey, Aunt Kumanina, the Karepins. There was silence from the living world outside. He had bitter thoughts of Mikhail dead and tortured himself about the children. As soon as he was discharged from the hospital and back in the prison hut he wrote to Mikhail through the censorship. There was no reply.

The summer was hot. When they worked in the brick field he stood on the bank of the river looking out on the vast empty Kirghiz steppe, a boundless plain stretching for a thousand versts beyond the Irtysh. There was the blackened tent of some Kirghiz far off, the woman beside it with two sheep, the smoke rising in the still air. A steppe hawk cried its wailing cry. For a moment he could forget the prison.

One warm night in September there was trouble with Alfonsky. They were locked in, the usual racket and eternal quarreling going on. There were groups playing cards and a few convicts tossing about on the sleeping platform, scratching against the myriads of fleas that swarmed with the cockroaches in summer and turned sleep into a sort of delirium. For some reason the convict posted to give warning of anybody approaching was momentarily distracted. Above the clatter nobody heard the door bolts grate. Major Krivtsov came quietly in with sergeant and escort and stood looking around.

There was an odd sort of pause. It lasted for several seconds. They all seemed to notice at once; everybody plunged in a wild scramble to cover up—and Krivtsov roared down the gangway, hitting out with his stick and bawling to the escort to seize the culprits. "Arrest them! Arrest! Sergeant, this man. Vodka, by God; arrest him!" He lashed out at Izay Fomich, who skipped under the sleeping bench. All at once Krivtsov stopped. He stood staring at Alfonsky. Alfonsky was standing, his head bent, eyes cast down, in a submissive attitude, in front of his place on the sleeping bench. He nearly managed to look humble but there was such an infinity of low, animal cunning and avarice about him that this came through all his acting. Krivtsov slowly walked around him. He bent down, pulled Alfonsky's bundle from under the platform, spread its contents with a kick. He knew there was *something* hidden but not where. The whole hut was looking on.

Major Krivtsov moved Alfonsky aside with his stick. He began tapping the boards under the platform. Alfonsky stood it for a moment, then began to fidget nervously, and at last jumped to the major's side gabbling. "There's rats there, your honor. They gnaw it all out. Gnaw all night, they do. They come from farther up there, sir."

"Let go! Take your dirty paws off me!" Major Krivtsov roared, thrashing at Alfonsky, who had actually touched his sleeve trying to draw him away. Everybody in the hut knew that Alfonsky stored his maidan goods in a box under one of the support posts of the platform; how he had managed to get them away there on the major's unexpected appearance was a marvel.

As if suddenly guided, Major Krivtsov grasped the post, tapped the floor board over the spot, and realized he had found something. He bent down. He was going to discover the whole stock in a few seconds. Alfonsky, who had been dancing, seemed to lose control of himself entirely, stared around the room, and said loudly and nervously, "Major Krivtsov—er—er—here's Namyetkin, you know. Namyetkin's here. Yes, yes, he's here, Major . . ."

Major Krivtsov paused, then straightened up. There was hardly a movement in the hut. Alfonsky skipped to the major's side and whispered in his ear. Major Krivtsov's face turned a deeper purple. Dostoevsky noticed a movement from Akim Akimovich just in front of him; Akim Akimovich had quietly pulled a knife out and held it close to his side. At the same moment Major Krivtsov caught sight of Akim Akimovich. "Sergeant—arrest him!" Akim Akimovich sprang for Alfonsky and Alfonsky twisted behind the major. The knife skimmed the major's shoulder, there was an instant of confusion, and then a rifle butt crunched on Akim Akimovich's head. All the guards were on him at once. They held him up. Major Krivtsov shouted into his face, "One of the

Dontremembers, eh? Dontremember. All right, Namyetkin. Now we'll see, eh? Namyetkin! Take him out. Chain him up!"

When they had gone and locked the door again the convicts hardly spoke among themselves. Dostoevsky said to Baklushin, "Who was he?"

"Namyetkin? He was a famous murderer in Tobolsk a few years ago. He killed a major, his wife, and three children—a whole family. Now he'll get God knows how many rods. They'll give him six or eight hundred—make sure he won't be alive at the end."

Alfonsky sidled unctuously up. "Well, Krivtsov didn't discover our stock, did he? He didn't discover it. No." He darted on, going around the hut saying, "They didn't get our stock, eh? Not them. We have to protect that, after all, eh?"

Nobody replied. The hut was silent. There was no gambling. Dostoevsky looked around as the candles went out. All the artel men were lying asleep on the platform.

A week later in the yard Baklushin said, "Alfonsky's asked to be put into solitary confinement."

"What?" Dostoevsky said. "He asked?"

"The artel are going to kill him."

Major Krivstov, they found out, agreed to the request but told Alfonsky maliciously that he could not go into a cell at once. Dostoevsky looked on with horror. At moments Alfonsky was in a state of collapse. He seemed to disintegrate with fear; he squatted every night by the door of the hut, his eyes going round. He avoided the crushes in the kitchen, watched for the moment when there were no convicts there, ran in like a pariah dog and hastily ate what scraps he could, darting out as soon as somebody approached. Gazin and the other members of the artel ignored him. Once, when Alfonsky was scrambling out of the way, Derevenko, the leader of the artel, said to him, "Don't hurry, Alfonsky. Siberia ain't big enough for you." There were coarse laughs.

Next morning Alfonsky was taken to the solitary confinement cells.

The autumn passed into winter. Every Saturday Dostoevsky was called out in his turn to the guardroom to have half his head shaved. The thought of release was constantly in his mind; what made it bearable at all was the sheer impossibility of accepting it, the provisional quality. Outside, a man was caught up in the movement of the world. In prison, as a matter of self-preservation, one thought of everything as temporary; one was on a visit. He saw with what confidence convicts faced sentences of twenty years or more. They looked on such periods as little and believed they would be as youthful and alert, still "have life before them," when they were released at fifty-five or sixty. Worst of all he felt the constant compulsory herding together with other men, the complete inability to escape from others for a moment. Never to be alone, never to have any reading material—ah, it was hard! He fled the harsh reality by recoiling into himself; he reached into the depths of his personality. He saw Durov in work gangs and in the prison yard; Durov, whose physique was going to pieces, had become strange, exalted and unapproachable. Dostoevsky saw the prison was destroying him. The class hostility of some of the convicts had lessened; but others lost no opportunity to poison his existence.

The spring was like the ghost of freedom. The rejoicing of all the living things outside made him melancholy and nervously restless. He thought of them taking out the double windows back in Petersburg. At the end of Lent he marched with a relay of prisoners to church to take the sacrament. It was pleasant walking over the hard frozen ground early in the morning. The guards marched alongside with their rifles. The service, the solemn prayers and prostrations all stirred the past. He remembered his father's house, the days of childhood, Alyona Frolovna. He remembered standing in church then and seeing the peasants crowding in at the back, humbly parting and making way for an officer pushing in, a fat landowner, an overdressed woman, and how he had fancied that the peasants must pray in a different way from other people, bowing down without shame, knowing their humility.

Now he too was standing in the background, marked and fettered as a felon. The people in the church seemed afraid of the convicts and avoided them; some gave them alms. And he felt the subtle pleasure in it. When the priest held the chalice and said, "Accept me, Lord, though a thief," all the convicts bowed down low and the united clank of chains echoed through the church.

Then, at the beginning of May, Krivtsov announced that the military governor of Omsk was coming on inspection. "If there is any trouble you had better look out!" He flew around in a congested fury for a week, ordering cleaning gangs to work. As a result, some of the filth disappeared for the day of the visit. When the governor entered the hut he said, "How do you do, lads?" The convicts shouted back the usual reply: "We wish health to your high nobility." He walked quickly around with a disgusted expression on his face.

But an hour later they heard that Petrov, who had been told off on special duty at the kitchen, had provoked some incident in front of the governor. They could not find out what it was. Petrov came into the hut looking pale. A group quickly gathered around him.

"Krivtsov has given me four hundred," Petrov said.

"What, Green Street?"

Petrov was making a cigarette. He ran the paper along his tongue. "No, rods. Tomorrow."

There was a murmur. Petrov rolled the cigarette carefully, tucked the ends of tobacco in, tapped it. He said, "I'm going to kill him." Everybody knew that Petrov was capable of the greatest ferocity. After a moment they all began talking at once, encouraging him, cursing the major. Petrov had decided that the major had treated him unjustly but wouldn't explain further. The convicts were in a state of tension all evening. Petrov drank vodka and put aside a small bottle of it, strengthened with snuff, ready for just before the flogging. Dostoevsky knew that the convicts would forgo the barest needs for six months rather than have nothing to buy vodka with before a flogging. "If you've drunk you don't feel the rod so bad," Baklushin said.

The flogging was in the evening. Golostchekin, the executioner, came into the yard. He was carrying a light wooden trough, like a feeding trough for ducks or hens, and a can of water. He was a man of ordinary height but he had the characteristics that are seen in a particular kind of congenital hunchback and male dwarf—abnormally large head with a long, loose-skinned face, a baying, metallic bass voice, a thick chest, and arms that seemed to reach to his knees. He dropped the trough, which was full of birch rods, and tipped the can of water over them. The rods kept supple in water. One of the soldiers with him put down a rough bench on which the man to be flogged would lie.

Petrov saw this. He ran into the hut and came out a moment later, his eyes watering from the scorching drink. He went up to Golostchekin and gave him money. Golostchekin nodded without a word. Dostoevsky watched for a sign that Petrov had a knife but saw nothing. A moment later the battalion doctor appeared, the drumbeat sounded, and the convicts lined up. The senior sergeant ordered Petrov to fall out and marched him between two soldiers to the guardhouse. When the punishment had been written down there they stripped off Petrov's shirt, marched him back, and reached the bench as Major Krivtsov drove up from the far end of the yard in his droshky.

There was something disconcerting about the appearance of the droshky; the major scarcely ever used it inside the prison area. Dostoevsky saw Petrov frown. But the major got out, came forward, and gave Petrov a glare. He looked drunk, as usual; his small red eyes blinked in a heavy way behind the glasses. Petrov made a movement, there was the tiny glint of a knife blade; Dostoevsky felt sick. The men in the ranks with him were very still.

Golostchekin took his shirt off, picked a rod out of the water, and bent it in his hands. There was an excited glow on his face. Petrov was standing apart just in front of two soldiers, Krivtsov about seven paces away from him to one side talking to Fedka, his orderly, and the battalion doctor. The senior sergeant and a corporal were on the far side. Petrov seemed to be judging the distance he had to hop, step, and jump. There was an instant's pause. All the muscles in Dostoevsky's neck tightened. Suddenly Krivtsov bawled at Golostchekin, "Go on, damn you. Get on with it!"

Petrov went pale, glanced toward Krivtsov, and bent springily at the knees. Golostchekin touched him on the shoulder with the rod, a signal to lie down. Petrov's right hand at his side held the knife hidden. At that moment Krivtsov spun on his heel, called out to the senior sergeant, "See that he gets all he can stand," and walked toward the droshky. Petrov stared at his turned back. Krivtsov had hardly reached the droshky, hardly lifted his weight in, before the driver, who had seen Petrov's face and evidently guessed something, whipped the horse forward. Krivtsov lurched into the seat cursing. Petrov did not move; he had simply not expected Krivtsov to go off like that and was unprepared for it.

"Come, lie down, brother," Golostchekin said. Petrov was as white as death, making a fearful effort to control himself. In a quick movement he bent, slipped the knife into his leg wrappings, then lay calmly on the bench.

Golostchekin said, "Look out, brother, I'll scorch you!" The first was "his" blow. He stood back, straddled his legs. He held the rod, his elbow crooked, behind his right shoulder. Instantaneously, he threw his arm, chest, his whole upper body upward and forward. Dostoevsky heard the hollow whistle of the rod through the air, Golostchekin

punch out his breath with the effort, his ape chest well
down. There was a squashy thud as it hit. He saw Petrov
actually bounce under the blow, then his shoulders rise,
muscles contracting, his head hanging forward, as he absorbed the shock. His knees bent and slid along the bench a
little. A blood-red ribbon lay across his back and curved up
under his left armpit.

Golostchekin rolled his movements; his whole personality
seemed to express itself in his chest and arms. He drew the
rod in toward him with aesthetic smoothness, crooked elbow,
and again there was the enormously powerful punching
smash. Petrov bounced again. The red ribbon thickened a
little. Golostchekin could hit along the same line fifty times
without varying more than a fraction.

Petrov did not make a sound. Golostchekin drew in the
rod, smashed, rolled back. Again it was along the same line;
he was not showing Petrov any favors. At each smash the
rod went *Fwittsh!* It traveled only a short distance, hitting
Petrov's back at maximum force.

"Ten!" the senior sergeant called out.

At thirty Petrov was no longer moving at each blow. The
rod struck his back with a thick sound. The weal was a high
crimson mound. At forty the rod split. Golostchekin kept
on with it for five more blows. The splintered ends tapped
together as he drew it in to strike; the sharp edges opened
the weal and there were small spouts of blood.

Golostchekin dropped the rod, picked another out of the
trough, and smashed again. Now he was laying it lower
down on Petrov's back. The fresh weal stood out brightly
on the white skin. The second rod split quickly, at sixty
blows. Golostchekin was sweating. By eighty Petrov's back
was turning from red to mauve.

Dostoevsky noticed the doctor was standing by eating
sunflower seeds, spitting out the husks with a peculiar
pouting of his lips. He was a Siberian of mixed blood who
was supposed to be one of Krivtsov's sexually perverted

creatures and only a medical orderly, not a qualified doctor.

"A hundred and forty." Petrov's neck seemed to have sunk lower on the bench. At two hundred the rod was hitting with a liquid sound, raising splashes of blood every time. There was blood in the dust all around the bench. The doctor sauntered over. Golostchekin stopped, wiping the sweat and blood spots off his arms and chest with a rag. The doctor turned Petrov's head around, examined him cursorily, stepped back, and nodded. Golostchekin smashed down the rod.

At two hundred and forty Petrov's arm, which had been lying along the bench, fell and dangled. He had lost consciousness. Golostchekin was using a rod that had split fifteen blows before; it was stinging his own hand and there were small pieces of flesh caught in the splits. Golostchekin threw it down and took another; he seemed intoxicated and looked horribly depraved.

The doctor came forward again at three hundred, felt Petrov's pulse, and glanced at his back. He said to the sergeant, "You'd better stop."

The convicts carried Petrov into the hut. They laid him on the sleeping bench, all behaving with great respect, consideration, exaggerated gravity. His back was like a blue jelly. They laid a wet sheet over it; in ten minutes Petrov shivered and came to. They kept soaking the sheet in cold water and laying it on his back as though he were in a fever. Then Derevenko, the artel man, took out a knife and began to extract the splinters. The blue and red jellied flesh was sewn with scores of splinters. They looked like roots of shaved hair under the surface. Petrov's lips quivered. Derevenko prized up the ends of the shallowest splinters and pulled them out. For the ones driven in deep he spat on the place, eased the knife point in, and probed.

At lockup time the senior sergeant came in. "You've got a hundred more, Petrov."

"I'll take them the day after tomorrow," Petrov said.

"This won't be healed, brother," Derevenko said.

Petrov spat weakly and said to the sergeant, "Tell Major Krivtsov I'll be ready for the rest the day after tomorrow."

My God, Dostoevsky thought. He had a strange impulse to rush up and kiss Petrov, his fellow sufferer, brother in guilt and misery. In all the brutality, there was something terrible and moving.

4

The snow began early. There were storms lasting two days, the drifts swallowing roads and barricading the buildings up to the eaves. As soon as the weather cleared and the sun came out they cleared the snow. Dostoevsky enjoyed it and saw with pleasure how all the other convicts set to heartily as well. The spade cut into the soft new snow, crisply frozen at the top and sparkling in the sun; he lifted huge blue and white cubes of it and threw it scattering into glistening powder. The convicts laughed and shouted jokes, invigorated by the fresh winter air, relishing the exercise. It usually ended in a ludicrous snowballing match.

Sometimes, with Dr. Troitzky's connivance, he stayed two weeks in the hospital ward. The doctor's wife sent him *Le Nord*, a French paper, and the doctor smuggled writing material to him. Derevenko and several others could not bear the arrival of another spring and "joined General Kukushka's army." The night before they escaped Baklushin came to him in the hut. "Why don't you change your luck, brother —come with us?"

"Thanks, Baklushin. I'd be no good, you know." He looked at Baklushin's good face and thought of him condemning himself as a brodyaga, everlastingly escaping and surrendering. He longed to be able to dissuade him but could not bring himself to try.

Baklushin said, "Listen, brother, there's tramping beginning all over Siberia now. God's people are going into the forests. You eat and drink what God sends you and you fall asleep in a peaceful place, brother. You're like a bird, you hop where you want!"

"I hope you manage it all right."

"Well, of course, you can have a hard time with General Kukushka sometimes," Baklushin said. He shrugged, giving Dostoevsky a quick glance. They had seen brodyagi brought in by the soldiers the summer before, their faces turned into swollen wounds, eyes buried in swollen eyelids, puffed nostrils and mouths covered with sores from the forest mosquito. And there were the Siberian peasants who sometimes spread through the forest and pitilessly exterminated the brodyagi they caught. Baklushin laughed in his simple way. "I'd have fifteen more years to do here—for my German! I'll shake that off."

"Wait a minute." Dostoevsky cast around for something to give him. And he had not a possession! At last he remembered a small tin with some Zhukov tobacco in it from a hospital patient who had died; Dr. Troitzky had given it to him. "Please take this, Baklushin." Baklushin smiled with pleasure and took the tin.

Next morning they made the break and escaped.

Only four days after this, returning from work, the men of the hut were surprised to find Alfonsky back in his place. He was jaunty, sly, confident, mocking at them, as good as telling them he was now safe. Derevenko, the leader of the artel, had gone; one of the other members had escaped with him. Gazin was in the hospital. Dostoevsky watched the rest of the artel. They were going to murder Alfonsky.

The long summer days were dry and warm. He worked strongly and willingly. He saw how the feeling of comradeship with the convicts had grown. Yes, he loved some of them. On their side there were many whose hatred had withered away. He could hardly treat the prospect of release as a reality. At first he was calm, patient, almost unconcerned. As the autumn rains began he grew more restless.

One evening Petrov, coming in from a task at the army barracks in the town, tossed him a smuggled, mutilated copy of *Annals of the Fatherland*. "Here, Fyodor Mikhailovich, you can read." Dostoevsky threw himself on it. Half the pages were missing but he read all night, the same pieces over and over, until daybreak. It was like news from a remote world. Petersburg, his former life, came back to him. Turning the pages, he tried to bridge the gaps of thought, to see how far he had dropped behind all that was stirring people's minds now. He found Turgenev's name, Nekrasov's; there were new names too. He became impatient and agitated. He was thirty-two years old! From that day on he was in a fever to end his sentence, to get away.

And at intervals in the endless winter evenings the atmosphere in the hut suddenly became tense. Nothing specific happened. The convicts worked, gambled, fought; the deafening racket, bawling and cursing voices, the clanking of chains went on as loud as ever. Then abruptly the tension seemed unbearable. He put it down to an impression caused by his own nervousness. Then he saw that the rest were waiting for the artel to kill Alfonsky.

Alfonsky was the only one who paid no attention. He no longer kept the maidan. But he was full of a sly, cocksure scorn and twice drank himself into unconsciousness as if he were sure the artel would do nothing.

They waited until his saint's day—he was named Evgenny Nikolayevich. The hut was locked up for the night. Four of them came over to him and took him to a space at the far end. They laid him on the floor boards, held him, and filled his eyes with powdered glass. Alfonsky shrieked. All the convicts kicked up a clatter, covering the noise, banging the platforms with their chains, bawling, looking at each other with their eyes shining, their toothless mouths grinning. The artel men crunched bricks from the stove onto Alfonsky's eyes, pressing down into the red froth. They had two freight sleigh-man's grappling hooks and caught Alfonsky on them and flung him. He became limp like a pierced sack of grain, they flung him, then cut away his clothes, slowly opened out his belly with their knives, and threw him into the excrement tub. He was still alive long after, his neck rag caught on the tub edge, his chin submerged. In the morning the guards took the body away. There was a cursory and vain inquiry. Izay Fomich cooed, "Krivtsov will keep him on the books!"

And then it was the last day. At daybreak he went through the huts saying good-by. Some of the convicts held out their hands cordially; others turned away with an oath; there were looks of hatred and indifference. The drum beat, and the convicts began to troop out to work. Dostoevsky gave his bits of rag, his fetter wrappers to Petrov.

"You'll be out soon, Petrov."

"Well—one day," Petrov said impassively. He shook Dostoevsky's hand; they kissed each other's cheeks. Ten minutes later the hut was empty. A sergeant called him out and he saw Durov in the yard. They went to the blacksmith's shop; it was strange going without an armed guard, only the sergeant. The convicts in the blacksmith's shop took their fetters off. Durov went first. Dostoevsky waited, then went up to the anvil too. The blacksmiths turned him around so that his back was toward them, lifted his leg up, and laid it on the anvil. They bustled, tried to do the task at their best, most skillful.

"The rivet, the rivet—turn that first of all," the senior blacksmith said. "Hold it—that's it, there. Now hit it."

The fetters fell off. Dostoevsky picked them up. He held them in his hands and looked at them for the last time; he wondered that they could have been on his legs a minute before.

"Well, with God's blessing, with God's blessing!" the con-victs said in coarse, abrupt, and yet pleased voices.

Yes, with God's blessing. Freedom! Resurrection!

He took the pen and wrote, scarcely able to put the words down fast enough.

"Mikhail, my brother. At last I can write to you openly. But before I say a word, I ask you why *in the name of God* haven't you written one single line to me? How was I to expect that? Sometimes in loneliness I despaired, thinking you were dead, and wondering for whole nights what had happened to your children, I cursed my helplessness. Then I bitterly reproached you. But that didn't last either. I forgave you, I tried to find justifications for you, and I never lost faith in you; I know you love me and keep good remembrance of me. I sent you one letter through the censorship. It surely reached you; but you didn't reply. They can't have forbidden you to write? It's allowed—all the 'politicals' receive letters. Durov had several. . . .

"Ah, you gave me a heavy heart! I said to myself, If he can't manage to get a letter to me, will he trouble when it comes to bigger things? Write to me as fast as you can, without waiting. Put everything in—everything—in detail, at length. I'm like a limb torn from you—and I want to grow back into place but I can't. . . ."

The date on the letter was February 22, 1854—seven days after his release from prison. He paused, lighted the cigarette that had gone out. Before him, through the window of the quiet room, were the streets of Omsk; a Kirghiz in his short sheepskin and red boots, a policeman with a big saber, a little cemetery with five shining crosses, a church with a green roof, and beyond a small group of windmills. He could just see the Irtysh and the camels crossing the ice on it like a string of tiny black seeds.

From the room below he heard the voices of Konstantin Ivanov, the engineer, and his wife, who had taken him in after his release while he awaited the second part of his sentence—transfer to a Siberian regiment. She was the daughter of Annenkov, the Decembrist. He turned back eagerly to the sheet, plunging into the past, the last night in

Petersburg, the journey to Siberia, the pain, longing, burning hopes. He conjured up his brother before him.

"Brother, don't forget me! My faith in you is still bright. You are my brother and you loved me. I must have some money and books. I must live, brother. These years won't go by without giving fruit. What you spend for me won't be wasted. If only I can live I'll repay your children and plenty over. Perhaps the authorities will let me publish something in six years or so; and this time I won't write rubbish. . . ."

The words raced from his pen. He filled pages. "I've had news of the others. Jastrzembsky is at Tara, Speshnev is in the Province of Irkutsk—and he has won the respect of everybody. Petrashevsky is just as ever, so is Mombelli. Pleshcheyev is in Orsk.

". . . Tell me everything, tell me about Emily Fyodorovna, the children, all the family and friends, those of Moscow, the living ones and the dead ones. Don't abandon me in the name of God."

He was still writing when Madame Ivanov knocked at the door and said, "It's lunchtime, Fyodor Mikhailovich."

In the evening he came up and finished the letter. "They are sending me to Semipalatinsk. It is almost on the Kirghiz steppe. Write to me: Second Class Soldier of the Line. Seventh Siberian Battalion, Semipalatinsk. I am starting out tomorrow."

PART TWO

Chapter Eight

1

He waded in the sand of the street, the rifle swinging on the strap and the folds of his white uniform tunic flapping. There was no pavement. The sand came over his ankles. This was the main street of Semipalatinsk. In the side streets it lay in drifts as high as a man against the ash-gray log houses. The garrison called Semipalatinsk the Devil's Sandbox.

He reached the gate with the striped sentry boxes and went in under the sign: Seventh Siberian Battalion; First Section. In the guardroom he unslung the rifle and stood it in the rack. He was just back from picket duty. "The general has just left," he said to the duty corporal, shifted the blanket roll across his chest, and wiped the sweat off his neck. There was a sort of mysterious satisfaction in the garrison life—the sentry duty, the drill in the sandy compound, and the endless parades. It was scarcely different in some material ways from the prison. The Seventh Siberian Battalion were a hard lot—serfs, professional soldiers, exiles. Half the officers were illiterates who lived for cards and drink with a strong interest in the local girls. But he got on with them well enough. After a few months they had allowed him to leave the barracks and live out.

He nodded to the corporal, went out, and trudged hurriedly along. A group of double-humped Bactrian camels loped by. The dark-faced Kirghiz men lolled on their backs, looking about with little beady eyes. Wooden mosques and minarets stood among the low wooden huts of the street.

In the whole of Semipalatinsk there was not a tree, a bush, or a blade of grass.

He crossed the Tartar market, catching the stinks of the Orient in the afternoon air. Flies sizzled up in clouds from the meat on sale and settled on again. He noticed a big Berkut eagle perched on a post nearby. Sometimes he saw the Kirghiz riding out, with the eagles perched on the heads of their horses, to hunt for wolves and foxes on the great steppe.

In a few minutes he reached Kapitolina Ivanovna's house where he lodged. The low gate in the fence made him duck —the attitude induced to catch would-be intruders, who could be banged on the head. He gave Kapitolina Ivanovna a brief salutation, quickly crossed the room, and stepped behind the curtain in one corner. There were fly-spotted woodcuts pinned up on the dirty whitewash, a bed, chair, wooden box for a table, and a stove. The ceiling was low and there were bugs in swarms; but it was the richest of privacy. Kapitolina Ivanovna, widow of a soldier, rented it to him and did his laundry for five rubles a month. Her daughters, Vatushka and Lubyenka, both under twenty, earned the rest of the family maintenance from the officers of the garrison.

Dostoevsky threw off the blanket roll and tunic, made a cigarette, and sat on the bed. But he could not sit still. He got up, lit the cigarette, and walked up and down. He had been feeling agitation and nervousness accumulating all day. The mental image of Alexander Ivanovich Issayev, the local excise inspector who clung drunkenly to him as a friend, came to him accusingly. He had half promised to see Issayev and since the morning he had been resisting the idea.

Issayev was a wreck. Dostoevsky had almost forgotten how they had met; it was intermixed with so many other thoughts and emotions about Issayev's wife, Marya Dmitrievna, and conflict about Issayev himself, a man of appalling weakness, of mean shabbiness, a soiler of beauty. One evening Issayev had been drunker than ever. Dostoevsky had helped him home and Marya Dmitrievna had appeared, to thank him, thin and fair-haired, big dark eyes in a pale face, her lips apart. He received the shock of her beauty. And he could see her saying to herself, It's only a soldier, one is not so ashamed before a soldier. She had begun to be kind to him. Kindness—when almost at once he was in love with her! She behaved as if she did not notice his feelings and yet entirely understood them. And he had found himself hiding behind Issayev, whom in a curious way he respected.

He drew with short nervous inhalations on the cigarette, walking up and down. She had soon understood he was not "just a soldier" and even when he told her he had been a convict she had become ashamed of her situation before him, ashamed of being the soiled beauty. They had never spoken about any of this, never discussed the situation, although there had been many moments when they skimmed it. But for her there was no "situation," as between the two of them.

She was ill, coughed a great deal. In quiet moments her face shone and she smiled in her intelligent-looking way when he talked about Petersburg. He saw she had already imagined all the life there. She listened smiling, carried away, exalted. "Yes, Fyodor Mikhailovich," Issayev said once, "my wife was educated in a high-class school for the daughters of noblemen, in Astrakhan. And when she left she danced the shawl dance before the governor and other personages and was presented with a gold medal and certificate of merit." He staggered drunkenly as he said this.

They had a boy of eight, Pasha. Issayev's drunkenness had dragged them all into the gutter. He had lost one post after another and at last drifted up like wreckage on the sands of Semipalatinsk.

A big spider darted out from under the bed. Dostoevsky kicked at it; it vanished. Ah, my God, he must resist going to see her! At moments there was an undercurrent of exasperation in their relationship that made him tremble when he thought of it. They had already had several raging scenes. She bore his outbursts of bad temper up to a certain point but then her own acerbity came out and they hacked at each other over nothing, over trivialities—because he was late, something she said about prison, a reflection of his on Semipalatinsk—until they were both pale and shaking, turned away from each other on opposite sides of the room with white lips. And an hour afterward or next day he was tortured with remorse, begging her forgiveness on his knees with sobs, calling her the most wonderful woman, thanking her for her generosity, she listening distressed and their explanations going on for hours afterward.

He fished up the watch hanging around his neck, an absurd crescent-shaped affair he had bought from a Kirghiz. It was past six o'clock. He was due at Lieutenant Colonel Belikhov's at seven to read the papers to him. Belikhov, the commanding officer of the battalion, could drink more than three Cossacks and outride a good many of them on his Kirghiz pony; but he was not a fluent reader. His fat wife treated Dostoevsky with scorn.

He crushed out the stub of cigarette, poured some water into his bowl, and began dousing his face. There was a shuffle behind him at the curtain. "Fyodor Mikhailovich, where shall I put this?" It was Vatushka, the landlady's younger daughter. She was holding a shirt of his which her mother had washed, her head slightly to one side, looking at him cunningly out of the corner of her black eyes. She was slim, with a golden skin, ankles and wrists a little too thick, loose-moving hips. The lower rim of her eyelashes was strongly marked and gave the eye a peculiar relief and beauty. The chemise she had carelessly tucked into her skirt was open to the waist.

"Oh, down there, Vatushka." He motioned with a wet hand and watched as she bent down to lay the shirt on the box table, seeing her breasts tilt forward, the dark pink smoothly rounded tip of one emerging from the chemise, seeing her pretending to clear a space for the shirt, stretching her skirt taut with her hips and legs. She looked up and laughed, put the shirt down, and came over to him.

"What's the matter, Fyodor Mikhailovich? Do you want me? For you it's one silver ruble." She leaned forward, the chemise touched him, and she gave a wriggle so that the round bare skin brushed his arm. When he smiled, however, she raised her shoulder defensively and looked at him over it with her eyebrows arching sadly. "Why do you despise me, Fyodor Mikhailovich?" And she burst out laughing, making him laugh too in spite of his nervous tension.

She noticed his tobacco and deftly rolled herself a cigarette.

"Where's Lubyenka?" he said, sluicing water.

"She's entertaining Lieutenant Sverlov. Ouf! I had him on Tuesday. He drives a girl to the devil. He drinks too much. Vatushka this and Vatushka that and wait till I have another drink. And then he goes to sleep and you have to stay there and listen to his concert of snores or he won't pay. And he wants to wear spurs. Pah!" She suddenly threw her skirt up and showed a cut on her thigh. "Look at that. Lieutenant Sverdlov!"

Dostoevsky was drying himself.

"What's all this writing?" she said, looking at the sheets of paper on the table.

"Some notes, that's all." They were notes he was making on the prison. "Go on, Vatushka, I'm in a hurry."

"Oh, I nearly forgot," she said, doing a pirouette. "His Excellency the count called for you this afternoon."

"Who? Do you mean Baron Vrangel?"

"Yes. I think he's handsome."

"Well, you'll be able to tell him so if you get into trouble, Vatushka—he's the Public Prosecutor."

She laughed. "He likes me, I can see it. Is he coming again?"

"Did he see you dressed like that?"

She protruded a hip. "Tell me about him, Fyodor Mikhailovich. You're his friend."

"Alexander Egorovich is a generous and handsome young man, Vatushka," he said. "But I—er—I don't think he's trying to outshine Lieutenant Sverdlov." Dostoevsky had struck up a warm friendship with the young Baron Vrangel, fresh from Petersburg. Vrangel had brought letters and books from Mikhail.

"Vatushenka! Vatushenka!" The landlady appeared at the curtain. "It's Captain Deryabin's orderly come for you, by the grace of God," she said. "Go on, my child—and do your best." Vatushka disappeared.

"Well, I must say, Kapitolina Ivanovna—you encourage them!" Dostoevsky said.

The landlady sighed. "Oh, Barin, you know how it is. Sooner or later they'd have gone to bed with the battalion store clerk or some corporal for a pound of nuts. And with the officers it pays better—and it's an honor. Excuse me, Barin, excuse me." She dropped the curtain and departed.

Dostoevsky dusted his tunic and trousers and hastened out. Lieutenant Colonel Belikhov lived in a gabled wooden house with flaking paint, garden benches outside, and a dried-up flower bed. As he walked up the pathway the front door flew open and Belikhov appeared, half lifting and half struggling with another figure and booming, "Yes, yes. Good night . . . you'll excuse me. Good night. We will discuss it another time." His uniform coat was unbuttoned and he looked annoyed.

The other man was Issayev, drunk and staggering. "But you see, my dear sir, it's a scandal," he was saying thickly. "Consider my position. Somebody must protest . . ." He waved his arms and lurched heavily against Belikhov. For a moment Belikhov stood entangled rather foolishly with him, keeping him upright yet unable to prop him on his feet.

Issayev, who did not know Belikhov very well, had evidently
made an unwelcome call.

Dostoevsky halted. An instant earlier he could have retreated. He looked around—but too late. Belikhov saw him
and seized the opportunity. "Dostoevsky, come here, come
here. Our friend doesn't feel well. You'll see him home. No,
no—never mind about the papers." He transferred Issayev's
weight to Dostoevsky. "There you are, my dear sir, Alexander Ivanovich, this man will accompany you. We'll discuss
your little matter another time. Good night. Good night."
He glared fiercely at Dostoevsky, making imperative signs
for him to take Issayev away—and, turning, slammed the
door on both of them.

Issayev looked up. "What, Fyodor Mikhailovich, is it you?
Everything's lost, everything. It's disaster." He seemed to be
on the point of breaking into tears, then made an effort,
stood firmly, and said, "Come, we'll go." He looked like a
defeated and broken clerk. His face, bloated from constant
drinking, had a yellowish tinge and red eyes that looked out
through chinks. There was bristle on his chin. He wore an
old greasy black dress coat hooked on lopsidedly by the one
remaining button, a canvas waistcoat, and a shirt covered
with spots. As they turned along the street he lurched again
and suddenly blurted out, "What do I care? Everybody
knows it already. I accept it all with humble thanks. Listen,
Fyodor Mikhailovich, do you *dare* to assert that I'm not a
pig? Do you dare?"

Dostoevsky said, "What has happened, Alexander Ivanovich?" Issayev had been suspended weeks before from his
duties in the excise service and in the resulting idleness had
sunk still deeper into alcoholism.

"I've been dismissed," he said. "I was expecting a transfer.
I've not been a success here, no. But they've struck me out
of the service. Yes, entirely! It's all over. I thought I would
appeal to Colonel Belikhov; he could speak to our governor,
Alexey Pavlovich. Well, I had a glass or two to pluck up

courage. And then, you see, I knew Belikhov would not like me calling at his house." He leered quickly at Dostoevsky. "So I went. Because I accept it all with humble thanks. I only suffer because of Marya Dmitrievna. Yes, I am a pig but she is a woman of noble feelings. And do you know, Fyodor Mikhailovich, that I have just sold her shoes for vodka? She prized them particularly and kept them hidden away from me. But I sold them. That's the sort of toad I am. And she is everlastingly cleaning those rooms of ours, tidying, letting out Pasha's old clothes so that they will last a bit longer, and even buying cabbage on credit. She's ill, of course; but you know she's terribly bad-tempered; and when she's excited her cheeks are bright red and her breathing seems to be scratching and scraping out of her chest. You've heard it. Well, Fyodor Mikhailovich, the moment I sold the shoes I saw her face, yes, in one of her worst moments; and I accepted less for the shoes because of that very image."

Issayev rambled drunkenly on and on as they made their way through the streets. His efforts at self-control lasted part of the way but as they came nearer to his lodging he kept staggering and clutching at Dostoevsky's arm.

"Do you understand what it is when you have nowhere to turn, Fyodor Mikhailovich?"

"Surely there's somebody in the service who can help you?"

"Th-that's just it. I've promised everybody to cure myself if they'd give me another chance. But what's the good of a last chance unless you enjoy it, eh?" He gave a helpless laugh and fell into the sand but refused help with a drunken, absurd dignity and staggered up.

Dostoevsky felt the excitement of approaching her. Issayev's disaster made the voluptuousness far more intense. He wanted to tell her he was in love with her. At the house, Issayev pitched in headfirst and flopped on the bench by the wall. The place was bare but clean. Marya Dmitrievna came in from the other room. Dostoevsky stood looking at her and then rushed over, took her hands, and kissed them, smelling the faint scent she carried and looking up to her black deep eyes. She had a broad forehead with hair parted in the middle. Her lips were pale like her face.

"Marya Dmitrievna, I wanted to see you very much." She allowed him to retain her hands long enough to transmit the hint of complicity and suddenly flushed and stood away. It was one of the flashes that recurred with her, an encouragement and withdrawal. Then she was past him and looking at her husband lying on the bench.

"I thought you were going to see the governor?"

"Masha, I saw Colonel Belikhov. Fyodor Mikhailovich will tell you." He made an effort and managed to sit up. "Listen, Masha—I took your shoes. I drank that too."

Dostoevsky watched her with desire. "My God!" she said furiously, took a quick breath as if she were going to cover Issayev with insults—and was seized with a fit of coughing. The sound raked up her chest and throat, her face reddened, she bent forward. Issayev gestured helplessly. Dostoevsky put out an arm and she leaned on it. When she had recovered she served a poor meal of cabbage soup, rice, and bread. They put the boy, Pasha, to bed and Issayev lay sleeping on the bench. The two of them sat together opposite as they had on many evenings before. The candle burned by the open window and they could hear the faint throb of the night watchmen's rattles outside. Dostoevsky spoke in a low voice about Petersburg, the great fetes in the Hall of the Nobility in Moscow. The color was in her cheeks. His hand caressed her arm, her waist, lightly smoothed the side of her breast. Issayev stirred on the bench. Dostoevsky felt her waist and the curve of her hips. She leaned toward him, her head came lightly onto his shoulder, and his lips touched her neck. She shifted away and got up. "Please go." He kissed her hand, turned, and hurried out in a fever.

2

As soon as he was off duty next afternoon he rushed to see
Vrangel. Baron Vrangel was beginning his official career as
Public Prosecutor when only twenty-one years old. He was
tall, lymphatic, as emotional as a woman, and wore his uniform with great elegance. His arrival from Petersburg had
thrown the wives and daughters of the town into confusion.
The officials were impressed, above all, by his refusal to take
bribes.

He and Dostoevsky became friends at once. At their first
meeting, when he had delivered the letters and books from
Mikhail, Vrangel began to speak of the execution scene in
the Semyenovsky Square. "I was there. I remember watching you," he said.

"What?" Dostoevsky's face changed; he recognized the
young man he had seen in the "last minutes"—the whiskers,
the clipped mustache, the expression of despair. "Yes, yes.
I saw you too, in the crowd." They had met almost daily
ever since.

He found Vrangel about to leave in his carriage. "I'm
going out to the Jardin des Cosaques to look at a house,"
Vrangel said. "Come along." The Jardin des Cosaques was
a suburb. Dostoevsky got in and they started. He was consumed with the need to tell Vrangel about Marya Dmitrievna; but as they drove he saw that Vrangel was in a
somber mood. The carriage floated silently along in the
sand like a boat on calm water. Vrangel sat looking gloomily
out without a word. They left the massed wooden huts behind, turned along by the Irtysh, and presently drove through
a high gateway up to a vast dilapidated house. A watchman
who evidently expected Vrangel was waiting. "It's as Lav-
renty Parfenyevich left it, your honor," he said. "He just
went out one day to go to Moscow and hasn't been back.
You won't see another house like it in the province."

They went up the front steps and entered. Layers of dust covered everything and seemed to muffle their intrusion. They felt the dust on the carpets and caught the dry smell and the taste of it on their lips. The candelabra were blackened. Dostoevsky lit a candle and they went wandering through room after room, their reflections moving faintly before them in the gray mirrors. As they stood again in the main downstairs room with the shutters thrown open, looking out at the big garden sloping down to the river, Vrangel seemed to brighten up.

"Alexander Egorovich——" Dostoevsky turned, paced along the room, and came feverishly back to Vrangel. "I trust and honor you. I need to tell you this, as a dear friend. I'm in love with a woman here. She is the most divine and wonderful creature, a woman of incomparable qualities. But it is hopeless—hopeless. She's married. I think of her constantly. And she is being disgraced, here in Semipalatinsk. You know I'm an uneasy man; but she's had nothing but cares and worries. How can she support it? You don't know her; you don't know her. She has the goodness of a child. She held out her hand to me. Oh, we've had quarrels, yes. But it was because I was an ungrateful pig. And she's ill, Alexander Egorovich, she's ill, upset, offended—offended at not being appreciated by people in this Godforsaken hole. Life and unhappiness have naturally worsened some things in her, but she is noble and honest and she is indignant at injustice. You don't know what they've become to me, those two—yes, he as well, the husband. He's a poor devil, but a truly noble soul, yes, yes. He's an educated man, he can talk on anything. If they hadn't existed perhaps I would have become hardened for good. And now I'm a new man, I've revived. Do you understand, Alexander Egorovich?" His face was flushed with excitement.

"Yes," Vrangel said. He looked ahead, out of the window. "It's the same with me, my friend. I'm in love too. I met her in Petersburg. That was where it began. I can have no pretensions; that is out of the question. She is also married."

"She is here, isn't she?" Dostoevsky said; he had guessed it some time back.

Vrangel nodded. They looked at each other, Vrangel sad, Dostoevsky glowing with restless anxiety. "Oh, my friend, what are we going to do?" Vrangel said.

"If only I were free. I've three more years to do! What will become of her in three years? I'll lose her, Alexander Egorovich, I'll lose her. You must come with me to see her. She's an angel. You will see. She's persecuted here; they despise and humiliate her, but she doesn't murmur. You'll show the people here that you see her goodness, my friend. It's only her misfortunes that have made her emotive and nervous. At heart she's gay and lively. Promise you'll allow me to introduce you."

"I shall be honored," Vrangel said.

"Ah, Alexander Egorovich—when you know her you'll see. She's an angel."

Vrangel took the house and moved in. Dostoevsky resisted his invitations to join him; he wanted independence. But he helped Vrangel install himself and went out to the Jardin des Cosaques several times a week after duty with the battalion. At night when he returned to his lodging he tried to put himself to the task of writing. It was a strange process after five years. Fear of the censor half paralyzed him, the writing instrument was awkward in his hand, and his creative thoughts led off in unusual directions. Apart from his notes on life in the prison which he was extending, he found he was tempted to try a comic genre, with plain straightforward action and caricature instead of analysis. He had two short novels in mind with provisional titles: *The Village of Stepanchikovo* and *Uncle's Dream*.

They were built on character and both, he felt, Gogolesque. He had been reading Gogol again and the "manner" had completely flooded him once more. The pivot of *The Village of Stepanchikovo* was Foma Fomich Opiskin, a posturing, hypocritical charlatan, a braggart with an unquenchable gift of the gab. He was a rich and enjoyable figure to do. Foma Fomich fastened himself onto Egor Ilyich Rostanev, a retired colonel, took over his household, tyrannized everybody, and tormented the life out of the weak, good-natured Egor Ilyich.

Dostoevsky wanted to give Foma Fomich the attributes of a Double— showing first his despotic nasty side, then, with a sudden twist, turning him into a honeyed, amiable creature, no less grotesque. He was going to do this by having Egor Ilyich rebel, throw him out of the house, and Foma Fomich return a changed man. One thing was particularly striking. Mentally projecting the story, he found the compulsion of the Double, the dual character, as strong as ever. He set great store by the book.

In *Uncle's Dream*, the uncle was Prince K, a senile, rouged, mechanical old corpse with stays, false teeth, and wig, doddering away his last years in a provincial town. The leading figure of the town, Marya Alexandrovna Moskaleva, made him tipsy and induced him to propose to her daughter. But a disgruntled suitor intervened; and as Marya Alexandrovna was about to give out the news of the engagement to gathered neighbors, the prince appeared, announced that everything had been a dream, and upset the whole scheme. There were amusing things in the story.

But after working a little on one or the other he jumped up, overcome by restlessness, tormented by thoughts about Marya Dmitrievna and a desire to see her. One day she said to him, "God knows what will become of Pasha. He is learning nothing at this school."

"I can give him lessons. Yes, yes, Marya Dmitrievna, I can repay some of your kindness and Alexander Ivanovich's."

He began to tutor the boy. Every evening he sat in her presence, his mind only lightly engaged on the lesson, watching her, talking to her, often teaching her with an intensity and fire that carried him away and bound her absorbed, elbows on the table, her eyes on him, her lips apart in the light humorous smile of admiration and marvel. Once or twice she met him with the boy outside and they walked rather self-consciously along the riverbank, Dostoevsky in his gray uniform overcoat, she holding the boy's hand between them. Vrangel found her "an exceptional woman" and said to Dostoevsky, "I haven't seen anybody like her since Petersburg." Then one day she consented to visit the Jardin des Cosaques. They drove out with Vrangel and spent a hilarious afternoon with his menagerie of dogs, eagles, pet foxes, and a colony of grass snakes they had found underneath the front steps. She had lost the touch of sharpness she had sometimes and was gay and entertaining in an excitable way. It was growing dark when Dostoevsky drove back with her. He was in a feverish state. She let him take her hand and he covered it with kisses until she drew it away again. He dismissed the driver a short distance from her lodging and walked on with her. There was a small open space with an incongruous statue to Suvarov tilting on its base in the sand and a bench in front of it.

"Marya Dmitrievna, please, one moment," he said in an intense way. As they sat down she turned and looked at some white-robed mullahs going past from the mosque and he saw she would not stay long. "Marya Dmitrievna, I wanted to say thank you for coming today. You don't know what you have been for me. No, no, you don't. All this, you—it's an entire phase of my life. A woman's heart, a woman's affection and compassion, they are irreplaceable for a man. I've found all that in you. I've never considered our meeting as an ordinary encounter. If you can feel that as I do——"

"Fyodor Mikhailovich, I must leave you. It's late."

"No, listen, listen." He put his arm around her waist, leaning urgently close to her. "I've lived for five years without anybody to open my heart to. I am in love with you,

Marya Dmitrievna. You know it. I have expressed it before without words and now I want to express it with all passion and humility. Yes, yes. You are the only woman, the first woman I have loved, Marya Dmitrievna. I swear that is true. For months I have scarcely been able to think of anything else except when I would see you again, when I could look at you, even when I'd seen you a few hours before."

"Wait, please——" He was trying to hold her closer, struggling a little awkwardly with her on the bench and somehow ashamed and pleased with the awkwardness. She disengaged herself and stood up. "Fyodor Mikhailovich, I —we shall be going away. Alexander Ivanovich has found a post." She paused at the expression on his face. "I should have told you before."

"Going? Do you mean from Semipalatinsk?"

"Yes. To Kuznetsk."

"What?" His heart gave a heave. "It's not possible. Kuznetsk—it's an immense distance. It's five—seven hundred versts. I'll never see you."

"Alexander Ivanovich has a post there. You understand, Fyodor Mikhailovich; it's so important for us, for Pasha." She was almost matter-of-fact.

"But isn't he out of the service? Hasn't he been dismissed?"

She looked pained and faintly irritated. "It is not a post in the service; he will be assistant at the tribunal, the civil court. Oh, of course it is nothing of any standing, much less than Alexander Ivanovich had here." She turned her head and muttered, "It's scarcely enviable."

"But you have accepted it too, Marya Dmitrievna?"

"Yes."

"When are you going?"

"In a week."

"My God!" He knew he would not realize it until much later; and then it would be worse than it was now; now was the almost pleasurable part of learning. There was a distinct pleasure in it. It would be painful later. "Yes, we must think of Alexander Ivanovich," he said. "Perhaps it will save him." She was holding herself back out of nobility of soul, he told himself. She was an angel.

She laid her hand on his arm. "I'm sorry; it is inescapable. Now Pasha is waiting. Good night." She turned away. He ran after her.

"Marya Dmitrievna, my angel. My angel." They were at the picket fence before the house. It was almost dark. "Is it possible that in a week we are going to say good-by, that we are not going to see each other again? No, no, Marya Dmitrievna, my angel . . ." He took her hands and bent over, kissing them feverishly.

"Good night." She broke away abruptly. In a moment he saw the faint light of the doorway, her silhouette in it, then she shut the door and he was looking at the dark. He hurried away in great agitation.

3

"But, Alexander Egorovich, she accepted it! She didn't protest." Dostoevsky threw himself into the chair; his face was gray and perspiring and his collar undone. "She hasn't tried to stop it. It's terrible."

"My dear friend, I——"

"Assistant at the tribunal. He is going to be assistant at the tribunal; that means at the best a clerk, probably a janitor. And she won't complain of it; I know her. She'll suffer, my angel. Yes, she will. Ah, my God!" He jumped up again and went toward the window.

Vrangel flipped his dressing gown over his leg and sipped his tea; he was still sleepy. Dostoevsky had arrived in a fever, very early, before the servants were awake, and told him everything.

"If you'd heard her. 'It's scarcely enviable,' she said. She is appalled but she won't say so. She is thinking of him, you see. Oh, he's a man of culture, after all; he feels the disgrace.

But she is sacrificing herself, Alexander Egorovich, that noble, pure creature."

"But it will be a fresh start, a new life, a new circle," Vrangel said. "That may change everything for them. She accepted because of that."

"Because it will change everything?" He looked at Vrangel with a tortured expression. "Yes, that's surely the reason."

"No, no. I didn't mean that," Vrangel intervened quickly. "I'm sorry, I expressed myself badly."

"Do you know, Alexander Egorovich, since it is like that, I want to tell you something vile," Dostoevsky said with a white face. "I feel secretly that the whole thing is an insult— her preference, the fact that she wants to go away to Kuznetsk with her drunken husband. You see how degrading such a thought is? I am ashamed of it; but I can't help it. I don't want to feel it and then, yes, I purposely encourage it. And in spite of myself I'm bound to have this unworthy feeling at moments of most intense love and respect for her. She can't go, she can't go, Alexander Egorovich! How can I lose her?" He sat down again, clasping his head and rocking from side to side. "Perhaps they won't be able to leave. Issayev has so many debts here."

Vrangel said quietly, "As a matter of fact, I collected them and paid them off."

"What? But, Alexander Egorovich——"

"I didn't think it would be painful to you," Vrangel said in a wounded voice.

"No. My God, no." Dostoevsky rushed over to him. "Thank you, thank you. It was a generous thing. I'm upset, you understand. Forgive me. She'll bless you for it, yes, yes. You've saved a noble soul. Now there's nothing to stop her. Yes, you've saved them both. They can begin a new life. I— I——" He embraced Vrangel and rushed out of the room.

Vrangel organized the departure. Dostoevsky came to him two days before and said restlessly, "I've just discovered they haven't the money to hire a carriage with. They can't even take their bits of furniture. There's nothing, not a kopeck. For the love of God, help them, Alexander Egorovich. Think of them, that truly good woman, the boy."

"Yes, of course."

Vrangel invited them all to drink a farewell toast at the Jardin des Cosaques on the day of departure; then he and Dostoevsky would accompany the Issayevs a little on their way. Dostoevsky was in a fever all day; it was late when he was released from duty and he did not reach the Jardin des Cosaques until almost dark. An uncovered country cart piled with furniture and baggage, with mattresses and pillows for the travelers, stood at the steps. Marya Dmitrievna was talking to Vrangel in the drawing room; she had on a blue traveling dress. He crossed the room toward her, feeling the ugly roughness of his appearance in the white and gray uniform and boots, his perspiring face, his eyes on her dark eyes and her parted lips. She smiled and he bent over her hand. There was her faint scent.

"Ah, there you are, Fyodor Mikhailovich." Issayev jogged him tipsily. "Bless the baron, eh? The baron is our benefactor, isn't he?" He swayed, putting his mouth close to Dostoevsky's ear in a reek of alcohol. "D'you know he gave us the money for a phaeton; we could have traveled in comfort. But I drank it, so we have that cart, that telega." He laughed. His chin trembled and with disgust and pity Dostoevsky saw there were tears in his eyes.

"Here, Alexander Ivanovich, your glass is empty," Vrangel said, taking his arm. "Fyodor Mikhailovich, will you give Madame Issayeva some champagne?" He tried to lead Issayev away but Issayev was in a perverse humor, twisted away, and rocked back, saying in a loud voice, "Our benefactor. Everybody drink to our benefactor. Look at this French—what's it? Veu—vo Cli—— Hold that bottle up, Fyodor Mikhailovich. Veuve Clicquot. I must kiss it, then I'll kiss you, Alexander Egorovich." He kissed the bottle and

embraced Vrangel with effusion, spilling the champagne
from his glass without noticing it. "But it's adieu. I must embrace Fyodor Mikhailovich too. Marya Dmitrievna, you must
sing a *hymne d'adieu* in French." He shook under a hiccup.
"*Mais, messieurs*—my wife's grandfather was a French
émigré, Monsieur Constant. '*Allons enfants de la pat*——' "
he sang, raising his glass and staggering.

He went on noisily, pushing Vrangel off when he tried to
lead him away, calling for Pasha, making drunken speeches.
Vrangel kept refilling his glass. Dostoevsky managed to take
Marya Dmitrievna to one side and they stood near the window looking at the last faintly green luminous patch of sky
in the distance. He was overwrought, anxious and unhappy.
"Marya Dmitrievna, I beg you, write to me as soon as you
arrive. A few lines, anything, anything. Think of me, my
angel, waiting here for a word. For the love of God, take
care of your health; put yourself in the care of a doctor.
Think of Pasha, think of the future. Ah, if only I could come
with you."

She put her hand on his arm and stood looking at him and
he was full of emotion and bitter happiness and pain. At last
Vrangel said they ought to start. Issayev was sprawled in a
chair, his head nodding; but when Vrangel tapped his
shoulder and said they were going he started up waving his
arms and exclaiming. "No—not going yet. Sing—'*senfants
de–la–pa-tr-ie*——' "

"That's right," Vrangel said. "You come with me in the
landau and we'll take a bottle of champagne with us."

"Bravo! Cham——" He could hardly stand. Outside, Vrangel's landau was drawn up in front of the cart. With a sign to
Dostoevsky, Vrangel half carried Issayev to the landau and
tipped him in. Dostoevsky put Pasha in the cart, helped
Marya Dmitrievna in, and got in beside her. Vrangel's carriage moved off, the peasant driving the cart snapped the
reins, and they started. Marya Dmitrievna covered Pasha
with blankets and the boy went to sleep at once.

They rolled slowly past the last houses of Semipalatinsk into the open country. The full moon was shining a greeny-white light on everything. There was Vrangel's landau ahead, the long straight empty road and the vast steppe all around. He knew it was all there, it was part of the invisible present of which Marya Dmitrievna occupied everything. He held her with his arm around her waist. They spoke quietly. The motion of the cart was softened by the sand and then the thick dust of the road.

"Oh yes, all this has been precious to me, Fyodor Mikhailovich. You know that."

"Isn't it more? Isn't it more than friendship, Marya Dmitrievna? I love you. You have changed everything—everything."

She raised her hand and caressed his cheek. He bent toward her, her lips were half open. He kissed her and she held him to her, her arms around his neck; then she laid her head on his shoulder and he took her hand, covering it with kisses.

The moon rose higher over the empty landscape. The night was warm. At last the cart slowed and stopped. Dostoevsky looked up and saw Vrangel's landau by the roadside just ahead. It was the moment of separation. His panic was restrained by the feeling of unreality. They climbed down. Vrangel was leaning inside the carriage, dragging out Issayev, who was unconscious. Dostoevsky ran up and helped him. Together they hoisted Issayev into the cart.

"Good-by, madame." Vrangel kissed her hand and walked back to the landau.

There were tears in her eyes. They threw themselves into each other's arms.

"Good-by. Good-by."

"It isn't the end. We shall see each other again."

She broke away and he went forward and helped her into the cart. A loud snuffling snore came from Issayev. The driver snapped the reins, the bells jingled on the harness, and the cart rumbled slowly forward. He walked with it a little way, then stopped. The cart gradually drew away. He could see her looking back, waving from time to time. The sound of the little bells was dying away in the distance. He stood still, looking after her on the deserted moonlit road until the darkness and the little cloud of dust following the cart hid it altogether. His tears fell in streams. His heart was brimming over. He was overcome with despair. He felt Vrangel's hand on his shoulder and turned and they went slowly back to the carriage.

Chapter Nine

1

He walked up and down the room between the red armchair and the table edge. The glass of some ornament vibrated with his tread as he approached the far end and then, just before he turned, another rattled. The lamp low down at one side threw his shadow across the wall and ceiling; the windows were open, giving the faint fresh earthy intimation of night.

The door opened and Vrangel came in blinking, looking dusty. "Good God, Fyodor Mikhailovich, what are you doing here?" Vrangel had been away for two days to a nearby town on official business. Dostoevsky rushed over to him and clasped his hands fervently. "They said you were coming back tonight."

"Do you know what time it is? Two o'clock."

"Excuse me, excuse me, Alexander Egorovich. I had to wait for you." He was in a state of high tension. "I've had a letter from Marya Dmitrievna."

"I hope she's settling down in Kuznetsk."

"My God, how could she?" Dostoevsky said in a trembling voice. "There's nothing but gossip in that place. Night and day. Issayev is titular assessor to the court. The post scarcely exists! He sweeps up, trims the lamps, and locks the door. They haven't any money. He managed not to drink a drop for forty-eight hours—and then didn't come home for three days and she had to go to the courtroom and see the judge and pretend he was ill in bed with fever. Ah, my angel, my angel."

Vrangel had taken a carafe and was pouring wine into two glasses. "But listen, listen, Alexander Egorovich. All that's painful enough, but listen." Dostoevsky was scrabbling a letter from his pocket. "This is what she says; listen to it. 'So my only real pleasure here is chatting with our new friend; he is a young teacher from the local school, a young man of excellent qualities, attentive and good.'" He seized Vrangel's arm and stared at him, trembling, at a pitch of excitement. "'A new friend'—what can she mean by it? A young teacher, a young man; she says 'young' twice. And 'attentive,' she says. My God, Alexander Egorovich, my God!"

"It's probably some ordinary acquaintance."

"No, no, no." He wrung his hands. "She wouldn't write like that about him. She hates the place. Issayev has disgraced her already. The neighbors spy on her and she is weak and alone. 'My only real pleasure . . .' He has seen she is alone and unprotected. He has seen she's a stranger, with no one near her, a noble, pure woman who is yearning for some small sign of affection, who'll trust herself——"

"You're upsetting yourself for no reason."

"But for God! Why should she write to me like that? Why should she talk about him? Why must she say he's her only comfort? I know her, Alexander Egorovich. I know her. And what can I do? If I could see her; if I could talk to her for an hour, a few minutes, I could settle everything. But I'm chained here. I can't move."

"Fyodor Mikhailovich, calm yourself. You are jumping to conclusions. Here—drink a glass of wine. Sit down."

"He has 'excellent qualities'—you see, she has considered them, she has thought about his character. He is in her thoughts."

Vrangel tried to reassure him but Dostoevsky would not be calmed. He went on marching up and down, talking until dawn came through the window, Vrangel sitting in the red plush chair, held, in spite of his fatigue, by Dostoevsky's inexhaustible fever, his racing thought.

Eight days later at the battalion headquarters there was another letter from her. He fingered the envelope, deliberately put it unopened into his pocket, and left it there until he was almost ill with suspense. When he read it there was no mention of the new friend. He seemed scarcely to be living in the intervals between her letters; he wrote to her fifteen, twenty pages at a time and wore down Vrangel in endless discussion. In a fit of anxiety he said to Vrangel one night, "I did the wrong thing this morning. I asked Belikhov for a few days' leave. He refused: he has orders from Petersburg that I'm not to leave Semipalatinsk."

"What are your times of duty? Sometimes you have a break of about forty-eight hours, don't you?"

"Occasionally. There is a period at the end of this week."

"Come, let's see. Write it down." Vrangel sat studying the times. Then he said, "I think I can manage to take you to see her."

"What? It's not possible—seven hundred versts!"

"We can risk being away for a day and two nights. Write to her at once, saying you will meet her at Zmiev—it's halfway between here and Kuznetsk. Say we will be there in four days' time. Next Tuesday, from 6 A.M. on, at the post station."

"My God, Alexander Egorovich, we shall never manage it."

"Yes, we will if we drive hard," Vrangel said. "You must write at once."

He sent the letter and lived in a fever for the next three days. But on the day they were to leave there was disaster. One of the political exiles, a doctor living in the local "free command," broke the bounds of his allotted area and went outside the town to attend a man who had been badly clawed by an eagle. He was arrested. In an excess of zeal, the governor ordered restrictions on all political exiles. Dostoevsky was called to the guardroom and told to report daily four hours after he went off duty.

He stood in Vrangel's drawing room in the evening overcome with anxiety. Vrangel said, "We'll find an alternative. We'll change the arrangements."

"But she'll be waiting. She won't understand what has happened if we don't arrive. We can't let her wait there alone, she'll have no money. It will drive her toward this new friend. Think of that, Alexander Egorovich. *What are we going to do?*"

Vrangel was tapping nervously with a paper knife; he threw it down. "Very well. I'll go and see Lamotte." Lamotte was the regimental doctor, a Pole deported to Semipalatinsk for a political offense, an intelligent, kind man. "We'll have to risk bringing him into it. I'll tell him you've had a fit today and have to stay in bed all day tomorrow."

"If he suspects it isn't true it will cripple everything."

"I'll plead with him. You won't have long with her—perhaps an hour. We shall have to be back by eight o'clock on Wednesday morning."

"By six! By six!"

"Stay here. Don't go outside." Vrangel left.

It was a fine, sunny evening. Dostoevsky wandered restlessly around the room. The sound of some wind instrument, trailing, breaking off, undulating, came from far off. He could not keep still—pursued by the thought of her waiting, lost, distressed, and humiliated, in the strange town; she might even be unable to return to Kuznetsk! The collar of his tunic pressed under his chin, the room was stifling. He tore the collar open. Above all, he must not have a fit now!

The face of the "new friend" tormented him; he had imagined it long since, a military face with little eyes, a narrow black mustache, and a woman's small mouth. He called him Oladyin. Oladyin had offensive breath; and she didn't notice it. Ah, that was one of the most outrageous things of all, that Marya Dmitrievna did not notice his breath! He always deliberately dwelt on the image when it came to him—Oladyin leaning close to her and saying something that made her laugh, open her mouth, and inhale his offensive breath. He had another idea about Oladyin—that she respected him. Perhaps Oladyin was a man of high qualities who had only sunk into baseness, but she greatly respected and even feared him.

He turned quickly around when Vrangel entered. "Well? What does he say?"

"Lamotte won't help. He won't give us away, but he said he will not be able to intercede if Belikhov orders you to be brought to the barracks hospital or wants to see you. Lamotte is a political himself. It's understandable."

"Yes, yes." He grasped Vrangel's arm. "We must go. Hurry —hurry!"

"I have already reported that you're ill. The horses are coming. Change your clothes." They had a suit ready, since Dostoevsky could not be seen in uniform. Vrangel told his servant, Adam, to keep the house shut all next day and not to let anybody in. But the horses he had ordered arrived two hours late. It was long past the time they had set as the last limit when they slammed the door and the carriage bounded out through the gateway.

The driver whipped up and they flew. By daylight they went still faster. The carriage leaped, the wheels spun in the air and crunched down in the sudden dips, banged against ridges so that everything was constantly shuddering and creaking and they lurched inside, holding fast to keep their seats. Vrangel reckoned that they would reach Zmiev by about six o'clock next morning—a run of about twenty-eight hours. Dostoevsky paled with impatience at the post stations. The boys sent out to bring the fresh horses disappeared. After vociferations, threats, and bribes the post-keeper yawned and scratched and sent messengers after them who also vanished and at the moment when all seemed lost they returned with the new team.

It seemed to Dostoevsky that they crawled. He hung out of the window shouting to the driver, "Go on! Faster— faster. Use your whip!"

"My God!" Vrangel dragged at his coattails. "If he goes any faster we'll overturn."

At one post station they walked straight into Zhiganovsky, the assistant mining engineer at Semipalatinsk, a friend of Belikhov's, who was traveling in the opposite direction. He greeted Vrangel with familiarity and was full of questions. Dostoevsky stood on the far side of the room with his back turned. As they left he saw Zhiganovsky looking after him curiously.

"Does he know you?" Vrangel said, with a pale face.

"He's seen me twice at Belikhov's; but he was tipsy. Anyway he is an unintelligent man. Driver, for God's sake—go *faster!*"

The road climbed the lower slopes of the Altai and pitched down bends strewn with boulders. They plunged toward rotten-looking bridges, the driver hastily crossing himself as they rushed down the slope, the carriage hitting the planks with a fearful jolt and the whole bridge rumbling and rattling and then the thumps and lurching beginning again on the far side.

It was full day when they reached Zmiev. He had proposed meeting Marya Dmitrievna at the post station or alternatively at the one hotel the town possessed, the Hotel Sibir. He was shaking, leaning out of the window as they drove up. There were two groups of people and several carriages outside the post station; she was not among them. He hurried inside. The room was empty except for a rosy-faced old man smilingly asleep on the bench. Dostoevsky banged on the door in the partition; a woman came.

"Is Madame Issayeva here? I've come to meet her. It's by arrangement . . ." The woman listened with a dense expression.

"No, Barin. Nobody like that has been here."

He paused, nodded thanks, and hurried out. "The Hotel Sibir. She's waiting at the hotel." He could hardly keep his seat beside Vrangel. The Hotel Sibir was on the main square, a one-story log building. From the front door he stepped directly into an odorous room with a board floor full of rat holes and thumbed paint on the walls. A man in a red flannel shirt was squatting on a stool, taking snuff in a prolonged way; he held a dish with some sort of food in it on his knees and sprinkles of snuff fell down into it.

"Please call Madame Issayeva," Dostoevsky said. The place repelled him; he wanted to take her away at once. The man said there were only two men staying in the hotel; he had never heard of Madame Ignatyeva.

"Issayeva! Iss-ay-eva." Dostoevsky stepped up to him, repeating it urgently; in the end the man shrugged and went away carrying the snuff-sprinkled food.

Dostoevsky rushed out. Vrangel was yawning beside the carriage. "She's not here. There is some mistake. We're missing her." They drove back to the post station but the woman there knew nothing more, nor did the hostlers. Dostoevsky was beside himself. "We must find her, Alexander Egorovich. We must find her."

They left the carriage while the horses were changed and drove through the streets in a droshky, scanning the passersby, stopping, returning. Dostoevsky ran in and out of churches, shops, the postal bureau, even the one-room Natural History Museum, full of forlorn, dusty exhibits assembled by an exile long since dead. Vrangel became increasingly nervous and kept looking at his watch. At last he said, "We shall have to leave."

"Let's try the market once more; she may be there." They searched the market vainly, then returned to the post station. The carriage with the change of horses was waiting.

"We have barely twenty hours to get back in," Vrangel said.

"Alexander Egorovich, *I can't go!*" Dostoevsky stared at him.

"Do you understand what the consequences will be?"

The keeper of the post station was beside them, holding

an envelope to his nose and reading out from it painfully, spelling out each syllable. "Dost-o-ev-sky. For you, Barin? My wife didn't know; you didn't say your name . . ."

Dostoevsky seized the letter and tore it open. It was from Marya Dmitrievna. "Honored Fyodor Mikhailovich, I am sending this to you at Zmiev in the care of the post station. I cannot meet you there. I would have written to you at Semipalatinsk telling you not to come but there wasn't time. I cannot leave Kuznetsk because Alexander Ivanovich is ill. I am quite unable to leave his side. Pray God he may outlast it; but he is very low. You can perhaps imagine my position. I will not say more in case this should fall into other hands. Your M.D.I."

He was crushed. He handed the letter to Vrangel.

They drove back at a furious pace. Dostoevsky, sunk on the seat, scarcely cared to hang on and was thrown about with the violent pitching of the carriage. Vrangel rushed out at each post station demanding horses, pretending he was traveling officially as Prosecutor. After a while Dostoevsky's desperation gave way to the torment of doubt. Was Issayev really ill? Had she stayed behind because of Oladyin? Ah, my God! Did it mean that? He sat up wrestling with these thoughts as the carriage raced along—and he was suddenly infected by Vrangel's anxiety about their arriving in time. Ten minutes later they lurched into a ditch with one wheel wobbling dangerously and had to proceed at a crawl for nearly ten versts to the next post station. Evening was coming on.

"If you don't appear at roll call tomorrow morning Belikhov will send to me," Vrangel said. "Lamotte may cover you up, he's a good fellow."

"No, no. They'll post me as a deserter. With this latest business I shan't have a chance. It will mean five or ten years more—back to prison again."

At the station he stood frantically watching the driver and another man doing their best to mend the wheel while

Vrangel went in search of another vehicle. At last, just as Vrangel returned unsuccessful, the repair was done, they sprang in and flew on again.

The night journey was frightful. The swaying and plunging of the carriage, urged on by both of them, was worse than ever. They were thrown hundreds of times against the sides and the roof; the ceaseless jolting, added to the nervous tension, gave Dostoevsky a blinding headache. They staggered into post stations across the massed bodies of travelers sleeping on the floor, gulped tea, and forced themselves back into the torture chamber of the carriage once more. At dawn Dostoevsky felt as if he had been beaten from head to foot with a club. They reached the Jardin des Cosaques at twenty minutes to six. He dragged on his uniform more dead than alive.

2

By a process that escaped him, he began to have debts. He seemed to have scarcely any needs, yet his pay and the fifty rubles Mikhail sent him at long intervals vanished and he was obliged to borrow. Vrangel departed on a mission to Bisk and left him a small sum.

Then one morning in mid-August he received a letter from Marya Dmitrievna saying that Issayev was dead. He stood reading it with great emotion. He felt in a familiar "double" state—recollections of Issayev's absurdity and repulsiveness mingling with feelings of respect. Issayev had been a weak and disgusting creature and yet full of authentic nobility. Marya Dmitrievna wrote that he had been carried off in two days, clinging to her and Pasha at the end and repeating, "What is going to become of you?" She was desperate. The funeral had been wretched. She had had to borrow from neighbors to bury him, she wrote. She was ill herself; she couldn't sleep and had no appetite. The wife of the police captain and another neighbor were helping her for the moment, but she had nothing—except debts at the grocer's. Somebody had sent her three silver rubles. "Misery forced my hand to accept. I accepted alms."

There was no mention of the "new friend." Dostoevsky could not suppress the exultation in his heart; Marya Dmitrievna was free! And the moment he thought of it he felt there was something shameful and furtive about his feelings. How many times he had blamed Issayev and cursed him—even wished for his disappearance, his death. He felt his face burning as guilty recollection mingled with the pathetic image of the drunken man and pleasure and anxiety about Marya Dmitrievna.

He could hardly wait until he was released from duty. At his lodging he flung himself down at the box table, writing to her, then to Vrangel pleading for money for her, urging, entreating.

Madame Belikhov was a slow, immense, barrel-stayed woman. She had a baby's tiny arched mouth in a glabrous face and mighty arms, was a great flirt, and generally considered herself irresistible. She came of an obscure family and had done well to marry Belikhov but had an altogether exalted view of her position and behaved with the self-satisfaction of a woman whose husband has been asked to accept a confidential mission for the Holy Synod.

"Allow me to offer you some tea," she said to Dostoevsky and leaned toward the tea things. Her glance suggested that she was struggling between hostility and coquettishness.

Vrangel's patronage had gradually brought Dostoevsky into Semipalatinsk society. The officers, civil officials, and their wives had grimaced at the idea at first; but Vrangel's own supreme eligibility, his quality as a member of what Semipalatinsk thought of with awe as Petersburg "high life" and his ardor on Dostoevsky's behalf, won them over. For Dostoevsky it was not unmixed joy; he entered the salons of Semipalatinsk with a faint return of the old perspiring awkwardness, feeling conspicuous in his soldier's uniform, the convict; the deadly provincialism, the difficulty of conversation with more than two or three of them, soon bored him, but he knew that it would be offensive to them if he withdrew now that he had been admitted. And there was a tang of humiliation in it which he found to his disgust he could not elude.

"Thank you," he said; and watched her pour the tea for him.

"Yuri Kondratyevich is with His Excellency," Madame Belikhov said, handing the cup. Dostoevsky was still having to read the newspapers to Belikhov; with typical coarseness Belikhov was now using their social relationship to keep him waiting, to be out when he arrived, as he was now. "I hear that Count Verbov's son has entered the Life Guards," she went on. "Such delightful people. I suppose you never knew them in Petersburg?" She gave a wriggle, meant to be girlish and fetching.

"No. I never had that pleasure."

"The count was attached to the secretariat of the Ministry of Home Affairs, you know," She was using her eyes on him. She and Belikhov had been in Petersburg once for a week, twenty-one years before, and she liked to pretend she knew all the fashionable gossip.

"Really? How interesting." He sipped the tea; he was tempted to say to her, "I know you would like me to be rude and I've a good mind to oblige you." After a moment her coquettishness melted into an expression of dislike because of his unreceptiveness to her. She had not forgiven Vrangel for making her "accept" a convict. She folded her fat fingers and sat back. "Tell me, Fyodor Mikhailovich, how is that young woman you were so attached to here, Madame Issayeva?"

He looked at her quickly, embarrassed. "Thank you, Olga Andreyevna; she is quite well."

"She's a widow now, h'm? Her husband has died, hasn't he—that shameless drunkard?"

"Yes. He was an inoffensive man, Olga Andreyevna, with many fine attributes. Above all unlucky."

"H'm." Smiling, she toyed with a chain on her mighty chest. "I'm told she is finding agreeable company in Kuznetsk with a young teacher. Did you know that? It's even a question of their marrying, you know."

"What do you say?" He flushed red.

"She is going to marry the young man."

"How did you hear of such a thing?"

"But it's quite serious. His name is—er—one moment— Ver——"

"Oladyin? Oladyin?" he shouted out, jumping up. "That's quite impossible! It is out of the question."

She was staring at him with a frightened expression. "His name is Vergunov."

"No, no!" His lips trembled; he tried to find some words, glanced around in a confused way, and at last managed to say, "Excuse me—I am not well," and ran out.

He saw nothing on the way home. As he entered the house a loud watchman's rattle startled him from the next garden. He realized he must have been wandering for three or four hours. He spent a sleepless night. Vrangel was still away. In the morning there was a letter from her. He could not open it. He kept taking it out of his pocket and turning it over and putting it back. At last he tore open the envelope and raced through it, noting fearfully the reserve in some of the phrases. Poor angel, she was ill. But there were fewer tender phrases, fewer confidences, and no word of their future hopes, as if that was shelved and she had ceased to believe in any improvement of his lot. "My head goes around at the thought of being here alone, in this spot, with a child. Astrakhan is so far off and my father is old." And then at the very end she said, "Tell me, honored Fyodor Mikhailovich, if there was a man of a certain age, with good qualities, a stable position, an assured future, and he asked me to marry him—what should I answer? Give me your advice; examine the matter coolly, as a *friend* should, and reply at once."

He was in a panic—overcome.

Next morning Vrangel returned unexpectedly, saying he was recalled to Petersburg. Dostoevsky threw himself on him and poured out everything. "She loves me, *she loves me*. I know it. Alexander Egorovich, what shall I do? Never in my life have I suffered so much. I'm consumed! I struggle with it all night. I call out, I choke, sometimes tears refuse to flow, the next moment they pour out. Don't blame me, Alexander Egorovich. Is it for me to give her up to somebody else? I've *rights* over her, d'you hear? Rights!"

He stepped away, then swung around abruptly. "I must have money. If only they'll let me publish things again I shall be able to live for the rest of my life. It's not as it was before; I've thought things out and, my God, I have the energy to write. I can do a novel in six months if they'll let me—better than *Poor Folk*. It will make an enormous stir. It'll sell, bring me some money, notoriety, call the government's attention to me, and I'll get back to Russia quicker. I only need two or three thousand rubles a year for myself, that's all. Isn't that being loyal to her? In a couple of years we'll be able to go back to Russia. She'll live well; perhaps we'll even have some to spare. Nobody knows my strength yet, my talent!"

Vrangel said, "What do you want me to do, my poor friend?"

"Alexander Egorovich, in the name of Christ, do what I ask you. I have written to Edward Ivanovich Totleben—yes, yes, the hero of Sebastopol. I knew his younger brother Adolf Ivanovich years ago at the Engineering School. Here's the letter; take it to him. He is a great figure, he can obtain anything. Get him to intercede for me with the Emperor. Tell him everything. Tell him I'll be a decent citizen. Surely the Tsar will listen. Tell him I must get out of this life, I must come back to Russia—above all, I want to publish things. *If I could be promoted, get a commission*—that would open the way. Can't you see young Adolf Totleben? He's my great friend. Tell him about me and he'll throw himself on his brother's neck and beg him to intercede for me. Yes, yes, he will."

"I'll see him," Vrangel said, putting the letter in his pocket.

But Vrangel was much taken up with official matters and their farewell was rather perfunctory. There was something in the unsatisfactoriness of it that unsettled Dostoevsky. He marched back to the barracks and on an impulse asked Belikhov for leave. Belikhov looked him up and down. "I'll give you eight days. You are not to go farther afield than Barnaul. If you're not back to the minute"—he stuck his cigarette back between his teeth—"I'll find you." He walked away.

The coach from Semipalatinsk reached Kuznetsk at midday. Dostoevsky found her address, two rooms in a wooden house in the worst district. At his knock she came to the door.

"Fyodor Mikhailovich!" He was covering her hands with kisses. She pulled him quickly inside. "How did you manage to come?"

"I had to see you, my angel." She was red in the face and, he thought, looked embarrassed. "Marya Dmitrievna, you don't know how many times I have thought of this moment, anticipated it." As he drew her toward him to kiss her she tried indecisively to free her hands and turned her head away so that his lips only touched her cheek.

"No, no. Sit down. Please sit down."

She disengaged herself, retreating, but he pursued her across the room with his arms stretched out to her. "Dearest Masha, forgive me. I've been longing to see you; I have upset you, I have tortured you with my letters."

"Let's not talk about that. Please sit down; I'll get some

tea." She escaped from him again in a flurried way, her face still red, and busied herself with the tea things. "Tell me about the journey. How is Alexander Egorovich? You've had a great many fires in the district lately . . ." She chattered nervously, warding off conversation about themselves.

He sat down, responding to her questions, following her with his eyes, unhappy and tormented. She was poorly dressed and her thin face made her eyes look enormous, her hair thicker. Suddenly he said, "Masha, I beg of you, speak to me, who is the man? Are you in love with him? Masha, I beg you to tell me the truth."

"No, no, no." She was wringing her hands, looking from one side to the other. "Not now, not now."

"But I've come here because I have to know, my dearest, my pure angel." He was about to throw himself on his knees before her, but she recoiled.

"You are making a mistake," she said. "I was only—only testing your affection."

"What? There's nobody, then?" He stood in front of her. "Masha, look at me."

"Yes, there is." She said pleadingly, "I don't want to hurt you, Fyodor Mikhailovich; you are good and upright. Please understand I would do anything not to harm you."

He was staring at her with a pale face. "Who is he?" And exactly at this moment he observed he was feeling intense pleasure. "Is it the teacher—Vergunov?"

She gave him a tormented look. "Yes. Nikolay Borisovich. He teaches in the district school here. Oh, he is only beginning his career. He comes from Tomsk and hasn't any patronage from Petersburg but he is loyal and hard-working."

In a shaking voice Dostoevsky said, "How old is he?"

"Twenty-four."

"What! You are intelligent, you've suffered, you have an independent mind, you know what life in Siberia is like, and you are going to throw yourself away on a miserably paid teacher five years younger than you are, condemn yourself, ruin yourself? What does he earn? Can he even hope to keep you and Pasha?"

"He will soon have nine hundred paper rubles a year."

"And you can speak of marriage. My God!" He stopped. "Do you love him, Masha?"

"Yes." She suddenly covered her face with her hand, her shoulders shrank. But before he could step over to her she looked up, tears running down her face. "I know how you love me, Fyodor Mikhailovich. I've treated you badly. I've been remembering all about Semipalatinsk. It would have been better if I'd never seen him. I could have lived with you. But now that I love him I need you even more as a friend. Please, please, I need your good heart." She looked completely wretched.

"Then everything is over? It's not possible. Masha——" She pitied him. That was atrocious to him; he accepted it, craved for it, and at the same time was ashamed of it.

"He is coming here," she said. "Don't blame him; don't laugh at him. He can't be judged like other people. He's a child; he may do something bad but one can't blame him. He'll forget me if I'm not continually with him. He is like that; other women attract him. And then what should I do? I'd be so miserable. I feel that if I'm not always with him, every minute, he'll stop loving me, he'll forget me and give me up."

Dostoevsky was violently agitated. "How can you love him then? You don't respect him, you don't even believe in his love. And you are going to ruin yourself for that. What does it mean, Masha? He'll torture you. You are throwing yourself away on him."

For a moment she looked lost, wavering. She held out her hands. "Fyodor Mikhailovich, we are two unfortunates——" But she was overcome by a sudden coughing. He stood by torn and helpless. As she recovered, there was a scratching on the door. They both looked at it in a sort of terror. A young man came in smiling. Dostoevsky saw at once that it was Vergunov.

3

He was short, with an oval, in some ways childish, face and blue eyes and was awkwardly dressed in a suit that had been made for somebody else; the sleeves were not long enough and left his red, bony wrists dangling. There was something in his movements, his expression, that struck Dostoevsky as complacent and at the same time egoistic. He thought that Vergunov looked simple at heart, weak, and confiding.

Marya Dmitrievna went toward him in a rather protective way. "Kolya, this is the friend I have spoken to you about, Fyodor Mikhailovich Dostoevsky."

He did not seem to notice her red eyes or her nervous state. He suddenly remembered he had not kissed her hand, snatched it to his lips, and looked up at Dostoevsky. "Oh yes, the friend of the late Alexander Ivanovich." Dostoevsky thought it particularly childish and irritating the way he said "the late" and continued to smile. So she had described him to Vergunov as a friend of her husband's. He bowed. Vergunov looked at him with perfect frankness and, still keeping hold of Marya Dmitrievna's hand, said to him, "I've been wanting to embrace you as a brother for a long time; Mary Dmitrievna has told me so much about you."

"I think, Kolya, it would be more convenient if we met later," she put in hastily.

"I only came to tell you what I've found out about getting Pasha into the Cadet School."

Dostoevsky felt that Mary Dmitrievna knew she would have mastery over him, would dominate him, even that he would be her victim. She was seeking the joys of torturing the man she had affection for, perhaps loved, and that was why she was in such a hurry to sacrifice herself by marrying him!

"Yes, but not now," she said. Vergunov smiled at her and said nothing. There was an awkward pause. He looked at Dostoevsky. Marya Dmitrievna stood near him, nervously fussing with the front of her dress, apparently afraid he'd say something embarrassing. Dostoevsky wanted to shout in his face: "Do you imagine you are going to marry her?" But to break the silence he said, "Marya Dmitrievna tells me you are at the local school here. What do you teach?"

"Oh well, I only assist. Writing and spelling. You see, I haven't got my full teacher's certificate yet. I expect to have it in a year or two and then I'll have a grade, you see."

And nine hundred rubles a year, Dostoevsky thought.

"Excuse me, Masha," Vergunov said. "I've found out a little for Pasha. It's not much but it's something." He raised his upper lip and sniffed. "I'll come later. Good-by, Fyodor Mikhailovich."

"Good-by."

Vergunov turned at the door, gave them another smile, and went out.

They stood still, looking at each other across the room. Faintly from outside they heard another sniff. Dostoevsky was shaking, white in the face. Her lips were parted, color glowed in patches on her cheeks. He tried to speak; he could not. Suddenly he threw himself at her feet and buried his face against her skirt, unable to stop the tears flowing. "Marya—Marya—it can't end everything for us."

"My dear." She bent over him, trying to lift him up. She was weeping too. "Don't cry, don't be unhappy. It's not all decided yet. It'll be you and I—nobody else."

He rose and feverishly clasped her arms, looking at her intently. "Will it? Do you mean that? You do—Masha, my love." He kissed her and she clung to him voluptuously; he felt her body against him. Her arms were heavy around his neck, her legs and hips molding close to his and her lips opening. He tasted the tears on her lips and felt her abandoning herself. She broke away and he watched her, thinking how much she would love torment, disputes, and death, would absorb them voluptuously as the incitement and preliminary to yielding and possessing in love. He saw he had known this all along and that he responded to it; he went toward her but she faced him and he saw her expression was different. She said, "How long are you staying in Kuznetsk?"

"Until the day after tomorrow." He sat down.

"Fyodor Mikhailovich, I wish you'd go back. It's no good, I can't decide with you here. I can't, I can't."

"But you said, 'It'll be you and I.' Masha——"

"Oh, my God! Why do you torment me? You are doing it purposely. You've seen him. Nothing is settled yet. I don't know what to do. I'm tired—tired. I must have time." She put her hand to her head. "Don't you see, I have to think of Pasha?"

"What?" He stared at her, then jumped up. "What does that mean? Yes, I've seen him, your teacher—a little Siberian who knows nothing, who has seen nothing, who is groping for his first thoughts, a dummy with no future! How do you think two people with outlooks, characters, and needs so different are going to bind themselves together for life? Won't you be unfaithful to him, in a few years, while you are still beautiful, desirable? Yes, and he'll wish you were dead."

"I beg you to stop." She was pale.

"Something like that is sure to happen. And what will you do, tied to Kuznetsk with a horde of children?"

"I can't leave as it is, can I?" she blazed up.

"Masha, listen to me. Love can pass, but not incompatibility. A marriage of that sort is going to ruin you."

"My God—and look at you! Four years a convict. Now a soldier without a kopeck."

"I don't reproach his poverty. I'm only trying to expl——"

"Do you expect me to wait forever, to live on your hopes that never amount to anything, promises? 'Oh, Marya Dmitrievna this, Marya Dmitrievna that'?" She was trying to find the insult that would hurt him. "While your rich friends in Petersburg use their influence. All of them!"

"Are you pleased I haven't more of them?" She had made him furious.

"I don't care! Perhaps I prefer the gutter in Kuznetsk to the gutter in Petersburg. It's cleaner. I'll tell you—Kolya has only four hundred rubles a year. Four hundred! There's the price—not much, is it? But Kolya is young and good."

"Yes, he's young." The phrase was on his lips; he knew it would wound her and in the sort of stinging enjoyment he could not prevent himself from saying it. "He'll say you have taken him for his youth. You've clasped him to satisfy your sexual appetite!"

"My God!" She stared at him, her lips white. "Those are things you think of privately when you are away from me to insult me with."

He turned away to control himself. They stood strained and silent, their faces set, neither of them looking in the other's direction. She sat on a chair. The silence lasted for fifteen minutes. Dostoevsky prolonged it out of excruciating secret pleasure; then he turned and picked up his cap. She looked at him mournfully and reproachfully. He rushed over and she crushed herself against him.

"Masha, forgive me, my angel."

"It will be all right."

He went to see Vergunov alone the next day and had it out, told him plainly of his own intention of marrying Marya Dmitrievna. Vergunov broke into tears and admitted he had "feared it." He said he could scarcely keep himself on his pay and could not seriously hope for more for years, since there was no opportunity for him in Kuznetsk to pass to a higher grade in the service. He wept several times and asked Dostoevsky for his "fraternal friendship." "You are a noble man and far superior to me," he said. Dostoevsky was tempted to behave brutally for a moment and said one or two sharp things, knowing he would feel horrified at them an hour later (perhaps even with that object in view).

In the afternoon he told Marya Dmitrievna about the interview. They sat in the shabby main room of her lodging. Pasha, a dark-haired boy with a yellowish skin, was playing with a ball; Dostoevsky sat on the arm of her chair, his hand lightly on her neck. He said quietly, "My love, send him out now. I can't——"

"He's going in a minute." She glanced at Pasha on the other side of the room and brushed her hand over Dostoevsky's knee, then over the mounded cloth, with fingers closing, enfolding, and passing.

Pasha clumped about more noisily than ever and at last said, "Mother, I promised to meet Alexey. Can I go? It's at his house."

"Yes," she said, rising. She fussed over him and took a long time to let him depart. When he had gone she locked the door and turned quickly toward Dostoevsky.

"Masha——"

The bed was high and when he lifted her onto it her legs hung over the side. The fabric of her stocking was faintly, sweetly odorous against his lips and she put one knee up in protection at the last nearness, her hand nevertheless caressing his head. She pushed him away and began to deal with the impedimenta of clothes, while he did likewise; but neither completed it. He covered her, lips on lips, and her arms held him as he adored and made her shudder with pleasure and the fear of love. After a moment he shifted. Her head was turned sideways, eyes closed. He looked at the line along the joint from the groin to the outside, the line adoringly accentuated on Greek statues. He kissed her and put his arms around her and she entwined him as the all-striving passed into the encompassing rings of unattainable seizure and containment and reaching holding for the springing self annihilating ending of all of all of all, all . . .

The shadows of the afternoon lengthened. In the end,

lying in the chaos of the bed, they were unable to stir any more, quite still, and the smell of love with them.

She came to the coach with him the next day. He was surprised to see her looking disturbed and anxious. As the coach drove away down the street the dust cleared for a moment and he saw her walking off—to meet Vergunov? He screwed himself up to sit out the long journey ahead and not to think, not to remember that those who are absent are always in the wrong.

Ten days later he saw everything was lost. Vergunov was with her, her lover. Two letters from her confirmed it.

He felt an irresistible desire to *help* them. The idea was intermingled with feelings of pleasure, shame, and pure sacrifice. He longed for Vrangel's presence, for someone he could pour his heart out to. Vrangel, of course, would be offended by the hint of pleasure and satisfaction. But pain wasn't the reverse of pleasure. The frontiers of those feelings were mysteriously shadowy, the very contrary to the hard fixed definition the world gave them. He remembered one day in his boyhood; his mother had taken him into a bookshop and asked him to choose what he wanted. There were several books he longed for. And then he had noticed a *Book of Animals* by somebody called P. Yurovsky and chosen that. He did not want it a bit; he positively disliked the look of it and knew it would bore him. His mother glanced at him doubtfully and said, "Are you sure you want that, Fedya, not one of the others, with stories and pictures?" No, he said, he wanted the animal book. And he knew his mother knew he really did not want it. But she bought it; he detested it even before it was wrapped up and felt the peculiar, elusive, pleasant regret every time he saw it thereafter in the house. He had recalled the incident hundreds of times and still remembered its subtle flavor of pleasure and misery long after he would have forgotten the conventional pleasure of one of the other books, years after!

He wrote to Vrangel, begging him "on my knees" to do something for Vergunov, pleading, "In God's name, in the name of heavenly charity, don't refuse. He must have a better post. Speak to your friends about him, the Ministry of Education, write to the governor—coming from you, that will be everything. Sing Vergunov's praises, say he is admirably gifted. He deserves it. He is dearer to me than a brother."

Unable to sleep, he spent hours walking up and down the small curtained-off corner at his lodgings. He had borrowed money to give Marya Dmitrievna and now he had debts of a thousand rubles! He read her letters in a cold sweat, fearing each time there would be the final news of her marriage to Vergunov. She wrote noncommittally.

Then on the last afternoon but one in October when he was on duty in the armory, Belikhov sent for him. There was something about the summons he did not like. In the past week Belikhov had vindictively punished several men. Belikhov tilted back his chair and hoisted his boots onto the table and, keeping his eyes on Dostoevsky, reached for a paper from the desk. "From the general, dated today, October 30, 1856," he said, and read out: " 'By order of His Imperial Majesty I am instructed to inform you that the soldier Dostoevsky, Fyodor Mikhailovich, Seventh Siberian Battalion, First Section' "—he paused, looked Dostoevsky up and down, tossed the paper back on the desk; Dostoevsky felt the color drain from his face—" 'is promoted to the rank of second lieutenant to date from this present instruction.' "

Belikhov threw his head back and roared with laughter.

He sat up almost all night writing feverish letters to her, to Vrangel, to Mikhail. "Masha—we're saved, we're saved! It means returning to Russia, to Petersburg. In six months I'll ask them to let me resign my commission, grounds of ill-health. I'll get my titles of nobility back. They are bound to let me write again—and then, my angel, we'll begin life."

He did not know how he survived until her answer came. She said yes. It was a simple letter full of happiness at the prospect of being his wife. He borrowed another six hundred rubles to hire rooms, buy a bed and chairs, pay for the wedding and their carriage from Kuznetsk. He burned up his nerves in the interval of waiting for leave. And at last he could go. He found her smiling and confident, but shaken by frequent coughing. When they discussed Vergunov she let him understand that she had settled that relationship. Vergunov came himself and greeted Dostoevsky a little tearfully and then became pressingly friendly.

"I have persuaded Nikolay Borisovich to be your sponsor at the church," Marya Dmitrievna said to Dostoevsky.

"Excellent." The incongruous touch appealed to him. The next moment he caught an ambiguous look between the two of them.

The wedding was simple. The Kuznetsk chief of police and his wife gave Marya Dmitrievna away. Dostoevsky, who had grown a light brown mustache since his promotion, was in officer's uniform with high-collared tunic, epaulettes, and sixteen buttons down the front and trousers striped light blue at the side. His face was almost plump. They all stood in the little Kuznetsk church, the sponsors holding heavy iron crowns used for the peasants' weddings over their heads. The church was rather dark and smelled of incense. The rumble of carts came in from the road outside. The chief of police clinked his spurs. Dostoevsky was too full of emotion to think of anything. When it was over they said goodbys. He was noticing Vergunov getting into a carriage when Marya Dmitrievna drew his attention to the priest bowing up.

The afternoon sun was sinking in a red ball as they set out. The road twisted and turned. Dostoevsky saw another carriage behind them; for a moment he had the impression it was Vergunov's but after a few versts it dropped back a long way and he dismissed it. The horses' hoofs flew and the bells jingled. He felt tremendously keyed up, as if every thought were flying faster and faster in his mind and sight, hearing, every faculty were sharpened.

"Faster!" he shouted out. The driver lashed the horses. Clods of frozen mud flew back from the flying hoofs. Evening came, the moon swam up, shedding pale light over the hills and gorges of the Altai. The carriage plunged and rocked.

"Faster! Faster!"

"Don't, Fyodor, you're frightening me."

"No, no, he must go faster!"

She shut her eyes and was silent. At last they saw the lights of Barnaul. They pulled up at the hotel; it looked fairly clean. The room was almost entirely taken up by a huge bare blanketless and pillowless double bed with peeling brass-covered knobs. They squeezed the luggage in.

Marya Dmitrievna shut the door and lifted a bag onto the bed. Dostoevsky had an instant of panic in his sudden need of her. He stepped over to her and took her arms. A breeze floated across his face, he experienced the inexpressible voluptuousness, the radiant instant of ecstasy, heard the cry far in the distance, coming nearer and louder. His tongue seemed enormous and his chin was wet. The sound burst from his lips, he contorted himself, choking, wrestling to thrust off the force that seized him. There was another terrifying scream at his side. In one flash he saw her recoiled, an expression of horror and loathing on her face, and the red curtain thudded down heavily.

PART THREE

PART THREE

Chapter Ten

1

It had been snowing in Petersburg all day. In places along the curb where it had been shoveled back from the roadway the snow, frozen solid, rose in ramparts higher than a man. Dostoevsky went forward with his collar up. Through the big wet flakes he could see the commotion on the square ahead. There were groups standing about and gesticulating —students. At intervals one of them shouted something and the rest cheered. Others were coming from a side street. There was defiance, revolt in the air. The whole city, for that matter, was stirring with excitement. The new Tsar, Alexander II, was the symbol of movement, change, the rush of new ideas.

Dostoevsky lowered his head as the snow blew harder into his face.

"You, there! Where are you going?" It was a police captain. Looking up, Dostoevsky saw police everywhere. The captain had two dozen sheltering behind the corner. There were more along the opposite pavement. They were expecting another demonstration. Farther down, at the square, he saw Cossacks on their horses, waiting.

"To Chernichev Street," he said.

"Pass this way," the captain said, gesturing down the side street. Dostoevsky was about to do so when somebody exclaimed, "What! Fyodor Mikhailovich." He turned. It was Adolf Totleben.

"My dear fellow, at last!"

"So you got back then?" Totleben said, laughing and chuckling. "It came off?"

They wrung each other's hands affectionately. Dostoevsky took in Totleben's prosperous look, the plump well-shaven face, the smart uniform, the major's insignia. He felt his own shabby appearance. "I've been trying to see you for months to thank you for all you did, and your brother," he said. "They said they didn't know when you'd be back."

"I've been in the Caucasus. I'm delighted to see you."

A shout from the students floated down to them. "Long live the Russian social republic!" They both turned.

"The government won't stand that much longer," Totleben said. "Look here, here's my carriage. I'm going to the Ministry of War. Let me give you a lift." He took Dostoevsky's arm, leading him, insistent. "I want to hear all about it."

As they drove Dostoevsky told him. "They allowed me to petition, as I wrote to you, released me from the army, and sent me to Tver. Ugh! I don't recommend Tver. Then a year ago they gave me permission to come back here—to the scene of my debts!" He grinned sardonically. "Oh, but I'm allowed to write. Yes, yes. I have all that back again. It all comes from your kindness, Adolf Ivanovich, and your brother's. Now Mikhail and I have started a paper here, a monthly review called *Vremya*. Oh yes, it's succeeding so far. I'm publishing my new novel in it, *The Insulted and Injured*. Mind you, there are a hundred administrative obstacles always cropping up. We struggle with the censorship seven times a week. I'm on my way to the Ministry of Home Affairs now to satisfy a senseless regulation. But we're moving. The whole of Russia is moving."

"How long have you been married?" Totleben said.

"Three years." They talked on, pressed each other with questions. The carriage went along the Fontanka. Over the parapet washerwomen were washing out clothes, cattle were being watered, some soldiers were pushing wheelbarrows full of stones, and boatmen with long poles were shoving off a barge piled with wood.

All at once Dostoevsky had an intense desire to offend

Totleben. It made him tingle. He knew it would be particularly outrageous at this moment when the communication of gratitude and friendship was flowing between them; but that somehow made it all the more imperative. Totleben was talking about the army. Dostoevsky interrupted him in a loud voice. "This will do for me. Do you know, Adolf Ivanovich, I detest being made to feel under an obligation. It is odious—abominably humiliating," and he tapped for the driver to stop.

Totleben stared at him uncomprehendingly, then said, "Wh-at?" and flushed as he realized he had heard correctly. Dostoevsky particularly noticed a small vein pulsing in his lower lip. Moreover, there was a barrel organ nearby playing *"Luchinushka,"* which somehow seemed especially appropriate.

"I'd better walk." He got down. "Good-by, Adolf Ivanovich." He could not help adding, "We must meet again soon."

Totleben was looking at him with a red, furious face, then he said something to the driver and the carriage crunched away over the snow.

Dostoevsky walked along toward the Ministry. He felt pleased. It had been a sort of test of himself. Nevertheless he was slightly irritated at his weakness in adding, "We must meet again soon," and there was one section of his thought which was utterly and painfully ashamed—but enjoyably so! He thought about the episode for a minute, then consciously turned his mind to Totleben's question about his marriage. Good God, yes—it was three years! If they had both known then how the marriage was going to turn out. He and Masha were not happy. He had found out almost at once that Vergunov had followed them to Petersburg—and he accepted it readily. Marriage ought not to bind the partners body and soul; that was what he believed. Neither had the right to interfere with the liberties of the other provided the liberties did not upset their own profound, intimate relationship, which was secret and apart from everything else.

But it was not that; it was the basic impossibility of their finding harmony. The fit she had seen him in that night of their wedding had deeply shocked and disgusted her, marked the marriage for her as a mistake.

They had blazing scenes. At the beginning when he had told her of feelings like the one with the animal book, she had replied with contempt; he had been a little offended. She could not understand, could not fit herself to his constant stimulus, his many-sidedness, his instability and uneasiness, his extreme violence of feeling, the passion of his nature. He felt her soured, shrewish, irrecoverably and sarcastically at odds with life—an unhappy woman. Even in the way, taking up his lead, she claimed independence of the customary external bonds there was something exasperated and spiteful. At the quietest moments their differences hung constantly unseen and menacing in the air. The slightest word was often enough to send the electricity crackling and flashing between them. In their quarrels they used unrestrained language. She bitterly complained that the marriage had been disaster for her. They tried to find words that would torment each other. Often she provoked him slyly at his most peaceful or expansive moments. And they ended these scenes, he pale as death, twitching convulsively, she, prostrate, with pinched mouth, clenching her handkerchief, the two of them sitting strained and silent for hours on opposite sides of the room. And scarcely had the wounds healed superficially than they cut them open again.

He had had more attacks of epilepsy too, some extremely violent. And debts. Three more years of debts! He saw it was especially harrowing for Masha, who so much wanted to "be somebody." He had lost sight of Vrangel, who was abroad.

The great portal of the Ministry rose before him. He went in and down the dingy corridors to the Bureau of Publications, already familiar to him. They had asked to see the *Vremya's* Publishing Certificate—a pointless request, the

whim of some bored general councilor, but one of the harass-
ments every Petersburg periodical had to submit to. Dostoevsky gave the certificate to a clerk and sat in the waiting
room. A man with a big mustache glanced in and then went
away.

The snow outside blocked up half the window and the
place was dark. He stared into the corners of the room, his
mind rushing with thoughts about his work on *The Insulted
and Injured,* his first full-sized novel since prison.

The plot was richly complex, the sort he liked, could
scarcely avoid. Vanya, the narrator, was a young writer
whose first novel, like *Poor Folk,* had been a great success.
Vanya loved Natasha Ikhmenyeva, whom he had known
from childhood. Natasha recognized and returned his feeling to a degree but made no secret that she loved Alyosha,
the irresponsible, weak, and not entirely unlikable son of
Prince Valkovsky. Alyosha was another dual character, a
Double; he half loved Natasha and half Katya, a girl of
seventeen. Though loving Natasha, Vanya helped her to
run away from home to Alyosha, met them together, and
undertook to do everything to advance their happiness, to be
their messenger, their "guardian angel." Further, both Natasha and Katya were ready to give up Alyosha to the other.

He was making Alyosha somewhat like Vergunov in
character. He wanted to convey the fleeting, elusive savor of
that particular incongruity that he had long ago hinted at
in "White Nights" and that he had since lived through himself in Siberia in the desire to "sacrifice" himself "on his
knees" for Vergunov. He was dissecting his own soul in the
book, opening its wounds to disperse pain and evil.

There were any number of other people in the novel,
including a victimized and ill-treated fourteen-year-old child,
Nellie, whom Vanya took in and who came to love him
jealously.

Dostoevsky tapped his foot with impatience. Above all
he was struggling with the writing, trying to give the figures

life. He had told Mikhail the book was ready; that was not true—and now, having to rush out installments, he was falling into melodrama and cheap sentiment. He was immensely excited by the character of Natasha, his first complete woman Double, who strove with desire to be Alyosha's abject slave and to dominate him. He felt he had given both Natasha and Alyosha a greater complexity and depth than any other other characters he had done so far.

He shifted about, scarcely able to contain himself. At length the clerk called out, "Dostoevsky," handed the certificate back, and he left. He hurried home. They were living in two small rooms on the third floor of a poor apartment house. He heard Marya Dmitrievna coughing as he climbed the stairs. She came out of the far room in a chemise with her hair down and he realized how much thinner she had become in the last few months.

"That Meyer creature has been here again with her bill. I've had her for half an hour—screaming, making a scandal! Bills, bills, bills! Never any money. I'm tired of it—worn out by it."

"I've already told Meyer she'll be paid at the end of the month." He wanted to be patient, conciliatory. "Masha, listen—as soon as the paper has printed the last section we shall have the book out. It will bring us something. I'm working on the prison notes——"

"Yes, and I suppose they will do us as much good as *Stepanchikovo*." He knew she had said that with deliberation —the humiliating reference to the failure of *The Village of Stepanchikovo*, the first piece of work he had brought out after their return from exile. It had taken him two years to write and he knew it had not been worth it. Katkov, the editor of the *Russian Messenger*, had flatly turned it down and asked for his advance back—which they had already spent.

"I don't see what more I can do. The paper needs money at present. We're growing, developing."

"Oh, the promises you made in Tver about the rich future! This is it—look at it. Yes, your brother and his German wife are fattening, no doubt."

"It's not Misha's fault that Madame Meyer put you in a bad temper." He knew she hated Mikhail and Emily Fyodorovna.

"Do you expect anybody to be gay in this hole?" She had a spasm of coughing, bending forward with the painful intensity, but even with the spittle running down her chin, gasped on. "I can't ask anybody here. When I go out I look like a servant. I saw General Vaganov in the street today and he barely gave me a salutation. I'm shut in here like a hermit. That's what you want, isn't it?"

"It is not!"

"Do you observe that I haven't a friend—or care?"

"But you don't want any friends. You're always saying you detest the people here."

"And I do! Filth—filth!" Her enormous eyes were blazing in her thin pink face. "I never wanted to marry you. Ah, my God, I ought to have listened to Nikolay Borisovich."

"You have ample chance now."

"And poor Pasha—he can never have what he needs, like a normal boy."

He said furiously, "Would he have any more if you'd married Vergunov?"

"Yes! He wouldn't be suffering through a convict stepfather."

"My God!"

"And seeing you in those disgusting—filthy—fits!"

"Wait a minute—wait a minute!" He was going to say something outrageous to her, some phrase with "Vergunov's bed" in it. But he checked it. With a green face he said, "We are now at the level of your discussions in Kuznetsk."

"Oh!" They were both silent, turned away from each other. He glared out of the window unseeing. Presently, amid his furious, bitter thoughts, he felt his attention being pulled,

nudged by something extraneous. He saw a man stationed
on the pavement below whose face seemed faintly familiar.
After a moment he recognized the mustached man who had
looked into the waiting room at the Ministry earlier. He was
being watched—still the political convict under surveillance.

2

Petersburg seethed like a cauldron. A new age was beginning. After the disastrous end of the Crimean War the old
rigid order in Russia was giving way in the upsurge of
liberal enthusiasm—at least, everyone proclaimed it so. When
an actor shouted from the stage of the Marinsky, "It is time
to tear evil up by the roots throughout Russia," the audience
rose, cheering in frantic exaltation. Russia was a giant waking
from sleep. Day and night people talked of reforms and
nothing else. The papers poured out articles on the practical
side of the new life—on railways, banks, joint-stock com-
panies, local government. Audiences flocked to dramas about
free trade; poets wrote sonnets to the law. There was to be
no more compulsion—only respect for human dignity. Russians began the struggle toward new hopes and destinies
with a touchingly naïve impetuosity.

On the nineteenth of February 1861 the Tsar signed the
decree for the emancipation of the serfs. Russia had been
talking of it for thirty years. Yet the deed was a shock. There
was something holy, dramatic, frightening in the event.

Dostoevsky worked like four men on the *Vremya*. He
begged contributions from the writers of the day—including
Turgenev, who had matured and dropped his former pre-
tentious posing and met him with cool amiability; he corrected proofs, wrote articles, his own serial contribution,
tramped around the town in the cold and slush to get subscriptions, encourage the selling agents, bargain over paper
and printing. Mikhail managed distribution, accounts, and

the business side. As collaborators they had recruited Apollon Grigoryev, disgraced soak, scandalous liver, a writer of brilliant gifts, unquenchable thirst, and infinite debts which had already landed him in the debtor's prison, and Nikolay Strakhov a young philosopher. Magazines and reviews were flourishing in the changed Petersburg atmosphere; Nekrasov's liberal *Contemporary* was the leading monthly, the *Annals of the Fatherland* the next. But *Vremya* was catching up. It was a success. The paper's tiny office, two dark back rooms with chaotic desks, piled books, an old sofa, was invaded by students bringing articles, heroic poems, manifestoes to be printed, resolutions to be announced. They came in, the girls with blue glasses and hair cut short in "revolutionary style," smoking cigarettes, ready to lay down their lives in defense of Darwin and talking of free love, "the new principles of sexual and marital ethics."

One morning in August as Dostoevsky sat at his desk amidst a disorderly accumulation of proofs and papers he heard the porter shove the door open behind him and say, "Here you are," to some visitor. He had the distant impression that the porter, a sour man, was being unusually agreeable. Grigoryev, who was in the office writing a theater notice, jumped up quickly, kicking the empty bottles under his desk, and went forward. Dostoevsky concentrated on the proof he was working on. Presently Grigoryev dropped a manuscript on his desk. "Here you are, my dear fellow, just what we need—a charming contribution. The authoress wants to offer it to you herself."

"What?" Dostoevsky looked up.

"This is Apollinarya Pankratyevna Suslova," Grigoryev said, and the girl came up, a slight, rather derisive smile on her lips. She was about twenty, tall, a touch of coarseness in her features, with glorious dark red hair, cut short, and a wide mouth. She moved slowly, her eyes on Dostoevsky with quite a hard look in them. He rose, pen in hand, his mind still on the proof.

"I do hope you can publish my story," she said with a soft intonation.

"Oh—er——" He glanced down at the manuscript. "I shall be glad to read it. Thank you for bringing it to us."

"I read *The Insulted and Injured*. It was splendid. So was *Stepanchikovo*. Foma Fomich is wonderfully Russian."

"Thank you. It's kind of you."

"I heard you give the reading from your books, you know, at the university last month. All my friends were there. You don't know how electrified everybody was."

"Oh, come," he said. She seemed very sure of herself. A phrase of the proof was recurring in his mind and he wanted to get back to it. "Your story—er—we'll do our best for it. Thank you, thank you." Bowing, he accompanied her to the door. She held out her hand, he took it in a somewhat flustered way and shut the door after her. He caught his reflection in the splinter of mirror nailed to the wall—big forehead, neat mustache, straight eyebrows; a young forty.

"Whew!" Grigoryev was looking at him with raised eyebrows. "She—is—delicious."

"What? Who—— Oh yes—I suppose she is a pleasant child," Dostoevsky said in a preoccupied way.

"Yes—a child!" Grigoryev laughed, lifted a bottle from under the desk, drank, and wiped his lips. "Did you notice the looks she was giving you? It's the fourth time she's called in the last two weeks."

There was no doubt that *The Insulted and Injured* had failed. But the installments of *The House of the Dead*, the account of the prison life, were highly praised. Strakhov said, "Turgenev is saying the bathhouse scene is 'Hallucinating—pure Dante.'" Dostoevsky wept secretly over this: he was returning; after all, he was asserting his talent. Ah, the heroic world of his youth, the gigantic visions of those days —they were not lost! He wept, opening his arms to them still. He must be the higher man, purifying his life. He clasped his young dreams of power and of rising to heights above everything.

He worked alone late, writing about the years in prison. He could not put everything in or it would all be stopped by the censorship. He laid it out in a loose order, as the memoirs of an imaginary convict, Alexander Petrovich, sentenced to ten years for murder, and at points dealing with some of the worst things he mentioned he had to add notes saying that all this had long since changed. "When it got dark we all used to be led to the hut and locked up for the night. . . . I always felt depressed at entering the hut from outside. It was a long, low-pitched, filthy room, gloomily lit by tallow candles, full of a heavy, stifling smell. . . ." He described it, the bestial existence, Gazin, Petrov, and the other convicts, giving them in depth, psychologically, as human beings, even sympathetically. He described Eight-Eyes Krivtsov, the artel, Izay Fomich, life in the hospital. He could only hint at the agonies of mind and obliged himself to give the account a positively detached coloring, as far as he could. Strangely, after the first few episodes he found this intensified the effects and continued with it. He was deeply stirred. Prison had been his spiritual death, annihilation and resurrection in pain. At the same time the underworld had become alive in his soul and he had caught recondite harmonies that were faint, distant, harsh, luring.

One night in September he was sitting writing in the office. The rain dripped outside. The single lamp threw a circle of shadow around the desk, the smoke of his cigarette curling up. The clock struck ten. A moment afterward he heard a small noise behind him and looked around. The door opened and as he peered a voice said, "Yes, it *is* you. Good evening," and a girl came in.

It was Suslova.

He rose—astonished, pleased, puzzled. "Good evening. Please come in. Why, you're wet." Her thick red hair glistened with rain and her dress was a little wet.

"Oh, never mind that. I'm glad to find you here." She smiled brilliantly, frankly, girlishly, standing with a straddle-legged girlish stance. "You published my story—how good! I had to say thank you at once. There I am, in *Vremya*. Oh, I'm so proud!" She threw back her head and laughed, a gesture overwhelmingly graceful and full of magic. He looked at her long legs, the slightly mounding belly and the breasts wide apart, the warm rich inviting fork molded under the dress.

"It was excellent." He was thinking: What a beauty. Her skin was not pale but had the rare creamy-brown tinge of some red-haired women. Her eyes were as yellow as a cat's.

"I have the plan for another one," she said.

"You are at the university?"

"Yes." She was smiling. "I brought our manifesto in last month, don't you remember? We went over it together."

"Yes. I—er—of course," he said confusedly. "Please sit down." He blushed, feeling acutely foolish at doing so before this girl—half his age—and unable for that reason to recover and also because of her sexuality, the sexual warmth and invitation that she gave out in a very subtle and elusive way.

"Did you really care for the story?" she said. "I admire your writing very much. I read *Poor Folk* long ago. What you are writing about the prison now, I read to my comrades. It is something apart for us, something fine, with great intelligence—yes, especially intelligence." She talked openly, in a young way, praising him, expressing admiration for him; her eyes shone, there was something magnificent about her enthusiasm. He saw her in a flash—the university comrade, the girl with a sort of special gift for personifying everything of the student life, living it more intensely than any real student, the feminism, the carelessness, cigarettes, the daring opinions, negligence about work, the eagerness for any sort of meeting, the defense of trivialities, the headlong, shining, impassioned youth. At the same time there were mysterious qualities that escaped all this.

"I've been reading *Netochka Nezvanovna*. Yes! In the *Annals of the Fatherland*, old copies," she said. "It hasn't your name on. It is excellent."

"Well—it seems a long time since I wrote it," he said. He was suddenly tempted to behave like a monster. He took her hand with a peculiarly abrupt movement. He even felt a definite pleasure in the abruptness. She looked at him with an expression of surprise. He again blushed furiously and, though a moment before he had known what he was going to say, he decided all at once that he would obstinately refuse to say anything of the sort. It was impossible to say at whom this "obstinacy" was directed and he was aware of this, yet something made him continue with it. There was a strange silence. When she tried to withdraw her hand he got up, rather nervously and feverishly, led her across the room, made a somewhat formal bow to her, and sat on the sofa. She sat beside him. She seemed to him enormously self-possessed, confident, even amused.

"Fyodor Mikhailovich——" she said, and stopped. He "obstinately" kept his eyes fixed on a paperweight on the desk. The continuing silence was an absurdity. He was in an agony and felt that he had already, in the last few minutes, shown himself to be almost mouselike, not at all the hero she had imagined! He knew he would remember these minutes with extreme discomfort, actually perspire at the recollection of making such a fool of himself. For this very reason he glanced at her face and saw a suggestion of contempt in her expression. He turned toward her, buried his face against her; his hand pressed her breast to his lips. He sought hungrily around it on the cloth of her dress.

"Fyodor Mikhailovich——" She jumped up.

He clasped her around the knees, imploring her. "Please— I'm in need of you. I need you—Paulina—Paulina——" The peculiar whining tone in his voice disgusted him and he knew that in this posture he must look ludicrous. Under his weight she sat heavily down on the sofa again. He clasped her, kissing her neck, leaning over her, covering her creamy neck with kisses. It hugely excited him.

"Please—no!" She struggled, his lips reached her jaw and rose and reached her mouth, covered it; he felt her lips quiver in secret pleasure. The embrace extended; she accepted his caressing. They were pausing in the long kiss, shifting gently.

At this moment, intensely intimate and tender and harmonious, the ugly image of Izay Fomich came to his mind. He was revolted and the greater efforts he made to dispel the picture with thoughts of the young girl he embraced, the more persistently Izay Fomich danced, picked over some old rags, and scratched his crotch; until he saw that he was positively conjuring up attitudes of the old man. The next moment his hand was lifting aside the encumbrance of the dress, he felt her helping, and he lay covering her. Her arms moved on his back. The warmth of her thighs bore him. The warmth and brimming soft acceptance touched and she drew him to her and enclosed and enveloped, the rich tight-seizing warmth pulsing unbearably. He had a moment of control, of cresting control, control, then all was plunging with the compelling drawing inability to continue, to remain, to withhold all in rings, all in waves of overreaching, grasping, ending and declining and fading and contracting in a last sharp brief ring-grasp and holding, holding and releasing.

The rain blew against the window outside.

He watched her reclining, showing herself quite unashamedly, the slight rose pouting under the dark curling triangle, the long legs as she adjusted the top of her stocking. She seemed quite cool—accusingly!—finished a rather complex arrangement of underclothes, flouncingly smoothed her skirt, and looked at him. Her hands began adjusting her hair. There was an almost indifferent look on her face. He was overcome by shame at her coolness.

He bent on his knees at the sofa, clasping her hand, covering it with kisses. "Forgive me, Paulina, my darling—I—

it was—I was overexcited. It was too quick, finished too quickly. I couldn't——" He felt he must continue to the full, humiliating acknowledgment. "You're not—I mean, you—you didn't get to the end? Nothing happened with you. Did it?"

She said to him with a smile, "Give me a cigarette, will you?"

He jumped up, turned to the desk for the cigarettes, and had reached it when she said, "I was hoping it would last longer."

He groaned. He rushed over to her, flung himself on his knees again. "Paulina—forgive me. I couldn't help myself. You are too wonderful. I had too much desire for you. It will be better later. The first time is never good."

She threw her head back in the graceful, magic way and laughed at him. He was unable to move. She said, "Where is my cigarette?" He gave it to her and lit it. "And I am called Pauline," she said. She exhaled a long jet of smoke, looking at him and smiling again with such amused cool majestic young mastery and mockery.

3

Sometimes he was ashamed, mouselike, enormously desiring her and imploring, at others he dominated her. He stood in front of the glass, tortured about his appearance, trembling at the possession of such a young creature, looking at his pale, now unhealthy-looking face with hollows in the cheeks and lines produced by his nervous tics, by his efforts to keep his muscles still, the thin mustache which he bit nervously, the deep eyes with the enormous pupils. He looked shut up, silent, locked with a key—a man from prison or a hospital ward.

She was independent and complex, intelligent and full of an aggressive pride. He knew she was attracted to him because of her romanticism; her admiration for him was genuine. When he talked, described his experiences, and explained the meanings he found in life, she was at his feet. But even then, dominating her, he felt his own ugliness and her desire to escape. He felt a resistance in her—and grasped at it because it heightened the pleasure of possessing her.

Sometimes when they made love she protested at his appetite, at his excess, his ways of intensifying their feelings; she was offended. He implored her. He wanted her to accept things which, for all her student boasting about sexual emancipation, shocked her, hurt her mentally—and yet she did accept them, was dismayed and ashamed afterward, psychologically upset. During these hours of love he excited her until she completely lost her head and didn't know what she was doing. He made her share shame with him in a voluptuousness which she fought, welcomed, desired, and could not escape. And her admiration turned to disgust. *She* dominated with her body—and he made her feel revolted by that!

At other times she complained that he was keeping her like "an ordinary mistress." She was drawn to the excessive in him, the element that made him go beyond ordinary limits. It answered something in herself. She felt herself an exceptional woman. And when they began meeting and making love with methodical regularity she became exasperated, reproaching him with spending too much time at the *Vremya* office, too much with Marya Dmitrievna, with behaving "like a merchant."

"It's repulsive! You're becoming a man who takes things solemnly, who's busy, does his duty in his own fashion, but doesn't forget his pleasure—me, my body! You want to be dissolute regularly. You're like the doctors who say a man ought to get drunk once a month for his health—you think working yourself off on me is indispensable."

"Pauline, I want you to——"

"Oh, go away!"

"Listen. I see you as often as I can. Do you think it is

amusing for me at home?" Marya Dmitrievna's health was worse. The rows with her were endless.

"Then you'll meet me tonight, and tomorrow," Pauline said. The week after she was wanting to break off but continuing to see him in spite of her "disgust." She was languid, moved slowly, with only a few gestures. Her father had been a serf, intelligent enough to earn money to buy his freedom, come to Petersburg, and set up a successful business. She was one of the new generation. She was sighing to go to Italy and sometimes they discussed going together.

He was working harder than ever at the review. The pressure was constantly greater since *Vremya* was thriving, increasing its circulation each month. He had the keenest pleasure from one story he wrote called "A Vile Predicament." Partly it grew out of his relationship with Suslova; it was another exploration of the feeling of shame and embarrassment which she was enlivening and renewing in him.

It was about His Excellency General Ivan Ilyich Pralinsky, forty-three years old, tall, handsome, and smart, walking home in Petersburg one enchanting frosty night after drinking champagne with two of his older friends and speaking of decent men's humanity toward their inferiors. On his way he passed a house where he heard the noise of a gay party with thudding dancing feet. One of his clerks, a cringing fellow called Pseldonimov, was celebrating having married that day. Ivan Ilyich, a little tipsy, went in on impulse to pay them a pleasant call, evoke their nobler feelings by his presence, quite on an equality with them, as a gentleman. His appearance struck everybody with stupefaction. Instead of welcoming him with deferent smiles and bows, the crowd of guests, poor clerks, tradesmen, and so on, were idiotic, dismayed, awkward, and overawed. Ivan Ilyich tried to "put them at their ease," but the more he did so the more horribly embarrassing the situation became. Yet pushed on by some uncontrollable force, he grew tipsier, more foolish, then hopelessly drunk as he saw he had wrecked their evening and at last in a climax of horror fell down unconscious and had to be carried for the night to the bed which had been meant for Pseldonimov and his bride. When he made his appearance at his office several days later, Ivan Ilyich was relieved to be presented with a petition from the crushed clerk Pseldonimov, asking to be transferred to another department. "Tell him," he said, "that I feel no ill-will. On the contrary I am ready to forget all that is past." And he and the chief clerk both flushed vividly with discomfort at the recollection.

Dostoevsky laughed and rubbed his hands over the story. Then in January there was revolt in Poland against Russian rule. It sent a profound shock through the country. The Russian liberals wavered. The Slavophiles were at a loss; they could scarcely condemn brother Slavs outright and urge Russian soldiers to suppress the uprising in blood. In Petersburg everybody's nerves were put more on edge by rumors of fire-raisers being about; and some fires did occur. But Polish insurgents were attacking Russian troops. Russian soldiers were dying. After the first pause Petersburg and the rest of Russia surged into vibrant nationalism. Turgenev sent a subscription for Russians wounded in Poland to a Petersburg paper with a special letter to the editor. Muravyev, whose cousin had been executed as a Decembrist, crushed the rebels at Vilno and chuckled, "I'm one of the hanging Muravyevs, not the Muravyevs who *get* hanged!" Grigoryev threw his pen on the desk in the *Vremya* office, drank from a bottle, and wiped his lips. "There you are; this delightful spring—the end of the great Russian liberal dream."

Three nights later Dostoevsky was lying in the miserable room he rented for meetings with Pauline. She was stretched out beside him, her back to him, perhaps asleep, the sheet fallen away from her, her long legs bent at the knees, her head forward, as if she were waiting to submit. He shifted on the bed toward her again, taken by the submitted offering curves of her back, the wide arching of profiled hip. Slowly, his knees, also bent, traveled down the soft yielding of recumbent thigh-back and, interlocking at her knees, joined all-being loins against the swelling but unmoving warmth. Smoothly following divide and tremblingly directing pressure to resistance, he was aware of her silent conscious acquiescence, continued pressure and felt counterpressure produce the beginning of achievement and heard her murmuring pleasure. He was captured in the encircling resistance, adoringly received furthermore, arching and furthest and furthest, the springs, the springs, the furthest clamping, quivering arching of all the upreaching flying springing spring.

She lay still, then shifted away from him. He thought there was slight irritation in the shrug away of her shoulder. It was a very conscious, alert-minded shrug. She kept her back turned and said nothing. She was still faintly shocked at their love-making in that way, thinking that physical pleasure should be orthodox, according to mysterious tribal custom and taboo which, in conversation, she said she had discarded but which she still, to his excitement, felt and tried to make use of by pretending that that fashion was selfish on his part since it gave him more instead of sharing the essential experience between the two of them. Yet each time she showed her desire for it herself, so that he believed she experienced as much as he did. But afterward she was often irritated. In some curious way it was an acknowledgment of his power over her which she resented.

When he awoke a little later she was dressing. The straps of her slip had fallen down and her breasts hung out as she bent to put the stocking on her foot. She rolled the stocking over her knee, up the thigh, and pulled it smooth; he watched the tilt of her oval breasts again as she put the garter on. She looked up and caught his eyes on her and for an instant there was an expression of disgust on her face; then she reached over to the chair, took a cigarette, and lighted it.

He got off the bed and knelt before her, burying his face in her lap, moving past the garter in the soft faintly odorous valley between the two columns of her legs. She pushed him away. He stood up; he was close to her, his expression imploring. She looked at him and then lowered her eyes. He bent down, lifted her head, and kissed her on the mouth. "Pauline—please—please." She pulled her head away but he caught it, turned it, and kissed her mouth again, standing close to her so that she felt him; and she yielded, her hand reaching and moving. He took the cigarette, stubbed it out, lifted her, and carried her to the bed and knelt over her.

Afterward as she put the slip on over her head again and languidly smoothed it, she said, "I received my passport today."

"You did! And you didn't tell me before."

She looked at him sideways, as if she regretted now having told him. "I don't know whether I want to go away with you. I—I feel soiled by you. Sometimes I hate you."

"Listen, Pauline, listen, please, my darling." He was imploring again. "Give me time. I'll ask for a passport at once. I think I can leave the review to Misha. There's so much to do. I'll manage it somehow. We'll go to Paris and Italy. Yes, yes!"

"I need money," she said. She was looking at him with contempt.

"I'll get it. You'll have it, I promise." She drew away from him.

He left her a few steps from the door of the house where she lived, kissing her hands fervently in the dark street. He hurried home in a strange mood. He still felt the excitement of the erotic experiences with her, turning them, savoring them in his mind's eye, seeing her with appetite turned from him, ready. And yet there was an infernal quality in her.

He reached the apartment house and went upstairs hearing Marya Dmitrievna's everlasting coughing. As he opened the door he was surprised to see Mikhail, Strakhov, and Grigoryev standing together in the middle of the room. They looked around at him and came quickly toward him.

"My God! We've been looking for you everywhere," Mikhail said. Dostoevsky glanced around at their strained faces. "What's happened?"

Mikhail said, "We have been ordered to shut down the review."

"What?" Dostoevsky stared at them. "We're suspended? That's a nuisance."

"No, not suspended," Grigoryev said. "Shut down. Shut down for good. Banned."

"It—it isn't possible." It was a crushing blow. "Surely they—— We've never been warned. They always give warnings first. No, no, it's a mistake. It's some overzealous new censor." He realized they were all looking at him in silence and stopped. "What reason do they give?"

Mikhail said, "Strakhov's article last month about the Polish rebellion."

"What—'The Fatal Question'? But it went through the censorship without a scratch!" He looked at Strakhov, who was overcome. "Perhaps I read it too quickly. Nikolay Nikolayevich, was there anything risky——"

"Nothing that the Slavophiles haven't said already," Strakhov said. "I talked about Polish writing and culture in the past. The whole point of the article was that, once Russia had predominance in literature and art and culture in Poland, there wouldn't be a Polish question any more—so those were the weapons we ought to be using."

"The Moscow *Gazette* has been screaming against us," Mikhail said, picking up cuttings from the table. "Saying we're pro-Pole and claim that Polish art and culture are better than Russian."

"I think I remember seeing something of that," Dostoevsky said. "They are trying to show their own orthodox purity."

"And now the *Revue des Deux Mondes* in Paris has reprinted Strakhov's article," Grigoryev said. "The *Deux Mondes* is anti-Russian. All this put together——" He shrugged.

Dostoevsky said, "We must appeal at once."

"My God—Fedya." Mikhail looked at him, fearful and pleading; it was something of the same look he had had on the night he had come to the Peter and Paul Fortress to say good-by. Mikhail kept a mistress and behaved like a Petersburg man of the world and now that all this was in jeopardy he was calling on his brother for strength.

"If only they will let it go this once," Dostoevsky said. "We are a success. It's a matter of three or four more numbers and we'll be home, we'll be accepted, permanent. They must let us carry on. If we're held up now it'll be terribly damaging."

"You're forgetting," Grigoryev said. "We aren't shut down for a number or two. It's the end of *Vremya*."

There was a pause. "No, no. It's impossible," Dostoevsky said. "There's a misunderstanding somewhere. It's too stupid. It's too *bête*. No, it's too *bête*. I'll go to the Ministry tomorrow."

"How can you?" Mikhail said. "You're not even legally responsible for the paper." The sound of prolonged coughing came from the next room. Dostoevsky felt overwhelmed with guilty feelings about Suslova. All this had happened, they had all been tortured and wretched, and he had been away from everything with Pauline. But he would have gone to her anyway! He would have told her about it and said, "And you see, here I am all the same. It's vile, isn't it? It is quite despicable, eh? But that is how I am. That's my underground soul. There, you see!"

His face went red. He said to Mikhail, "I'll go tomorrow. It doesn't matter about being legally responsible." Something infernal but irresistible urged him to reassure them all deliberately and shamelessly. "I know exactly how it can be done. I've just thought of it. Of course! Rely on it, I'll settle it tomorrow in an hour!"

The next day he woke up rather late. Masha was tapping

about in slippers, looking bedraggled; she was thinner than ever and kept holding her head and spitting painfully into a handkerchief. He wriggled uncomfortably as the previous night's conversation went through his mind again, especially his own words about arranging for *Vremya* to continue. The idea of lying in bed seemed to him particularly disgraceful, even disagreeable; moreover the room was untidy and there was a bad smell coming in from the courtyard below. Altogether it was distinctly distasteful.

Mikhail and the others had been surprised at his saying he could save the review. He had told them all sorts of lies! And acted. In the end he had been acting the "good and noble" man who took all their cares on himself and would settle them all in a spirit of altruism. Ugh!

"Are you going out this morning?" Marya Dmitrievna said contemptuously; she had heard them talking last night.

"Yes." He got up and dressed. When he left the house he did not turn toward the Ministry of Home Affairs but went in the direction of the Offizierskaya. It gave him a shameful tingling to think that they were all believing he was on his way to intercede with the officials, all of them—Strakhov, Grigoryev, Mikhail, his mistress and wife, their children perhaps. They were all probably having a lazy morning, thinking they could leave it all to him! And he was not going there at all. There was something so disgusting in it that he kept saying he could turn aside, take the next street, and go back. He even slunk rather artificially along close to the buildings. He had not only raised their hopes; it had ended by their going away quite reassured, even happy. How was he going to manage it? they had asked. "I have made the acquaintance of a general, exceptionally influential," he heard himself saying—and remembered that he had even put on an injured, martyred look as if he were sacrificing something for their sakes! He had done that! It was loathsome. And it was done and could never be undone. One couldn't correct life like a printer's proof. An action was done forever. There was something exceedingly painful and yet agreeable in thinking that. And inwardly gnawing himself for it, consuming and despising himself, he tasted the enjoyment, the acute consciousness of his degradation. He would not have exchanged it against anything!

He reached a building with false columns against a yellow façade and went in. At the far side of the imposing hallway was a dingy corner with a man in a tight coat sitting at a table.

"Where is the Authors' Fund?" Dostoevsky said. The man gaped soundlessly and raised three fingers. Dostoevsky went up. There was a carpet on the third floor, two potted palms and a lot of polished brass, an air of comfort. He found the door with a plate outside it: Fund for Assistance to Needy Men of Letters. A bell tinkled as he opened the door into a well-furnished office. A woman looked up from a desk. He was at once sharply aware of his shabby clothes; there was a particularly large yellow stain on the knee of his trousers. The woman was advancing toward him with an assumed, meaningless smile; she was small and brisk-looking with hard eyes.

He bowed, with surprise saw her walk past him, and as he flusteringly caught himself she shut the door which he had left open behind him. He went red with vexation. With that one action she had "put him in his place" at once; her attitude expressed that. There was something intensely Russian in that too! He felt an urgent desire to live up to her expectations. He would just blurt out rudely what he wanted. "I beg your pardon—er—good morning." He bowed again. (There, you see! he said furiously to himself. I can't do it. I begged her pardon. Ugh!) "I have come to ask for some money. My name is Dostoevsky. I need help. You exist for that purpose. I—er——"

She looked at him with the wings of her fleshy nose moving like the gills of a fish. "You are inquiring about the formalities?" She was retreating, eying him up and down. "You wish to know how to qualify? The regulations are laid down by the committee."

"I am qualified. You will find all about me from the official records. Dostoevsky. I assure you the committee knows of me."

She paused mistrustfully, then said, "I will fetch Mr. Karminsky. Kindly wait." She disappeared into the next room, shutting the door ostentatiously.

He waited. The quiet of the place added to his tension. He sat on the edge of a chair, hearing the woman's voice and a man's in the next room. His position was already humiliating and he knew in advance that he was going to behave contemptuously in front of Mr. Karminsky because there was simply no escape from it. One couldn't change oneself; even if one believed in one's ability to become a different man, one probably wouldn't want to—or wouldn't do anything about it, because really there was nothing left for one to change into! But that was nonsense! He decided that for that very reason he would be offhand with Karminsky.

The door opened and Mr. Karminsky came in with the woman. Dostoevsky sprang to his feet with unnecessary alertness—and went crimson. He was already doing exactly what he had sworn not to! Mr. Karminsky was tall and bony with glasses and he looked particularly dull-witted, which made it worse.

"Mr. Dost-o-ev-sky?" He enunciated with extreme punctiliousness. He had, of course, noticed Dostoevsky's abject overeagerness; his expression showed that he put it down to deliberate obsequiousness and made clear that he was superior to such "tactics."

"Yes. I want to borrow three thousand rubles," Dostoevsky said. "It's essential I have the money, you understand?"

"Oh, no doubt, my good sir," Karminsky said in a sarcastic way; his eye traveled down from the large yellow stain and up again; he did not disguise his contempt. "No doubt. There are certain pre-lim-in-ar-ies, of course. H'm! Perhaps the committee will agree to consider your case. Please sit down." They all sat; the woman looked on rather disapprovingly. Karminsky took a paper and pen. "Be so good as to answer my questions." He began asking about dates of publication, rights to Dostoevsky's books, contracts.

In the midst of replying, Dostoevsky interrupted. "Could you let me have something now?"

"Er—no." Mr. Karminsky looked at him with the greatest dislike. There was something particularly insulting in the pause. At that moment he moved his arm and the sheet of paper on which he had been writing fluttered from the table and landed on the floor between them. Dostoevsky leaned quickly forward to pick it up, then checked himself, but too late. He could not conceal it and turned crimson again. Karminsky (as Dostoevsky was agonizingly sure he would) at once made the most of it. "Don't bother, I'll pick it up," he said loftily—but only when he saw that Dostoevsky was not going to, and even then he managed to do it so that he gave the impression of forestalling him. Dostoevsky felt utterly disgraced; he felt that he had as good as picked up the paper himself.

Karminsky was saying patronizingly, "We have to make inquiries; those are the rules."

"But I need the loan at once."

"For what reason?" Karminsky said, raising his eyebrows and giving him a peculiar stare. Dostoevsky saw he believed it was for some mean purpose. He was tempted for a moment to make a confession, to give some intensely intimate and private details about his relationship with Suslova. He said in a deliberate voice, "I would rather not say." He knew this was almost the worst possible answer and also that it was absurd, that he was exaggerating again. Karminsky looked at him with positive disgust, said, "H'm," and wrote something.

Dostoevsky began to believe he would get some money because Karminsky felt his superiority was acknowledged!

It would be too sickening to flatter him. He had no sooner thought this than he managed, with a white face, to bring out one or two flattering remarks; Karminsky received them with a sarcastic look.

At last, after some argument, Karminsky agreed to advance half the sum he had asked for—fifteen hundred rubles—on the security of all his published work and an undertaking to repay the money before February. Dostoevsky signed, took the money, and hurried out.

He went straight to Suslova's house. She shared a room with a girl student named Brylkina but would be there alone at this hour. She answered the door holding a wrapper around herself with one hand at her hip and smoking a cigarette. She was surprised, and seeing his agitated face, she paused; then she held the door wide and he went in.

"What's happened?" she said.

"Here, look here." He stepped up close to her, pulling the money from his pocket. "The money for Paris. I promised it. A thousand rubles." He thrust the notes tremblingly into her hand, cramming the rest into his pocket. "Pauline, my darling." He put his hand on her arm. Her expression of a moment before had completely changed and she was looking at him with a humble face. He felt a strange disturbance in his heart. She was "pure and good," asking to be dominated by him; and he was overcome with guilt, half mistrusting her and yet tormented by the idea that he was ruining a good woman. Her wrapper fell open. She had a small garment around her waist and wore nothing else. He buried his face against her breasts, bending her backward. He lifted her to the bed. He was like a tiger. Her head lying back, spasms crossing her face, she pushed him away, protesting, but needing, desiring him, claiming, claiming, containment never enough.

She knelt by the bedside afterward, smoking and looking impassively at him. There was a quality about her which made him uneasy; he shifted and got up. She watched him

with the same "good, humble" expression. At the door he
kissed her hands and hurried away. He walked quickly
through the streets. The thought of Mikhail and the others
waiting for his news did not affect him as much as he had
thought it would. When he opened the door of the flat Mikhail and Strakhov came forward, smiling confidently.

He said, "I failed. The general—er—he couldn't intervene.
But we'll find something. But we'll find some way."

The liquidation of the review was interminable. He was
eaten up with impatience. Exhausted, his nerves on edge,
he struggled with administrative details which drove him
into insomnia; there were an infinity of letters to write,
payments to juggle with. Mikhail was too discouraged to help
much. The tenant from whom they had rented the office suddenly died and his agent, an old man, refused to deal with
business at all and had his servant slam the door in their
faces. The chief accountant got a job in Moscow and went
off to it. In the midst of this Marya Dmitrievna's health
became much worse, and during a lull in their disputes
she agreed to move away from the damp of Petersburg for
a while. He borrowed more money, took her to Vladimir,
and returned.

Pauline was longing to start for Paris. When he begged
her to have patience until he had finished winding up the
review's affairs she said, "But of course," quite happily. One
afternoon in the middle of June he went to Dominique's,
bought an expensive box of chocolates, and sent them around
to her. He reached the *Vremya* office some time later and
found a note in her handwriting. It said: "Fyodor Mikhailovich, I am leaving for Paris this morning. I thought it best
to let you know in this way or you might have been upset.
I shall be staying at the Pension Baillet, 6 Rue Soufflot. I
shall expect you in a few days. Pauline."

She had gone! He rushed out of the office. At the flat
Brylkina was sitting with two young men. "She said she'd

sent you a letter. She left this morning." The three of them exchanged glances. "Are you feeling all right?" Brylkina said.

"Yes—yes, thank you." He staggered out.

He lived in a fever, in a continual agitation, working from morning to night to complete the liquidation. Days passed into weeks. The thought of Pauline alone in Paris tormented him. When almost everything was settled there was a difficulty over his passport. As a former political convict he had to have the permission of the military governor of Petersburg to apply for one. He was nearly prostrate at the prospect of a new delay. It was cleared up and he wrote to her that he was coming.

Then he found he had forgotten the three advertisements in the *Official Gazette* to warn creditors of his intended departure. He inserted them—and waited the regulation nine days in an agony for one of the ghosts of the past to appear with an annihilating bill in his hand. None did. He caught the train on the nineteenth, incredulous that it should be a reality at last, in a state of tremendous excitement, the wheels of the coach pounding Pauline! Pauline! Pauline!

Chapter Eleven

1

The steam billowed up under the great glass cage of the Gare de l'Est. *"Porteur, m'sieu?"*

"Voilà, m'sieu, porteur!"

He shook his head, gripping his one bag, hurrying through the crowd out into the Rue de Strasbourg. *"Cocher!"* One of the station beggars sprang forward and held the door open. "Hotel Pascal, Rue des Lions," Dostoevsky called; somebody in Petersburg had recommended it as cheap and decent. They clipped through the Paris traffic. It was nearly noon, a hot dusty day. His heart was bounding. At the hotel he jumped down, forgot to pay the driver, turned back, and overpaid him. He was given a small clean room on the third floor. He walked up and down trying to contain his excitement, not knowing how to start matters. He decided to send a message to her, wrote a note giving the address and saying he would call at six o'clock that evening, and hurried downstairs. The proprietress, a woman in black with hennaed hair and inquisitive greedy eyes, said, "You want the post, monsieur?"

"Yes—no! This must go at once. By messenger. Please send it at once."

"Mais oui, monsieur." She ate him with her eyes and took the note as if she were going to read it through the envelope with her fingertips. He did not know how he got through the afternoon. At the pension in the Rue Soufflot another woman in black sent his message up and showed him into a salon with lace curtains. In a few moments Pauline came in.

"Good evening," she said in an uncertain voice.

"Pauline." He clasped her hand joyfully. She was alternately avoiding his eyes and glancing at his face. "What's the matter?" he said.

She withdrew her hand. "I didn't think you'd come."

"What?" He was staring at her. "Why not?"

"After the letter I sent you."

"What letter?"

"Telling you not to come."

"But—Pauline, why? I don't follow."

"Because it's too late."

He stretched out his hands in a quick movement of appeal, stopped, wavered. She was suddenly unattainable and he felt defeated by youth, by the condition of life, and dropped his head. The next moment he said, "Pauline, I must know everything. Let us go somewhere and tell me or I shall die."

She hesitated, then said, "Very well. We can go to your hotel."

In the cab they did not speak. He kept calling to the driver, *"Vite! Vite!"* The driver looked around several times in a puzzled way. Dostoevsky's mind was in a ferment. He clasped her hand convulsively and once she said in a frightened way, "It's all right. Be calm. I'm with you."

When they got into his room he locked the door and fell at her feet, clasping her knees, kissing them through her dress and sobbing. "Pauline . . . Pauline . . . I've lost you. I knew it." She did not move. He managed to calm himself a little and rose; he held her hands, begging, thinking he must look absurd to her with his forty-year-old, pale, tear-stained face, and not trying to lessen the absurdity but with bitter pain accepting it. "Who is it? Tell me, Pauline, tell me." She did not answer. "Perhaps he's young and handsome? A good talker? Ah, but you'll never find another heart like mine."

She looked at him with melancholy detachment, still without replying.

"Have you given yourself to him completely?"

"Don't ask me that. It's not fair," she said.

"Who is he, a Russian? A Frenchman?"

"Fyodor Mikhailovich, I am in love with him—very much."

"And you're happy?" he said.

"No."

"What? You're in love with him and you're not happy? How is that?"

She avoided his eyes. "He doesn't love me."

"He doesn't love you!" he shouted, clasping his head in despair. "But you love him like a slave. Tell me, I must know! You would follow him to the end of the world, wouldn't you?"

"No. I—I'll go away into the country." She burst into tears.

"Pauline, my dear." He bent over her as she sat on the bed, his arm around her. She wept. There was a strange feeling of joy mingling with the despair in his heart; he had never seen her in tears before. Perhaps they meant everything was not yet over between them? When she had recovered he said, "Tell me, who is it?"

She was still sniffing, compressing her handkerchief in her hands. "He's called Salvador. He's Spanish, a medical student here. I met him soon after I arrived. He's good-looking, has excellent manners. With you, there was—I don't know, I was struggling. Salvador is something else. I gave my heart to him. I didn't know myself. I—oh, I love him, that's all."

"You mean you're his mistress?"

"I love him."

He sat in a chair opposite her, upright. He felt an irrepressible desire to find out everything, to make her confess to the last details. He wanted to know everything as a sort of voluptuous torment.

"Pauline, you went to bed with him?"

"Yes." She was looking at the floor.

"The first time? You did it in bed with him the first evening?"

"No, it wasn't like that."

"Tell me, Pauline. I want to hear." He was trembling; he had a feeling that some devilish impulse in her was pushing her to explain.

"Oh, we met. It was in a restaurant, a students' restaurant. He was with several comrades and they were all charming; I was lonely. He made me laugh a great deal. He is always lighthearted and cares for nothing. They were all gay and happy and begged me to go with them; there was a *bal* nearby, a hall where they go dancing. I went. Salvador was attentive and charming. He——"

"He showed he wanted you? What did he do?"

"Don't, Fyodor Mikhailovich. Don't."

"Yes, please! What did he do?"

"But I can't—I can't," she said.

"Polina, darling."

"When we danced he held me . . . so that I could feel him."

"And you responded?"

"Yes."

"Go on," he said. "Did he take you somewhere then? Did you do it that evening?"

"No."

"You must tell me. That first night?"

"It was after we'd met two or three times." She looked at him and said in a hard, rather angry voice, "Why are you asking these things, Fyodor Mikhailovich?"

With a pale face he said, "Please, Polina. What did you do the first evening, after the dancing?"

"Very well, you'll hear it. You've asked, after all." She spoke in a loud, irritated tone which he thought at once was exaggerated. Yes, she was distinctly exaggerating there. "We went into the corridor at the *bal*. He kissed me. He is dark and very attractive." But all the same she did not go on.

"And he caressed you?"

"My God!" she said angrily. "I knew you would do this. I knew it. Yes, then! He kissed me and caressed me. There, now you know! Damn you—and I liked it, I liked it! My God, why did you come here?" She stopped abruptly and looked at him with a changed expression. She said in a particularly imperious way, "And yet why should I mind? Why should I hate you? You are my slave. You have come here as my slave, haven't you?"

"Yes, yes, that is so," he said. "Polina, afterward, when you went into bed, where was it?"

"In his room—one afternoon."

"Did it—did it last long?"

She looked steadily at him. "We stayed there all afternoon. He is young and big and vigorous. Big and hardy."

"I mean, you completely——"

"Yes. Completely. All, all."

"Even my—even our particular way?"

"Everything! Do you understand? Everything! Why do you think anything is 'your particular'? I am his. I belong to Salvador with all my body and my heart and mind! I am *his* slave in everything. He does all he wants with me."

"You behave like a love-slave with him?"

"Yes, I do." Her face was flushed and he saw with a sort of secret joy that he could not explain that he had angered her. She rose and went to the window. "I wish you had got my letter."

"Ah, Pauline, you were bound to find somebody else sooner or later. I knew it. Your feelings misled you when you gave yourself to me, didn't they?" He crossed to her. "Listen, my darling, do you know that when you told me how he was just now—attentive, always lighthearted and caring for nothing—I had a low shameful feeling. I felt relieved that he wasn't an intelligent man. No, no, I beg you, don't misunderstand that; you know what I mean perfectly. Sit down, Pauline; stay with me for a while. I know how lucky I've been to have someone like you, even though I've lost you."

She sat down again rather reluctantly. "You see I'm calmer now," he said. "Whatever happens, we must remain friends."

"Give me a cigarette."

"Will you promise?"

"As you like." Her expression softened and as he held out a match she took his hand. He had an overwhelming temptation, which filled him with a peculiar sense of disgrace, so that he blushed.

"What are you thinking of?" she said, noticing it at once.

"Pauline, what are you going to do?"

"I don't know."

"Couldn't we go to Italy together as we planned? I mean as brother and sister? Yes, yes I'll be a brother to you, nothing more."

She flashed him the look of an experienced cocotte and smiled sarcastically. "You would never be able to do that."

"I swear it, I swear it."

For a moment longer her smile mocked him; then she frowned and stood up. "I want to go."

"Are you meeting him?"

"Yes."

"To get into bed with him? You're going to do it in bed?"

She stubbed out the cigarette. "I hope so. Particularly tonight."

"Ah, yes." He felt as if he had received a blow. He took her to the Rue Soufflot. She said good night, promising to see him next day. He walked back to the Hotel Pascal in a fever and threw himself on the bed, unable to beat out of his mind the visions of her making love to Salvador, giving herself—now, now, this minute, this very minute.

He waited for her all next day and she did not appear. At noon the day after he was unable to stand it any longer and went to the Rue Soufflot. She came down to the little salon with a touch of her imperiousness but looking worried.

"Pauline, excuse me." He made a deliberately formal bow. "I very much wanted to see you. I present the respects of your humble slave. I thought, I won't put her out by calling; but here I am, you see. I was nervous, waiting. Excuse me, excuse me." All that was exaggerated, of course; while he was speaking he told himself he was overacting in an idiotic way and even that she saw through it. But he didn't care. Indeed, it occurred to him that it was the moment for some disgraceful trick, and for an instant he actually cast about for one; but he had with regret to give it up because he was more and more struck by her anxious expression.

"Is something the matter?" he said.

"Oh, I don't know what to do." She sat down on a chair and put her hand to her head. "I've had a note from a friend of Salvador's. He is terribly ill. He has typhus."

"Salvador has?" He could not help the sudden feeling of joy.

"Fyodor Mikhailovich, is he going to die?" she said in a distressed voice. "Can they cure typhus now? A sudden case like this, I mean?" She spoke as if he were the most natural person in the world to ask. The joy mingled with a strange feeling in his heart; he thought in a flash of Masha and Vergunov in Kuznetsk.

"Yes, they can. You mustn't worry. There are excellent doctors here. They'll apply emergency treatment. He's young, strong—and vigorous, isn't he?" (That's exaggerating, too, he thought; but I really do feel differently about him all of a sudden.)

She gave him an intent look. "No, please Polina——" He snatched her hand. "I'm speaking hopefully; I mean he'll have strength to overcome his illness if he has your love, your constancy. You must assure him of it. You must make Señor Salvador feel that." He was especially pleased with the "Señor Salvador"; it gave him particular satisfaction. "And you'll call on me for anything you need, won't you? I rely on it. I absolutely insist on my privileges, you know. Yes, yes. I positively have a right to put myself in first there. And your duty is to call on me, for *his* sake. Why are you looking at me like that, Polina? I assure you I'm serious. I shall be offended if you think otherwise." And he actually was ready to take offense. He was sure that if she had expressed a word of doubt he would have been greatly offended!

For a moment she shifted awkwardly. Then she stood up, proud and overbearing. "I have a headache, Fyodor Mikhailovich. I would rather not continue our conversation. I will send you a note later. Good-by." She walked past him out of the room.

He went back. He did not know why, but he felt extraordinarily content with his behavior. The sun blazed down. All at once, without noticing how, he found himself standing on the pavement at the door of a small church. In the mysterious gloom inside he could see the candle flames, looking small, strange, and unreal. It looked cool inside. He thought of the Lenten service with the convicts, the chains clanking, his emotion at taking the sacrament. Ah, but he had lost that faith again now. He thought of the passionate discussions with Shidlovsky, with Belinsky. "What! You are going to supper—and you haven't settled the existence of God!" He had never grasped at belief without doubt in his mind. He knew it would remain so to the grave. His thirst to believe still cost him tortures; and it was a thirst which was all the stronger in his soul the more proofs he had against it. Yet God sent him serene moments; and he believed that there was nothing more beautiful, more profound, more sympathetic, more reasonable, more manly, and more perfect than Christ. He turned away up the empty street, feeling miserable and lonely.

Next morning a knocking at the door of his room woke him.

"One minute," he called out. Wrapping his threadbare

dressing gown around him, he glanced at his watch—seven o'clock—and opened the door. It was Pauline, her face blotchy and tear-swollen. As he stared she advanced into the room.

"You must come to the Rue Soufflot at once. At once, do you understand?" She was angry.

"But what's wrong?" he said, and the incongruous reached out to him and he was suddenly ashamed of his bare feet protruding beneath the shabby dressing gown; he had the recollection of the same absurd feeling on the night of his arrest in Petersburg. "Excuse me, excuse me." He climbed into bed again and drew up the clothes.

"I can't tell you anything here," she said impatiently. "You must come to see me. I will explain everything then." She went to the door. "I expect you at once."

"But, Pauline——" She was gone. He jumped out of bed. The street door below slammed as he hurried feverishly into his clothes.

She came out of the pension dining room eating a piece of bread. "You see, I'm quite calm now," she said, and smiled.

He looked at her with a sort of terror. "Who'll ever understand you?"

But when they were in her room she said, "Do you know who I met in the Rue de la Sorbonne yesterday? Salvador."

"But he's——"

"Rubbish!" She laughed in a strange way. "It was all a lie." She was walking up and down. "He is perfectly well. I understood at once. We had a short conversation. He didn't even try to make an excuse; he was chuckling. I went home and had a fit of hysterics. I thought I was going to be very ill and it was even pleasant to think of. Then I wanted to kill him. I haven't slept all night. And I came to you this morning. There, you know everything."

He struggled to conceal his exultation. "My dear—it is no use tormenting yourself. You've sullied yourself, but that's incidental. He was a young fellow who needed a mistress, you turned up, and he seized the opportunity. Why not? A pretty girl satisfies all tastes."

"Oh, I know. But I feel—I feel—if I could tell you! I must have revenge—I must, must, must! How, Fyodor Mikhailovich? Help me." There was blind anger in her face. He felt crushed. She had called him in to ask him how to pay back a jilting, that was all. "What can I say to you?" he said.

"Listen, Fyodor Mikhailovich, I've written a letter to him; I was writing it half the night." She snatched up the pages from the table and began reading rapidly, rather incoherently, her baffled passion flushing her cheeks. The letter was full of insults; but before she had finished it she was struck by a new idea. "I must send him money. I must. I can't bear the thought that he spent money on me. I want to fling it in his face. Can't I send it back to him? Can't I?"

"No, no. Calm yourself, Polina."

"When he is laughing at me? My God, I want to kill him!" Abruptly she stopped and sat down. "You're right," she said. "He is an insect. All that is beneath contempt."

He took her hands. "Polina, my darling. You'll be better away from here. Let us go to Italy together. As brother and sister. I will be your brother." He felt two tears rolling down his cheeks.

She took her hands away. Then, giving him a strange look, she said, "Yes. All right, I'll come with you. We'll start tomorrow. Leave me now. We will start tomorrow."

2

The guard put his head in at the window and shouted, "*Baden-Baden, meine Herrschaften!*" and they clasped their sides with more laughter. One of the bags fell off the rack and spilled its contents, which set them off again.

"Quick, we must get out," she gasped.

Laughing and spluttering, they stuffed the bag full, hauled
the others onto the platform. The train whistled and pulled
out. They stood wiping away the tears of joy, recovering,
aware of the glares from the respectable Germans. The two
of them had been gay all the way from Paris. Dostoevsky
had brought out a flow of comic rhymes, acted and played
the fool. She had responded delightfully. Once, shifting
close to her, he said, "I'm glad you broke away from Paris
so energetically. I have hopes. Definite hopes." She smiled
but didn't reply.

The platform was bustling. She looked around with curiosity at the fashionably dressed crowd. As they walked
behind their porter she touched Dostoevsky's hand.
"Brother!"

At the Hotel de l'Europe the clerk bowed and said, "We
have a double room and suite on the second floor."

Dostoevsky wet his lips. Seriously, if the pattern were set
now, from the beginning, she would accept. Yet there was
a doubt. . . . The moment seemed to magnify itself. He saw
the clerk's glassy eye loom up, the end of his nose balloon;
the stock tie around his neck was enormous. "My cousin and
I—that is, we shall want two single rooms," he said.

The clerk bowed. "Just so, sir. Would you kindly register?"
Under "occupation" Dostoevsky put "officer." She saw it and
simpered. The clerk was bent over the room plan, muttering,
"Two rooms . . . two rooms . . ." to himself. Dostoevsky was
in a torment. As the clerk raised his head, about to articulate,
he said, blushingly furiously, "Two *communicating* rooms,
if you please." There was a fractional change in the clerk's
expression, gone in a flash; he said, *"Natürlich, mein Herr."*
Dostoevsky fussed with passports, avoiding her glance.

An hour later they were out strolling. Four o'clock was
the hour of the fashionable promenade in front of the Kursaal, the Conversationshaus, as they called it. A military band
was giving a concert in the pavilion. They strolled down the
Lichtenthaler Allee. Everybody wore the latest European

modes. The men had waisted coats, light-colored, fancy trousers. Their tall hats glistened. The women wore crinolines. In their landaus the adventuresses drove by, showing a little lilac stocking at the ankle, their black eyes enormous in their pale faces. Crowds were entering the gambling rooms.

Dostoevsky felt nervous and on edge. Her mood had changed again and she was showing only the vaguest, most tenuous interest in him. At one point, while they sat on a bench, he saw her return the prolonged look of a man who was passing, a Frenchified-looking creature, then drop her eyes and smile in a way that was positive encouragement to the fellow. As they went back she was humming amusedly. She said she did not want dinner and he dined gloomily alone and went upstairs. He tried to sit still and could not. All at once there was a turn of a key and she opened the communicating door. "I've ordered some tea; would you like some?"

"Yes."

"Come in, then," she said. The faint smell of her scent hung in the room. She had unpacked and had evidently spent the early part of the evening writing letters. It was after nine o'clock and nearly dark. She lit an extra candle and they sat drinking tea and exchanging phrases almost cautiously. Then she got up, stretched, bending back and pulling the material of her blouse tight over her breasts; and, kicking off her shoes, she lay on the bed. He looked at her enviously, with appetite, his eyes following her legs. She held out one hand and said, "Come and sit a little closer." He pulled the stool to the bedside and took her hand.

"I was cruel and unjust to you in Paris," she said in a soft voice. "You must have believed I was thinking only of myself; but I was thinking of you too, Fyodor Mikhailovich, only I said nothing so as not to hurt your feelings."

Her cool fingers caressed his hand. She was wearing a broad belt which accentuated her hips and he felt an intense desire to encircle her waist, to feel her straining hips against him, her long legs, knees lifting outward. He glanced away and his eye caught her foot. The muscles of him stirred, he could not restrain himself. He rose, bending toward her—and at the last moment turned away, took two paces, stumbled over her shoes by the bed, and hurriedly turned around and sat down again. He was shaking.

"Where were you going?" she said.

"To—to shut the window."

Her eyes remained on him. "Then shut it if you want to."

"No, it doesn't matter." He was struggling violently with himself. "Do you know what happened to me just now? I wanted to—to kiss your foot."

"Oh! What for?" she said in a mock-startled way and drew up her feet.

"It was a desire I had. I decided to kiss it." He paused. "Do you want to go to sleep?"

"No. I want to be with you."

He got up, hand in trousers pocket, and went restlessly to the window. She said from the bed, "I think I'll undress, after all. It's late. Is that maid coming back for the tea things?"

"No. She won't come back." He approached the bed again and stood there.

"Don't look at me like that," she said. "It makes me feel uncomfortable."

"I feel uncomfortable too," he said, trying to smile. She hid her face in the pillow, then a moment later looked around at him. "Are you sure that maid isn't coming?"

"Yes, I'm sure."

"Then go to your room. I want to sleep."

"All right. Good night." He bent over her and kissed her on the mouth. Her lips trembled under his, his arms went around her, and he pressed her to him with passion, gradually reclining, feeling her beneath him, lying on her—and then her arms were pushing him away, her body lifting. He broke away and got up and went into his room. Pushing the door half to, he sat on the edge of the bed, tortured with desire for her; at the same time he knew he was acting; he was waiting for her to get undressed and in a minute he would go back, pretending to be surprised and overcome by it. The minutes passed. He could wait no longer and went in. She was still lying on the bed as before, her skirt slanting across her thighs where he had rumpled it. She did not move.

He went up to her. "Why don't you undress?"

"I will," she said as if she were only waiting for him to go. He sat beside her. He could see a creamy band of her skin above the top of her stocking. "You undressed with Salvador, didn't you?" he said.

"Yes."

"Altogether?"

"Sometimes not," she said.

"Why not?"

"Sometimes there wasn't time. It was urgent."

He said, "Urgent for whom? For which one?"

"Oh, for me, quite often. Do you think it is always urgent only for men?"

"You asked him, you mean?"

"Yes, I did." She stirred lazily; the band, showing the inside of her thigh, widened. They looked at each other. She was faintly smiling; and then he saw a small change in her expression. "Please take off my stockings," she said as if he were her slave. He leaned forward and with trembling hands took the garter, slid it down to her knee, his fingers lingering over the firmness of her leg. He felt an enormous desire to press his lips to the creamy band at the top; he bent his head down and kissed her there but she pushed him away. He took the stocking; she tightened the muscles, lifting the leg as he rolled the silk stocking and took it off her foot.

"Now the other." She lay quite still. He lifted back the

fold of skirt and took the second off. At once she got off the bed and stood up, removed the wide belt.

"You'd better go to bed now," she said; she was unhooking something at her waist, the next moment her skirt fell, and she stepped out of it. He watched as she did the same with an underskirt and a slip, laid them on a chair, unbuttoned her blouse and removed it. She was moving about the room, lit a cigarette, took no notice of him. He rose. Her back was turned and he saw she was freeing herself from her bodice; their eyes met in the glass and she paused, the cigarette between her lips, the light curving shadows under her breasts.

He was white-faced; he took two steps toward her. She turned around, the cigarette still in her mouth, and said, "Good night, Fyodor Mikhailovich." She moved a hip and her nude breasts swayed.

"Good night." He went quickly through to his room and shut the door.

He lay in bed in the dark. The night was warm. A faint luminosity from the window showed up the outlines in the room. He did not know how long he lay staring, trying to keep off the thought of her in the next room. At last he got up. He was naked. Silently he turned the handle of the door and opened. In the faintly luminous dark he could see her before him sleeping, turned toward him, the bedclothes loosely about her. He stood with the yearning strength of his loins craving, undeniable, and stepped softly up, seeing her parted lips, her neck in shadow, the swell of her breasts before the yearning of him in the darkness. She moved her arm a little. He scarcely brushed her, so lightly, caught his breath and fled, unable to shut the door, reaching his bed and throwing himself face down on it all springing and outward bursting, shaking and overwhelmed in the dark still room.

She tantalized him. She drove him to anger and despair.

One minute she was delightful, confiding, full of laughter. The next she was proud, imperious, completely selfish. In the secret moments she could have given lessons to the Marquis de Sade. After that first evening she left the communicating door unlocked and he was constantly seeing her undressed. She seemed to take no account of him, which infuriated him. When he tried to embrace her, to kiss her, she encouraged him for a while, was crude and enticing in her special way, then turned him away. "No. You promised, Fyodor Mikhailovich. We are brother and sister." And the moment after, she was inviting him again.

He sat in her room watching her while she stretched languidly half dressed on the bed—until he could bear it no more and rushed out, ill with frustration. She called him in on some pretext at moments when she was drawing a stocking to her thigh or sitting with a loose wrapper on, pretending not to notice his looks. He was wildly, tormentingly, impossibly in love with her. Her youth and beauty were magically attractive, yet he felt she would commit a crime with the greatest coldness and indifference. He wanted her to come to him and say, "I love you"—and if she wouldn't, then what was there to care about? All he wanted was to be near her.

She provoked him to talk of his love for her, to amuse herself. She liked to work him into a state of misery, to hurt him with some display of contempt. He was indignant, obeyed, even acted in the most humiliating way to please her, and then found she had forgotten about him. Another thing. She tried to anger him to make him pay for her allowing him to ask questions about herself, about her affair with Salvador. She disliked his questions but said, "It amuses me to see you so furious. You must pay for my permitting these liberties."

He said, "I consider I am entitled to ask you any question simply because I am ready to pay any price you want for it." She laughed.

The relationship provided constant new turns. She knew that he loved her and showed that she knew. She allowed him to speak of his feelings for her; and then with exasperation he saw that it was only a refinement she had invented for showing contempt for him—letting him speak without restriction as if she cared so little for his feelings that she didn't mind how much he talked of them. This led back to her attitude about the questioning. For, since she treated him as a slave, she sometimes behaved as if there was nothing for her to be offended at in his curiosity and so she did not seem to notice his questions at all. It left him weak, baffled, longing for her, detesting her.

She was love and hate. She made him understand how intimately hate may be interwoven with love. She teased his appetite for cruelty and showed him again what he had understood with Marya Dmitrievna, how close suffering was to desire. She was superb. In the style of her soul, he felt intensely, she was a perfect Russian. When she refused to leave the hotel room he spent hours in the gambling rooms and lost steadily.

One morning they were sitting in the gardens after a night of utter frustration when she had allowed him for a long time to lie beside her, kissing and caressing her breasts, and then turned him unconcernedly out of the room. He said intensely, "Polina, do you know, I shall kill you one day? Not for jealousy or because I don't love you. But because I want to eat you—to devour you, yes, yes, consume you——"

"Oh, stop!" she said. He saw she was breathless with anger; and secretly rejoiced. "How disgusting!" she said.

"I don't care," he said. "Sometimes I feel an irresistible longing to beat you, to strangle you. And do you think it won't happen, Polina? You're driving me beyond anything." She was glancing around; they were sitting in a quiet alley of the gardens where there were not many strollers. "It's all right," he said in a loud voice. "I'm not afraid of a scandal. I love you without hope and I know after this I'll love you more than ever." He seized her hand. "If I kill you I'll kill myself too. And do you know something incredible, something quite unbelievable, Polina? I love you *more* every day and yet that's impossible. It's impossible!"

"Let go of me!" She tried to free her hand. "What absurd talk."

"Absurd or not, I don't mind."

She looked at him with prolonged fixed attention. "Are you a coward?" she said.

"I don't know."

"Will you kill a man if I tell you?"

"Who—Salvador?"

"Whoever I say. Answer me! You told me last night you were ready to do anything for me—'something heroic,' you said. Or were you exaggerating as usual?"

Perhaps she was half joking; but he knew she was capable of an enormity. "You wouldn't ask it."

"Ah, you see! You're simply a talker. I wouldn't ask you such a thing. Do you suppose I'd care about what happend to you? I'd look on."

"What!" Her bluntness shocked him; she was crudely asserting her rights over him. A humiliating phrase came to his mind; he struggled not to say it and then gave way in a sort of secret satisfaction. "It is worse than slavery or insignificance."

She threw her head back, laughing. "You said you liked this slavery. I thought you found it pleasant."

"You thought I did!" he exclaimed, feeling a subtle enjoyment. "That's either naïveté or it's very clever. Oh yes, there's pleasure in utter humiliation and insignificance."

She was laughing again. Suddenly she said, "You see that man coming along here? Go and say something to him in French." It was the Frenchified man she had smiled at on their first afternoon; they had seen him almost every day in the gardens. Pauline never failed to glance at him and twice even smiled again, which, to Dostoevsky's fury, the man seemed to find most encouraging. He hated the fellow.

"Do you think I won't?" he said. "But it's just a stupid idea. There's no point in it at all." He understood perfectly that she was insulting him again—reducing his "something heroic" to this.

"And suppose it is? I don't want to discuss it!" she said venomously. "Simply go and get yourself thrashed, that's all. I want to laugh."

Dostoevsky looked at the man again. He knew exactly the sort of creature he was and she, of course, had seen it at once. He was one of the special class of men, usually former officers, found in Russia, Poland, and sometimes in France, who were extremely dangerous because of their reckless insolence and thickheadedness. They were bored; they were experienced swordsmen and pistol shots and were always fighting duels. At some time in their lives they had performed some completely fearless action, done something defiant, even horrifyingly daring and foolhardy—perhaps having boasted of their ability to do it beforehand and then actually doing it—gaining a reputation and living on it for the rest of their lives. Often the action was quite senseless, something disgraceful, and had brought some honorable family into scandal. They were idlers, rakes, reckless gamblers at cards, and though they displayed an offhand manner they were in deadly earnest and never let pass the suspicion of an insult.

"Very well," Dostoevsky said. "I'll go." He rose, walked to the path, and waited. The man approached. He was of medium height, elegant in a close-fitting waisted coat, tall hat, and carrying a stick, rather dark-faced with a military mustache. His eyes went to the bench where Pauline sat alone and he smiled to himself, evidently thinking he was going to make her acquaintance; then he saw Dostoevsky.

Dostoevsky took off his hat and said distinctly and carefully in French, "Monsieur, I am accompanying that young lady and I beg to bid you good day." Then he bowed, put his hat on deliberately, and walked away.

He felt sick and his head was spinning. And yet some impulse pushed him to go further, to aggravate the whole thing. He stopped, turned, and, giving another bow, said loudly, *"Oui, Prince. Exactement!"*

"Hein?" The man had stopped and was staring at him.

Dostoevsky remained in expectation. With his heart pounding and yet with a sickening inner delight, he struck a *respectful* attitude—yes, it was positively respectful!—and gazed at the man with a smile.

"Hein?" the man said again; his face was beginning to darken, blood coming into it and suffusing his neck. His eyes fixed Dostoevsky's unflinchingly.

In a flash Dostoevsky thought: A duel's certain. It's quite certain now. And suppose he refuses to fight—this man? I'll catch him just as he's leaving and scream at him, "You can drive a man to desperate lengths!" I'll shout to the crowd, "Look at this scapegrace, this puppy who let me insult him in public. I spit in his face—there!" That, of course, will end everything. I'll be arrested, sent to Siberia. In twenty years when they release me I'll hunt him out in some town. He'll be happily married, surrounded by a family. I'll say to him, "Look, you monster, at my hollow cheeks and my rags. I've lost everything through you—career, happiness, art, the woman I loved—and I forgive you." Then I'll fire my pistol into the air and disappear forever.

He thought all this in a flash; and felt intensely sorry for himself and yet he knew quite well it all came from Pushkin's *Silvio* and Lermontov's *Masquerade.*

"Vous êtes fou?" the man said. He was looking mystified.

"Oui, Prince." He gave the word "Prince" a particularly prolonged nasal sound, drawing it out and in fact managing positively to sing it. He waited for the quick, stinging, one-two flick of the man's hand across his face.

The man opened his eyes wide. Then he showed a set of

perfect even teeth in a smile (even at that moment Dostoevsky thought how such men always had perfect teeth)—and
walked on.

Dostoevsky felt utterly humiliated. The man had taken
him for an imbecile. It was almost as if she had arranged
it expressly. As he reached the bench she rose. "Well, I've
done what you want," he said.

She shrugged, hardly glancing at him.

Suddenly the money ran out. They left Baden with a
hundred and twenty francs and traveled through the Swiss
and Italian autumn pawning watches and rings, dreading
hotel bills, and waiting for loans from Mikhail and the
family in Petersburg. But there was not a letter from Petersburg. Not a single one. At one point in Rome, with the hotel
asking for payment, he wrote to Strakhov, pressing him to
raise a loan on a novel about gambling. "It's the next novel
I'm going to write. For God's sake raise three hundred
rubles. Offer it to Boborykin." Boborykin was editor of a
rather second-rate Petersburg paper.

Polina was captivating, baffling, expensive, exhausting.
There were moments when he could have strangled her.
And yet he adored her. When she left him alone and went
out "to visit a museum" he raged inwardly with jealousy.
For days she was hard, with scarcely a tender moment, and
accused him of "hanging around her neck." Then she re-
versed all this, twined her arms around his neck, rubbed
herself against him, and yielded voluptuously to his kisses
and caresses—and in the end refused and escaped from him,
leaving him physically aching, pacing the room ready to
smash the furniture in rage and frustration.

He began trying to avoid ending the evening with her;
but she was also possessive in her torture. She came and lay
beside him on his bed in the wrapper that gaped to her
waist, raising a long bare leg toward the ceiling, joking and
laughing, lying there sometimes for more than an hour,

accepting his lips lingeringly on her breasts and, as his weight became heavier, drawing away, getting up and lighting a cigarette and laughing and turning about the room in a dancing spin.

One night he was questioning her as they sat idly in the room. "My God! I won't answer," she said.

"Oh, you want to. You know, I consider myself at liberty to say anything to you and ask you any question, however candid it is. You can't be offended at a slave, can you?"

"That slave theory is ridiculous."

He said, "After the first time with Salvador, did you always do it in his room?"

"No. Other places."

"Where?" She did not reply. "Outside? In the open?"

"Once. In the park at Versailles. I was afraid somebody would see."

He said, "Did that make any difference?"

"It made it very exciting." She looked at him venomously. "You want it all, don't you? Well, it was good. I enjoyed it immensely. In fact I wanted it again. There!"

He was watching her. "Yes. Go on."

"No." But in a moment she said, "We—we saw someone else first. We passed them, a couple. That was partly what began it." He could see she was recalling it with enjoyment. "Afterward they went away."

He bent forward and kissed her but she did not respond. His hand moved along her leg and felt the soft warmth at the top. She allowed him for a moment, then pushed him away. He got up, lighting a cigarette, and leaned, smoking it, over the end of the bedstead, looking at her.

"Why do you refuse? Is it worth it?"

"I have my own reasons—which I needn't tell you of."

"Yes—caprice, the idea of torturing me."

"Why should I want to?"

"You can't forgive me for the fact that you once gave yourself to me. You're taking your revenge; it's like a woman."

She said coldly, "Do you think so?"

"Yes. And you know, you can make a man suffer for just so long. At the end he won't wait any more."

"What do you mean? No! Fyodor!——"

He stubbed the cigarette out with a move and caught her as she twisted away, holding the wrapper to her. For a moment he grasped her wrists with one hand and pulled her against him, then she freed her hands, beat his face, suddenly entwined her arms warmly around his neck, pressing her body to him, saying to him, "I want you, I want you, all—wait, wait—dearest— dearest—dearest—I want——" and slipping free, escaping, leaving the wrapper in his hands, smiling at him and running nude lightly across the room. He shrugged and lit a cigarette. She climbed like a cat voluptuously into the bed. She raised her arms to him and, when he came over, embraced him in one of the sudden moments of tenderness. "You've done so much for me—and it was all pleasant for me," she said.

"*Eh bien, ma chère*. It's one o'clock in the morning. You're warm and waiting in bed. I am humiliated to leave you like this. But—good night." He smiled and saluted from the door and went out.

There was a letter from Boborykin next morning saying he had sent the three hundred rubles to a local bank and one from Moscow saying Marya Dmitrievna was very ill.

He said to Polina, "I must go back at once. What will you do?"

"I'll go to Paris."

The train carried them north. He was in a fever of self-accusation.

Chapter Twelve

1

Moscow was crowded and deep in the first winter snow. There had been more fires and cheap rooms were hard to get. Dostoevsky walked down Teterinsky Street toward their poor two-room flat carrying the provisions, a cabbage, black bread, and half a rabbit wrapped in newspaper. Ahead, the bells of the Andronov Convent sounded, light and cheerful; then, at a little interval, far off from behind there was the deep bell of the Kremlin.

He turned into the alley, entered the building, and went upstairs. Even in daylight the staircase was dark. The door on the second-floor landing led directly into a formerly spacious apartment now split up among several families; a clerk in the Public Debts Department with his wife and child occupied the outer "room" (formerly the entrance) and the other tenants the rooms giving off it. Even so, the clerk, a pock-marked man with a great thirst, had succeeded in letting out a corner of his room to a still more downtrodden creature, a sort of adult waif who subsisted on God knew what.

As Dostoevsky entered, the clerk's daughter, fifteen years old, was alone, washing herself at a basin. She smiled at him and he glanced at her arms and breasts marbled with soap and water. He was about to speak to her but there was the twanging of a guitar from behind the right-hand door and all at once Marya Dmitrievna's voice screaming, "For God's sake, shut up! Shut up that noise!" then a fit of coughing. He stepped quickly inside. Marya Dmitrievna gasped at him from the bed, "Get that fool away from here. Ah . . . ah . . . I can't stand it. He is driving me mad."

"I will, my dear." In the few days since he had returned and moved her into Moscow, she had become much worse. Before he could put the provisions down, Pasha sauntered into the room holding a guitar to his chest.

"What's the matter now?" Pasha said. "Why can't I play? Can't do anything here." He was a dandified youth of sixteen with a puffy, spotted face and an expression of lazy selfishness. Dostoevsky looked at his new clothes, glistening boots, a watch chain dangling from his fob. He had left the boy in Petersburg with a tutor while he was abroad and had been horrified at his extravagance with borrowed money. Bringing him here with his mother had not been a success either. Pasha did not know how to behave with a sick woman and was quite insensitive; Marya Dmitrievna's illness made her irritable to the last degree and she flew at him every other moment.

"Your mother needs quiet, Pasha," Dostoevsky said.

"He tortures me!" she gasped, and began coughing again. Pasha put the guitar down on a chair and turned away pettishly. At the same second Marya Dmitrievna wrenched herself up onto her knees, reached out and snatched the guitar, swung it, and with furious energy smashed it against the foot of the bed, the strings jangling, the wood splintering and flying as she kept raising and smashing it down again in a mad rage until she was clasping only a remnant of the shattered fingerboard in her hand and collapsed. Dostoevsky held her in his arms. Pasha shrugged indifferently.

She revived, with white lips and burning eyes. "I don't want him in my sight," she said.

"You'd better stay in the other room, Pasha," Dostoevsky said.

Next morning he took the boy to the station and put him on the train for Petersburg. Pasha went off whistling.

Dostoevsky knew she was dying. As the winter dragged

through she acquired the grim ferocious superficial energy of consumptives. His helplessness was bitter to him; he had to stay by her. She made continual scenes. With her eyes blazing she screamed, "Devils! Devils! They're here. I can see them!" And flapping a towel, he opened the door and pretended to chase the devils out. He was overcome with tenderness for her. They had had love together, even if not always. Sometimes, her mind seemingly strangely lighted up, she stared at him for a long time. He heard her mention Vergunov under her breath, as if Vergunov were there beside her. He was fearful of his own health; in the first week of his return he had had two epileptic fits, one very severe.

It was terribly difficult to work in the flat, sometimes impossible. But at night he sat at the table, hearing her coughing on the other side of the room, and poured the torments of his soul into a piece of writing. He had started it as a short piece and it carried him on with extraordinary force. He called it *Notes from Underground*. It wasn't a novel, only partly a story, and the beginning was even like a philosophical and psychological study. But above all it was a confession. He trembled with intense feeling as he wrote; he was greatly moved by it and felt it by far the best work he had ever done. He searched the dark recesses of his mind, laid bare the tormenting impulses, and opened his wounds; he followed emotions down strange corridors where opposites came together, suffering was desire, hate and love intermingled, and the incongruous was spur and reward. As the Man from Underground he explored the tortures and delights of shame; he pretended, put on a false mask, exaggerated, postured, boasted, and behaved in answer to a rationalism that one could reach only after jumping several hurdles. He remembered the humiliations of his schooldays and put them in, including the episode with Arekin, Glazov, and the other cadets when he had walked up and down in the restaurant. In it he was a superior intelligence but the nastiest, most absurd, and envious of all worms on earth. His heart pounded as he showed himself the Man from Underground persisting in an action which he utterly "condemned," prolonging an awful moment, even just because it was awful and knowing that he would remember it with shame all his life! Why were people so unshakably, so triumphantly convinced that only the normal and the positive, only what was conducive to welfare, was to man's advantage? A man loved something besides what was called well-being. The something else itself was well-being! Perhaps suffering was just as great a benefit as conventional well-being? He thought of his mother and the *Book of Animals:* of the impulse to insult Totleben, of all those other moments of the same sort when his life had suddenly become marvelously more real. He tried to convey all that. And from this he wanted to affirm his ardent belief that a man may seek out evil for the sake of evil, knowing it to be evil, desiring it. What a man wanted, what he shattered all the scientific principles of behavior for, was his own caprice, his own free, independent choice. Reason satisfied the rational side of man's nature; but it was by his will that he manifested *every* side of his life, including impulses. And it was his dreams, his vulgar follies that he clung to simply to show that he was not something like a piano key, something which the scientifically delineated laws of nature controlled completely. Yes, yes! A man could consciously, purposely desire what was apparently injurious to himself, or what was very stupid, simply to have the right to desire even what was very stupid *and not be bound by an obligation to desire only what was sensible!*

His mind teemed with these thoughts; they followed so quickly that they obliterated each other and he could scarcely write them down. And then Marya Dmitrievna would call for him weakly and he would hurry over to support her and reach for the basin she spat into.

Then Mikhail wrote that he had managed to get permission to start a new review! Dostoevsky hurried to Petersburg. They made most of the arrangements in a few days, though there was a delay when they proposed calling the new paper *Pravda*. The censorship rejected this as "too dangerous." They named it the *Epoch*. He returned quickly to Marya Dmitrievna; but from then on he began to go regularly back and forth. Turgenev was persuaded to contribute a story called "Ghosts." One day Dostoevsky ran into Alexey Milyukov, from the Petrashevsky days, and Milyukov agreed enthusiastically to contribute. Mikhail managed to borrow ten thousand rubles from Aunt Kumanina to launch the review: nevertheless they had to struggle and watch every ruble. Dostoevsky started *Notes from Underground* in the second number.

On the fifteenth of April Marya Dmitrievna had a terrible hemorrhage and nearly stifled. She lay like wax. He held her in his arms for a long time and said gentle things to her. He sent a telegram for Pasha to come. The next day she was quiet and the coughing had nearly stopped. He sat by her and she stroked his hand and smiled. Aunt Kumanina, his sisters, and Marya Dmitrievna's relations came. The priest stood in the room chanting prayers. Pasha arrived in a flashy suit, smoking a cigar; he had a new ring on one hand. Marya Dmitrievna did not seem to notice. At seven o'clock in the evening she died quietly, passing almost imperceptibly into death.

When they had laid her out on the table Dostoevsky stood looking at her yellowed, sunken face, the pitiful arms crossed on her chest. There were deep shadows all around and only the little light from the ikon in the corner over her head. The terrible thought of eternal separation overcame him, he felt in great need and the old burning question that he had struggled with all his life filled his mind. Is there a God? Masha, shall I ever see you again? He looked at the holy image of the ikon and fell on his knees.

He felt a strange reluctance to return to Petersburg. He

went to the Nicholas Railway Station three times and came away without a ticket. In a moment of reasonless panic he wrote to Pasha saying he was not coming, then destroyed the letter. Suslova wrote to him from Petersburg with a mixture of accusation and friendship. Then one morning he got up early and caught the train. He sat looking out of the window; now he was on the way he felt how irrational he had been. It was spring. The weather was delightful. The snow had melted early and the countryside was green.

They found the *Epoch* office buzzing with activity. The review was going fairly well, no one could say flourishingly. The trouble was that the Petersburg literary world seemed to know they had no money; and they could not persuade good writers to contribute. Dostoevsky was still running *Notes from Underground*. He handed the new installment to Mikhail.

"I see there are some new subscriptions this month."

Misha gave him an unhappy look. Dostoevsky slapped him on the back. "My God! Cheer up, Misha. A little longer and we'll be over the worst." Misha smiled. Dostoevsky said, "Here, give me those address bands. I'll do them. And those proofs—yes, all of them; hand them over."

They managed to get the May number out in June, nearly two months late. Misha was away ill. And then Dostoevsky felt the uneasiness which had hung over him becoming more definite. He was incredulous; he could not accept the idea it suggested. Misha was dying. Early in July, Emily Fyodorovna and her four children knelt by the bedside as he died. The bright sunshine outside showed through the drawn curtains; it was not yet half past seven in the morning. They had watched all night. Dostoevsky walked out into the street. People hurried by; an officer bumped into him roughly. The street glittered, bathed in the brilliant morning light of summer. The dirty gray, yellow, and green façades of the houses had lost their gloominess; and he looked up at them

as if he had been startled. He was alone and frightened. His
life was broken in two. That first part, which had all gone
now, had held everything he lived for. In the second, which
lay before him, all was unknown and new, without one heart
that could replace the two he had lost. He shrank from
starting some new life, forming new ties. He felt the cold
and emptiness around him. All at once he turned and went
back to the house.

2

They sat grouped at the desk in the *Epoch* office. There
was one lamp burning and the desk was littered with papers,
account books, full ash trays, and teacups. The clock struck
eleven. Dostoevsky pushed back his chair. "Well, we have
twenty-five thousand rubles in debts, fifteen thousand of
them in bills of exchange."

Strakhov said, "And we are pledged to deliver copies for
the next six months to the people who've already paid
their subscriptions."

"Yes," Grigoryev said, bending over the accounts. "And
the printing bill for that alone is going to be eighteen thousand."

"Is there anything on Misha's own side?" Strakhov said.
"I mean, in the way of cash?"

"He left three hundred rubles," Dostoevsky said. "Just
enough to cover the funeral."

Silence.

"So we owe thirty-three thousand rubles." Another pause
as they took it in; Mikhail had somehow kept the *Epoch* alive
on credit. Dostoevsky looked around at them. "I'm going to
carry on. I have to. Misha always gave me everything he had
when I was in need."

"But you're not responsible for the bills of exchange,"
Strakhov said. "Misha signed them. You only have to show
the subscribers and creditors these figures; they can't dis-

pute them. If we stop the review now, sell all the equipment, they'll get part of their money back."

"No, I can't, Nikolay Nikolayevich. I cannot. I can't leave that mark on his memory—bankruptcy. No, no. I'll take everything on myself."

"But what about these?" Strakhov indicated a separate pile of bills. "You agree some of them are doubtful, if they haven't really been paid."

"No. Everything," Dostoevsky said. "I'll pay everything —somehow."

The other two looked at each other. "All right." Grigoryev put his arm around Dostoevsky's shoulder and kissed him. Strakhov took snuff and said, "*Mon cher*, it's all very well; I'm sure it's admirable. But will they *allow* you to keep the paper going? You're an ex-political convict."

"What? My God!" Dostoevsky stared. Strakhov was right. "Then you do it, Nikolay Nikolayevich; simply declare it in your name. It's only the mere formality of declaring yourself the editor. All the rest will be my responsibility. You will, won't you?"

"After my article in *Vremya?* Do you think they'd allow me to take over any more readily than they would you?"

Grigoryev said, "I want a drink. Hasn't anybody even got a drink?" He got down on his knees and began searching among the empty bottles in the kneehole of his desk, suddenly exclaimed, and appeared grasping a bottle with three fingers of vodka in the bottom. He drank it at a gulp and said, "I'd like you to ask me, my dear Fyodor Mikhailovich. But that would be bad. I don't advise it. I can get vodka out of a stone—out of a creditor." Dostoevsky was walking up and down. "On the other hand," Grigoryev said, "there's Poretsky."

"Poretsky! That's it—exactly the man!" Poretsky was an earnest middle-aged man, devoted to the review since it had printed a couple of small contributions from him. "We'll nominate him. Go and tell him, Strakhov, at once, at once!"

Strakhov said impatiently, "But we need five thousand rubles' worth of paper by next Friday. It's impossible!"

"I beg you to tell Poretsky. I'll raise the money. We must have it. Wait a minute." He broke off with a sudden idea. "Listen, Nikolay Nikolayevich. There is one real chance for us. I am going away. I want you to see the printers, carry on the editorial work as if we were publishing as usual, see that Poretsky registers himself as new editor. I shan't be in Petersburg tomorrow. Wait for me here on Wednesday evening. Is that agreed?"

"Very well." Strakhov shrugged.

When they had gone Dostoevsky locked up the papers and account books. He had already told Emily Fyodorovna that he would take on her upkeep and the children's, that they need not worry. He sat at the desk and wrote a hasty note to her in case she should think he had fled in face of the difficulties. He counted the money in his pocket—nine rubles, eleven kopecks. The third-class return fare to Moscow by the passenger train was nine rubles. Well, no dinner.

It was a fine night outside. He posted the letter to Emily Fyodorovna and walked to the Znamenskaya Square. The waiting room at the Nicholas Station was full of sleeping bodies. An official in a red cap said the train for Moscow left at eight o'clock in the morning. Dostoevsky found a place on the floor and lay down to try to sleep.

Good old Aunt Kumanina. She kissed him three times on the cheek in the way she always did and said, "Yes, my son. I gave poor Misha ten thousand and you shall have ten thousand too. I feel a lively interest in the *Epoch*."

He hurried back to Petersburg and burst in on Strakhov. "I've got it. I've got it! We can carry on." Strakhov's face was expressionless. "What's the matter? Don't you understand? I've got ten thousand rubles."

Strakhov said, "It's no good."

"Why isn't it?"

"Look at this." Strakhov held out a letter. "The censorship says it cannot allow us simply to carry on the paper. We must apply for an entirely new permit."

"But you told them Poretsky would be editor?"

"It doesn't make any difference."

"Oh, my God! Then let's apply. Quickly, quickly!"

But the censorship had its own pace. Angry subscribers were soon invading the *Epoch* office. "Where are my copies of the review, sir? I sent you the money for them!"

"I haven't had my June number yet. Not out yet? But we're in August. It's a scandal—outrageous!"

Dostoevsky smoothed them down as best he could and turned back to the mountain of work. He was editor, proofreader, messenger, credit raiser. He spent hours wrangling with the censorship, dealt with the entire correspondence, rewrote contributions, somehow persuaded the printers to continue producing the review. He began work at six o'clock in the morning and dropped exhausted on the sofa at 1 A.M. In spite of enormous efforts he could not get the December number out until well into January 1865. He heard that Vrangel was in Copenhagen and wrote to him, "Ah, my friend, I'd gladly go back to prison for the same term if it would pay off my debts and free me from this. It's all anxiety, bitterness, cold nervyness. And I'm alone. Yet it still seems that I'm getting ready to live. Laughable, isn't it? The vitality of a cat!"

But then he could defer the moment no longer. One spring afternoon he flung himself down at the desk in a fever. The cashbox was empty. He had three rubles and one of the old five-kopeck pieces in his pocket. Subscriptions to the review were down to thirteen hundred, not enough to cover expenses. There were bills, bills everywhere. He had written nothing himself since *Notes from Underground* except hack journalism. His reputation was failing. He couldn't raise money on advance projects. The Petersburg publishers were receiving him with skepticism, refusing to listen to his explanations of unwritten novels or to advance cash on them. He had told Krayevsky of a short novel he was thinking out called *The Drunkards,* with a portrait of Issayev; but Krayevsky had shown marked lack of interest. "The trouble is, my dear fellow," Nagorny said, "you're notoriously unreliable." Boborykin was pressing for the return of the three hundred rubles he had sent to Italy for the promised novel about gambling.

He picked up a letter that had arrived with the afternoon post. It was a formal court summons. He must pay twenty-one hundred rubles, two old debts he'd forgotten, within twelve days or be arrested for debt and have all he possessed put under constraint. He felt extremely perturbed. He took out the envelope he had been stinging himself with for an hour and fingered it; it was from Pauline. He tore it open and read it with shaking hands; it was only a page long, she was spending a few days in Salzburg, she had written at night when she had been in a mood of tenderness and loving reminiscence—yet she ended with a stab. "The hateful moments are still here with me too; and perhaps they are the most precious."

Ah, he still loved her deeply. The thought of the days with her in Baden was unbearably exciting. Germany! He suddenly jumped up. The only way to save himself was a big win at gambling. He was going to shut down the *Epoch* and clear out. He scrabbled hastily through the chaotic papers on the desk and found his passport; yes, it was still valid. It would be a mere formality to get the exit visa renewed. He would persuade the Authors' Fund to advance him money again. He would have to pay the worst creditors and leave at once. Quickly he wrote a letter to Pauline. "I am leaving for Germany—with holy recollection of you there. Can't you join me in Baden or Wiesbaden if you'd like a new setting? I beg you, Polina, on my knees. There is a union in our two hearts that, after all, survives these separations. . . ."

He looked at the clock; five-thirty. There was just time to reach the Authors' Fund. He adjusted his tie at the glass, noticing the dirty collar, cursorily brushed his worn swallow-tail coat, and took his hat—and at that moment the conviction overcame him that the Fund would refuse him. He could see Mr. Karminsky's sarcastic look. He paused. No—he *had* to try! Otherwise it was certain jail. He pulled open the door. Facing him on the doorstep was a big-bellied man with a flowing tie, a square face, and gray eyebrows who leaned on a walking stick and regarded him impassively for a moment, then smiled, showing three gold teeth at the side of his mouth.

"Good afternoon," he said in a rich bass.

"Stellovsky." Dostoevsky recoiled. Stellovsky, the publisher, was one of the most dreaded figures in Petersburg. He lived on the flesh of writers, a literary vulture watching for those in trouble and pouncing on them mercilessly. He had exploited Glinka, Pisemsky, many others.

"I was just calling on you," Stellovsky said, entering, steering his belly before him. "You have five minutes?" He said it as if he didn't care anyway what the reply was since he was going to stay and say what he wanted. He put his hat down on the desk, looked around, dusted a chair with his gloves, and sat.

Dostoevsky was staring at him horrified.

"Sit down, sit down," Stellovsky said. Dostoevsky shut the door and came forward. "I hear you're in trouble," Stellovsky said. He took a cigar out of his pocket and examined it closely. "It's very unpleasant getting into bad trouble like that, eh? You're going to have your property seized? They are going to put you in the debtor's prison and shut your review? That is very unpleasant." He lit the cigar. "And you are looking a sick man too. I don't wonder. Very unpleasant."

"Excuse me, I was just leaving. If we could——"

"Leaving? Where for?" Stellovsky's narrowed eye fixed him.

"No—er—I meant I was just going out. It's nothing at all. Nothing." This made Dostoevsky even more nervous than before.

"H'm." Stellovsky gave him another piercingly suspicious glance, then settled on the chair, making it crack, and said, "Do you know, you have been disappointing me, Dostoevsky. Do you know that? It's foolish for a man to get into such a mess, eh?" He lifted his stick, inserted the end under the disorderly pile of papers on the desk, and stirred them with a look of distaste.

With fascination Dostoevsky watched him convey the utmost fastidiousness. Stellovsky appalled and disgusted him. And for some reason, perhaps because of the over-excited state of his nerves, he was tempted at that moment to behave toward him like a mouse; positively like a mouse. He said with gratuitous obsequiousness, "Yes, isn't it? It's stupid, Osip Timofeyevich," and actually curved his back a little. He was immediately shocked at Stellovsky's not even seeming to notice the obsequious tone, as though it were quite natural! He stepped quickly to the desk, snatched two handfuls of papers, and threw them into the waste-paper basket. He was quite certain that Stellovsky would despise him for doing such a thing, and stood smiling in a particularly foolish way. Then he said, "All the same, I feel hurt that you should say it," and blushed. He did not feel a bit hurt; it was ridiculous. He could not think what had made him say that. His red face was tingling.

Stellovsky looked at him uncomprehendingly, then laughed cynically. "I should have thought you would have written another novel, made yourself some money," he said.

"Oh, but nobody is interested, you know," Dostoevsky said in a strained way. "I've proposed one or two things. Perhaps I have too many creditors in Petersburg."

"You have! You're far too much of a risk." Stellovsky's bass laugh made his belly shake. He particularly gave the impression of enjoying himself at Dostoevsky's expense. Then he made a broad gesture. "I'm only interested in an impersonal way, of course. I'm a man of broad ideas. I called in to tell you I can do you a service. I'll print a new edition of all your work in three volumes."

Dostoevsky looked at him. This, he knew, was the opening of the shark's jaws, the very display of the terrible teeth. He said in a humble voice, "Yes—er—for what——"

"You want to know how much, eh? You're all alike. It's always money. Why don't you get this office cleaned out, Dostoevsky? It smells bad. How can you do business in an office that smells bad? I don't understand it. I tell you, your reputation as a writer is ve-ry small nowadays. Nobody wants Dostoevsky any more. You've proved it yourself, eh? You haven't written anything lately, so you can't expect much. I'll give you a thousand rubles each for the three volumes and you won't get more."

Dostoevsky was shaking. Stellovsky offended him more every minute he sat there. But he was offering three thousand rubles. Freedom! He imagined Mr. Karminsky at the Authors' Fund shaking his head. "I very much regret, my dear sir, we can't help you this time. . . ." He said to Stellovsky, "Very well, I'll accept." There was always time to change his mind.

Stellovsky put his hand inside his coat and produced a paper—a ready-made contract! He said, "Since I'm taking the risk, I'll even help to give you a fresh start. You write me a new book by—say the first of November next year."

"Is that included in the terms, Osip Timofeyevich?"

"That's right," Stellovsky said, unfolding the paper. He rattled a pen in the inkpot. "Here, sign it."

"The three thousand rubles covers the new book also?"

"Yes. What do you suppose?"

Dostoevsky felt physically ill; his head was throbbing and his nerves were at extreme tension. He felt the same compulsion about Stellovsky as he had felt all those years before about Speshnev. "What if I can't keep the contract?"

"You can't expect me to throw away three thousand rubles. Be reasonable. Look at the risk I'm taking. And I'm putting you onto the market again. I'm rescuing you! If you can't deliver a new book on time you pay me a fine and give me sole ownership of all your work—including what's to come. I must have some chance of getting my money back."

"But you will be publishing the three volumes."

"At three thousand rubles I'll be out of pocket."

"But *all my work*——"

Stellovsky shrugged and got up. "All right, go to prison." He reached for his hat. Dostoevsky watched him, appalled. He suddenly wanted to show himself that he was not afraid, to show Stellovsky that he was not a spiritless creature and could survive even such terrible conditions. At the same moment the absurd recognition flashed into his mind that he was seeing himself as one of Pushkin's or Schiller's heroes, standing on some mountaintop "braving damnation" and "the powers of darkness"; and he admitted to himself at once that all that was cheap, revolting romantic stupidity—grandiloquence at such a moment!

"Give it to me," he said. He took the pen and signed the contract.

He sat in the train counting the money that was left. After all he had had to borrow from the Authors' Fund to leave some for Emily Fyodorovna, her family, and Pasha. Now he had exactly one hundred and seventy-five rubles left. Stellovsky had insisted on paying the three thousand rubles through a notary—who, it turned out, held the creditors' bills of exchange. It was plain now how Stellovsky had played the trick. He had bought up the bills at a low price and started the prosecution to put him in prison. So that what he had given with one hand he had taken back with the other. He had obtained that contract for practically nothing.

But what did it matter? The train was rolling for Germany. Pauline had written to say she would try to join him. He knew she would come. And he was free; he was free!

3

The roulette wheel spun, the ball clicked across the numbers. It was late, but a large number of players still crowded around the table. Wiesbaden was full and the gambling rooms were a great attraction. Many of the people shouted and pushed in a gross way. Dostoevsky sponged his face. He was exhausted but could not tear himself away. All the same, he thought again, what an unbelievably trashy atmosphere there was—nothing like the newspaper tales, especially those of the Russian papers which had flunkyish articles every spring about the extraordinary splendor and luxury of the gambling rooms on the Rhine and the heaps of gold piled on the tables. There were no piles of gold—indeed scarcely a gold coin.

He looked around at shriveled men and sharp emotionless women. Aging unsuccessful actresses, with dyed hair and their wrists full of bangles and their death-mask faces, sat beside stiff ladies in old-fashioned jewelry and lace dresses that had surely been worn decades ago at some long-forgotten German general's ball. Some of them plainly suffered tortures waiting for mysterious lucky portents before they could bring themselves to play. He understood that! Others went in for a quick game of changing chairs, moving toward the coveted place of fortune. From time to time a few ancient figures tottered in and looked on with watery eyes.

With a great effort he turned to go; he had played all afternoon and evening. At first he had been utterly confused by the table, the odds, the different ways of staking, but had asked questions and understood, won up to ten friedrichsdors, and then lost them all again. As he walked away from the table, his fingers playing with his last gulden, a croupier's voice came throught the din: "*Messieurs, mesdames, les jeux sont faits!*" He ran back and, thrusting his arm between the players around the table, just managed to throw the coin on Even. "*Rien ne va plus!*" the croupier called. The wheel spun, slowed down, and the ball dropped into a number. It was eleven. He had lost. He walked out through the warm night back to his hotel, rather unnerved by the evening's excitement and the beginning of this new phase.

Next morning there was a letter from Pauline. She was arriving in three days' time. He went to the gambling rooms with the last of his money and lost it in two hours. As he re-entered the hotel the manager was standing behind the desk with the clerk; he felt their eyes on him and deliberately pretended not to notice—then looked toward them. The clerk bowed slightly, the manager, a Rhinelander with a fleshy, pear-shaped face, inclined his head—very little. Dostoevsky felt they knew he had just lost his money, that he had nothing left, even that they knew exactly *how* he had lost it, at roulette. They were too experienced. And *he* was too experienced not to recognize the expression, that glint of intimate and exasperated conviction! He wanted to ask them for a room for Pauline but did not dare. He bowed, hurrying into the dining room. Oh, they already knew all about him, eying his shabby swallow-tail coat, nodding over his scanty linen. They were wary of him, that was what their attitude said.

It was a small hotel with an inexpungeable third-rate air, one of those which is never so third-rate, he thought, as when it is also, in a peculiar way "respectable." It was threadbare, dusty, finger-marked; he was amazed at the number of greasy finger marks and mysterious stains there were on everything. Smells hung permanently in the dark passages and stirred from the curtains, the worn upholstery. There were potted ferns and aspidistras and bony red plush chairs. He had chosen it because it was cheap.

The loss of the money did not upset him unduly. Pauline would have some and he was confident that with a new start at roulette he could make a big coup. He pawned his watch the following day, went to the table, and won steadily all evening; then in four turns of the wheel everything disappeared. He groaned and accused himself; he had become too worked up, he had lost control of himself.

He spent the day after walking about the town and the surrounding countryside, bored and impatient. In the afternoon, as he was sitting in the gardens reading a newspaper somebody had left there and yawning from irritated boredom, he caught sight of Turgenev crossing a path nearby. He positively ran up to him. Then, just as Turgenev saw him, he stopped himself, wanting to go back and sit behind his paper. Of course he could not (though for a second the thought flashed through his mind that he ought to have run up solely for the purpose of turning back at the last minute).

"Ah, there. Well, indeed," Turgenev said, looking him up and down.

"Hello, Ivan Sergeyevich."

But Turgenev apparently decided he would go further than noncommittal exclamations and Dostoevsky blushed with fury at the aristocratic and pharisaical way Turgenev embraced him and offered his cheek to be kissed. He completed the gesture of greeting as quickly as possible and said, "I had no idea you were in Wiesbaden. How long are you staying?"

A smile seemed to play fugitively in Turgenev's beard at this; he looked amused, condescending. "Oh, until the next train south, *mon cher*, that's all. I should be in Baden by now but I missed the connection. Here I am without a bag. All my luggage has gone on to the Europe. And I must confess I find Wiesbaden a bore."

My God, Dostoevsky thought, he puts on monstrous airs! He was tempted to say to Turgenev: "I have never met anybody who so clumsily displays all the wounds of his vanity, *mon cher* Ivan Sergeyevich." Instead he said, "Yes, there's no doubt of it, Baden is on a different plane. German civilization is at its best there."

Turgenev looked at him intently. They exchanged a few more words, then Turgenev saluted him and they parted.

And at last Pauline arrived. He pushed through the crowd at the station, seeing her from a long way off. She was wearing a dark blue dress with a fashionable full skirt, a tiny adorable hat with blue ribbons, and carried a little parasol. She had painted her lips slightly and held her head in that proud way—her whole figure expressing suppleness and sexual appetite and magnificent youth.

"Pauline."

"Ouf! I'm glad to be here; that train!" He had forgotten how hoarse her voice sometimes was. She leaned forward and let him kiss her three times in the Russian manner; then saw his intense nervous pleasure and smiled. "Well, how is it? Are you enjoying yourself? What's entertaining to do here? Is there a fashionable crowd? Many Russians and French?"

"Yes, yes. There's everything one needs. You'll see, you'll see. Don't ask me to explain; I'm too excited. Polina, my darling, how was your journey? This way, this way."

She linked her arm in his and with a porter carrying her two bags they went toward the exit talking. Outside she said, "How far it is? You booked me a room?"

"Er—no—that is, I was waiting. It's not far. We can walk."

"Pay the porter, will you?"

He said, "As a matter of fact, Pauline, I haven't any money. Could you pay him?" She took out her purse and paid the porter. Dostoevsky was soon sweating, carrying the two bags in the bright dusty sunshine. A military band which was parading through the streets had brought out a big crowd. He struggled, red-faced, nervous, and overanxious to keep the bags from bumping into massive crinolines, to squeeze through after her, trying to shout conversation to her above the blare of the band and the voices of the spectators, feeling himself ridiculous and uninviting for her with the sweat running down his face, yet so anxious to keep up, to keep moving, to get out of the crush, that he could not stop to wipe it off.

But when they did arrive at the hotel she laughed and was in the best of moods; she stood there cool and entirely self-possessed and he was delighted to see how the German clerk fawned on her, stammered, and even deferentially bowed to him. "*Aber natürlich, Fräulein.* A room near that of *mein Herr* your cousin. Quite so."

They went upstairs together. Alone in his room he rushed to change his damp shirt, to sponge his face, comb his hair, and look at himself in the glass. Presently, when she had refreshed and tidied herself, she knocked at the door. Quickly he let her in, took her hands and kissed them ardently, drew her to him, embracing her, his lips on her neck, her face, her lips. She leaned away, resisting at first, then accepting, leaning back with him pressing against her, opening her lips to his kiss, her arms winding around his neck, prolonging it, a thigh moving against his—then breaking away breathless and trembling.

"Polina dearest——" He fell on his knees clasping her, kissing her skirt. "I love you. You are everything in my life now."

"Oh no!" She laughed, throwing her head back. "It's too like the first time."

"I won't get up until you let me kiss you here—here—here." He actually felt a little light-headed; perhaps it was the walk in the sun. She was still laughing; there was something in her laugh that was distinctly scornful and he couldn't help thinking of the scene in the gardens and her urging him to insult the man. It was as if she secretly despised him; but instead of his usual acceptance of that (and acceptance with pleasure), he felt a sudden desire to cast aside meekness with her, to treat her brutally and disregard her finer feelings altogether. Holding her fast, he grasped her skirt and the mass of petticoats and hoops and wrenched them roughly above her knee and pressed his lips burningly to her leg. She struggled but he kept his lips there, her intimate scent exciting him tremendously. He ran his lips up her thigh until she managed to free herself. She stepped back with a pale face; then suddenly burst out laughing. He was distinctly pleased, as though he had gained something over her and yet at the same moment his tender feelings for her were intensified, were actually more precious to him.

"Are you ready to be more reasonable?" she said lightly. Eying her rump, he rose to his feet; she was adjusting her hair at the glass. She was infinitely more dear to him than she had ever been. She took out a cigarette and lighted it.

"Polina, I—there's something—that is, I have something of great importance to ask you."

She was looking at him with a faint smile. "Well?"

"Do you know—" He wet his lips, suddenly afraid of having chosen the wrong moment; then blurted out, "How much money have you brought with you?"

"That isn't what you wanted to ask, is it?"

He shifted nervously. "Polina, I've lost all my money. I haven't a kopeck. It's maddening. I only lost because I couldn't keep calm. Lend me what you've brought with you and I'll win everything back and some more. It's simply a question of keeping one's nerve. It's only that. There was a man opposite me, a Swede or something, who kept winning and winning; he didn't move a muscle. In that way it's impossible to lose."

"I haven't any money," she said.

"What!"

"I only just managed to scrape together my fare here. To be exact, after paying that porter, I have three thalers."

They faced each other—and the next moment were laughing together. "Isn't there anybody you know staying here?"

"Not a soul." Then he thought of Turgenev. With a sort

of exquisite shameful pleasure that passed into horror he thought he could borrow from Turgenev. She was leaning against the table with her skirt billowing out around her; and then she turned and crushed out the cigarette and he looked at the wonderful graceful line of her neck, her breast and outstretched arm. He was in a sort of panic at the idea of losing her. He said in a loud voice, "No, no, I was only joking about the money. I've got plenty; that is, I'm expecting some in two days. Polina, my love, my love; let me show you the splendors of Wiesbaden." He clasped her lightly around the waist, took her to the door, slammed it behind them, and made her skip a ridiculous dance with him down the corridor.

A light somewhere outside made a pattern across the ceiling. At long intervals there was the sound of a carriage going by. She was lying with her hands caressing his back and shoulders as he lingered over the grove, and pushing him away at too much insistence and holding him again fiercely. She moved gently. Riding, they strove in the wished-for sweet agony and yearning and yearning of delay. And trying to preserve and at the same time to end it violently with all containment, she raised scissors of knees and at once dropped one knee, pleadingly defended, turning her head from side to side. Abruptly he disengaged himself and sat up, back turned to her to delay further, sitting separate, apart. Her arms sought him, twined around him, lips imprinting and exacting, she encompassed all desire and kept it softly and languorously in soft sweet content containing all. He could not stir. Then a spring twanged with their quick shifting, she scarred his shoulders in acceptance, all taking and now urgently reaching to attainment, the center and being of all fulfillment rising and consumed in the beat and demand, beat and demand, losing and taking, claim and exaction, eagerness, reaching, cadence of love, all into all dissolving, ever and ever and ever and ever.

He sat over her afterward, his hand on her breast. After a while she opened her eyes. "You've exhausted me. I thought I couldn't—even once more." She smiled and in a moment of extreme tenderness took his hand, pressed it to her face, and kissed it.

"Polina." He was entirely overcome. He put his hands under her smooth shoulders and kissed her on the mouth with trembling lips. He could not speak. Then, in a minute, he said, "Polina, what I wanted to say this afternoon—I wanted to ask you to marry me."

She was looking at him.

"Polina, my dear——"

She turned her head away. They were silent. Presently, with her head still turned, she said softly, "Will you go." She was inaccessible. He moved away. A few moments later he opened the door and went out.

Next morning as he waited for her in the entrance hall after posting the letter to Turgenev, the clerk said, "Herr Dostoevsky. *Ja.* If you please!" and laid a paper before him on the counter—the bill. He was a round-faced man with a pale complexion and a tiny doll's mouth that he managed to pinch up even smaller. Dostoevsky could feel his disapproval.

"Thank you." He picked up the bill and began folding it.

"It is a rule to pay bills weekly," the clerk said.

Dostoevsky pretended not to hear, put the folded bill into his pocket, and was about to turn away when the clerk leaned forward and said loudly. "Herr Dostoevsky, if you please! The bill is paid every week."

Dostoevsky felt a cold shiver go through him. To his own surprise he flew into a violent temper; that is, it was not entirely a surprise to him, it was also partly prepared, so that he did not know exactly how much was something that surged up in him or deliberate pretense on his part.

"What? What are you saying?" he shouted. "How dare you! Are you a policeman as well as a clerk?" That's stupid, he thought, but it is frightening him all the more. "So that is the sort of client you have here, is it? And you were going to pluck me by the coat. Yes, you were! I saw it!" The clerk had recoiled. "You had your wretched paw out to do it! I won't stand for such familiarity. Understand that!" He felt an intense gratification. He flung away to the far end of the entrance; in a glass he could see the clerk, rather white, discountenanced, whispering to the manager.

He lighted a cigarette and looked at the clock; half past eleven. Writing the soliciting letter to Turgenev had strung him up. He had felt an indefinable pleasure in that too; and of course he had exaggerated there as well! He had deliberately "put it on." "Dear Ivan Sergeyevich, I am ashamed and disgusted to bother you with my affairs but you are precisely the only person I can turn to at the moment. Besides, you are more intelligent than the others and to apply to you is therefore easier for me morally." Whereon he had asked Turgenev for a hundred thalers and added, "It is possible I shall not be able to pay you back for three weeks." He had even felt a resentment at Turgenev on account of this letter! It somehow added to his complete disgust at the whole thing and also to his satisfaction. He still felt it at this moment.

Then he saw Pauline coming toward him. He noticed at once that she had changed; she was in one of her "infernal" moods. "Well, have you got a carriage?" she said in a cold voice.

"A carriage? What?" He ran after her into the street. "Pauline, listen, my darling——"

They walked aimlessly. He was in a fever of anxiety over her. She treated him sarcastically and made a scene in front of a fashionable restaurant where she wanted to lunch and he had to beg her to return to the hotel where they could still put it on the bill. "What did you get me here for?" she said to him with her eyes blazing. In the afternoon he bundled two shirts and his spare trousers into a newspaper and ran out to sell them; after nearly an hour he managed to find a

pawnbroker willing to give him a thaler for them—barely
enough to buy one meal.

He hurried in distress to the post office three times next
day. But there was no money from Turgenev. At night
Pauline locked her door. As the days passed she became
increasingly bad-tempered and exasperated at the hours they
spent in the gardens, walking about the neighborhood in
the heat and dust, listening to the everlasting German bands
or sitting like prisoners in the hotel. "I'm sick of it, do you
hear? Sick of it—sick of it!"

Since they had no money between them they were obliged
to cling to the hotel for food. He sent off letters in all directions begging for loans—to Herzen, who he heard was in
Geneva, to Katkov, the editor of the *Russian Messenger* in
Petersburg, to Vrangel in Copenhagen. She softened, then
scoffed at him. "I thought you were going to win a fortune?"
In some way she made the acquaintance of a Russian who
appeared in the gardens, a man with a depraved look who
was said to have been involved in some local crime, and
flirted with him until Dostoevsky went pale with anger.

"Ah, my God, it's too much!" she cried when he reproached
her with it. "Do you realize that this is preposterous, that it's
hateful, all this? How is it possible to put me in such a false
position? I can't even buy a ticket to get away."

On another occasion he said to her, "You can't love anybody with your heart. That's true, isn't it?" He was almost
running alongside her in the gardens at the time. She was
pale and imperious. "I don't admit it or refuse to admit it.
If I say anything else you'll invent something, you'll begin
to twist it with your damned imagination."

Two days later the money came from Turgenev: fifty
thalers instead of a hundred. He rushed to the gambling
rooms. He was going to win and pour everything triumphantly into her hands! On the steps he paused and on
an impulse turned back to the hotel. Pauline was in her room.
She said through the door, "Who is it?"

"Polina, please let me in. I've got some money."

There was a pause; then apparently she made up her mind and opened. She was half dressed; as he entered she went back to the bed and began languorously pulling on a stocking. In a moment she looked up again and saw him immobile, pale, his eyes fixed on her legs. "Well?" she said, not moving. "Don't look at me like that. I've told you before. You make me feel I'm on exhibition. Damn you! You always choose these moments, don't you? What do you want?"

He stepped up, caught her, and pulled her to him. He felt the hardness of her legs against him. "No!" She dug her fingers into his face, freed herself, and back off. "Keep away from me. Oh, my God, I couldn't. It's enough to remember it." She shuddered. "My God!"

His lips trembled; he thought he was going to faint. He put the money on the table and said, "It will pay your bill and you will be able to leave." Her eyes went to the money. "You are going, Polina, aren't you?"

She turned away impatiently. "Yes. To Paris. Now go. Go!"

He saw she was looking after him with hatred as he shut the door.

They said good-by at the station next morning. She was cool and kept turning on her heel and giving glances at a French lieutenant of hussars in the carriage. He rushed back to the hotel in a ferment.

4

The hotel dining room was a sort of basement with only one window forever steamed over. It smelled everlastingly of cabbage, cooking fat, and stale remnants of meals and as usual it was crowded and noisy. The guests at the big *table d'hôte* in the middle were all talking at once, vociferating, clanking knives and plates and reaching out for dishes.

Dostoevsky hurried in; after a tormented, restless night he had fallen asleep well after daylight and awakened late. He felt strangely lightheaded and wondered if he were going to have a fit. Everything seemed to be moving a little faster than normal.

He was annoyed to find his usual table occupied by a fat German woman and a fat blotchy-faced schoolgirl, evidently her daughter; he turned to the approaching waiter, but the man brushed by him. Dostoevsky hovered a moment, then crossed to an empty table on the far side and sat down. It was a particularly nasty place, cramped up next to the door to the kitchen. The door kept opening just beside him as the waiters came and went, letting out over him a nauseous wave of cooking smells and heat amid the clash of pots and pans and the loud shouts of the waiters giving their orders. The tablecloth was stained and once or twice the waiters actually dropped scraps of food from trays upon it.

All at once he was startled to see the Russian whom Pauline had flirted with in the gardens sitting at the central table and looking at him in a peculiar fixed way. He had the uncomfortable idea that the man had come there to persecute him; that perhaps, even, he had been sent by Pauline to make a scene. The man turned to speak to his neighbor, who wore some sort of uniform, and Dostoevsky saw that there was a party of them, including two women; they were all drinking a lot and making a noise. He was more convinced than ever that they were there for the purpose of getting up a scandal. It increased his nervousness; he felt horribly tense and shaky.

"Waiter! Waiter!" The waiters kept passing him; they were slovenly and careless, fit for nowhere but this sort of hotel. At last he could bear it no longer. He actually stood up and touched a waiter who had consistently ignored him and was standing with his back to him. "Look here, who is serving this table?"

The man turned; he had a big red nose and unshaven chin.

"Who's asking you to punch people about, eh? Who are you?" he said in a resonant voice.

Dostoevsky went pale. "What? Punching? How—how dare you? I am waiting to be served. I insist on being served."

"Oh, you do? And what do you expect to be served with?" the man said.

Dostoevsky stared at him. "Are you mad?" he said. With terror he noticed the sudden silence in the room. Everybody was looking toward them. The Russian and his party seemed particularly interested.

"We have orders not to give you anything," the waiter said.

"Orders? What orders?"

"It's always the same with such parasites." The waiter was addressing the room. "They do nothing but shout, 'Hurry up there! I'm waiting to be served'—and they haven't a penny to their names."

The Russian at the central table laughed in an extraordinarily insulting way. In an instant the whole table was laughing uproariously. The Russian rose provocatively in his place and for one mad moment Dostoevsky imagined himself actually grappling with the fellow. Then, with his head in a whirl, he rushed out. The manager was at the desk in the entrance. Dostoevsky almost threw himself on him. "I have just been grossly insulted by one of your waiters. He refuses to serve me lunch. He insulted me in front of everybody. He said he had orders not to give me anything."

"Will you kindly not shout!"

"I am not shouting! I'm speaking quietly. You're the one who's shouting. And if you are so keen on correctness, why are you smoking that cigarette talking to a guest?" In spite of his rage, he felt especially pleased at having said that.

"Ah!" The manager gasped with anger. "It's none of your business, is it?" he shouted even louder. The clerk came out from behind the rear curtain. The manager had tiny eyes like prune stones and his jowls quivered. "You don't pay

your bill. Do you expect to go on living like an archduke
here for nothing?"

"Like an archduke—here? My God!"

"The waiter is quite right. I have forbidden the staff to
give you anything until you pay up. Anything, d'you hear?
What's more, I've told the police and they won't hand over
your passport before everything is paid. Now do you understand?"

"But—but——" Dostoevsky stammered. He looked at the
manager as if he were completely at a loss; and at the same
time he knew he was, in a certain subtle degree, acting.
The clerk smiled contemptuously. The manager was looking
at him with an expression of condescending triumph, as
though saying, "And how do you like that? How do you feel
now?" Dostoevsky saw it plainly. And what was extraordinary, the triumphant look actually gave him enjoyment. Yes
—it was genuine enjoyment. He felt a sudden desire to say
something exceptionally agreeable to them. He said, "I am
sure you will overlook my being rude just now. I beg your
pardon. There is no doubt I was ill-mannered. Excuse me.
You see it's a little awkward. I am expecting some money
in a few days. I have five thalers here; if you will kindly take
it on account." He reached into his pocket; he had kept five
thalers from the money Turgenev sent.

"Your bill is thirty-nine thalers one florin," the manager
said.

"Yes, yes," Dostoevsky said. "It certainly must be that.
To be quite truthful, I gave some money to a young woman.
Oh, honorably. It was quite honorable. You see, I was in
love with her. I still am somewhat. I asked her to be my
wife—even though she is an angel sometimes and an infernal woman the next——"

"We are not asking you for these private details," the
manager said, and Dostoevsky saw that the clerk was looking
especially contemptuous as if everything in his opinion had
been *confirmed!* He felt extremely excited; he scarcely knew

what provoked him but went on, speaking quickly and insistently. "Excuse me. I understand that. It isn't necessary. I'll tell you though. The fact is at the beginning she couldn't forgive me for being married; she knew what my wife was like (she's dead now, by the way, my wife, I mean) but the proud and haughty side of her nature couldn't bear——"

"These private affairs are nothing to do with us," the manager interrupted roughly with the trace of a sneer. "You can't pay your bill and I have given orders that you're to have nothing."

The clerk chimed in, "That's all we care." And there was something so casual and scornful, even familiar, in his tone and the attitude of both of them that all at once, in one instant, Dostoevsky felt utterly sick, in an agony. He could not understand where the feelings had come from that had made him force himself on these two. Yet he plunged on further.

"But I must eat. If it's only lunch, a light lunch. I'm hungry."

"No, no. You don't deserve lunch," the manager said in a peculiar way.

"*Deserve?*" Dostoevsky was white.

"That's right—deserve," the manager said. "Tea, that's what Russians live on, isn't it? Tea. You can have tea. And it'll go on the bill. And that's all!" He waved his arm and disappeared with the clerk behind the curtain.

Dostoevsky staggered away.

The hotel staff treated him with contumely. They snickered at him in the corridors. He came in and found his things shifted to a tiny back room, more like a cupboard than a room, with half the wall paper off and a bed with broken springs. He might ring the bell twenty times; nobody came. He left his shoes out to be cleaned; they remained there muddy. He was sickened.

To begin with, out of pride, he left the hotel in the

mornings and returned after dark. But he found the day in the open made him terribly hungry and he changed plans and stayed all day in the room so as not to work up an appetite. One of the servants brought him tea in the morning and evening, but shrugged indifferently when he asked for a biscuit or a morsel of bread and several times even refused him a candle for the night.

The first few days of voluntary confinement to the room were bearable. He lay on the bed or sat writing in his note-books, sketching out the ideas that pursued him, that perhaps he could work into a new novel. Sometimes, lost in emptiness, he drew men's heads and strange Russian merchants' houses and did copperplate penmanship with curly p's and r's on the pages between the maze of finely scrawled notes.

There were ideas in his mind of portraying one of the younger Russian generation, one of the "advanced" young men of the new nihilist movement who liked to imagine themselves "destroyers" and were ready to wade through blood if necessary to achieve their ends. At the same time he was passionately drawn to creating a meek, submissive opposite, another Double,—and he became lost in the complications that the two involved.

He wanted somehow to pursue, to extend, the ideas he had stated in *Notes from Underground,* to show the virtue, even the necessity of caprice, freedom from the tyranny of reason. He was tremendously stirred up by the thought that he could do this by showing the failure and destruction of a man trying to live purely by intellectual theory, by a mechanism that would settle existence for him.

But then hunger made it absolutely impossible to continue. He had to eat. Sometimes he sat on the bed not daring to go out, quivering with nervous timidity like one of the figures of his books at the thought of meeting a servant on the stairs —and then in despair he rushed out. He roamed the streets. All around the Kursaal, like a parasite growth, there were pawnshops and banking houses. Some of the pawnshops, the ones most prominently placed, were disguised as smart jewelers. They had imposing marble fronts, plump uniformed doormen, and windows blazing with diamonds and emeralds. A little farther off, they became less magnificent and displayed old-fashioned brooches and the silver forks and pepper pots of vanished families. These were already undisguisedly pawnshops. The ones still farther away were noticeably more doubtful—and so down to the dirtiest dens.

He stared into the windows. He had nothing to pawn!

Searching through his possessions again, he found a pair of cheap metal cufflinks in the pocket of his traveling bag. The pawnbrokers shook their heads and some sneered aggressively, "What are you up to, bringing such rubbish? What do you expect for it, eh?" He wandered the back streets of the town, going into the dark shops that smelled of old clothes where Hoffmannesque men and women appeared as if they were rising from another world. There was one shop made with clocks, all striking. Another was piled to the ceiling with rags, old hats.

He walked the streets till his feet were sore. He called at the post office every day but there was never any reply from Katkov, Vrangel, or the others. The clerks eyed him curiously as they gave always the same negative answer to his inquiry whether any money had arrived for him. Now and again he saw one of the shrunken spinsters of the Kursaal gambling rooms hurrying to some cheap restaurant and watched hungrily. He tried to sell his traveling bag; it had a split near the hinge and the pawnbrokers infallibly noticed it. Standing waiting for their suspicious, mistrustful eyes to judge, for their disparaging words, their shoulders to hunch slowly, he lived in a sort of terror; he observed all the nuances of their scorn, he became acquainted with the infinite variety of their techniques for decrying. At last a man gave him a florin for it. He rushed and spent it on sausage and bread, ate ravenously on a bench in the gardens, and fell asleep and awoke after dark, cold and soaked in a thunderstorm with the gas lamps shining from the Kursaal and the carriages rolling up.

He spent a ferverish night wrestling on the bed with endless streets and faces passing in front of him. In desperation the next morning he took out his overcoat to pawn. The shop that had taken the bag was shuttered. A few minutes later he noticed that nearly all the other shops round about were shut too. It was some sort of holiday.

He walked on carrying the overcoat. It was a blazing hot day. He felt lightheaded and ill. He found two pawnbrokers open, miserable shops he had been into before; but the shopkeepers flicked at the coat and scoffed. They only lent on gold, they said. The dirty men and women in their rags looked as if they were in the gutter—but they only lent on gold!

The smell of mortar, dust, bricks, and stagnant water, the heat and airlessness, brought back Petersburg in summer and worked on his nerves. There was the stench of the wine and beer shops in the wretched streets. A band of street boys skipped around him shouting and mocking, twitching at the coat from behind; they darted off to a distance when he stopped threateningly, then jeered and chorused again and began slinging dirt and he was only saved by their being drawn off to some other attraction. He was in a strange state, completely overwrought, harassed by thoughts of debts everywhere, of being so far from home, even of having failed utterly as a writer.

In spite of the sun he felt cold and began to shiver. He walked on aimlessly; sometimes his thoughts were flying, at other times he halted, unable to remember what he had been thinking about the minute before. Early in the afternoon he saw smart carriages and fashionably dressed people. Then he was in the poorest district again, abruptly looking up under the heads of some horses. The driver of a huge beer dray shouted at him and gave him a lash with his whip across the back. Dostoevsky sprang away, furious at the lash—and only then realizing he had been walking in the middle of the road. He wanted to run after the dray but it was rumbling quickly down a slope and passers-by were jeering at him.

"Got what he deserves."

"Look at him, the rogue. Pretending to be drunk. Trying to put it on."

"Getting honest people into trouble!"

Rubbing his shoulder, he went on. He had the impression he was going to have a fit and began to hurry, looking for somewhere to shelter, for a "convenient spot." All at once he found himself in a dirty courtyard where there was a shop-window with broken panes boarded up. In one place on the window letters had been pasted long before and he read the outline of the words "Pledges Accepted." A pawnbroker's. He stared at the shop. His head ached and he felt dizzy; he made a violent effort to steady himself, shook the over-coat out and folded it again over his arm, and went forward.

The shop entrance was in a passage at the side. It was quite dark in the passage and he took another minute to find the bell. It gave a faint tinny tinkle, like the bells of all such miserable houses. He waited and presently the door opened a tiny crack; he saw a little eye watching him from the darkness.

"Good afternoon," he said. "I have something to pawn; this coat here. It had a raccoon collar once. It's a good coat." The crack was no wider; he thought he had better reassure whoever it was. "I'm a visitor to Wiesbaden—at the Hotel Burger." There was another pause, then by one of those chances that determine things a cat appeared at his feet and began nosing at the door with its tail straight up. The door opened to let it in and Dostoevsky saw there was an old woman with a puffed dirty face and little malignant eyes. She held the door wide and he stepped in. She was short and stout, dressed in some colorless rags with a mangy yellowed fur cape over her shoulders, and stood just inside the door, evidently still mistrustful.

He bowed and said, "Excuse me, perhaps you were not expecting business today? I didn't know. If you'd be so good as to look at the coat" and he held it out to her. The entrance was dark. He glimpsed the shop faintly through a glass-paneled door on the right. He could hear no sounds from the interior. The old woman kept her eyes on his face as if hesitating once more, then pushed open a door and said, "Very well, go in." As he entered he heard her shutting the front door. The room, a sort of sitting room, was lighter but still dingy. He looked around at the cumbrous ugly furniture, a great sofa covered with faded pink plush, a huge oval table, oval looking glass, chairs around the walls. Through a curtained doorway he saw another small room with a bed which was covered with a fringed shawl; underneath the bed he caught a glimpse of a chest.

"Well?" the old woman said, coming back and confronting him. "What is it?" She spoke in a sharp way and stared straight at him.

"It's this coat," Dostoevsky said. "What will you give me for it?"

"What do I want with coats?" she grumbled, taking it from him, fingering it, and peering at it. "I can't everlastingly take people's left-off rags. I haven't got the space for them. Besides, it's worthless, such stuff." She shuffled over with it to the window to see better, turning the coat inside out and muttering to herself. "What's the good of this? It's all worn out, every bit of it. Here's a hole—and here's another; the lining's gone; anybody can see the lining is good for nothing. It won't keep the cold out for you, my beauty. Bah, it's rubbish—and look at these buttonholes . . ."

Dostoevsky stood watching her. Except for her mumbling, there was a peculiar silence all around. He could hear nothing from the neighboring flats and nobody seemed to pass through the passage or the courtyard. Her thin greasy hair was especially repulsive, her whole figure hideous; she was like some gray spider. Here was this spiteful, filthy, evil old woman, he thought, useless and ailing—and, outside, young people wasting for lack of help, gasping, strong men and women who could be saved from hopeless situations, given a new chance, with her money. She certainly lent on gold like the rest. She had a hoard somewhere; in the chest under the bed?

His head ached worse than ever. A phrase occurred to him with exceptional force: "the service of humanity." With her gold one could devote oneself to the service of humanity. Eliminating her would be no more than squashing a spider. And once one had her gold, how magnificently that single crime could be made up! With her money he could eat, live—be secure—live! With piercing intensity he thought: Life is only given to me once. The minutes before the execution came to him terribly clearly. Life is only given to me once and *I shall never have it again*. I want to live! He had to take the first step to make himself independent, to get means. Then he would write great books. Yes, yes! They would make a profound impression for good. They would add to the world's good. He would explore the secret places of the soul where antitheses were resolved; create the meek, humble, the proud and holy, all for good. Yes—all for good! And when future generations saw that, would they think of this dirty old woman's death? Wouldn't the world be better off? Wouldn't he have not only wiped out the one crime but enormously benefited mankind? All at once, with a shudder, he noticed an iron bar with bolt holes, apparently meant for the shutters, standing against the wall.

Yes. He was going to murder her.

Immediately he had a curious feeling of emptiness. The decision itself aroused nothing in him at all. His eyes went from the iron bar to the old woman. He judged the distance; two paces to reach the bar . . . he would have to swing it above the table. Abruptly she looked up and noticed his expression; there was a gleam of sharper mistrust in her eyes. Dostoevsky felt he was giving everything away, struggled in a moment of blind confusion, and managed to say, "Give me two thalers for it. You won't have to keep it long. I'm expecting some money and then I'll redeem it."

"You can have two florins for it and that's all."

"What! Only *two*——"

"And I'll take the interest in advance."

Her little eyes were watching him. He wet his lips.

"All right—hand it over." He held out his hand—and realized that he had accepted too readily; but he did not know how to go back on it. The old woman said nothing; she fumbled under her apron, produced some keys on a ring, and went into the bedroom. From where he stood he could not see behind the curtain, but heard her unlocking a drawer; that was where she kept her money, her gold. He listened intently. He was in agony. His attention concentrated with the utmost intensity on the sounds the old woman was making; he moved stealthily toward the iron bar. At the same instant he thought: What if it is not heavy enough? I shall have to bring it down on her head; it will make blood. Is there really room to swing the bar? Good God, I mustn't make a mistake.

He caught the faint chink of coins. In another step he could reach the bar. And he suddenly became quite cool. It was extraordinary how calm, even icy, he felt. In a flash he wondered whether it would not be better to wait, to take note of everything now, all the details, so as to make no mistake, and come back to kill her later. But he decided no, now was the time. Curiously at that moment his mind had begun to race on why most criminals left such traces behind, positively signing their crimes. He had long since come to the conclusion that their will power failed at the critical moment when they most needed reason in all its strength. At the very moment of committing the crime, he had decided, they were actually suffering from something like disease—atrophy of the will and reason—which passed off afterward. He would not allow that to happen to him.

He could hear her still fumbling in the bedroom. She must be counting the coins six times. This was the best moment to pick up the bar and hold it by his side ready to hit her when she came back. But then an absurd question occurred to him; it was a legitimate question but nonetheless absurd and he felt bound to answer it at once. If Napoleon had been standing here now, in his place—if he hadn't had the battle of Toulon, Egypt, the passage of Mont Blanc for a beginning of his career but, instead of all those splendid and monumental exploits, there had merely been some horrible old hag of a pawnbroker who had to be murdered for her money (for his career! yes, to secure his career, that was the point!) —well, would he have recoiled? Would he have found it an abject deed, nothing at all splendid or monumental?

He knew the moments were passing and that if he did not snatch up the iron bar now it would almost certainly mean a struggle with the old creature. There would be noise, the neighbors' attention would be attracted. But he could not do anything until he had answered the question. He stood there in the pawnbroker's sitting room struggling with that question!

But if Kepler or Newton, he thought, hadn't been able to make their discoveries, or have them accepted unless they had first killed somebody, killed ten people, a hundred—even more, more!—they would have been right to kill them off. Good God, they would have been absolutely obliged to—so that the world could benefit by what they had discovered. Wasn't it true that scarcely any of the "great men" from Lycurgus and Solon to Mahomet and Napoleon and so on had hesitated to shed blood when it was to their advantage? And they were given laurel wreaths, called saviors, benefactors! All great men had to be ready for that; otherwise they couldn't raise themselves above the common herd. They

spilled blood like champagne—and were crowned with
glory for it.

But . . . but . . . an old woman; the meanness of stealing from under her bed? What! he shouted in his mind. Did
it have to be aesthetically attractive before one did it?
Picturesque? Was there an aesthetic law? No, no! Murdering
people by bombarding them in a siege was no more glorious.
Napoleon wouldn't have had the smallest scruple about
killing the old woman; he wouldn't have flinched for a second
but would have strangled her with his own hands. *It would
even have been splendid, monumental to him!* Ah! He shut
his eyes for a second. Power was only vouchsafed to the man
who dared to stoop and pick it up. He had only to dare—
nothing more. *He longed to have the daring.* He wasn't
really going to kill her for the money or to become a benefactor to humanity. That was all rubbish. He wanted to kill
her for his own sake, for himself alone. He wanted to know
quickly whether he was a worm like everyone else or a man.
Dare he stoop and take it or not? Was he a trembling
creature or had he the *right?* It was the same thing as the
Arcade and the child Natasha.

His coolness had suddenly left him. He was pale and
covered with sweat. He glanced at the iron bar. At that
moment he was startled to see the old woman's head come
around the curtain. She was still standing in the bedroom but
had evidently decided to give a precautionary glance out at
him. Yet she did not speak. He was horribly upset by her
standing there glancing out at him like that. He fancied she
had guessed what was in his mind. He struggled to speak
and at last got out, "What are you staring at me for?"

"What's the matter with you?" she said.

"It's nothing."

"You're pale."

He was horrified; he felt he was losing his head, that
he was frightened. Everything was going out of control.
"I'm hungry," he said. "Besides, I've got fever."

To his acute relief, her head disappeared again. He wanted to ask her why she was being such a long time. He stepped cautiously toward the iron bar but before he could reach out and take it she came back. She saw at once that he was not in the same place. It did not matter, he thought. Now was the moment; he had only to reach out. He foresaw all his movements though he was shaking.

He said, "Are you always alone like this? You are alone, aren't you?"

Her eyes glinted at him suspiciously. "What's it to do with you?"

"Only not to come at the wrong time, next time." He stared at the top of her head, the greasy rattails of hair.

"Here," she said, holding out the money. "One florin eighty kreutzers. That's less twenty kreutzers interest for a month." She gave him the pawn ticket and turned, impatient to get him out. "This way."

Her back was turned. Now! Suddenly as he reached for the iron bar the image of Gazin, the Tartar convict, came into his mind. It was a shock. Giddiness came over him. He was filled with loathing and disgust. He felt intense repulsion. It was all loathsome; the idea of having considered such a crime was awful. His jaw fell, he gasped, wrenching at his collar; he was utterly horrified. He sprang forward, brushed past the old woman, out of the room, flung the front door open, and rushed out.

He was trembling violently. The street was as hot as an oven. The parching dusty afternoon descended on him like iron. He almost ran, staggering as if he were tipsy, scarcely seeing anything around him. In a moment he was jostled by two men, halted, and saw that he was outside a beer shop. He noticed he had a burning thirst; he went in, ordered beer, and gulped it down. It was good and made him feel better; he called for a second glass. Fleetingly it occurred to him as curious that he should be spending the money on beer instead of food.

But his mind was invaded by a scene in the old woman's room. He saw a young student, a penniless young man with Napoleonic pride and ambition, in the old pawnbroker's sitting room, going there to do the murder—and doing it, killing the old woman. Yes, yes! That was what he wanted, it was what he had been searching for. That was what he must write. All his mind was working on this one overwhelming idea. He was beside himself. Good God! It could be a masterpiece. All those things he had felt, the intense struggle about his "right" to kill the old woman, all that must be worked out in the book, all of it. Now—now! He couldn't wait.

He jumped up, knocking the glass over, and hurried out. Sometimes he was running on the way back to the hotel. He did not see the clerk, the sneering porter. In his cupboard room he flung himself down at the table, pouring out notes, sheet after sheet of writing, a burning man.

It was like struggling with two opponents. It was contending with good and evil. The young student, whom he named Rodion Raskolnikov, lived in the room tormenting him. "Do you believe in God? Do you believe in Lazarus's rising from the dead? Fully? Do you believe it fully?" The passionate discussions with Shidlovsky returned. It was the everlasting question: Is there a God? He *desired* to believe, yet he did not believe. At night he paced the tiny room— three and a half steps forward, three and a half back. The force in Raskolnikov was of both God and Satan. Each of them pulled him the opposite way. He loved and hated both.

The motivation of the story was enormously complex. As with everything he had ever written, Dostoevsky was torn between opposites; he could not renounce one or the other. Raskolnikov was the supreme double man. He was going to call the book *Crime and Punishment*. He wanted to express the ideas about the "new movement" of nihilism, about the vanity of trying to live purely by intellectual theory, of "life

replacing dialectics"; and in addition to the theme of drunkenness (which kept recurring to him with such sharp
recollections of Issayev), he was sketching the outlines of
more Doubles—the good prostitute, the cynical self-willed
rake who has something noble in his soul.

But it was too much! It was too big! He could not see
how to grasp it, to embrace it all. Could he do it as a diary?
Or by an omniscient narrator? At one moment he thought
of doing it as Raskolnikov's confession. He worked day and
night, blocking out the book first one way, then another. He
filled his notebooks with the ideas, outlines, detail.

He lived entirely on tea. The clerks at the post office
became exasperated at his appearing every day to ask if
money had arrived, insulted and made fun of him. At one
crisis in trying to work the book out, he rushed to the
Russian church and knelt praying like a beggar. As he was
leaving, somebody touched his shoulder. Dostoevsky started;
it was a man with a plump pink face and a beard. The man
said nothing, put some coins in Dostoevsky's hand, and went
away. Dostoevsky looked down—two thalers.

He made the money last by eating once every other day.
When it was gone he lived on the watery hotel tea again.
He was gradually coming to grips with *Crime and Punishment*, though he had made false starts and given them up.
In the second week of September the weather turned cold
and he was frozen, sitting in the room, going without a coat
to the post office. He particularly dreaded one clerk who
reminded him of his old orderly Arkady, a man with hair
en brosse, pince-nez, and white hands who clearly ascribed
the most serious importance to his duties and position, had
a solemn air, and without a word expressed the most immeas-
urable contempt; he indicated that Dostoevsky could not be
noticed in any other way than a dog's dirt on the curb. One
morning Dostoevsky stood at the counter while the man
ignored him, served others, turned his back. Dostoevsky
appealed to two of the other clerks; they shrugged and

referred him back to the first. Dostoevsky began to feel weak; he rapped on the counter and said loudly, "You, there! I demand an answer. Has any money come for me?"

The clerk pivoted. "Order! Order! Do you dare? Do you understand whom you are talking to? I am a government official. I shall call the police!"

"I beg your pardon." Dostoevsky had a horror of the man; yet hardly knowing what he was doing, he said, "I'm a foreigner. You understand that I didn't mean any disrespect?" The clerk was quivering in exalted indignation. "One forgets oneself," Dostoevsky heard himself say in a sort of mad furious inner rage. "If you would kindly overlook it. It was most unnecessary and regrettable."

The clerk's face expressed even more profound derision than ever.

"If you would, nevertheless, be so kind as to see if anything has come for me. My name is Dostoevsky."

The clerk gave a sort of tolerant snort and looked along with a twist of his mouth at the other clerks, who were all grinning too. "With a *D* or a *G*?" he said. He asked the same thing every time, to annoy, and Dostoevsky went pale. "*D*," he said. The clerk reached into a pigeonhole for a bundle of money transfer orders awaiting collection and turned to Dostoevsky, holding them with deliberate delicateness in finger and thumb. Everybody at once understood that by counting them out he was going to demonstrate that nobody had ever heard of "Dostoevsky." He was going to demonstrate that Dostoevsky did not exist. He was going to crush him for good, to annihilate him once and for all. One by one he delicately let the orders drop on the counter, pronouncing the names. "Harz, Weissberg, Flugel, Kempenstock, Boehmer——" He stopped at the last order. His face gradually became pink, then scarlet. "Dost—Dosto-evsky."

With a grimace Dostoevsky said, "I beg your pardon." It was intensely pleasant saying that!

"One—uh—one hundred thalers." The clerk was coughing, growling, already recovered and imperious again.

On the street Dostoevsky could scarcely believe it. He gripped the money in his fist. It was from Vrangel. Thank God for Vrangel! The accompanying message said that Vrangel had only just returned to Copenhagen and found his appeal for money and was sending some straight away. Dostoevsky bought the first cigarettes he had smoked for weeks and flew back to the hotel.

"I want to pay my bill!"

The manager handed it to him majestically. Dostoevsky gaped at it. It was for one hundred and twenty-five thalers. "But—but this can't be right. I haven't had anything . . . except tea . . . that bad room . . ."

"And what do you do if you borrow money, my good sir? Tell me that," the manager said. "Do you get it for nothing— with service and shelter at the same time? Tell me—tell me. Do we throw you out into the street? You are lucky we do not charge you more."

Dostoevsky was crushed. "I can pay you ninety-five thalers now." He gave the money with shaking hands and went quickly out, walking through the gardens, jostling people, striding. He was a prisoner. Even if he wanted to run away, even if he had his passport, he hadn't the fare back to Russia. And now he was gasping to return to Petersburg. He couldn't write here. He would be lost. He needed Russia. He must return home to work.

He did not know how long he walked. He was in despair. Suddenly he thought of the Russian church, the priest there; he might help. At the church the priest, Father Yanishev, sat in a little room that smelled of scented powder and had red silk covering the walls. To Dostoevsky's dismay, Father Yanishev, who kept chewing something and moving his lips in a peculiar way, said, "Yes, but how are you going to pay it back?"

"I am beginning to write a new book. I shall soon have a thousand rubles' worth done, Father. It will sell, I know it."

"H'm. Well—I will tell them at the hotel to leave the bill with me for security, until you can pay it." Continuing to chew, Father Yanishev went to a box and put some coins on the table. "That will pay your third-class fare home. There, I have made a note of the total debt for you. I rely on your settling it soon. I will say nothing about interest. I leave it to you."

Dostoevsky bowed.

The unheated train next day was bitterly cold. He ran up and down the platforms to get warm. But he was going home! At the frontier he was sick with anxiety in case the Petersburg creditors had obtained an order for his arrest. The police handed him back his passport after the usual questions and let him through. He climbed the stairs to his rooms, shaking. All was the same but covered with dust. As he felt in his pocket for the two rubles fifty kopecks that he still had left, the little light breeze began to blow across his face gently, he had the wonderful ecstatic feeling of enlightenment and joy and perception, reached the door and hauled it heavily open and began calling downstairs for help, hearing the distant cry and then shouting it as the curtain stifled everything.

He had scarcely started the writing of *Crime and Punishment* for the *Russian Messenger* when Katkov, the editor, announced it and he had to rush. As soon as it began appearing in January of the New Year, 1866, creditors came knocking at the door holding out copies of the review. "Here you are getting money, my dear sir, and not paying me a kopeck." Emily Fyodorovna and her family hung on him for their support. Pasha moved in with him and harried him with demands. Dostoevsky begged from Katkov, borrowed everywhere he could. He struggled to keep up the monthly installments of the book—and often only succeeded because the *Russian Messenger* came out late. By April, half the book had appeared.

But it was a success. Petersburg was excited, full of enthusiasm. People spoke of Dostoevsky with Tolstoy and Turgenev. He was famous. One morning he was at the table writing when there was a knock at the door. It was Milyukov and Dolgomostyev, another contributor from the *Epoch* days.

"I say, Fyodor Mikhailovich, do you know what Stellovsky is going about the town saying?" Milyukov said.

"Who?" Dostoevsky went pale. "My God."

"Stellovsky. He says he is going to print an edition of *Crime and Punishment*—and everything else you write."

Dolgomostyev, a short man with pebble glasses, said, "Katkov asked him what he meant and Stellovsky said you signed a contract. What's his idea?"

"It's—it's true. I'm finished. It's the end." Dostoevsky put his hand to his head. "I forgot. I've been in the middle of this other work, I——"

"You mean you did sign a contract—with Stellovsky?"

"I couldn't help it," Dostoevsky said. "I needed the money. My God, Alexander Petrovich, what is the date today?"

"October the first," Milyukov said.

Dostoevsky said, "I have to deliver a new full-length novel to Stellovsky in thirty days from now—or he has everything I write from now on for nothing. That's the contract. Thirty days. I can't do it . . . I can't do it."

They stared at him. "My God."

Chapter Thirteen

1

"Sit down, sit down. Yes, there." He motioned the girl to a chair, went out, returned, excused himself, walked up and down the room. Ah, why had he fallen in with this idea of a stenographer? Milyukov had heard of some school in Petersburg where they had started teaching stenography, a new thing, and had contended it was the only way to get the book for Stellovsky done in time. But dictate a novel! He could never succeed with it; he needed to see what was written on the page. But Milyukov had arranged it and now here was the girl, looking up at him, lowering her eyes demurely, waiting for him to begin. Moreover, this morning he felt exhausted and uneasy. He stubbed out his cigarette. "Have you been doing stenography long?"

"About six months."

"I see." He glanced at her again. She looked prim—about twenty, with fair hair parted in the middle, gray eyes, a long oval face, and a decided nose; not pretty. She was dressed very ordinarily in black and was probably the daughter of some minor government official. "Will you have a cigarette?" he said, offering them.

"No, thank you."

"Do—do. You're saying that out of politeness."

"Oh no. I really don't. I dislike seeing women smoke."

He coughed, lit another cigarette himself, and went restlessly to the window. "Forgive me—it's a great nuisance; I don't know whether we shall be able to work today. I'm epileptic. I've just had a fit, this morning. I have convulsive spasms; the effect takes some time to pass off."

She was looking at him with astonishment, then averted her eyes, staggered at such blinding frankness.

"I suppose since you're here we'd better try," he said. "I'll see if it is possible. I doubt it, I doubt it. I'll read something first. Are you ready?"

"Yes."

He snatched up a copy of the *Russian Messenger* and began reading rapidly. "Please! Not so fast," she interrupted. "Please dictate at a normal speaking rate, like ordinary conversation."

While she wrote out the copy he fretted, walking up and down the room and at last burst out, "But why is it taking so long?" He picked up the finished sheets. "And it isn't accurate! Look here—you've left out a semicolon here. And there's no accent here. It won't do at all!"

He began to roam about the room again—but it was impossibly difficult to begin! Sitting there silent and unmoving with her pencil poised, she prevented the first sentence from forming in his mind. She became twice life size. He kept having to avoid glancing at her; details about her drew his attention—she had ugly shoes, the brooch she was wearing was old-fashioned. Her notebook—oh, damn her notebook! It was all nonsensical. And if she would only budge, instead of sitting there like an idol. He struggled, managed to turn his thoughts away—and came back with a start to her sitting primly waiting. "It's impossible! I can't dictate anything. I can't *think* of anything! Come back this evening; eight o'clock."

He spent the afternoon trying to write and tearing the sheets up. When she returned he was still nervous. "Miss—er—I've forgotten your name."

"Anna Grigoryevna Snitkina."

"Yes, yes—sit down—that is——" He cast about for some means of putting off the dictation; he couldn't help it. "Tell me about yourself. Why are you a stenographer?" She sat firmly upright as he questioned her about herself; she lived

with her mother, brother, and sister at Peska, a district of
Petersburg that was filled with drays and the smell of rope.
Her father had died six months before. This was her first
job; she worked because she wanted to be independent. She
answered with an unsmiling circumspection that showed
him amusingly her resolve to protect herself from familiarity;
and yet when they began to talk of other things he saw that
she had read a good deal of his work and developed from
it a girlish adoration for him.

"Oh, but Vanya in *Insulted and Injured* was wonderful,"
she said.

"Who?"

"But——" She looked astonished. "The hero."

He smiled. "I can hardly remember the book. I must
reread it."

The door flew open with a crash and Pasha came in. He
wore a new bright blue coat, narrow trousers with a fancy
seal dangling from the fob, and smelled of pomade. "Hello,
who's this—the new secretary?" His face was sallow, his
hair crinkly; he laughed, showing misformed teeth. "You do
stenography, do you? Let's have a look." He picked up her
notebook rudely, looking at the signs.

Dostoevsky said, "This is my son, Paul Alexandrovich,
Miss—er—excuse me——"

"Anna Grigoryevna Snitkina."

"H'm, funny stuff," Pasha said, dropping the book onto
her lap. "Well—so long." He turned at the door, said airily,
"I shan't be home till late," and went out. She gave Dostoevsky a look of embarrassment but he had not seemed to
notice anything untoward.

"Have a cigarette, my dear," Dostoevsky said.

"I don't smoke."

"Oh. Have a pear then. I've got some here." He jumped
up and offered a paper bag. They both began to munch
pears—and the atmosphere suddenly changed. She relaxed
and he noticed with pleasure that she smiled. It seemed to

her that she had known Dostoevsky for a long time—and that was a magical feeling. As a result of some turn in the conversation he started telling her about the "execution" in the Semyenovsky Square. He spoke with passion, losing himself in the recollection of those minutes and telling her of his feelings and the return to life and shouting his joyful singing in the Fortress cell. When he stopped she was watching him intently. Besides being moved by the account, she was overwhelmingly astonished at his candor, that he should have exposed his soul so freely to her, almost a child, whom he had seen for the first time that day. She was enchanted, glowing in the enormous force of his personality, the intensity of his conversation. And at the same time she felt his loneliness.

All at once he saw the time. "You had better go home, my dear."

"But you've dictated nothing all day."

"Ah! We'll have to begin, we'll have to begin." He clasped his head and jumped up. In a moment he began to dictate but after twenty minutes, with many pauses, he gave up. "It's no good. I can't do any more tonight. Besides, it's too late for you; nearly eleven. Come at eleven o'clock tomorrow morning."

He held a lamp over the stairs for her, showing her down. "Good night."

"Good night." She went down, thinking that for the first time in her life she had seen a man, intelligent and good, as unhappy as if he had been rejected by everybody; and a feeling of profound compassion stirred in her heart.

He was tremendously agitated next day when she didn't appear. He had forgotten her name and didn't know her address. She arrived half an hour late. "I thought you weren't coming back, that it was too difficult," he said.

"I'm sorry to be late," she said. "I was making the copy of your dictation last night. If I'd intended staying away

I would have told you in the correct way and dispatched last night's dictation to you."

She was so solemn, he thought—and certainly no nihilist! But when she was seated with her pencil ready she seemed to be manning a barricade. He walked up and down. "My God, it's the fifth of October—we must get this novel moving. And I haven't more than the barest outline. It must be done by November first."

He told her about Stellovsky and watched a blush of indignation come into her face. She said softly, "Don't you think you could try to dictate something?"

"Yes, yes. I must try." In a moment, when she had read him the previous day's copy, he began. It was a struggle. He faltered continually, reflected, went on for a little, asked her to read back what he had said. After an hour he said, "That's all for today," and threw himself on the sofa. "We'll go on tomorrow, Miss—er——"

"Anna Grigoryevna Snitkina," she said.

"As a matter of fact I'd remembered. Here, Anna, have a cigarette."

She looked at him—and they both burst out laughing.

So every day Anna came at noon, took his dictation, and returned with the copied sheets next morning. Soon the difficulties dwindled; he could dictate more fluently. Between the dictation they made tea and talked. The pile of manuscript grew. The story was called *The Gambler* and he was building it around his affair with Pauline Suslova on the first trip abroad with her to Baden-Baden; with a few changes he had even brought in her daring him to insult the Frenchman in the gardens and later was going to introduce her desire to fling the money into Salvador's face. He found a secret pleasure in re-creating the scenes of humiliation before the innocent young stenographer, his "slavery" to Polina, his questions to her, the baffled moments when he could have strangled her. He asked Anna, "Are we going to finish in time?"

"Yes. I'm confident, Fyodor Mikhailovich." She was cheerful, dependable, sympathetic; he admired her independence. She told him about herself; she had two suitors, she said, but wasn't going to marry either since she believed in marrying for love. She talked to him as if he were an uncle or some older friend and asked him about his life. He told her about the Fortress, Siberia, places in Europe, showed her the photographs of Marya Dmitrievna. She knew he was poor in spite of the success of *Crime and Punishment*. One day she said with a laugh, "Now I know what you live on—buckwheat porridge."

"What makes you think so?"

She looked at a spoon on the table. "It's always better when you eat it with a wooden spoon."

"Well, my dove, you're wrong. I haven't any money, so I pawned the knives, forks, and spoons."

Sometimes he called her "my dear" or "my dove"; she took it as if he were addressing a young girl, almost a child. She saw with pleasure that he was growing calmer, working more steadily; and she was proud to be helping a celebrated writer. But there were still moments of agitation and despair. Once he said, "Oh, my God—the only thing for me is to go off to the East, to Constantinople, Jerusalem, and stay there for good. Or throw myself body and soul into roulette. Eh, what do you think, Anna?"

She looked at him in distress; such ideas seemed fantastic to her. She said quietly, "I think you should get married again, Fyodor Mikhailovich, and find happiness in a family."

"So you think I could still find a wife?" he said, smiling. "What sort should I choose, intelligent or goodhearted?"

"Intelligent."

"No, no. If I had to choose I'd take the goodhearted one." Then he had three fits in quick succession and could not work for several days. She fretted. It was the twenty-fifth of the month and there was still a lot to do with the book. They hurried on. At midday on the last day of October she brought him the copy of the final pages. She had put on a lilac dress for the occasion.

"Anna, it's charming, delightful." He took her hand, making her turn. "It makes you look taller. And the book's done! Mademoiselle, my zealous collaboratrice, I bow to you!" He bowed and capered joyfully.

"Done in twenty-six days," she said.

"Yes, and it's longer than the contract calls for. I'll look through the last section and we'll take it around. Will you come, Anna?"

"Yes. Thank you." She blushed with pleasure. While he read she made tea. With a good deal of difficulty he obliged her to take the fifty rubles they had agreed on. She said, "Your spoons are still in pawn——"

"Anna, this is the first money you have earned. And you *have* earned it." They put the sheets together and made a package. As they left it began to snow. They hurried, heads down, through the big wet flakes; they ran between the carriages, ducked under the horses' heads, bumped into passers-by. Stellovsky's office was in a big shabby commercial building. The clerk looked over the counter at them.

"Mr. Stellovsky is expecting this manuscript," Dostoevsky said, giving his name.

"I'm sorry, Mr. Stellovsky's not here."

"But I have to deliver this to him today."

"I don't know anything about that. Mr. Stellovsky won't be back until the end of next week. He's in the provinces."

"Well, it's a nuisance. However, here is the manuscript. Please give me a receipt for it."

The man sniffed with a twitch of his nose. "I can't take manuscripts from anybody who comes in here. You'll have to see Mr. Stellovsky."

"What? But this is something he is expecting."

The clerk said, "That's what you say. Mr. Stellovsky didn't leave any orders with me about it. Come back at the end of next week."

"But it will be too late!" All at once he saw it was a trick. Moreover, the man's face suggested that he knew. Stellovsky had gone away so as to be able to claim he had not received the manuscript in time—and the terrible retribution under the contract would begin. He looked at Anna in a panic. She was white-faced.

"But you've got to take it!" he shouted at the man. "Take it—here, take it!"

"I don't know who you are. I'm not taking any manuscript —and you can stop shouting." A porter like an ape looked out from behind a screen; clearly Stellovsky was used to awkward scenes in the course of his business affairs and had provided for them. Dostoevsky was gasping, shaking. Anna touched his arm. They went out. On the landing she said, "Can he really have left? Isn't there anywhere he might be in Petersburg?"

"Come on!" Clutching the package, he was pulling her with him already. They hurried through the snow from one address to another, looking for Stellovsky. The sky darkened, the gas lamps came on in the streets and shopwindows. The snow fell thicker than ever. They could not find Stellovsky. At last she pulled him panting into a doorway. "Fyodor Mikhailovich, we'll never find him like this."

"But what can we *do?* In a few hours it will be too late."

She said, "There's only one thing. I've heard you can deposit things at the Central Police Station. It will prove you delivered it in time if Stellovsky tries to contest it. But they're sure not to accept anything after six o'clock."

"My God, it's after half past five now."

Turning toward the Grand Sadovaya, they wove and bumped through the crush of people coming against them on the busy pavement and he dropped the package in the gutter. "We shall never do it like this," she said, and called to a droshky, "Isvostchik!"

"Anna." He held her arm. "I haven't a kopeck."

"I've got fifty rubles." She smiled at him. For a moment

he stood there looking into her face with the coral lips, the flakes of snow falling and melting on her red cheeks. Then she drew him toward the droshky, jumped in, and he followed. "Quick! The Police Station on the Grand Sadovaya."

A police sergeant with a black mustache took the package and gave a receipt with the date and time on it. Outside, Dostoevsky said anxiously, "Surely Stellovsky has to accept it. It's legal proof we were in time." He touched her arm. "Anna, I'd have been lost without you." He was discovering the brilliance of her eyes, the lovely curves of her lips.

"No—no," she said, and looked down. Then she said, "Well, I've enjoyed my first job in the world very much. Now it's done. I shan't forget. Good-by, Fyodor Mikhailovich." She shook his hand. This was the minute she had dreaded; she was going to turn and walk back into the empty life that he had banished for twenty-six days.

"I'll come and call on you," he said.

"Yes. Good night."

"Good night, Anna Grigoryevna. Thank you for all you did." She walked away. He was looking after her. "Anna! Anna Grigoryevna!" He suddenly called out and struggled through the people and ran up to her. He took her hand. "My dear—listen—I—I've still some work, the end of *Crime and Punishment*, you know; it isn't done yet. You can help me a great deal. Won't you come tomorrow as usual?"

Her face lighted up and then she blushed in the way he found so wonderful. "Yes. Tomorrow as usual, then. Good night."

"Good night, Anna Grigoryevna."

He stood watching her walk away and disappear in the crowd.

He was waiting for her next morning. "Come in, my dear. Come in." He took her coat and led her to a seat.

"What's the matter?"

"Nothing—I'm so glad to see you." He smiled at her.

As she arranged her notebook and pencils she said, "No, but has something happened? You look as though it had, Fyodor Mikhailovich."

"Oh, it's ridiculous." He laughed. "I had a dream, I think a lucky one. Dreams certainly mean a good deal—and mine are always prophetic."

"What was it?"

"I was rummaging about in that old box I brought from Siberia and saw something glinting at the bottom. Every time I tried to see what it was, it disappeared; the next thing, I'd thrown all the papers out and was reaching into the box and picking out a little diamond. That was excellent, wasn't it?"

"They say you should interpret dreams by their reverse," she said.

His face suddenly changed. "Do they?"

"No, no," she said quickly, seeing his lightheartedness had gone. "I don't know how to explain dreams; I don't believe in them anyway."

"Listen, Anna." He sat down opposite her. "I want to tell you about this new book of mine. I'm trying to work it out and the end is elusive, especially the psychology of the young girl in it. I could ask my niece Sonya in Moscow, but I think you can probably help me better. It's—er—about a painter, not a young man, about forty-five, my age. He's had an unhappy life, marries a woman he loves but who gives him a great deal of torment; she dies, he is full of debts and ill; and yet—er—he longs for a new life. He has a good heart, you see. One day he meets a girl, a young girl, say about your age, twenty. We can call her Anna for the sake of the story, it's a pretty name."

"Is she pretty?"

"She's not a beauty; but she's not bad-looking. Anyway, I find her attractive. The more the painter sees of her, the deeper is his conviction that he could be happy with her. It—er—it would be a terrible sacrifice for her. She would probably regret it later; she twenty and he forty-five. Anna, do you think it's likely that a young girl who is separated by all that in age and character could love him? Would it be psychologically wrong?" His voice trembled. "Put yourself in her place a minute, my dear. Suppose I was the painter and I said I loved you and asked you to be my wife. What would you say?" He was pale and considerably agitated.

She said, "I'd say that I love you and that I'll love you all my life."

He jumped up. "Anna——"

She was in his arms.

They were married on February 15, 1867, at eight o'clock in the evening at the Troitsky-Ismailov Cathedral, a little way from the Semyenovsky Square. The candles blazed and shone on the crowns held over their heads. The choirs sang. There were many people present.

Afterward Dostoevsky led her before his friends in her white wedding dress with the long train. "Look how adorable she is."

2

He tapped his pockets, searching for matches. He looked in the drawer, rose and searched the room, then shouted in a sudden fury, "There are never any matches in this house!" The fits were recurring with shattering force and regularity —one a week. He felt his mind was becoming deranged. He had wild moments. Pasha, lounging in the corner, took no notice. The door opened and Anna came in with the tea. "Pah!" Dostoevsky gave up the matches with an exasperated shrug, snatched the teapot, and tipped it up with such a violent jerk that he spilled some. "There isn't any sugar."

"I don't know what's happened to it," Anna said in a contrite voice. "I can't find any." She felt miserable, though she tried not to show it. Everything was amiss lately.

"What! No sugar either?" Dostoevsky said.

"I've been looking everywhere for it."

Pasha started whistling in the corner. "But you had that packet this morning," Dostoevsky said. He was shaking with irritation. "We can't afford to buy sugar twice a day."

"You see?" Pasha interrupted in a sly voice. "Now perhaps you'll admit things were better when I was running the household."

"It's you—that's who it is!" Anna flared up at once, turning on Pasha with her face red and furious. "You've hidden it. You try to find ways to annoy people, you——"

"Annoy, Anyechka dear? I haven't the time," Pasha said.

"Where is that ruble from the kitchen?"

"If you can't manage things——"

"Stop it! Stop it!" Dostoevsky shouted. Then, as they subsided, he said to Anna, "You ought not to quarrel with Pasha." She stifled her tears, turned quickly, and ran out of the room. Dostoevsky looked after her in mingled distress and annoyance.

Sucking his teeth, Pasha said, "The fact is——"

"All right, Pasha!"

In a moment there were sounds of visitors arriving from the entrance. He recognized the voices. Emily Fyodorovna and her four children—Fyodor, the elder boy, older than Anna, two girls over twenty—were now living in his old flat; after the marriage he and Anna had moved into this brighter one, taking Pasha, though he still paid the rent of the old flat for Emily Fyodorovna. As dowry Anna had brought a piano and some furniture. And nowadays Emily and his nieces and nephews were almost living with him; they arrived at any hour, stayed for lunch, dinner, only left at midnight. It was quite different from their former rare, brief, purposeful visits. Well, he thought, perhaps that was necessary also.

"What's the matter with Anna?" Emily Fyodorovna's fair hair had grown thin and fuzzy and her face with its meager eyebrows had a tendency to blotchiness. She held her cheek for Dostoevsky to kiss.

"I don't know," he said rather inattentively. "It's all the process of getting used to running a household, I dare say."

"Well, the children will cheer her up."

"No doubt."

"You must understand she's young, Fyodor Mikhailovich," she said. "She likes young people. You mustn't try to monopolize her or she'll think you're a bore. She needs people of her own age or younger, not older. And if you try to force her away from them she'll take a dislike to you. It's extremely delicate, believe me. Young girls are like that. You must try to understand."

He sat slowly back in the chair, looking at her with irritable uncertainty. "Do you think so? Yes, yes, you're probably right." He stared ahead for a moment, fidgeted nervously, then jumped up and said in a savage tone, "Can I never be left alone! I *must* get on with this." He swept up the writing things from the table, went into the next room, and slammed the door.

Pasha said, "He's getting so jumpy lately it's impossible. I'm fed up with this hole. Why can't the old fool make some money and get us out? Do you know I want some new shirts and he can't pay for them?"

"And catch you doing any work, eh?" Emily Fyodorovna laughed.

"I don't want any insults from you." Since she continued to laugh he said, "He's finished, that's the trouble—worn out."

"Not for his young wife," Emily Fyodorovna said.

As Pasha began crowing like a cock, Anna came in with red eyes. "Fyodor, I've found a little castor sugar." Silence. Seeing he wasn't there, she glanced at Emily Fyodorovna, then turned toward the door to the far room.

"Anna, my dear, one moment." Deftly Emily Fyodorovna caught her elbow. "Don't disturb him. He has gone in to work. It's something he must finish." She sighed windily. "Ahh, you don't realize, you're so young for him. Your naïve conversation doesn't really entertain him. He's a serious man and he needs to reflect on his work. You can't possibly help him in that—only get in his way. Go out for a walk with the children: Katya and Marya will go. I brought them around expressly. I'll look after the tidying up and so on." Emily Fyodorovna took the tray with the castor sugar out of her hands.

Anna eyed her remorsefully. "Oh, very well." She felt hurt and miserable and bewildered. Stifling her tears, she went out.

Gradually Dostoevsky became used to saying, "Oh, Emily, will you bring me the paper?" instead of asking Anna; or "Emily, this is good tea; where did you get it?" Emily and her grown-up children, aided by Pasha, took control of the household. Almost daily in front of Dostoevsky, Emily Fyodorovna found occasion to criticize Anna's incapacity as a housewife, her waste of money. And money was going faster. He had spent everything he had earned from *Crime and Punishment.*

Then, one evening in the fifth week of Lent, after a nervous row with Anna, he came home from a dinner visit and found her weeping on the bed. "But what's the matter?" He sat with his arm around her.

"Nothing. Nothing."

"You must tell me, Anyechka." He insisted quietly, gently. At last she said between sniffs, "Do you know, you hardly spoke to me all today? We're breaking apart. And I can't bear this life any more, Fedya. I can't, I can't."

"But what life, my sweetheart?"

"It's Emily Fyodorovna, too, but mostly it's Paul Alexandrovich." She would never call him Pasha. "He's poisoning my life, Fedya; he's setting you against me. An hour ago, when you were out he said you'd been an idiot to marry me, that I was a detestable housewife and squandered the

money that belongs to them all. And he said he'd noticed"
—she could hardly restrain her sobs—"that you've had
more fits since we were married." She broke down completely. When she could go on she told him of Pasha's tricks:
hiding things, telling lies so that she was blamed, insulting
her, sending Fedosya, the old servant, out on long errands
at the busiest times, stealing. "And he's succeeding, Fedya,"
she said, dabbing her swollen, tear-stained face. "The admiration I had for you is diminishing at a frightful speed.
Instead of defending me you let them take command here,
let them eat my dinners, and mock me for my inexperience.
I don't think you love me any more. You never come and
ask my advice as you used to."

He was irritated and regretful. "It's been my fault. I didn't
see for a moment. You never complained about Pasha. How
can you doubt that I love you just as well, with all my heart?"
He comforted her and kissed her. "What we need is a change
from all this. I tell you what! I'll try to get another advance
from Katkov and we'll go to the country."

"Couldn't we go abroad, leave Russia altogether for a
month or two?" she said.

He looked doubtful, caught. "I don't know. Perhaps."

"Please, Fedya."

"I'll have to go to Moscow first. I need to see Katkov
anyway."

From Moscow he sent a telegram announcing his return.
Anna insisted on preparing the dinner herself and Emily
Fyodorovna, for once, let her have her own way. Dostoevsky
arrived in high spirits, telling them laughingly about a man
he had met on the train. "He kept telling me about his con-
stipation, all about it, in front of the full carriage. I was so
ashamed. And he wouldn't stop!"

They all sat down to the table together, Dostoevsky, Anna,
Emily Fyodorovna, Pasha, the children, Fedosya, the old
servant. Helping to serve, Anna was glowing with happiness

at having him back; he seemed changed, more lighthearted; the journey had done him good.

"Ah, it's good soup," he said. "Nobody makes it like you, Anna." She smiled at him. "And Katkov's a splendid fellow," he went on. They were all quietly watching him, poised. "He advanced me a thousand rubles." Anna clasped her hands in dismay; he should never have blurted it out. There was a chorus of voices.

"Then we can take a house in the country."

"The fine weather's starting."

"I'm willing to sacrifice myself to run it," Emily Fyodorovna beamed.

Dostoevsky said, "We're not taking a house in the country. I'm going abroad with Anna."

The others exploded with laughter, then looked uncomfortable. They began to remonstrate loudly. "I need three hundred rubles for new clothes," Emily Fyodorovna said.

"You promised me two hundred," Pasha bawled.

"Uncle Fyodor, I owe fifty rubles . . ."

They were all talking at him at once, gesticulating. He saw his mistake. Anna was biting her lip. He shrugged, slowly, helplessly. At last he called above the voices, "You can't have it all. I'm willing to give some. . . ." There was prompt silence. "I promised a hundred to my brother Nicholas," he continued. "I'll give two hundred to you, Emily Fyodorovna, a hundred to you, Pasha—and that's all. We'll be back by August; I can't manage any more."

They howled at him, they protested. Emily Fyodorovna said, "I can't do with less than seven hundred for myself, the children, and Pasha."

All at once there was a loud rapping on the door. With unusual alertness Pasha jumped up, answered, and slouched back. "It's Madame Reimann's son."

"My God!" Dostoevsky said. It was one of the creditors. "He says he holds two thousand rubles' worth of bills

against you and wants five hundred now." He slipped Dostoevsky a sly look.

"But we're paying them heavy interest," Anna said.

Pasha shrugged. "If he doesn't get it he'll call the bailiffs
and seize the furniture."

Dostoevsky got up hurriedly and went out to the man.
Anna caught the odd expression on Pasha's face—and understood. He had somehow wormed news of their projected trip
out of his stepfather before Dostoevsky went to Moscow and
now sent this creditor to prevent their leaving. In a moment
Dostoevsky came back, looking suddenly tired. "I had to give
him three hundred. And he wants eleven hundred more in
six days."

"Oh no! What about us? Where's ours?" Emily Fyodorovna
cried.

"Seven hundred, you said. It belongs to us," Pasha was
shouting. "You're not going to give it to those people before
us!"

Dostoevsky stood looking at them for a few seconds. Then
he opened his hand and let his wallet fall on the table. As
they snatched the money from it, he shrugged to Anna.
"Well—at any rate there's nothing left for us to quarrel over."
She pressed her hands to her face and ran from the room.

They were walking down the Voznesensky Prospect the
next day when she said to him, "Do you see how they are
spying on me? Pasha has been watching me every moment.
They don't want me to be alone with you."

"You're imagining it."

"Fedya, we can't stay here. It will soon begin all over
again; it will get worse. We must have two or three months
of peace together or they'll break us apart for good." She
covered her face, weeping.

"Anna, Anyechka, don't——" He tried to comfort her, in
a panic.

"If we don't go somewhere abroad it's the end of our marriage."

"But we haven't ten rubles, Anna. You saw——"

"I can pawn my dowry things, the piano, furniture, those bits of jewelry."

He looked at her in great distress. He was confused, harassed by the worries of debts, the fits were becoming unendurable. He knew that he would go with death in his soul. Now that the time had come he shuddered at going to Europe, whose moral influence he believed to be very bad, without any material to work on and with a young, inexperienced wife. She would be borne down by his disposition —and yet she seemed to need the trip so urgently. "Yes. All right," he said.

"You will? You'll take me?"

"Yes, my dear."

"Fedya dear, dear Fedya. Oh, you're wonderful!" In the midst of the passers-by she threw her arms around him and covered his face with kisses.

They told the family at dinner. It was a complete surprise. Pasha shouted that he must have more. Emily Fyodorovna expostulated and wrung her hands. Dostoevsky said, "It's not my money. It's Anna Grigoryevna's."

Three days later they left for Germany.

PART FOUR

Chapter Fourteen

1

She was a child. She took a naïve delight in everything, exclaiming when she saw her first donkey-chaise, laughing, and liking Berlin, a place he detested. The three-room apartment they took in Dresden she found charming, though it was ordinary enough. When he took her out and bought her a white straw hat with roses around the brim and two loops of velvet, she paraded beside him as though it were the smartest hat in the world. "Oh, Fyodoritschka, you're so good. It's wonderful!" She applauded all the German bands. Every day she sat secretively and childishly writing shorthand in a diary. "What are you putting down?" he asked, his arm around her. "Relieving your mind about me, I suppose?"

"It's nothing. Things for me." She looked up at him smiling. There were all the new impressions she wanted to record. But he was the real reason why she made notes. He was so mysterious and unfathomable to her; and she thought that if she put down his thoughts and expressions it would help her to understand him. She had told him she was pregnant the day before.

Dresden was windy, staid, and full of hunchbacks, cripples, and yellow mail vans. Dostoevsky worked a little at night, got up at eleven o'clock in the morning when they had breakfast. At two o'clock they went to the picture gallery, at three had lunch at Helbig's restaurant on the bank of the Elbe where there were five courses for twenty-five groschen, including marvelous blue eels and Niersteiner wine.

Moreover the restaurant took Russian newspapers, which

he read—with enormous nostalgia already! They walked on the Brühl Terrace, in the gardens, listened to the prize bands and took out books from the lending library, tried their luck at all the shooting stands, and at nine o'clock were back at their rooms for tea. He read a little before starting work.

He was writing an article on Belinsky for Babikov, of the *Svesda* review, and it would not come as he wanted. He strove with it, groaned and perspired over it. He wanted to say everything and yet because of the censorship he was obliged to throw away precious things. And what was left was miserable, mediocre stuff. He had half believed that once out of Petersburg, away from creditors and family, he would be able to work. But now after hours of struggling he snatched the pages from the desk, ripped them up, and threw them on the floor. He sat with his head in his hands. What was he doing here? Where were they heading? Apart from anything else, he was dying of boredom. This life in Dresden was overwhelmingly tedious; they were vegetating. The Germans made him furious. As days passed his exasperation came out in bickering arguments with Anna. In the rooms on either side there were plasterers beginning work at four o'clock in the morning. But Petersburg meant the knock on the door, the voices demanding payment. If only they were clear of debts. By the end of three weeks he was in a state of acute tension. One evening he threw the pen across the room and jumped up. There was only one thing to do; he must have money—and there was one method of gaining it. He looked into the bedroom; Anna was sleeping. He returned and walked up and down the room excitedly.

He told her the next morning. She was putting on her hat to go out with him. "Listen, Anyechka, we can't last more than another month here at this rate. There's no money coming in and Frau Zimmermann has been hinting she'll want more rent soon. If we're going to see some of Europe we need money. I know a way of getting some; it's quite certain. We'll have all we need if I can spend some time at roulette. It absolutely cannot fail."

He was irritated at the consternation on her face but contained himself, took her hands excitedly. "It isn't gambling. The element of chance is reduced mathematically. I have a system. Provided one continues to a certain point, it isn't possible to lose. Do you understand?"

"I don't know, I——" She was shocked and uneasy. The idea seemed fantastic to her, incomprehensible and frightening.

"You don't mind?" He hesitated again. "It'll mean my going to Homburg."

"Do you mean, leaving me here?"

"For a few days, that's all, a few days," he said hurriedly. The feeling of guilt overwhelmed him; and yet he was urged on by it and actually felt a sort of stinging enjoyment. "There are no tables here; the best gambling is in Homburg. It'll be nothing, my dear. Just the time to win our fare to Paris, Madrid—wherever you say."

"I see."

"Better still, I tell you what. As soon as I start winning I'll send you word and you can join me there and we'll live happily together, eh, Anyechka?"

She longed to say it would be better if he didn't go at all; but she couldn't. "Yes, I understand." She didn't want to dash his eagerness; and he looked extremely overwrought, as he did sometimes before a fit. "It'll be all right. Let's go out, it's a lovely day."

He deliberately waited another day in a fever. They passed the hours in a strained way with sudden displays of attention on his part, testy answers he couldn't suppress, and silences. At three o'clock in the afternoon they went to the station. He leaned from the carriage window, holding her hand; there was a strange feeling of anguish and exultation in him, pleasure and excitement inextricably entwined with misery. He said to her, "Anna, I know it's mad for me to be doing this. It's vile and weak—but there's a faint chance in it. Do you see?"

"Yes. Don't worry." The whistle blew. She said, "I love you."

He looked at her. "Thank you for saying that, Anna." As the train began to pull out, her resolve crumbled and tears came into her eyes. She was embarrassed at the stares of the bystanders and in her acute distress, before he had gone, tried to cover her face. He signaled with his hand, shouting above the noise, "I'll be back in four days. *Four days!*" She couldn't help running alongside for a little while and heard him say, "Don't cry, Anna."

The distance widened. He looked back, seeing her young figure sadly waving to him from the platform, and he felt a terrible remorse. Why had he left her there, alone in a strange town? A wall intervened, cutting her from view.

2

It rained steadily in Dresden all the week. Anna went to the station early on Sunday and stood under the dripping wooden canopy on the platform waiting for him. Everything was steamy. The rain fell straight down.

A man with a cane and checked trousers kept walking jauntily past, eying her impertinently, and she was more and more afraid he was going to speak to her; but she did not want to go into the waiting room for fear of missing Fedya. The train from Leipzig was the one for passengers from Frankfurt and Homburg. It was already twenty minutes late.

The man moved nearer. She kept her eyes down as he passed but she could feel him pausing in front of her. She longed for Fedya to arrive. She had sent the money he had asked for, though Frau Zimmermann, the Swiss landlady, had sharply disapproved and advised her not to. She had very little left. The four days had extended into ten and it had all been so miserable and Frau Zimmermann, tall, thin, and goodhearted, had been kind. She braced her shoulders; it was past and she wouldn't think of it any more. A bell began ringing and everybody looked along the line. Through the rain she could see the swirl of black smoke made by the arriving train.

"*Eh bien, mademoiselle,* it'll be good to get away from such weather, *n'est-ce pas?*" It was the man with the cane; he spoke French.

She looked at him, her face reddening with confusion.

"I hope I may have the pleasure of accompanying you," he said.

"Please——" She turned, but he stepped in her way.

"Allow me to present myself. Henri de Cheptal. Oh, don't run away." Clutching up her skirt, she tried to escape; he unashamedly walked alongside her, eying her, talking rapidly. "How far are you going, my child? I'm sure I can be of assistance to you. Oh, you blush delightfully. Do you know that? Where are you stopping the night, h'm?"

"Please go away. I'm waiting for my husband."

"Ah, you are Russian! My dear child, allow me to offer you the benefit of my experience, a seat in my carriage——" He took her arm.

"Oh! Leave me alone." She freed her arm. She did not know what to do and ran out with beating heart beyond the canopy into the rain. He did not follow. She stood alone in the downpour, full of distress and longing for Dostoevsky. He had lost everything and written for more money, which she had sent. The train was stopped at a signal a little way down the line. In a few minutes she was soaked. The white straw hat which she had put on specially for him hung shapelessly down on her forehead. She tried to protect her scarf but it became a sodden rag. She touched the little packet of chocolate cigarettes she had bought for a present for him. At last the train moved forward. As the first carriages passed her she had a moment of panic at the idea that he might not see her and ran back along the platform to the exit. The man with the cane was standing with his back turned, watching the train come to a halt. The carriage doors were thrown open, there was all the noise, shouting, bustle of arrival. She stood searching the throng of people with her eyes, looking for his broad figure, his face among the others. They went past her through the exit in groups, singly, in bright-faced couples. She was pushing back strands of wet hair, dabbing the sodden sleeves of her coat and her collar with a handkerchief. It didn't matter; what did anything matter with Fedya arriving? A smiling young man and woman went by and she smiled herself in happy anticipation.

Then there was nobody more to come. She looked along the platform; people stood at the carriage doors talking to passengers. But he hadn't come. The man with the cane stepped down from a compartment nearby and came toward her. In her confusion she hurried out to the ticket collector.

"Please, when does the next train arrive from Homburg?"

"Nothing with passengers from Homburg before tomorrow."

"Tomorrow?" She turned away. The loneliness and disappointment overwhelmed her. Her wet skirt trailed in the mud as she looked at the rainy desolate town beyond the station steps. She climbed into an omnibus to go home.

She waited at the station next day but again he did not come. As she arrived back at the lodging Frau Zimmermann poked her head out into the hallway. "There's a letter." Anna turned quickly to the rack and ran upstairs. Her heart was beating painfully. She opened the letter and read it with trembling hands. "Anna, my dear love, my wife, forgive me; don't call me a wretch. I have committed a crime and lost everything you sent me, everything, everything, to the last kopeck. When I got the money I went to the table with the idea of getting a little back, to increase our resources. I was only thinking of a little win. At the beginning I lost a trifle, but I wanted to get it back and lost more. I went on playing without realizing and then I was playing just to get the money to come back with and I lost everything. Anna, please, I beg you, have pity on me. Don't condemn me. If I were to lose your love now! I want to get back to you as quick as I can. Send me ten imperials to pay the bills here and my fare back, even if it leaves you with nothing. My angel, I won't gamble that away too, I promise, I promise. I give you my word of honor I'll leave straight away, in spite of the cold, rain, everything. I kiss you, my love."

She threw herself on the bed and wept. Frau Zimmermann was solicitous and often looked in for chats. She was a good-hearted creature, lonely herself, longing for another husband and fond of spicy confidences about the local scandals. But Anna shrank from the pain of explanation and began staying out of the house. This cost a little money, sitting in the confectioners' shops for an hour over a cup of tea, going to the municipal picture gallery. So she walked the streets and when the rain was too heavy stood in doorways. Occasionally she felt sick. She thought constantly of Dostoevsky's return.

On the third day after sending the money she left the house early, spent the morning looking once more in the shops, and went on to the station. The train arrived on time. The last of the passengers went by. She stood at the barrier, still waiting. He wasn't there. She was standing, biting her lip, trying to understand why he hadn't come. He had promised; he had given his word not to gamble away the money again at roulette. She was unable to control her tears and went quietly away, seeing the stares of the German women and trying to hide her face. She did not feel bitter but terribly unhappy and lost and lonely and frightened. At the lodgings she heard a man's voice from the stairs and as she reached the landing there was a German policeman at her door. Her heart heaved; she stopped with the shock. The next moment Dostoevsky was coming out talking excitedly to Frau Zimmermann.

"Anna! My God—where have you been?" She threw

herself into his arms. "Frau Zimmermann didn't see you go out. We've been running around looking for you everywhere. I went for the police. Anna, my Anyechka——"

"I was waiting for you at the station."

The policeman gave a good-humored chuckle and went away with Frau Zimmermann. It appeared that Dostoevsky had come by the early train which reached Dresden at six o'clock in the morning and, while he had waited so as not to wake her too early, she had gone out.

He sat with her in the room, his arms around her. "All the torment and pain I've put you through, can you forgive me, Anyechka? I need you much more than I can tell you. All these last few days I've been hounded by one idea—something had happened to you."

"Oh, nonsense. You see what a spoilsport I am."

"Anna, my love, you can't say such things." He kissed her and got up, still excited. "I don't know what we're going to do. I don't mean the future, that's unfathomable. I've never seen further ahead than six months in my life. But now I'm counting on work. The next book has to be better than *Crime and Punishment*. Yes, yes! Then I'll have all of them in Russia with me. I believe in it, I believe in it for us! The only thing is, God knows what will happen if we go back to Russia with all those debts. Katkov will help us in the long run, I'm sure of it. But how are we going to wait?" He paused. "How much have you got left?"

"Twenty-eight thalers. That makes forty-nine florins." She looked up at him with her open childish expression. "I tried not to spend it, Fedya. I——"

"Anna darling, you of all people have nothing to reproach yourself with."

She turned to the window. "Look at that. It's the first day it hasn't rained for a fortnight. Let's make some tea and then go out. There ought to be some sign of spring."

There was a knock on the door. It was Frau Zimmermann. "This came this morning. With all that fussing and rushing and running, I forgot all about it." She held out an envelope.

Anna opened it. "Look!" She waved it. It was a money draft. "It's from Mother."

"Twenty imperials. We're rich!" He put his arms around her waist and they skipped around the room in a furious mazurka. Panting and laughing, she stopped him.

"Listen, Anyechka, let's leave here; let's clear out. Let's go to Switzerland—Geneva. I can work. There's no gambling there anyway."

"Oh yes, yes!" She was overjoyed. She flung her arms around his neck. "Oh, Fedya, I love you."

They said good-by to Frau Zimmermann and took the train next day. The weather had brightened and the lovely German countryside ran by, green and refreshing. They talked happily and laughed. At Leipzig, where they arrived at ten o'clock in the evening, they had to wait an hour for the onward train and reached Frankfurt at half past nine next morning. They spent the morning looking around the town and caught the two o'clock connection for Switzerland.

At first Anna dozed and then as they ran down the Rhine Valley she sat exclaiming at the splendors of the scenery.

"Look at that castle!" She glanced at him; his face was lighted up.

"Extraordinary, yes, yes!" He chuckled, clasping and unclasping his hands. "Extraordinary!"

She began watching him cautiously. She had the impression that something was stirring him up. As dusk came on she became more and more certain of it. He was loquacious, fidgety, the muscles of his face working. After Oos, where their two German fellow passengers got out and left them alone in the carriage, he could not sit still. He turned between the windows, peering out one side, then the other, sat, got up again, lit cigarette after cigarette. Presently the train began to slow down and they passed signal boxes and the freight yards of a station.

"Where's this?" she asked.

"Baden. Listen, my dear." He flung himself down beside her, clasping her hands. "Let's change plans and stay here for a couple of weeks. It's a delightful place. We're in no hurry; the weather has improved. And you'll like it better than Dresden, you'll see."

"But why, Fedya?" She was looking at his white face apprehensively.

"The whole trouble in Homburg was that I was anxious about you, what you were doing, whether you were sick. You were never off my mind. I couldn't concentrate on the play, I couldn't keep my attention on it, don't you see?"

"You want to gamble again?"

"My dear, it's not gambling. It's—it's a—a way of attacking the table, that's all. There are not only losers at roulette; people win. It really is extremely simple. Whatever happens, you must not get excited. You have to be clearheaded, composed, cool, free of worry. That's the whole thing. If you stick to that it's simply impossible to lose, you're bound to win. You understand that, don't you?"

The lights of the station ran by, the wheels squeaked, and the train jerked to a standstill. There were the shouts of the guard and porters. She looked into his face with acute anxiety and dread. She struggled to think of some objection that would not give him pain.

"But what about our tickets to Geneva?"

He seemed not to hear. He was sitting on the edge of the seat, greatly worked up. "I could have won every time in Homburg if you'd been there. That Jew! You should have seen him. He had nothing to distract him—and he won every day, every day! They were afraid of him. He took away a fortune. Now you're here with me I shall be like him. I'll be icy. You'll see. Once I'm like that I can't help winning."

She turned her face away, trying to summon the courage to refuse. He managed to wait a moment. "Anna—my dear——"

Doors were banging along the train. "Anna, we must get out!"

"You said you weren't going to gamble any more," she said, still turned from him.

"But it's our chance to win a fortune!"

The carriage door opened and a fat woman with a stringy servant came in, lifting brown paper bundles and suitcases.

"Anna, please, look at me." He clasped her hands again. There were shouts from the platform outside and more doors banging. She turned her head. "Think of the debts in Petersburg. I want to work, Anna. I want a little security, that's all. And we can win!"

She could not hold out; she wanted to weep, to bury her face in his shoulder and weep. She smiled. "Yes, of course, you're right."

Somebody slammed the door. The guard's whistle blew.

"Quick!" He seized two of their bags, shoved past the fat woman, flung the door open, and threw the bags on the platform. As he turned back for Anna the guard and another official ran up, shouting and blowing whistles. Anna was struggling to pull down their last bag. "Leave it! Get down, quick!" He pushed Anna toward the door, wrenched the bag from the rack, knocking the fat woman's hat sideways, tried to apologize, and as the train began to move leaped out into a group of gesticulating railway officials while heads poked from all the adjoining carriages in a general jeer.

They left the station to protests about "*Streng verboten*" and threats from the German officials. Dostoevsky was quivering, triumphant. "Anyechka, you'll see, you'll see. This is the turning point. Now we're going to make the big coup!"

3

"*Cinq, rouge, impair et manque.*" The morning sunshine outside dimmed the table lights. A woman with a painted face, a great hat, and a feather boa sat next to the chief croupier. Anna could see her eying the men professionally. The place smelled of stale smoke and beer. She looked up at Dostoevsky beside her. His face was drawn with excitement. He caught her glance and smiled. "Well, what do you think of it?"

"I thought it would be more impressive," she said.

"Don't you want to try, Anna? Here——" He gave her a five-franc note. "Put it on *impair*," he said. She did so.

"*Rien ne va plus*," the croupier called. She lost.

"Oh—I'm sorry," she said involuntarily, then put her hand to her mouth, feeling herself blushing. Dostoevsky reached out and placed coins on a combination of numbers. When the wheel stopped the croupier raked everything away. She could not bear to look. They moved around to different places. After a while Dostoevsky took her arm. "Let's go home, Anna." She saw the effort he was making to pull himself away. As they went out he said: "We've won twenty-five thalers. It's the beginning."

They had rented two tiny low-ceilinged rooms in a house over a forge on the Werderstrasse. The rooms had worn old-fashioned furniture that creaked at a tread, a sofa, dusty wool mats on the floor; the landlady had agreed to supply them with a midday meal for a florin a day. The smell of the forge came up from below and the clang-clang of the smith's hammer on the anvil, the sounds of the horses shifting position on the cobbles and the men's voices. Anna had to go outside to the lavatory on the landing to be sick. Marie, the landlady's smiling but dirty servant, put a lunch of sausage, potatoes, and bread on the table.

"I won't have anything; I don't feel like food," she said as they sat down. And there seemed to be constraint between them. All the uncertainty had come back; she could not understand the attraction roulette had for him. She felt all this was strange and terrifying; and she dreaded the future.

After lunch Dostoevsky moved around being attentive to

her. She saw his underlying ferment, the almost irrepressible desire to rush off to the Kursaal again. The nausea would not leave her; she went into the bedroom and he helped her lie down on the bed. Through the open door she saw him take something out of the small bag in the trunk where they kept their money and go out. She was tired and wanted to sleep.

When she woke up she lay wondering what the time was. They had no watch since Dostoevsky had lost his in Homburg. In a little while the clock outside struck four.

The bed was high with a mahogany frame and bore her up away from the tiny room in a way that intensified her sense of isolation. It was a bier on which she was dying. She tried to shut her mind to everything. She lay high and lonely above the strange room. The afternoon dragged by. She heard five o'clock strike; then six; then seven. The strokes reverberated. The clang-clang of the smith's hammer came up oppressively from below and there was a child crying down there. The changing of the afternoon light, the sense of the foreignness of the place weighed on her spirits. She had thought he would be back earlier and would bring some bread. She kept thinking of bread. She was hungry and felt horribly sad and anxious. At last she climbed from the bed, went downstairs, and asked the landlady to send for two rolls from the baker's. The landlady, a red-faced garrulous woman, all hair wisps and breathless untidiness, gave her an irritated look and sent Marie.

The light began to go. The window of the room became livid. She sat eating the rolls of bread, watching the shadows invade the room. The clanging below stopped. It was very still. The terror of dusk came out. She sat, gripped by a sort of horrible depression, until it was almost dark. When she lighted the lamp the room was uglier and more hateful than before, a room of strangers in an unfriendly place. Nine o'clock struck. Then ten o'clock. All at once she thought perhaps he had had a fit there—he'd been so overstrung—

and couldn't say where he lived. She jumped up, clasping her hands. He might be dying and she'd arrive too late. She tried to control herself, putting on her hat. There was a noise outside. The door flew open and he came in. "Anna."

"Oh, Fedya—are you all right?"

"Yes, yes, you've been pulling me toward you for the last three hours so strongly I could hardly resist." He was haggard, in a passion, and began frantically tugging at his pockets and emptying money onto the table. "They're Baden ducats. There are a few of them left. I had more than four hundred francs' worth. Ah, my God! It's terrible." He seized her by the shoulders with an agonized expression. "I was longing to be with you, I was tormented about your being sick, every minute, every minute—and yet *I stayed there!* I wanted to win more, more! I couldn't tear myself away. I wanted it in spite of you. Forgive me, Anna, forgive me. I'm a miserable wretch, unworthy of you." He bent his head, covering her hands with kisses.

"Poor Fedya, poor Fedya. You mustn't torment yourself. You see nothing happened to me while you were away. All that is of no importance at all."

After a while she managed to make him a little calmer. "Come, I'll make you some tea and then you must sleep."

"Do you know, there was such a scene tonight! Red came up twenty-six times running—*twenty-six times!*" He walked up and down, talking, talking, full of an unquenchable excitement.

In the morning while he was sleeping she counted the money in the bag. There were seventeen of the gold ducats, a florin, and small change in kreutzers; she took the kreutzers, went out and bought some milk and fresh bread, and when she came back he was dressing and singing in great good humor.

After breakfast he lit a cigarette, moved uneasily about the rooms for a while, taut, nervy again. "Don't those children

of the landlady's ever stop howling?" He went to the bag.
"Anna, I'm taking five ducats. I shan't be back late."

She looked at him. "Are you going . . . ?"

"Why don't you go out for a walk? It looks like a fine day."
He already held his hat, kissed her, and the next moment was
gone. She stood with a plate still in her hand looking at
the shut door as if he were coming back, then sat slowly
down by the table. All the unbearable affliction and loneliness came over her; she knew he was going to lose everything and come back in despair and she flung her arms on
the table and burst into tears.

The rough voices of men with horses at the forge came
through the open window; there was the mingled smell of
fresh horse dung, burned hoof, and soot, the clink of chains
and clip-clop of hoofs and, beyond, the shouts of the passing street vendors; the child had stopped crying. After a
while she recovered. She put the bag of money in a drawer
and resumed clearing the things away. The day stretched
before her emptily. She tried to concentrate on giving the
room an extra cleaning; dust in quantities seemed to fly
up from the forge. About an hour later there was a step
outside and he came in avoiding her eyes.

"I've lost," he said furiously; he went rapidly past her to
the window and suddenly turned. "It's weakness, it's the
most damned and contemptible weakness. I know, I know
it, and it doesn't make any difference. Anna——" He rushed
over to her and said in a moved and trembling voice, "Whatever may happen, believe that I love you. My dear sweet
Anna, I love you. You're an admirable woman and I'm unworthy of you."

"Oh no. That's not true." She said it with absolute childish
warmth and spontaneity.

He kissed her repeatedly and kissed her hands in a fever
and she saw the pleading in his looks. "Give me a little
more, Anna," he said. "I can win the other back. A little
more."

She was overwhelmed at his asking her. "Not now, Fedya. Come out. Show me around Baden."

"Please, Anna, now, now. I must go back!" He was shaking.

"Tomorrow perhaps." She released her hands, clenched them behind her back; she wanted the strength to refuse, though it broke her heart. "No more today. You'll only lose it and reproach yourself again."

"Only five ducats. Only three if you like. Give me three, Anna, give me three."

She shook her head.

"It's only so that I can relax a little. I'm worked up. I——"

She couldn't hold out; she wanted to throw her arms around his neck and beg him with all her love not to go; but she opened the bag and said, "All right; here you are —five ducats."

He kissed her hands. "Anna—you won't think I'm a scoundrel who'd take your last scrap of bread to gamble with?"

"You know I'd never think that." She raised her chin, managed to turn calmly on her heel, almost nonchalantly. "After all, you're absolutely free to lose it if you want to. Why not?"

He was giving quick glances, looking away again. She saw his enormous haste to get away. "Go on, my dear."

"Yes, yes. I will."

As she heard him clattering down the stairs she had a terrible impulse to run after him; she crushed the knuckles of her hand into her mouth so as not to call out—unable to stop the sobs that shook her, she wept unrestrainedly.

His unhappy face kept accusing her; it was worst of all to see him in that state. And what was going to become of them, without resources, in a foreign country? All at once the voice of the smith's wife came noisily from the stairs, talking to someone. Anna quickly blew her nose, dried her eyes, and managed to compose herself. She moved about the two rooms, superficially busy, pretending for the sake of the landlady who was not there! Presently she thought of going out; but the landlady was at some prolonged operation on the stairs and she shrank from passing her, submitting to her sharp glances and questions. She took up some sewing but could not get on with it, turned to washing some clothes in the basin, and managed at last to recover herself in the sheer dullness of this.

As the servant finished setting the table for lunch Dostoevsky came in. He began fretfully making a cigarette, sitting at the table, getting up. "I've lost everything."

"Fedya, never mind. It's of no importance."

He moved away from her restlessly. "Turgenev's here. I just ran into Goncharov. He said Turgenev saw me yesterday but avoided speaking to me."

"Why?"

"Knowing that 'gamblers don't like being accosted,' says Goncharov. Can't you hear Turgenev saying it? Can't you? My God!"

"Do you still owe him money, Fedya? You told me so once."

"Yes, yes. Fifty thalers."

She said, "You ought to call on him or he'll think you're afraid he'll ask for it back."

"I'm sure of it," he said impatiently. "You have to be careful of people you borrow money from!" Then he turned abruptly and appealingly toward her and took her on his knee. "Anna darling, I beg you—give me another five ducats. Will you? I must go back."

"But—there are only seven. After that we'll have nothing left."

"I know! I know!" He put her away from him, sprang up, and flung across the room. He shouted at her, "Is it too much to ask? Five ducats! I can *win!* D'you hear? *Win!* Do you want fifty thousand ducats? Or do you want debts? Everlasting debts—*debts?* DEBTS?"

With a white face she said, "Fedya, try to calm yourself."

"How can I be calm? My God, I'll go mad!"

"We'll have nothing to live on—nothing for food. Wait till tomorrow, darling. You'll do better then."

"No, no, no!" He was moving around the room like a caged animal. "If I stay here I'll kill myself with impatience. I'd rather get everything over at once than endure this torture."

She went to the bag and gave him the money.

"Thank you." He kissed her.

"Have something to eat," she said. "They are sending it up now."

"Save it. I'll come back later." He hurried out.

When he had gone she found she was unexpectedly calm. They had only two ducats and a florin left—but what of it? It was nothing to cry about. She felt the pain of anxiety as if it were dampened, kept momentarily from the forefront of her mind by some system of self-defense. She ate lunch alone and afterward lay down. The afternoon drew on. She began to feel the brief allotment of assurance running out. Just after four o'clock he came in again. At once she saw from his face that he had lost. He said nothing. She climbed down from the high bed and went to him; he was standing at the window looking out. She took his hand, then saw that he was checking himself with difficulty. He turned to her. "Anna—I need two gold pieces. I pawned my wedding ring. They said if I don't redeem it straight away it's lost. Give me two pieces, will you?"

With the strength of desperation she said, "Of course. Take them, my dear."

He gave her an almost wild look, crossed the room, and sat down on a chair in the far corner, leaning forward and holding his head in his hands. She took out the bag and put the money in his pocket. The coins made a little chink. For a moment he sat without moving, as if he had not noticed, then jumped up and went out.

An unhappy revolt and rage overcame her; she cursed the gambling, she cursed Baden, her own weakness, she buried her face against the bed, ashamed to be weeping again but swept on by her misery and wretchedness. After a while she felt better. She changed her dress, carefully did her hair, taking a long time over it, and went out. It was warm and sunny; she was entertained watching the overdressed strollers with their enormous Parisian bustles and long trains. She longed for him to be with her and suddenly thought he might be waiting for her at home and hurried back; but he was not there. She made tea rather disconsolately and sat down and wrote a concealingly optimistic letter to her mother in Petersburg. At intervals she stopped, listening, thinking she heard him on the stairs, but there was a group of carters with their horses making a great noise at the forge. She knew he was at the roulette table again. Had he redeemed the wedding ring? What was happening?

She was in the bedroom when she heard him come in but he did not answer her greeting. "I'll make you some tea," she said. She did not want to question him, but she could not help herself. "Did you get your ring back?" Without speaking he held up his hand, showing the ring. "Was it— what luck at the table, Fedya?"

He was sitting in a careless attitude on the corner of the table, rolling a cigarette. "I won a bit; about ten pieces," he said in a toneless indifferent way. "I've been at the Reading Room."

She looked at him with panic, feeling the sudden distance between them. It was she who had brought him here; she had made him leave Russia. She longed to be back in Petersburg herself, to see her mother, brother, and sister; writing the letter had painfully intensified her thoughts of all those things. But Petersburg meant Paul Alexandrovich, the insults, the everlasting quarrels again. They would be surrounded by hostile people, all hostile to her. Paul Alexandrovich would be there to drive Fedya mad, to drive both of them apart. She had brought him away to circumvent their attempts to take him from her. But now the gambling was destroying everything. He was becoming indifferent. Was it better than Petersburg, after all, the uncertainty of this life?

"Fyodor!" She crushed herself against him.

He shaved rhythmically, keeping the strokes in time with the reverberating clangs on the anvil below. He had got up late. The smell from the smithy rose up agreeably in the late morning heat.

"You'd think that man shod half the horses in the Duchy of Baden," he bawled out.

He felt in an odd state of mind, with an undercurrent of excitement. He was obliged to call on Turgenev; it wasn't possible to put it off any longer, though he could not pay the fifty thalers. In a way the idea of the meeting was unpleasant; he could foresee Turgenev's patronizing manner, his superciliousness. For some reason at this moment he particularly detested the thought of Turgenev's being accepted as a specialist in tact and the social graces, simply because he was so "favored by the gifts of nature." Even in the days of Belinsky, Turgenev had behaved as if all that were accepted—as it had been! And the recollection of the casualness with which Turgenev had ridiculed him at Prince Odoyevsky's all those years back (that had been the worst, the casualness) made him tingle even after such a lapse of time. Now Turgenev had certainly been despising him for his abjectness and lack of spirit in not calling on him before; and yet he was sure that, as soon as he arrived, Turgenev would behave as if it were all the other way round (that was the maddening thing), as if he were contemptuous of Dostoevsky's not having the courage to stay away and yet would manage to convey that he was flattering him in receiving him at all! Oh yes! That was exactly what Turgenev would be like. He thought of it with disgust.

After breakfast he took five gold pieces, said good-by to Anna, and went out. It was half past eleven. Turgenev lived on the Schillerstrasse, in the fashionable area near the Villa Plessen. Dostoevsky went down the Friedrichstrasse trying to suppress his growing agitation. He felt something scandalous was about to happen. There was even something humiliatingly agreeable about the situation. He went so far as to indulge in a short fantasy, imagining there was a whole gathering of notables, not merely Turgenev, awaiting him; he subdued them all by his elevation of thought, was absolutely triumphant, everybody else was dust and ashes and, compelled to acknowledge his superiority, went down on their knees to beg for his friendship; he forgave them all. He was the great poet of the age, the romantic figure, a new Alexander of Macedon, swaying them all by "the good and the beautiful." He gave orders that the millions of money that were suddenly his should be distributed to the poor and he went forth on a new pilgrimage while humanity poured out its grateful tears and blessings. He would not allow Turgenev to be entirely crushed but would raise him up and they would drink to their everlasting friendship.

For a moment he enjoyed it as if it were real. But he felt too many bitter and humiliating pangs. He knew he didn't need anything of such imaginings; he didn't care in the least about crushing Turgenev, subduing him, or winning him over.

At last he reached the Schillerstrasse, found the house, an elegant one with columns, and rang the bell. A servant, pompous and yet stupid with a crafty glint in his eye, typically German, showed him into a room with a bay window and glistening furniture. Turgenev was sitting on the sofa with a little table in front of him eating his morning cutlet, either his late breakfast or early lunch, with half a glass of red wine. Dostoevsky had seen him doing the same thing in Petersburg and, from what he had heard from others, Turgenev was always found eating his cutlet and usually ate it without offering his callers anything.

"My dear fellow. It's been ages," he said, getting up and

dabbing his lips with his table napkin. *"Excellent ami."* He leaned forward, offering his cheek, and Dostoevsky could not help asking himself which of them deserved greater contempt—Turgenev, embracing him just to humiliate him, or he himself, accepting in spite of his scorn. He positively refused to kiss Turgenev's cheek so that their faces just brushed each other in an absurd way which Turgenev evidently found perfectly satisfactory, though the unmixed delight on his face, Dostoevsky knew, was merely there as an expression of his distinction, his illustriousness.

"Sit down, *mon cher*. You must tell me everything about yourself," Turgenev said, as if on the spur of the moment one could give an account of one's entire life.

But that was the height of *chic* again, this sort of exaggerated interest and friendliness. Yet he was taken aback. It was not exactly happening as he had expected! There was a sort of circumspect formality in Turgenev's manner. He had expected Turgenev to break into his usual shrill laugh and start making his sour jokes; in fact he had been getting ready for them the day before. But there was a note he hadn't counted on. He hadn't expected quite this high, rather formal condescension. Not to this degree. Clearly Turgenev regarded himself as immensely superior to him in every respect! If it had only been an insult it wouldn't have mattered. But he seemed with the utmost earnestness to believe himself superior, altogether on a higher plane, and could only look at Dostoevsky in the most patronizing way. Dostoevsky gasped. He understood with absolute certainty that if, at that moment, some prince or archduke or even a baron had walked in, anybody Turgenev was in awe of, he would make it his sacred duty to forget Dostoevsky's existence, with the most insulting heedlessness, like an insect, a chip of wood, before Dostoevsky even had time to get out of his sight. He looked with detestation at Turgenev's rather fleshy nose, his beard, his graying locks falling artistically over his temples on each side.

"You don't want—er—you won't have anything?" Turgenev said. Dostoevsky took this to mean that he expected a rather obsequious refusal.

Dostoevsky had an intense desire to be perverse. "Yes, one of those cutlets will do nicely," he said in a deliberately rude way. "I'm quite hungry this morning."

Turgenev looked up, astonished and annoyed; then with a shade of fluster, rang the bell; and Dostoevsky couldn't help noticing his loud, irritated, decisive tone (meant to intimidate) when he ordered the servant to bring the second lunch.

"And a glass of wine, thank you," Dostoevsky blurted out, burning with a sort of mingled shame and delight. "I say, Ivan Sergeyevich, have you got bronchitis or something?"

"What? Why?"

"That jacket." Turgenev was wearing a sort of thick smoking jacket with a tasseled belt and a white muffler.

"No. I like to keep warm." Visibly Turgenev made an effort. "Tell me, are you working on something new?"

"I've not written anything for weeks. And you? Are you still having to respond to the persistent demands of your fellow countrymen?" He gave a loud and pointed laugh; it was actually a guffaw, a vulgar noise which he would have been ashamed of at another time but which Turgenev seemed positively to bring out.

Turgenev looked at him. "You've been reading the reviews of *Smoke*?" His vanity and his desire to speak about his own writing were too strong for him, Dostoevsky thought. Turgenev's latest novel, *Smoke*, a love story interspersed with tirades against "Russian barbarism," ignorance, animality, and general backwardness, had been very badly received in Russia. Turgenev was red in the face, evidently anxious to justify himself, even to somebody he was contemptuous of. "They tore it to pieces in *Golos*—the idiots. I have been slandered by the youth of Russia. And do you

know, our precious Russian aristocracy—they've been trying
to exclude me from their society!"

"Well, you couldn't have expected them to bow down
before you when you maintain that all intellectual, educated
and cultured Russia is nothing but smoke. Or perhaps you
did expect it? Russian art——"

"Russian impudence and conceit!" Turgenev's face was
dark with anger. "Where is it—Russian art? They praise a
lot of bloated nonentities and say other people have nothing
to compare with them."

"What? Pushkin, Gogol, Tolstoy, Glinka?"

"They only prove what I am saying. Kukolnik, Timofeyev
—fourth-raters like that is what they want! The poor be-
nighted barbarians. For the Russians an artist is of the same
species as a weight lifter. How dare they say other people
have nothing to compare with them! I tell you, when I went
to the Crystal Palace in London——"

"Yes, yes?" Dostoevsky looked at him eagerly.

"I can't forget it. There was everything there, everything
devised by mortal ingenuity—machines, marvelous machines,
implements, beautiful things, statues of great men. I kept
walking around and looking for the Russian things—where
were the *Russian* contributions? And I saw that our dear
mother, Holy Russia, could sink through the earth, disappear
utterly, with everything she had invented, without disturbing anything in the Crystal Palace—not a nail! Why, you
couldn't do the same with the Sandwich Islanders. You'd
miss them! After all, they did invent certain types of canoes
and spears which you would see were missing. We didn't
even invent the products for which we are most famous—
the yoke and the knout! The rest we got from western
Europe. And we talk about Russian art, the independence
of Russian science! Twice two is four with us, but you
reach the result more ingeniously."

"On the contrary, twice two is four for Euclid, but not
necessarily for Lobachevsky!"

"What? What?" Turgenev said, puzzled; but he rushed on. "We can't even invent a machine for drying grain. The farmers are still shoving their sheaves into ovens as they did eight centuries ago. The Germans don't need a machine, so we can't think of one. The Russians pick up some old bit of rag cast off by Saint-Simon or Fourier and treat it as a sacred relic. Oh yes, we're capable of that all right. Rubbish dropped by somebody else, we treasure it. Or getting up an article on the significance of the proletariat in France— oh yes, we can do that! I'm always hearing about the rich Russian nature, its multiple attributes; but what does it amount to, eh? Slobberings, half-animal sagacity. Something magnificent to boast of! I can't stand the smell of that triple extract of Russian muzhik!"

"Well, I can!" Dostoevsky couldn't help shouting. He suddenly decided to assume truculence; it was all pretense and he knew he was exaggerating. "I remember all that, all you've just said, from *Smoke*. It sounds as if you were so pleased with it you memorized it!"

Turgenev threw him a confused, angry look and flushed again.

"I didn't realize that the failure of *Smoke* and all the nasty articles about it exasperated you so much. I assure you it isn't worth it, Ivan Sergeyevich."

"What! Who—who——I'm not a bit exasperated!" Turgenev's face was purple. "I—I—my God!"

At that moment the servant came in with the second lunch and set it out with slow dignity on the table. Turgenev got up, visibly infuriated at the whole interview, and began walking up and down the room for exercise. Dostoevsky, eating, noticed that each time he turned he gave a slight but jaunty quiver of his right elbow. There was something excessively vain and self-satisfied in the movement. He quickly finished the cutlet and wine and lighted a cigarette.

"Then when are you going back to Petersburg?"

"I'm not!" Turgenev said testily. "I don't know that I'm ever going back. There's nothing in that barbarism, superstition, and obscurantism that tempts me at all. I've no faith in the Russian God. I prefer Germany. We ought to grovel before the Germans. Crawl in the dust! There is only one universal road, that of civilization, and all attempts to create a specifically Russian culture are pigheaded folly. I'm writing a big article on the Slavophiles and their stupidities."

"What you ought to do is to get a telescope," Dostoevsky said.

"Eh? What's that?"

"A telescope—and train it on Russia. Otherwise you can't expect to see what's going on there, let alone understand it."

Turgenev stopped and pushed back the hair from his brow; he stared with anger.

"You don't believe in the Russian God?" Dostoevsky said.

"I don't believe in any God! I'm an atheist. I believe in science, reason."

Dostoevsky jumped up. "Allow me to tell you that's nonsense. There hasn't been a single nation ever founded on science or reason alone. Absolutely from the beginning, science and reason have played a secondary part in the life of nations and so it will always be. Whether you like it or not, nations are moved by something different—the assertion of their existence, the spirit of life. If you like, 'the seeking for God.' No! Listen, listen! Every national movement you like to take is only a people seeking for its own god. There has never been a nation without a religion, without an idea of good and evil. And the stronger a people the more individual its god. But when it begins to share the same gods, it's a sign of decay. If a great people doesn't believe that the truth is to be found only in itself alone, exclusively, if it doesn't believe that it alone is fit and destined to raise up and save all the rest by its truth, it becomes ethnographical material, that's all, and not a great people. There you are! And one nation is 'god-bearing' and it is the

Russian. I believe, I cling with passion to my faith in the Russian people."

"And I believe in the German."

"What! Germans?" Everything that he had been silently harboring against the Germans since Petersburg boiled up in Dostoevsky. "Nothing but rogues and rascals. You meet them everywhere! They're a destestable race, far worse, far more disreputable than ours. And more stupid. No, no, no! There's no question of it. You throw their civilization in my face—but what has it done for them? Eh? What right have they to exalt themselves at our expense?"

Turgenev glared at him, absolutely breathless with anger. "You mean to insult me personally! I'd like you to understand that I have settled here permanently. I consider myself a German and I am proud of it."

"I deplore it. I did not know it and I deplore it." Dostoevsky rose. They moved toward the door.

All at once Dostoevsky had an overwhelming temptation. He positively shuddered at it; yet the idea at once became essential to him. Turgenev was standing ready for him to go. There was an expression of anger and contempt on his face; and it occurred to Dostoevsky in a flash that the temptation could not have arisen without that. His throat was parched and he had difficulty in controlling his voice. Turgenev noticed the change come over him and began looking at him with mistrust. Now, now! He wanted to test himself. He wanted to plunge into the abyss. The feeling that accompanied the dreams of power, his enormous height above everything, rushed over him.

"Ivan Sergeyevich, I—er—I have something to say to you; that is, it's a personal thing. Perhaps it will take some time . . ." He was crucifying himself. He felt horrified and yet something pushed him on.

Turgenev's face showed exasperation, tinged with a sort of crafty uncomfortable curiosity. He hesitated, then waved to a chair. "Pray sit down."

Dostoevsky said, "I wanted to tell you of this episode. I think you'll agree it is interesting. It happened in Petersburg a good many years ago. I was going home one day from meeting some friends, as a matter of fact it was from Petrashevsky's, and I happened to go into the Arcade. You may know how it was there at night with women, boys, a scandalous traffic of all sorts. This was the afternoon, and of course the place was full of ordinary people, families and so forth."

Turgenev was suddenly bolt-eyed.

"I went in in a peculiar state, greatly worked up by the meeting and in particular by a relationship with one of the group. Naturally, there were one or two women there, operating discreetly, and one accosted me. I enjoyed that intensely. I remember I had four hundred rubles with me and I was tempted to spend it all at once, in an orgy—that is, with several women at the same time—though perhaps it was only the thought of it that I enjoyed. I imagined reclining on cushions, with only a narrow scarf around my chest—I can't imagine why the scarf, but it was there very vividly—and having the women attend to me, all at once, in various delightful ways. I would have done so, perhaps, except that farther along the Arcade I happened to notice a young girl with her governess.

"She was about thirteen with a budding little figure, a creamy skin, and big eyes, a little charmer, still in a short frock. They were absolutely respectable of course. The child was even expensively dressed and evidently came from a good family. I stood there pretending to look into the shopwindow next to the one they were studying but eying the child and feeling myself quite shaking and weak. All at once she turned her glance and looked at me innocently and I couldn't breathe!"

Turgenev had become pale. He was not moving. There was absolute quiet in the room.

"At first when they went on I let them go. I simply stood

looking after them. The governess was holding the young girl's hand and walking along with her, very properly and modestly. They stopped from time to time to look into a shop. Then I decided in a flash. I walked quickly behind them. The governess was leaning forward at a shopwindow full of lace and fancy embroidery and I went around to her side and stood looking in too. She turned her head and I gave her a pleasant smile. 'Good afternoon,' I said. 'What agreeable things they have in here.' For a second, I saw, she wasn't going to answer; then she evidently thought better of it, smiled faintly, and said, 'Yes.' I summed her up at once. Oh yes, at once! She was about forty, with an oval face, rather bulging cheekbones, and pinched in underneath. You could see she had been a governess all her adult life and had only had the most respectable employers. But there was a tiny fleeting expression in her eyes that told me everything I wanted. I made no attempt at finesse. I said to her, 'I'd like the little girl for an hour. I'll give you three hundred rubles.'

"You should have seen the expression on her face! It was as if in all the years she had been walking out her charges she had dreamed of this happening to her once, just once. I swear her heart was beating nineteen to the dozen at that moment. She had also dreamed of those three hundred rubles. I saw it! I saw it! She did not take her eyes off me. The little girl was fortunately absorbed in something on the other side and didn't follow any of it."

Turgenev said, "Do you mean to say——"

"Don't interrupt!" He was plunged in shame, drowned, overwhelmed by it. He wanted to rush from the room and yet also tell everything. "The governess swallowed and said in a whisper, 'No, sir. Oh no, no, no.' I said, 'You can have three hundred and fifty. I'll bring her back to you in an hour. Just introduce me to her as one of her cousins, Alexander Ivanovich. Come, here's a hundred rubles in advance.' I pressed the note into her hands. Her bottom lip was trembling violently. She said very low, 'Very well. But not more than an hour.' I could have fallen on her neck. I asked the little girl's name and she told me it was Natasha. My own heart was beating at a sickening rate, but I raised my voice at once, stepped around to where the girl was standing, and said, 'Hello, Natasha, don't you remember me?' She looked up, held my eyes, and blushed faintly. 'No, I'm sorry.' The governess intervened. 'It's your cousin—er—er—Sozont Alexandrovich. Listen now, my dear, I'm just going to Praskovia Ivanovna's around the corner. You go along with Cousin Sozont and we'll meet here in an hour.'

" 'An hour and a half,' I said, smiling. She hadn't been prepared for that and positively shrank with fear; she scuttered off like a rabbit. I took Natasha's hand and turned away. A little way along the Arcade was one of those bath establishments. They stay open half the night and of course don't ask any questions. I took her in there. I forget exactly how I put it. She came quite willingly. I saw her sent to a room, waited a little, then gave the attendant a tip to take me to the same one and open the door with her passkey. They're used to it and take no notice. Natasha was undressed, hanging up her slip. I locked the door after me . . ."

He clasped his hands, which were shaking as he went on with the recital. He felt all the acute voluptuous torture. He explained everything in detail and described his own feelings fully. Turgenev sat as if he were stone.

"And as we walked back, you know, she held my hand just as before. We had been away an hour and three quarters and the governess was in a fearful state. I deliberately gave her only another fifty rubles instead of what I'd promised. It gave me a special satisfaction. She did not know what to say. I was suddenly exasperated with her—no, it was more, I was infuriated with her. I wanted never to set eyes on her or the girl again. The governess was shaking and hurried away with Natasha, who was extremely calm. I couldn't help being struck by Natasha's absolute calm. She said nothing, just kept her eyes down. They disappeared outside."

There was a silence. Slowly Turgenev's white face became pink. Dostoevsky deliberately prolonged the silence so as to heighten Turgenev's embarrassment. Turgenev rose unsteadily. He said, "I regret . . . I much regret . . . I . . ."

"It was the behavior of the worst sort of scoundrel, wasn't it?" Dostoevsky said. "Even criminal." Suddenly he gave a loud laugh and said, "As a matter of fact, I invented the whole thing."

Turgenev stared at him. There was bitter offense in his face. He seemed unable to speak.

"I must go. Good-by, Ivan Sergeyevich. I mean, *auf Wiedersehen, auf Wiedersehen, mein teurer Freund. . . .*"

Mechanically Turgenev rang the bell for the servant. Dostoevsky hurried along the Schillerstrasse. He was in a tumult of excitement. The confession had brought him to a tremendous pitch. It had been excruciating to tell that to Turgenev, of all people, the man he detested more than any other! He had done it out of pride, out of sheer pride! He had shown his greater will, the will of the hero on the heights, defying everything, everything! He was not afraid of the truth, even with a man like Turgenev. He felt somewhat annoyed that he had exaggerated it, worsened it; that had been a quirk on the spur of the moment. He did not know why he had done that; he couldn't account for it. But he had needed to suffer the whole experience. And Turgenev had understood that he wasn't afraid. Ah! He was exultant; burningly ashamed and exultant.

Chapter Fifteen

1

Suddenly he had a big win. They counted out a hundred and sixty-two gold pieces—ducats, Russian imperials, gold double thalers, Prussian friedrichsdors, Napoleons. He sent some to Emily Fyodorovna and Pasha in Petersburg.

The same afternoon there was an incident at the Kursaal. The crowd of gamblers was pushing, vociferating at the table. At one end, a French *lorette* with enormous painted black eyes played recklessly, losing and laughing and showing her brilliant white teeth—playing also for a fat merchant two seats away who was eying her nervously.

Dostoevsky sat with the crowd pressing behind his chair, leaning over him, ten arms, a dozen, reaching out at once to put down stakes and snatch up winnings. He gripped the table edge trying to keep calm. He was winning—more and more. He had begun with ten gold pieces and had won forty. He staked ten on black.

"*Dix-sept!*" He had won again—another ten. He could hardly sit still.

"*Faites vos jeux!*" He reached out, distributing stakes. The wheel spun.

"*Vingt!*" He had lost on the combination around the 8. But there was his square of numbers: 19, 20, 22, and 23. Another win! It was an unbreakable vein of luck. He picked up the winnings—twenty-four ducats. Now, now that his luck held, he could make the coup he had dreamed of. He fidgeted nervously with the two stacks of coins in front of him, watching the table.

"*Mais—monsier! Monsieur!* That was my money you

picked up" A hand shook his shoulder violently. He looked up at a man with an imperial and waxed mustache à la Napoleon III, evidently French. "On the 20–22. My money, *monsieur!*"

"But—I—it was my square."

"Non, monsieur. Non, non, non. You were on 22–26. I saw you put your stake on. That is mine."

"What?" Dostoevsky was thrown into confusion. He believed the Frenchman was right. He had picked up the wrong winnings. Quickly he took the twenty-four ducats from the pile and held them out. "I beg your pardon. It was inadvertent, a foolish mistake. I apologize, *monsieur.*"

The man took the coins. "Mistake?" He stood glaring offensively with large watery blue eyes. *"C'est trop facile, monsieur.* A very nice game, such inadvertence, *hein?* You cannot lose. *Non, non,* it is somebody else who loses by the inadvertence."

Dostoevsky forced back his chair and sprang up in a fury. "What do you mean? What are you insinuating?" Startled faces were turned to them. "I demand an explanation, *monsieur.* Are you insinuating that I took your money on purpose? Are you?" He was trembling, in a blind rage.

The man stepped back, coughed, braced himself, coughed again. "What I said—ahum—I said."

"Then you're a scoundrel, *monsieur.* A rogue! Do you hear? And a blackguard!" He shouted it; he was already fighting the duel. The Frenchman was purple in the face; he recoiled, defiantly clinked the coins in his hand, and with a toss of his head suddenly turned and pushed his way through the onlookers. Dostoevsky flung himself down at the table; he was seething, he could scarcely take in what was before him. People were eying him curiously. The muscles around his right eye and his neck began twitching. He felt completely unnerved by the incident, snatched up a pile of coins, and began staking, hardly able to remember the combination of numbers. He lost, quickly staked another twenty pieces on red, changed his mind and moved it all to black at the last minute, and in a sort of confused horror watched the ball spin—and fall into red. Ten more—another ten! He flung the coins out. He won five back, lost another twenty. He played in a fever. In a moment he had only two ducats left. He staked them blindly, lost, shoved back his chair, and rushed out.

At the lodgings Anna was washing his shirts. He paced up and down telling her about it. "Anna, give me twenty pieces. I'm wasting time. I have to go back."

"Don't play any more today, darling. You know we can quite well manage to live on what's left."

"I want to *lose* them!" he said loudly, fidgeting all over. "I want to show that winning doesn't go to my head, that I can stake just as high when I'm losing." Suddenly he choked in a prolonged coughing fit that doubled him up and sent his face purple. She tried to hold him, frightened; then when he had recovered she took out the bag.

"Give me thirty," he said.

By the evening they had only twenty gold pieces out of the hundred and sixty-two.

Anna was feeling sick in the morning and wanted to lie in bed a little. Dostoevsky kissed her and went off to the Kursaal. He was soon back, saying he had lost the five ducats she had given him and wanting another five. She gave them; he lost these and another five. After lunch she gave him four of the last five.

She waited a long time for him to come back. It was raining steadily. For once the house was silent; none of the usual hammering from the smithy or the crying children below. Occasionally a carriage rolled by on the cobbles outside. She sat at the streaming pane, not knowing how to while away the time; she had nothing to read and couldn't bring herself to sit down to write; she had broken her needle and there was no thread so that she couldn't sew.

She began to sing softly to herself, looking out on the street; she knew that she only sang when she had something on her mind and never when she was at peace with herself. She felt oppressed and uneasy. At last the door opened and he came in.

"I've lost it all," he said. He looked so wretched that she held him tight in her arms as if she were protecting him, kissing his face like a child's.

"It's all right. Don't upset yourself. It's all right."

"Give me three more ducats," he said.

She said gently, "My darling, there's only one five-franc piece left."

"Then give me something to pawn." He could not conceal his agitation. She took off her earrings and her brooch and held them in her hand, looking at them. He had given them to her and there were no belongings in the world more precious to her.

"Dear Anna, I'm so ashamed of myself. It breaks my heart to take your things from you."

She kissed the earrings and the brooch as if she were saying good-by to them. "Please, Fedya, only pawn them for a month. I'll write to Mother and ask her to send us some money and redeem them. I couldn't bear to lose them."

She put them in his hand.

"Anna." He took her on his lap and began kissing her breasts and her hands. "You're the best and dearest girl in the world. What would I do without you?"

He kissed her for the last time, put on his wet coat, and went out. The door closing seemed to cut him off from her. In an access of unreason she wanted to shout down the stairs for him to come back; with her fist to her mouth she held herself back, briefly heard his footsteps going away through the rain outside, and threw herself on the sofa sobbing bitterly and convulsively. She was distraught. Everything seemed dark and despondent. The sobs which she could not suppress hurt her chest and she got up, walking up and down the room, crying and sobbing insupportably. She felt terribly lonely. But all at once she stopped, her face red and swollen, her hair disordered, holding her hands to her head; she was afraid of his coming back! She had a sudden and awful dread of seeing him return saying he had lost everything. She wanted him to stay away as long as possible—for days, days, so that she could lie asleep in a dark room. She was trembling violently and thought she was going out of her mind.

She lay on the sofa again and hid her head in her arms; for a long time she stayed without moving. She heard the clock strike outside. The room became prematurely dark with the heavy rain clouds. It began to seem a long time that he was away. It was more than three hours, she saw. Sitting there, she became uneasy and dared not stir. Suddenly the door handle moved; she started up with a scream.

It was Dostoevsky. She stood facing him, digging her teeth into her lower lip, rigid, torn by distress and dread. He came in looking drenched and exhausted, walked straight up to her and with the faintest sad smile said, "It's all gone. Even the money on the earrings." She did not move. He took his coat off, sank onto the sofa, and held out his arms to her.

She was flooded with pity for him and knelt down to comfort him.

"I swear it's the last time I'll ever gamble in my life," he said; and he covered his face with his hands and wept. "Now I've stolen your last things from you and gambled them away."

"They were yours too, darling. I gave them to you with my love."

She could not stop him from weeping. It distressed her infinitely to see him. He told her the pawnbroker had given him a hundred and twenty francs on the earrings at five per cent, so that they would have to pay a hundred and twenty-five francs to get them back at the end of the month.

They lay on the sofa in each other's arms. The rain stopped. Presently he said, "Anyechka, let's go out for a little while."

"Yes." The evening was still and full of fresh smells after the rain. They strolled arm in arm. Little by little his spirits began to pick up. He talked of all sorts of plans for getting them money, becoming animated, excited. "And I can write to Aksakov, suggest collaborating with him. He ought to accept; he's bound to. Or Katkov. He'd send us some, I'm certain. It's only that writing from here is awkward; when he gets a letter from Baden he'll know we've lost everything gambling. It would make a bad impression. Wait a minute! I can try Krayevsky. Now there's an idea. Anyushka, we're saved! I'll tell him he can have the proofs of a new novel by January."

"But, Fedya, it's not possible. You're already committed to Katkov for a novel. It would be too much work."

"Couldn't I do it, though, Anna?"

She glanced at him, her heart bursting. She felt terribly unhappy in his presence, yet when he wasn't there she was sadder still—though she could at least cry then. With him, she had to do her best to seem in good spirits, laughing and telling entertaining stories. And he thought it was admirable of her, not to let adversity break her spirit, still to "carry her head high." Perhaps, she thought, all this trouble was atonement for the great happiness she had been given in marrying him.

"Shall we have one more try with that last five-franc piece?" he said.

"All right, Fedya."

As they lay together that night in the dark, sleepy, he said softly, "You know I love you with all the strength I have. I'm as dependent on you as a child and I'm terrified of making you miserable. I'll never forget how good you've been to me, dearest sweet Anna."

"Fedya, that's wonderfully sweet and tender to hear. I love you."

2

He wanted to wait till early afternoon, his "lucky time."
At one o'clock she took the five-franc piece out of the
moneybag and gave it to him. He had another acute coughing spell that frightened and disgusted her. They walked
together to the Kursaal. Outside she said, "I'll sit on the
bench here a little; I want some air." It was a cloudy, uninviting, rather cold day and she was uncomfortable but sat
on out of a pointless obstinacy which she recognized but
somehow could not throw off. As she was getting up to go
at last she saw Dostoevsky among the people between the
columns of the entrance. He ran to her excitedly, shaking
his head. "No good. No good! I lost it all." He was extremely
worked up. "My God! I had twenty gold pieces half an hour
ago. I had them in my hand."

"No!" She flushed with impatience.

"I risked them. I risked them and lost everything." He
was frantic, kept clasping his head, exclaiming, gesticulating
so that passers-by stared. "I pawned my wedding ring on
the way and that's gone too."

"My poor Fedya." They owed the landlady for their last
three meals. And the eight florins for the rent was due
tomorrow.

At the lodgings she began to look for something to pawn.
She came in from the bedroom with the Chantilly lace shawl
that she and her mother had bought for her trousseau. "Here,
darling, take this; we can redeem it later. Yes, yes, please,
Fedya."

He was shifting restlessly about the room and looked at
her with misery. He accepted without a word, put his coat
and hat on while she wrapped the shawl in old newspaper,
and went out with it under his arm.

It was raining in torrents. He walked with his head down,
clutching the parcel, the rain spouting from roofs and gutters.

He did not know where to go, then thought of the shop where he had pawned his wedding ring. The man was dark-skinned with black greasy hair falling over his face. "I only deal in gold. Try Weissmann."

"Where is he?" The man gave complicated directions, repeated them unwillingly so that Dostoevsky, out of some perverse impulse, was nodding and saying, "Yes, yes," as if he were following perfectly when he understood nothing. He went out into the rain and walked. Horses and drays splashed by; the gray, soaked, cobbled streets with steaming dollops of horse dung stretched before him. He was wet through and suddenly noticed that the paper around the shawl was sodden and thrust the parcel under his coat. Once he caught a glimpse through a steamy restaurant window of fat men with napkins tucked around their necks. A boy of eight or so darted out of some shelter holding up a basket of violets; Dostoevsky passed on.

He tried to stave off the harassing thoughts that kept coming to him of things he could write about. It was as if he were thinking about writing now to intensify all the pain. They punished him, the thoughts of writing. Art: the life of art. Oh, my God, he thought, my God.

He saw a pawnbroker's shop and went in. The woman shook her head. "Only gold. Try Weissmann." He managed to follow some of her directions, then was lost. The rain spouted off his hatbrim. He walked on and on. He thought of Anna waiting for him and quickened his pace. A waiter standing idly in a doorway told him to retrace his steps; he did so but couldn't find the place. There was a cabman huddled in his seat behind tarpaulin and a drowned horse. "Can you tell me where Weissmann's is?" Dostoevsky shouted.

"*Weiss nicht.*" The man shrugged.

He wandered into alleys and back courtyards. Under an archway he tripped on a stone and fell into a broad puddle, struggling frantically up to save the shawl from dipping in the water. Farther on there was an old woman with a basket of cat's meat under her arm.

"Weissmann? Around the corner," she said. He found the shop—small and dark with scratched glass cases of rings, watches, brooches, the smell of dust and some sweet-smelling bread. Weissmann had bright eyes, a smile, and a hump. Dostoevsky picked the paper in scraps off the sodden package, apologizing.

"Clothes, they are not interesting." Weissmann raised his palms. "Gold you have got, no? Women's clothes, that is not much good; it costs me money, *schon*."

"But this is very fine work. Look at it."

"What should it be fine work for me for?" Weissmann eyed him. "You are wet. Here, I'll give you some paper to wrap it in."

"Couldn't you tell me of somebody who'd take it?"

"For this you should try Madame Etienne, yes. In the Platz."

He trudged again through the unremitting downpour. He had to go twice around the Platz before he could see Madame Etienne's, a narrow shop next to a beerhouse. It was a hanging forest of secondhand clothes—blouses, coats, dresses, scarves, hats, wraps, bustles, crinolines, under-clothes. There were standing rows of women's high buttoned boots. A timid-looking, shriveled woman parted fronds of petticoats, peered at him, wrung her hands as if she were in pain. "Madame Etienne—that is my sister—she is not here. I ought not to take it without her seeing it. Can you come back tomorrow morning?"

"Very well." He went back to the lodgings. His head was aching and he dropped exhausted into a chair. Anna took out the shawl and folded it carefully and lovingly as he told her of the expedition. And then when he had changed his wet clothes he was taken up with a sort of depressed, fidgety idleness.

She said, "Darling, it's so tedious for you here; why don't you go to the Reading Room for a little while?"

"How can I go off and amuse myself and leave you sitting in this prison thinking God knows what!"

She stood before him in despair and pity. She pulled off her wedding ring. "Dearest Fyodor, please take this and pawn it and go to the roulette."

He looked at her with intense pain, his lips trembling. "You can't—Anna, you cannot——"

"Yes." She put the ring in his hand and kissed him. She went on her knees and he stroked her hair; they did not speak. He left when it stopped raining. She went out soon after, passed the Kursaal, looked through the window of the Reading Room, and thought she saw him reading a paper with his head in his hands. She strolled on, lonely, and was suddenly frightened and ran home, stumbling in tears up the stairs and throwing herself on her knees in the room to pray. "Oh, God," she prayed, "give me strength to bear all this. There is so much misery in the world that ours is only a tiny drop among all the rest. Dear God, why am I so petty-minded? It's only that this fear keeps gnawing at my heart. If Fyodor would come back, then I couldn't cry. *I couldn't*. And even when I do, the tears don't take the weight from me, as they used to. Oh, God, I want to have Fyodor here with me and yet I don't want him, because it means seeing how full of misery he is and how wretched."

The prayer made her feel easier. She rose. After a while she noticed the sun shining from the clear evening sky and put on her bonnet to go out and try to get a little coffee on credit. As she shut the door behind her Dostoevsky came up the stairs onto the dark landing. He seemed to be carrying something in his hand. They went back into the room. "These are with my love," he said—and handed some flowers to her, a bunch of red and white roses. "I was coming home and bought them—and then went back. I managed to save five francs." He gave her the coin too.

"Darling, it doesn't matter," she said.

He lay on the bed. "Wake me up in half an hour, Anna." She was arranging the flowers and for some reason stayed in the bedroom. As the clock struck he got up, came over, and kissed her. She thought he needed something and said, "What do you want, Fyodor?" He had already turned away but came back toward her and had a fit.

There was the scream. She recoiled, horrified, then clutched him and tried to get him back onto the bed but could not. She propped him up between it and the wall and he had the convulsions, half standing, half squatting. He began to wrestle and fling himself violently about and she couldn't hold him. His eyes were starting. She was terrified he would kick her accidentally. She threw two pillows on the floor and managed to push him down onto them. He writhed there with blue lips, shouting out in German, "Leave me alone! What's that? What are you saying?" His face was red and after a struggle she managed to undo his waistcoat and trousers. Then he lay still, unconscious. She wiped the foam from his lips and crouched beside him. She felt the cold sweat all over her body.

"Anya," he said in a faint voice. "I'm sorry."

"Don't try to speak, darling. Can you just move this foot a little?" She repeated it. Evidently he did not understand anything.

He said, "Give me some money . . . five ducats, five ducats, twenty . . . play the zero. I'm going now."

At last he came to. He looked at her with an extraordinary trace of suspicion in his eyes so that she was stabbed to the heart, got up and began buttoning himself and walking in a strange springy way about the room. "Where's my hat?—put my hat? Who's had it?"

"Fyodor, where are you going?"

He made a curious gesture and said in French, *"Comme ça."*

She took his arm; she was afraid and hated all this but pitied him so much. "You must lie down."

"No! You torment me! You laid me down there before."

For a moment he stood there, then veered drunkenly across the room and crashed onto the bed. She knelt by him; slowly he reached out and took her hand and put it to his lips.

3

She began watching the Apostle Peter, the weather vane on the clock tower outside. Their affairs prospered when the Apostle faced them with his key in his right hand; when he turned his back it meant bad luck.

The landlady took up talking loudly and abusively of them with neighbors at the street door and raising her voice on the stairs. She had a flow of speech such as Anna had never heard before, inexhaustible; she seemed to gabble without taking breath. They obtained a little money by pawning the shawl, his overcoat, shirts, underclothes, handkerchiefs, her shoes and light dress. Anna was constantly washing, since they had practically no linen left. She went about in the house in a worn wrapper; her old black winter dress, which she had had to let a piece into, was much too hot to wear in the blazing August weather and she had to reserve the only other one left, the lilac one, for going out. She tried to keep Dostoevsky out on longer and longer walks so that he would not go to the roulette. He was on edge and irritable. One evening when they returned after a rather silent walk she lay down on the bed. She woke up and found him stumping about the room mumbling resentfully, annoyed because she had dropped off to sleep.

"But why should you mind?" she said.

"It's nothing to do with you since you've apparently decided not to speak to me."

She said in a normal voice, "Please, Fyodor, don't make

such a noise with your boots. The landlady will be furious if you wake the children up."

"If you shriek at me like that I'll jump out of the window!" he shouted. He clutched his head, shouting despairingly, "I know it's all my fault we're in such a mess. All my fault. I know it better than anyone." He turned on her. "I hate you. I detest you!"

She burst into tears. "You used to say I brought you luck, now suddenly you hate me." She ran into the other room.

He crawled in to her. "Forgive me, Anyechka. I didn't mean to hurt you. I was so distracted . . . this penury . . . You used to take it much more lightly."

"I was happier then," she couldn't help saying. "There were fewer troubles. Oh, let's stop talking about it." She was bitterly hurt.

At night he tried to work. She listened to him walking up and down the next room. He never came to bed before two o'clock in the morning. One day he returned from the Reading Room in a great state. "There's an extraordinary case in the paper, a trial in Tula, a child of fifteen, Olga Umetskaya, accused of trying to burn down the family house. They've been treating her in the most savage way for years. It's come out in court. They whipped her, kicked her for nothing at all, tied her up. When she was only eight they tied her up in a stinking outhouse and when she didn't complain they smeared her face with pig's excrement and left her there all night in the icy cold. My God! It's appalling. I keep thinking of Shidlovsky . . . years ago. We used to talk about things like this and we kept on asking, 'Why does God allow it?' "

He was pacing the room, speaking with animation. "All that has twisted the child's mind; one can see it. She has been giving all sorts of strange and mixed reasons why she did it. It's splendid material. I must use it. I can make her the heroine. It's all bringing out the old favorite idea I've been wanting to do for a long time but haven't dared to—

trying to portray the positively good man. I've been trying to shape the idea around an idiot but it won't come. It's terribly difficult."

"What?" she said. "A good man is?"

"There's nothing in the world more difficult! All the writers who have tried to do it have failed—in Europe, Russia, anywhere. Do you realize how enormous the problem is? The good is an ideal; but nobody has completely worked it out yet. There has been one positively good man in the world—Christ. Think of Christian literature. Who is there? Don Quixote—he is the most perfect. But he is only good because he is ridiculous at the same time. And he hasn't any judgment." He stopped, catching her smiling. "What?"

"I was going to say Pickwick," she said.

"It's the same thing; it's a perfectly good example. Pickwick is good but he only succeeds by virtue of being ridiculous too. You feel pity for the ridiculous man who doesn't know his own worth as a good man, and so you feel sympathy for him. That's the secret of humor, this awakening of pity."

"There's the man in *Les Misérables*," Anna said.

"Jean Valjean. I agree with you. Hugo made a fine attempt there. But Valjean stirs your sympathy because of his horrible misfortune and the injustice he suffers. I don't want anything of that; nothing. So I'm terribly afraid I shan't succeed."

But he clung feverishly to the idea of winning at roulette.

"I want thirty thousand francs to go back to Russia with," he said. For two days he had ten florins, then lost them all. The day after was Saturday, when they had to pay the rent. They owed two weeks now and five meals. They sat caged in the airless, dusty room. The shadeless street outside was grilling in the noonday heat; the landlady's children were crying and the ceaseless jingling, clanking, tapping, hammering came from the smithy. Everything was pawned; they hadn't a single coin, nothing to read; they had even run out of tea and sugar. She had said good-by to her clothes and jewelry; they would never be redeemed now.

"Come out for a walk, Fyodor."

"No, for the third time! Damn your walks. Do you think I want to go tramping around in this dust and heat in a crowd of sweaty Germans?" It was a sort of exaggerated, "justified," anger. Ugh!

The landlady's penetrating voice rose angrily from below. Anna said, "I can't ask her for another meal today; she has been so disagreeable and she doesn't need an excuse to refuse."

He sat with his coat and collar off, shirt sleeves dangling loose, tapping his foot, nervous, untidy. He felt all the untidiness, discomfort, and cheapness with voluptuous enjoyment. The despair itself was enjoyable. There were the most acutely intense enjoyments in despair. Especially when one was sharply aware of the hopelessness of one's position. Oh yes, the scenes of his falling on his knees and asking her forgiveness were part of that too; he wriggled uncomfortably. He longed to get up, move about purposefully, do something to "put order" into their affairs; but the more he thought of it the more painfully he felt the discomfort and futility of everything around him and for that very reason obstinately declined to stir.

Anna went into the bedroom and took out her lilac dress. She tidied herself, put on her hat.

"Where are you going?" he said.

"To Madame Etienne's, to pawn this. She ought to give us twenty-five francs for it." She was folding up the dress.

"No, no. I'll take it." He got up.

"I don't want you to have to go back there, Fyodor. It's so painful for you."

"I'll go!" he said angrily.

She gave way. In the middle of wrapping the dress up she said, "How are you going to get it past that woman below?"

"Under my coat. Wrap it up small."

"She'll see it." They tried it and decided he would carry his coat over his arm with the dress hidden underneath. She looked at him. What they had come to—smuggling clothes past landladies! In a few moments he went out and she stood still and tense. She heard the landlady raise her voice, Dostoevsky saying good day to her, ignoring her abuse, then his steps receding; he had got by.

She took her wrapper off and sluiced her face and shoulders. An hour passed. Two o'clock struck and she began to wonder whether he hadn't gone to the roulette with the money; but just then she heard him coming up the stairs.

He was sweating, threw off his coat, and she thought he looked a little evasive. "Did you pledge it?" she said.

"Yes. With Weissmann. He always makes a fuss about taking clothes. Here you are." He held her out the money.

"What?" She frowned, counting it. "Only six florins. Is that all they gave?"

"He gave fourteen florins. I lost eight at roulette."

It was as if he had slapped her face; she was incredulous and bitterly upset. "Really, it's too stupid!"

Suddenly he shouted, "It's your fault, your damned fault!" He struck his forehead and banged his fists against the wall. "If we'd gone for a walk I wouldn't have lost it."

"I begged you to come out. My God—how can you be so unfair! You are trying to fasten your own guilt on me. The money was for the rent."

"Couldn't you have said so?" he said furiously—but she had run into the bedroom and shut the door. He wrenched it open. "And for God's sake stop sniveling! I can't stand it. It gets on my nerves."

"Do I say that when you have your fits or that hateful coughing? Such egotism—it's disgusting." She pulled the door shut again and once more he pulled it open. She faced him, unable to restrain herself. "I can't help crying with the horrible life we've led ever since we've been here. I want to go—go—go! This everlasting gambling and gambling, hoping for a big win. When are we going to get out of this accursed swamp? Sometimes I feel we're going on here for all eternity, playing and playing and playing. You'll never be able to tear yourself away from the table. And since I'm your wife, I'm your property, so I can suffer all kinds of wants and wretchedness. You can send money to Emily Fyodorovna; she can live in clover. I have to pawn my coat so that she can have one. And it hurts me, do you understand? It hurts me that anybody I love can be so thoughtless and imperceptive."

"It's my duty to stand by Misha's family; they stood by me."

"Haven't you a duty to me too? Haven't I devoted my life and soul to you? Surely I've shown I'm ready to put up with everything to make you happy?"

"You don't in the least understand my feelings for you."

"And what about mine? You never took my part in those quarrels with Pasha."

"That's stupid and not worth talking about. Pasha is quite sensible and wouldn't dream of wanting to hurt you."

"There you are! What sort of existence is this? I'm forever trembling at the thought of where the next meal is coming from."

He shouted, "It's nothing to do with anybody else! I'm my own judge!"

"I'm the last person to judge you ever. Marya Dmitrievna never stopped calling you an idiot, a criminal, a jailbird, and you were like an obedient dog to her!"

"My God! I'm a gambler. I know it, I know it, and I'm quite impervious to your advice on it! For everything else you're the piper and I dance!"

"Yes. And you scatter your winnings. You're a benefactor to humanity."

Dostoevsky was pale and shaking.

"Oh no, no, Fyodor—all that's so unjust and horrible."

She threw herself into his arms. "I don't mean any of that, my own dear, darling husband."

"Anna, I've been a scoundrel and a criminal. Please forgive me. I take back everything, everything. I'm always ashamed of myself for behaving so abominably to you when you're always so tender and gentle."

They made it up. The talked, moving among the hidden reefs, shifting once again in the same idle, aimless, maddening way about the room. The midafternoon heat became intolerable. He said, "Come out for a little air."

"All right." She put on the thick winter dress, perspiring in it after five minutes. Her look struck him as so despondent that he cast around in desperation for something to buoy her up. "Let's go to the post office."

The street was blistering. The Lichtenthaler Allee and the gardens were thick with carriages and strollers and the cafés filled with customers sipping cool beer. They walked slowly past the Kursaal to the Leopoldplatz. Anna's red face was running with sweat. She longed for a parasol.

As they entered the post office she detached herself from his arm. "You go," she said; she couldn't face the disappointment once again of being told that nothing had arrived and stood near the door wiping her face with her damp handkerchief. The next minute he was calling, "Anna! Anna!" and beckoning excitedly. "There's something for you. Look, from Petersburg."

She signed for it and tore it open. "From Mother; a draft for sixty florins. She's sending some more straight away." At Meyer's Bank where they had the money counted out to them she said, "Fyodor, let's redeem the things. Now, at once."

"Yes, yes. And the wedding rings and earrings. We must try to get them back. Come along, we'll go home for the pawn tickets."

But at the lodgings she felt sick and tired and sank onto the sofa. "I can't go out again in this heat. Go without me."

He was getting the pawn tickets out of the trunk. "Fedya, don't go to the roulette again, will you? Give me your word of honor you won't."

"What?"

"Oh, God, if you won't give me your word of honor I won't let you go alone. I'll go with you."

He jumped up angrily. "What do you mean, 'go with me'? How can you stop me going to the tables if I want to?"

"I implore you, I beg you. I go on my knees to you."

"No," he said impatiently, stopping her movement. He looked at her silently, took his hat, and left. She stood in the middle of the room pressing her hand to her face in terror and despair. Her thoughts were in complete confusion. She stared at the ceiling, her mouth gaping, her fingers pressing into the skin of her face. I have to believe he won't go, she thought. She undressed and lay on the sofa with her eyes closed; she was full of uneasiness. All at once she started up; there was a dribble of spit down her chin as if she had slept. She looked at the clock outside; he had been away nearly an hour. She was in a panic. He would gamble everything away if she did not stop him. She put on the thick dress which now seemed to her so ugly. By good luck the landlady was not at the street door. She went as fast as she could but had to stop several times, out of breath. In the entrance hall she was so unsettled that she sat down for a moment to steady herself, then went into the gambling rooms. She saw him at once, sitting at the roulette table, started forward, and then halted. If he thought she had come to stop him playing he would be furiously angry and make some disastrous gamble with what he had left and there would be a tremendous scene once they were alone.

She stood hesitating, aware of two men eying her from one of the seats by the wall. Of course, that was the method. She approached the table and touched Dostoevsky's elbow just as he reached out with his stake. His eyes were staring at the table and he could not even turn around to her.

"*Sept.*" He had apparently won, looked at her, waited for his money, and then came to her. His face was horrible—violently flushed, his eyes red; he looked drunk. "What is it?"

"I've been in the Reading Room. There was a man who kept speaking to me and when I went out he followed me. It made me nervous, Fyodor."

He glared around. "Where is he? Point him out to me. Which one, which one?"

"I think he stopped at the entrance."

"What sort of face? What was he dressed like? Show him to me." He was shaking with anger and excitement as they went out. "I'll have five minutes with him. My poor Anna, my poor little Anyechka. You understand, I couldn't turn around when you touched me. Look what I've got. I've been winning, winning!" He produced a fistful of notes and gold and silver coins from his pocket.

"What? Is it true?"

"Where is he? Can you see the fellow?" He was almost running among the crowd at the entrance, pulling her with him. She was struggling to keep a straight face and yet she dreaded that he would insist on going back to "keep his luck in." "It doesn't matter, Fyodor. Let's forget it. It's time to go home anyway."

"Show him to me. Show him. We'll see if he's still at the Reading Room." They hastened there.

"No, he's gone," Anna said.

Back at the lodgings they emptied the money onto the table and counted it. "Four hundred and sixty-five florins!"

He paused, giving her a sharp look. "Do you know," he said in a quiet voice, "I thought at first you'd come in to stop me playing?"

"You're not serious? You know I'd never do such a thing."

"H'm." A pause. "What are you laughing at then?"

"Oh, darling," she spluttered. "I'm laughing because you've won—out of happiness—out of love." She went off into a long irrepressible laugh, catching hold of him and starting him chuckling, beaming, and laughing as well.

They could leave for Geneva. In the morning the new draft for two hundred florins came from her mother. With the four hundred and sixty-five they had already it made over thirteen hundred francs—enough to keep them for three months without worry. She decided not to cash the draft at once and kept it apart.

At noon Dostoevsky went off to the gambling rooms, taking the odd sixty-five florins. Before she could go out to redeem their belongings he came back, said he had lost it all. "Give me a hundred and twenty."

"But, Fyodor, it's far too much at a time. Why are you staking such big stakes?"

He flared up. "If you don't stake big how, for God's sake, can you win big?"

She shrank from going out in her shabby old dress but was afraid that if she stayed in he would be coming back for more and more. She seemed to communicate this to him by some look or gesture because at the door he said, "You're staying here, aren't you?"

"No, I'm just going out."

"You must stay, do you hear? Stay in! I want you here!" He banged the door with his fist and slammed out.

All through the afternoon he kept coming back for more money. She pleaded with him: "Stop playing. It's an unlucky day, can't you see that?"

He was beside himself. He shouted, "It's got to turn sometime. If it doesn't now, it will in a minute. Give me forty."

She could not stand it. She put on her hat, took a book, and hurried out. It was another sunny day; she walked up the steps toward the new castle. She felt a physical fear that he would find her and every minute was expecting to hear his voice calling or see him hurrying behind her, saying he needed more. She was in anguish and couldn't fix her mind on the book at all; she kept looking down to the town and once caught her breath in terror, thinking she saw him approaching in the distance. But it was somebody else. After two hours he came up looking white as a corpse and exhausted. He sat beside her on the seat, breathless, extremely tense.

"I told you the luck would turn. I was winning. Then I did one or two stupid things and lost everything. Anna, I must have forty more. I *can* win, do you understand?"

"I've only eighty florins left and we haven't redeemed anything."

"I can't help it. Come down now and give me the money. There is a man who has won twenty thousand francs. I saw it. Twenty thousand francs!" His face was twitching.

"Fyodor, I beg you, have some dinner first, go later on. You'll be better when you're calmer."

"*I want it now!*"

Her head was aching and she was dizzy. She felt that if she sat there a minute longer she would scream, have a hysterical attack, roll down the steps, kill the child and herself. She got up and began to run down the steps, people staring. He ran beside her, imploring her not to run, to stop and rest. She ran on. She only wanted to throw the rest of the money at him, then leave him, go off alone with the money her mother had sent. She was half sobbing and kept saying, "I don't care, I don't care. I'm sick of it. I can't stand it any more."

The landlady was in the passage; she pushed by heedless, rushed to the trunk, and was going to fling the money at him when he caught her arm.

"Anna, for God's sake, don't be angry."

"I'm sick of all this. I'm sick at heart."

He clasped her hands, kissing them. "Forgive me. I won't go there. I promise; I don't mean to torment you." He was almost weeping, reproaching himself, imploring. And as always there was the transfer of feeling; poor Fedya, she pitied him and her anger and revolt subsided. After all, only one thing could save him, some sort of harmony between the two of them. "It's all right, my dear."

They made peace. After dinner he begged for the forty florins and went out with them. He came back late with a basket of fruit. He had won two hundred florins.

She knew she could not hold him. She watched him shaving next morning, seeing the seething undercurrent in him. He kept laughing and joking.

In two visits to the tables he lost a hundred and sixty florins and came back saying, "It was stupid. All my own fault—simply bad play. Give me forty and I'll redeem the earrings and wedding rings on my way home." She could not help marveling at the conviction he spoke with, as if there were not the smallest doubt. "Don't worry, I'm going to do well," he said. And perhaps there was some mysterious transmission of that to her. He was away so long she had a feeling he had won and suddenly everything seemed bright and favorable to her. She was persuaded they were going to leave, cleared her trunk, and packed some of the smaller things. Then she ran to the window, hearing the children singing gaily for once outside, and leaned out laughing at them. Everything in the street seemed joyful and optimistic. In a moment she saw Dostoevsky coming along and she laughed with love at his quick nervous gait. He was always in a hurry; he had been in a hurry all his life. She turned as he came in the door. "All right. I know those 'I've lost everything' tricks," she said, and ran and embraced him.

"What? I really have lost it." He was looking at her uncertainly.

"I know you have!" She kept her arms around his neck, smiling. "Show me your purse." He pulled it out; it was empty. She flushed, all at once confused and upset, released him and went into the bedroom.

After dinner he asked her to come for a walk; but she had

lost her chignon. "I'll go and get the things out of pawn," he said. She gave him a hundred and eighty francs. At the last stroke of eight she heard the door slam and said over her shoulder, "Fedya, bring me a drink of water, will you?" He did not answer. She looked around, saw him staring at her, and suddenly he shouted out, "I've lost it all! Every florin. Everything you gave me to redeem the things with. Ah, my God!"

He stormed about the room in an outburst of rage and tears and at last flung himself down at the table in despair. She couldn't reproach him. She put her arms around him and begged him not to accuse himself. "After all, what does it matter? If you've lost, you've lost. Nothing is worth getting into such a state about, darling."

"No, no. You've no business to forgive me. You're too good, too good, my dear, sweet Anna. I'm an unutterable scoundrel."

"Fedya, you didn't do it out of malice," she said; but he wept bitterly.

When she had managed to calm him he said, "We must leave here. We must clear out. Let's go to Switzerland tomorrow."

"Do you mean it?"

"Anna, come to the station now; we'll find out about the trains. We can redeem the things on the way. Hurry up!"

It was late by the time they had retrieved the jewelry. All the way he was kissing her hands and effusively asking her forgiveness. At the station a guard said there was a train at five minutes past two the next day for Basle and they decided to take that. They would look around Basle, then go on to Geneva. They counted their money—a hundred and ninety francs. "Won't you let me have a hundred, Anna?" he said. "I can easily win and provide for us."

"I can't. I will not."

"Fifty, then."

"Nor fifty, Fyodor."

"Forty. What's forty francs?" He went on and on, becoming increasingly agitated, and she saw he would never rest until he got them. She wanted to appeal to him to stop but somehow she could not. She gave him the money with despair. He was like a man who has received a drug and calmed down immediately. "I'll play them tomorrow," he said.

It was a golden morning. Anna got up soon after six o'clock and left the house to redeem her lilac dress. He was awake when she returned. They finished the packing and had a long and disagreeable settlement with the landlady. The hammering on the anvils below was worse than ever and they were all shouting above it; she asked for all sorts of extras and, when they had got rid of her, flounced back claiming another eighteen kreutzers for a broken pot. The trunks and other luggage were strewn about the room; everything looked forlorn and untidy. Anna began to feel horribly nervous. She dreaded something happening to prevent their leaving.

It was eleven o'clock. Dostoevsky kissed her. "I'll have half an hour at the Kursaal." She turned away; she had great foreboding but wanted to shut her mind to it. There were still things to do. She wrapped up their books in her black dress and tied them, then sat down to write to her mother. As she finished, she looked up and saw him on the far side of the room; he had a cigarette in his mouth and was smoking it with nervous gestures and tics, giving quick glances at her, then looking away. "Is everything ready?" he said.

"Yes."

"Anna, I lost the forty francs. I pawned my wedding ring for twenty more and lost that too."

"Oh no." She was overwhelmed. "How could you do it?"

"I don't know, Anna. I don't know." He fell on his knees before her. "I deserve the worst punishment. I ask your forgiveness again, your pardon, Anna."

"But you *knew* I only had just enough. We need a hundred and thirty-four francs for the train alone."

"Anna dearest, I humbly ask your pardon." He buried his face against her dress. She lifted him up.

It was nearly one o'clock. She took out the money, put twenty francs aside, and counted the rest. "We've got a hundred and twenty francs. We can't get to Geneva. It's not enough. . . ."

She went to the window and back, trying to think, trying to calculate; then she took out her earrings. "We'll have to pawn these." It meant saying good-by to them forever. She handed them to him. "Try to get a hundred francs for them and redeem your ring."

He was in the depths of misery. It distressed her to see him so down at having lost the money and she wanted to console him, to tell him it truly didn't alter anything between them, to cheer him up for their departure; she wanted to tell him how much she loved and admired him. "Fyodor," she said. "And take twenty francs and try your luck, darling, will you?"

He stopped at the door, looking back at her. There was anguish and bright joy mixed up on his face and he ran back. "Anna, you're without things you need. You know I'll probably lose. And all the same you give me twenty francs?"

"Of course."

"There is a saint in you. I'll remember—I'll———"

"Hurry up or you'll have no time. Meet me at the station; I'll bring the luggage. Don't be late. The train goes at five minutes past two. Go on, hurry up."

He ran out. She collected the last things together and sent Marie for a carriage. The driver came up to fetch the luggage and took a great time loading it, then ambled his horse at scarcely more than walking pace up the Luisenstrasse toward the station. She was nervous and kept urging him to hurry but he took no notice. They reached the station at twenty minutes to two and there was already a busy crowd waiting for the Oos train. He was not there. She told a porter to weigh the luggage and paid ten florins for it.

It was hot and dusty. She looked at each arriving carriage, watched the surrounding streets and the station clock hand moving with a periodic jerk and a quiver up toward two o'clock.

At eight minutes to, the train came in. There was a general noisy rush by the people on the platform. The porter kept coming up to her uneasily. "Are you getting in, *gnädige Frau?* Your luggage will go without you."

She could feel the sweat on her face. She scanned the approaches. He wasn't to be seen. The train seemed to be full. Some official kept calling out that it was on the point of starting. She had a terrible picture of Dostoevsky sitting at the roulette table, staring at the wheel, trying to win more, more, more. He wasn't coming. He wasn't coming! "Oh, God," she prayed, *"I cast my bread upon the waters. Let him come."*

Two o'clock struck. He suddenly sprang out of a carriage in front of her, white as death. He grasped her bag and flew for the tickets. The starting bell clanged as they ran down the train searching for places. "In here!"

They clambered in panting, squeezing past the knees of the other passengers, and managed to sit down. He was gasping, laughing, half sobbing. "I lost everything except ten francs. I was down to one ten-franc piece and I got it all back. A hundred francs. I got it back, Anna. I got it back for you, I got it back."

The ringing bell on the platform covered his voice as the train moved past it.

PART FIVE

Chapter Sixteen

1

The night wind hummed down the street and rattled the window. The paper calendar hanging on a string stirred faintly, showing May 1871. Dostoevsky sat at the table writing, scratching out bits of phrase, sometimes half a page, clutching his head, then bending forward, hardly able to put the words down fast enough in a long rich intense rush.

It was developing into a huge piece of work. Katkov had been running it for five months in the *Russian Messenger* with the title of *The Possessed*. He had begun it as a medium-length piece about the nihilists, specifically Sergey Nechayev, the young nihilist who had created an enormous stir in Russia with a revolutionary conspiracy. But it had taken on a sort of Homeric growth of its own, leading him into profound questions of morality, social organization, and religion. The eternal question "Is there a God?" kept pursuing him throughout it. He despaired of ever getting the book done. He knew that if he had two or three years entirely for this novel—the time which Turgenev, Goncharov, or Tolstoy took for their books—he could write something which would be talked about for a century afterward. The idea was so splendid that he did reverence before it. Just as after all these years he knew that the idea of the Double, the story of his youth, had been wonderful and only killed by Belinsky's bad judgment. But to write the book in eight or nine months was awful. He would have to condense, the people would only be sketched in, there would be unsustained passages, superfluities, prolixity. A great many beautiful things wouldn't get into the book at all because inspiration depended on time and many things. Yet he had to go on with it.

The candle flame flickered in the draft. He threw down the pen, poured another cup of tea, stewed almost black as he liked it. Anna and the child were sleeping in the next room. He walked up and down with the cup in his hand. Ah, without Russia, life was a torment. Europe was becoming more hateful to him. If he had to stay away from Russia much longer his talent would wither up and die; he would never complete this or any other book; he was losing his energies, his faculties. It was worse than deportation to Siberia. They had had nearly four years of it—Geneva, Vevey, Milan, Florence, Venice, Prague, and now back to Dresden. If they had known when they left Petersburg that they were going to be away four years! And how much longer? He was working like a locomotive. He had scarcely stopped since they had left Baden—first *The Idiot,* the story of the "positively good man," then *The Eternal Husband.* Now *The Possessed;* the book had a tremendous compulsion and intensity for him. The Nechayev case, which he had started as a short story and gone on and on with, offered an opportunity for penetrating to the criminal essence of the new nihilist revolutionary movement which he reviled because it was leading Russia to moral and spiritual destruction. There were hundreds of arrests all over Russia because of it. The papers were full of it.

Sergey Nechayev was the son of a village priest. He had once been a divinity student in Petersburg but turned out a ruthlessly cold-blooded creature, proclaiming that the cause of revolution and the destruction of the existing order sanctioned every crime from murder to sacrilege. He was an unbounded liar, nerveless, icily brave, and ambitious beyond measure.

Early in 1869 the Third Section police, who still kept the sharpest watch on the universities, gave him a close interrogation and thereafter put him under the annoying routine of police supervision. Nechayev eluded the watch on him, managed to sow the story among fellow students that he was being taken under arrest to a prison fortress, and escaped from Petersburg to Geneva. There he went straight to Mikhail Bakunin, the apostle of world revolution. The two obtained money from other exiled Russians and in August Nechayev returned to Moscow to organize the People's Avenger, a secret political society which would launch open revolution on February 19, 1870, ninth anniversary of the liberation of the serfs. But in November the Moscow police found the murdered body of Ivan Ivanov, a student at the Petrovsky Agricultural Academy, in a pond with stones tied to head and feet. They made arrests, found it was Nechayev who had murdered Ivanov, and discovered the revolutionary conspiracy. Before they could catch him Nechayev fled; he was believed to be in Switzerland with Bakunin again. The newspaper accounts said the arrested people had admitted that Nechayev had formed secret cells of five, each a revolutionary committee. None of the groups knew of the others but were all co-ordinated and directed by Nechayev. Ivanov had either rebelled against Nechayev's control or been about to betray them and Nechayev had killed him to get rid of him and to bind the others to him in a crime of blood.

Dostoevsky was using the conspiracy and the murder as the central plot of the book. With it he was interweaving ideas, topics, and a romantic strain from another vast novel he had been thinking of longingly and making notes on for the past eighteen months, called *The Life of a Great Sinner*. But it had been overwhelmingly difficult to fuse the two elements. After wrestling with them and writing three hundred pages, he had suddenly changed it all and destroyed everything—the work of a whole year!—and begun again. And it was all in the midst of debts, debts, the everlasting pawnshop, no money for firewood with two days' snow on the ground, Anna pregnant and the new child

Aimée being born; no money to post off manuscripts, even his trousers pawned to pay for a pleading telegram. In one moment of torment he wrote home to Milyukov: "And people demand artistic finish of me, poetry without strain, without an impression of waste, and they point to Turgenev, to Goncharov! Let them look at the conditions I have to work in." No doubt they would growl at *The Possessed* as well. It *was* savagely tendentious; he was satirizing the nihilists. But he cherished the artistic ideal as well and was resolved to go on with it.

In the last few years since his observations of bourgeois morality abroad, he had shifted his political view and become convinced that the European radical movement, imported with other Western ideas, was the cause of the increasing revolutionary agitation in Russia. He was startled at the way Western ideas were corrupting the essential spirituality of the Russian people.

The Greco-Russian Christians, who had not become split up into innumerable rival sects like the Christians of the West, preserved the true ancient spirit of Christianity, the meekness, resignation, and brotherly love which Christ had taught. It was essential not to let this be destroyed. He was not against Western culture; how could an intelligent man be! But he was against its wholesale, uncritical adoption by Russia. For one reason; Russia had a different social and political organization from western Europe and the social and political ills she suffered from could not be cured by the remedies that had worked in the West. The broad Slavonic nature could not be satisfied by the thin dry Western rationalism, the reckless individual selfishness which was destroying western Europe. The nihilists, he believed, were the same as the revolutionary terrorists like Karakosov and Berezovsky, who had already tried to shoot the Tsar. He reckoned himself a liberal; but he did not want to be taken in, to be lulled over it. And in the nihilists he couldn't see anything but retrogression. In an extraordinary way they were the spiritual and intellectual sons of the old liberal Westerners. So that, with them, one ended with a direct contradiction of the original idea one started with, the ideas of the Petrashevists. Starting from unlimited freedom, one ended with unlimited despotism. They did not take human nature into account. They didn't want a living soul, so they reduced everything to a question of comfort. The whole secret of life on two pages of print!

He felt the novel had begun wonderfully well with the portrayal of old T. N. Granovsky, history professor at Moscow University in the forties, a lovable, ridiculous idealist and Westerner. In the book he was calling him Stephan Trofimovich Verkhovensky, the father of Peter Verkhovensky, the monstrous chief conspirator and enemy of society who stood for the Nechayev of reality. He could hardly wait to write the scene when Peter Verkhovensky, drunk with the desire for power and violence, would speak of the new Russian revolutionaries. "We'll proclaim destruction. We must have a little excuse. We'll set fires . . . we'll set legends. Ah! The great Russian gift for mendacity, it'll be used, you'll see! And every mangy 'group' will be of use to us. I'll search you out from the fellows who won't shrink from shooting and will remain grateful for the honor. Well, the upheaval will begin! There's going to be such an overthrow as the world has never seen before. Russia will be plunged into darkness. The earth will weep for its old gods."

So much of the book was in the characters; he felt already that he was giving them great vitality. One he took straight from his heart, thinking of Speshnev and the Petrashevsky days—Nikolay Stavrogin. Stavrogin was the center of the romantic part of the book—proud, aloof, handsome, demonic, a man who revealed himself to nobody. He was also portraying Turgenev as the "famous writer Karmazinov."

And he wanted to express his own ideas, his response to the revolutionary anarchists. The Russian radicals must return to the people and to the soil, to the Russian Christ, without arrogance and with humility. Western civilization with its Catholicism was selfish and materialist whereas in Russia moral force and brotherhood were still for the moment dominant. Europeans were individualists; among Slavs social attributes were foremost. So that a European, cut loose from his nationality or normal social status, survived by his individuality; but the Russian became a cipher, nothing. Therefore, instead of trying to become European, the Russian must show Europe the way.

There was all that yet to be written.

He took the two coins from his pocket: four thalers. He needed a thousand rubles to get back to Russia. In Petersburg the creditors were waiting.

He heard Anna stir in the next room. He snatched up the pen. There was never time, never enough time!

2

"Anna, I'm going to the gallery," he said, taking his hat next morning.

"Ouf—it's too hot for me."

"How is Mr. N. N. today?" He put his hand on her belly. She was seven months pregnant and "Mr. N. N." was their name for the child.

"It feels as though he were turning somersaults." She kissed him good-by.

It was the first time since their return to Dresden that he had been to the Picture Gallery. He stood for a long time in front of the Sistine Madonna and then walked through the other rooms looking at the Riberas, the Wouverman battle pieces, the Ruysdaels and genre pictures of David Teniers. There was scarcely anybody else there. The attendants were the same; he recognized them all. It was like visiting the past. He caught the strange impression of being back four years in time and sat quickly on one of the red banquettes to prolong it. But it fled and only stirred up other things—bits of the four past years that returned, intermingling illogically, sweet and incongruous, irritating, painful and comic. . . . The good figure of Katkov, without whom they couldn't have lived; Katkov had practically kept them the whole time; there had been the maddening boredom and exasperations of Geneva; Sonya, their first baby, dying there, three months old; Florence in the heat . . . debts . . . the ridiculous impersonation scene with the Belgian count in Milan . . . rare letters from Suslova . . . Aimée's birth . . . Anna pawning her skirt.

Well, they had lived it. He hadn't the temperament for prolonged regrets, for melancholy about what was gone. He rushed forward to meet everything; life was a battleground. And he had worked; he had written good things!

He had begun *The Idiot,* the novel about the "positively good man," after they had left Baden, had taken more than a year to finish it—and it had failed! People had not understood it. One critic, Burenin, had even called it "absurd, the worst Dostoevsky has written, whole pages of it incomprehensible." He shifted restlessly, thinking of that. My God! It wasn't a portrayal of contemporary life; it was much more —much more—a spiritual essence! Of course there were flaws in the book; it did not give a tenth of what he wanted. But he loved its idea and felt he had expressed transcendent truth in it. He had had the same arduous struggle to grasp the character of Prince Myshkin, the central figure, as he had had to imagine Raskolnikov's personality, and he had scrapped seven different draft versions of the book.

At first he had made the Idiot the younger epileptic son of the Umetskys, the cruel family he had read about in the newspaper, and had Olga Umetskaya, the ill-treated child of real life, follow him from home and suffer rape by him. After this draft he had striven with a tangle of other plots and situations, with new characters constantly springing up and fresh ideas pulling at his mind. The third plot, optimistically marked "final draft," had been the story of a struggle between love and hate. And he knew how much he owed to Suslova for his vision of the "infernal woman." In the fourth draft he had introduced a humble, simple, and noble young man who was in conflict with those about him—and once more Dostoevsky had recognized the everlasting dual personality he seemed inescapably impelled to create. In the fifth plan he had cast off one aspect and suddenly made the young man, named Ganya, a pure, nervous, deeply Christian youth whose nature was dominated by feeling. But there was some jarring note and he scribbled, "No good—the chief idea about the Idiot doesn't come out."

Katkov, who had advanced the money on the novel long since, was pressing for the first installment for the *Russian Messenger*, and Dostoevsky had to drive himself even more feverishly to find the spiritually good man he was seeking. In the sixth draft he had sent the young man, the Idiot, to Switzerland and brought him back to a life of sensual passion in Russia. But the Idiot was still a split personality, proud, childish, Christian yet devoid of faith, and Dostoevsky beat his head with despair.

At last in the seventh version he managed to reduce the original idea of a dual personality to new terms. The Idiot became a meek, submissive Christian, an epileptic prince, almost a child, with many human failings yet a personality of radiant beauty. Excitedly, Dostoevsky realized it was what he had wanted. Yet even after that, when he had begun to write, he had thrown away weeks of work and started afresh. It was appalling to try to put a figure with Christ's spiritual attraction on the page! But he had found one way to make Myshkin appealing without being boring or ridiculous— through innocence. He had written the book with joy and anxiety and been lifted up by the theme, driving himself to keep up the installments, penniless, constantly having fits, sometimes loathing the book to nausea. He illuminated the Idiot's goodness by putting him among base, villainous, and sensual people. And in the end, though he believed he had failed to bring the book off, he had created a Christ-like image of moral beauty in Myshkin—'Prince Christ' as he thought of him—the submissive, meek, but radiant epileptic Idiot of the story.

The story began with the simple, penniless, and innocent young Prince Myshkin, an orphan aged twenty-six, arriving by train in Petersburg from a long treatment abroad for epilepsy. In conversation with his fellow travelers, Rogozhin, a brutal voluptuary, and the toadying Lebedev, the prince at once revealed his character. He was blindly candid, willing to tell the first stranger the most intimate details about himself, without a trace of pride, weakness, or sentimentality, butted into other persons' affairs without guile, and was impervious to hostility. At the same time everyone instinctively noticed his extraordinary psychological insight; at times it was an almost mystic vision of the future, like the moment of clarity and pure harmony before a fit. Prince Myshkin went to call on the Epanchins, his nearest living relatives (though very distant ones); made the servants gasp indignantly by behaving as an equal with them, laughed when he was insulted by General Epanchin and when he was mocked at by others, and disarmed everybody by his innocent frankness. Almost immediately he was caught up in complex intrigues with the Epanchins, Rogozhin, the beautiful "good prostitute" Natasha Philippovna, and her friends the Ivolgins. In this grasping, sensual, vain, and perverted world, Myshkin drew everyone to him by his serene moral goodness. He loved them all and by the intensity of his love and belief in them made the worst of them good and innocent again at least for a moment. He was an almost supernatural creature. At the same time, because of his essential passiveness he was unable to save them. He offered to marry Natasha Philippovna, knowing, when she refused, that Rogozhin would murder her. He was unable to prevent the crime any more than he could save his other friends from themselves. And he lost himself, became finally mad. Yet he had illuminated the surroundings he had passed through with a dazzling, pure, and unforgettable light. Thinking of him again, Dostoevsky smiled, nodded his head. He knew he would live and perhaps grow in the world.

A gallery attendant and a group of visitors passed through the room. When they had gone he turned to Murillo's Madonna. The serene face looked back at him. The passionate arguments in *The Idiot* and now in *The Possessed* were part of his own struggle to believe, his desire for faith contending with his skepticism. There were times when he believed fully—as he always felt that he, like everybody else, shared in the general guilt and so could suffer for the sins of others. After all, the mathematicians who were working on the non-Euclidean geometry were finding parallel lines that met and the angles of a triangle adding up to something less than two right angles, so that reality was evidently not merely what the human mind could grasp. There was something else. One day, he thought, he would still write the huge five-book novel he had planned, *The Life of a Great Sinner*, a spiritual epic.

He felt hungry and, thinking he could take the edge off his appetite by smoking, he went out. It was a bright windy day. By a church clock he saw it was nearly three. Ah, to be back in Russia. In the midst of the cobbled German street the desire for the stillness and smell of a Russian forest suddenly came back to him: the tiny buzzing of bees and insects and the elusive smell of grass, leaves, bark that he had tried so eagerly to catch in Europe and had never found. Once again he had begged Katkov for money but Katkov had already sent more advances than he could work off. He had written asking Strakhov to sound out the Authors' Fund in Petersburg for a loan—and Strakhov had replied saying the Fund refused!

He began to feel a little lightheaded, as if he were going to have a fit. He hastened his steps toward the lodgings. There was a letter on the table and Anna said from the next room, "I went to the post office. The old clerk gives me your letters now."

"It's from Katkov." He tore open the envelope nervously and read. "My God! He's going to send us the money to get back to Petersburg. Anna—Anna! Where are you?" She had gone into the kitchen with the child and he ran after her, waving the letter, then in the midst of explaining he stopped, seeing her expression. "What's the matter?"

"Do you think we can go back?" she said.

"Eh? I don't understand."

"I've had a letter from Mother. She says she had written three times without an answer. I asked at the post office and the letters have never come. I didn't tell you because I didn't want to worry you but I thought something was happening to our correspondence and I asked once before, two weeks ago."

"What? They're watching us?"

"Katya Sokovina says the new Russian priest is a police spy." They had met the Sokovins among other Russians in Dresden. "Come here. There's something else." In the next room she unlocked a drawer and handed him a small paper pamphlet. "This also came in the same post, addressed to us."

He took it. It was entitled "Secrets of the Tsar's Palace"— a clandestine pamphlet against the government and imperial family. He saw that he and Anna were mentioned several times among the "exiled heroes of the oppressed fatherland." It would be enough for the Third Section to arrest anyone on.

"It's some sort of trap. Who would send it to us?"

"Burn it, burn it; here, give me the matches. No! I'd better reply to it. Wait a minute—I don't know." He was walking about the room, highly strung up. "My God, we are going back. The child is going to be born in Russia. We are going back whatever happens, if they arrest me at the frontier we're going back, Anna."

There were also the creditors to think of. His work had been appearing regularly in the *Russian Messenger* and if it became known that he had returned they would be flocking around demanding payment at once.

"I wish we needn't go directly to Petersburg," Anna said. "Ginterstein and Reimann swear they will put you in the debtors' prison."

"We *must* go to Petersburg."

But they waited on through May and there was nothing from Katkov. At the beginning of June the police, who had evidently intercepted their letters saying they hoped to return, intensified their watch and correspondence began disappearing in quantities. They could not write to the family and racked their brains to think of addresses of intermediaries they might ask to pass on messages.

"But why should they stop the money?" He beat his head. He was in great uneasiness.

In the second week they found an anonymous letter at the post office. It was a single sheet saying they were under surveillance, that orders had been given to open their correspondence and to make a special search of their luggage at the frontier.

The next day the money arrived. "Anna, we can go home! We can go home!" He ran in, red-faced and beaming, forgetting anxiety, kissed and hugged her with joy, picked up the child and capered with it. "Home, my little Lubochka, that you've never seen yet."

They paid a month's arrears in rent and tradesmen's bills, redeemed the pawned bits of clothing and their wedding rings, and bought the railway tickets. That evening he brought out a suitcase full of his papers, sat down, and began passing thick bundles of them to her. "Burn them, Anyechka."

"What are they?" She looked; there were the manuscripts of *The Idiot* and *The Eternal Husband*. "Oh, darling, no, let me keep them."

"They are going to search us, Anna. They need only the smallest pretext. Burn them, they're too dangerous."

"I can't, I can't! They are too precious to me."

He looked at her tenderly. "My dear, sweet Anna, they'll confiscate them anyway. Go on, burn them." She laid them in the fireplace and put a match to them.

"And this." He threw over another bundle. It was one of the discarded variants of *The Possessed*. They went through their clothes, turning out pockets for scraps of paper, looked at all their books, and decided to leave half of them behind. "No sealed letters, they'll seize them," he said; then suddenly remembering, "My God! Didn't you buy a lottery ticket once, in Berlin, just after we left Petersburg? We must find it—they strongly disapprove!"

The train for Berlin left in the evening. They changed and took the train for Petersburg, a journey of sixty hours. At Wirballen on the frontier they caught sight of the first Russian uniforms at the police and customs post.

Anna was nervous. He tried to comfort her, carrying Aimée in his arms. They gave up their passports and stood waiting. Dostoevsky noticed that the police captain separated their passports from the rest and took them away with him. Other passengers left. At last the police and customs men turned to their luggage and began to take everything out, putting books and papers aside. They stood there in the bare hall, Anna longing to sit down, shifting from one foot to the other, Dostoevsky holding the tired child, the police and customs men emptying their trunks and cases, spreading out all their belongings. All the other passengers had gone; they were the last; when everything had been examined they hurriedly crammed back the things into the trunks while the police leafed through the books and studied the papers one by one.

"We're going to miss the train," Dostoevsky said. "It's going on without us."

Then the child began to ask for something to eat. Anna

hushed her but she kept on. Dostoevsky could see the small complaining, tirelessly insistent voice getting on the police captain's nerves. "I'm hungry, I'm hungry," and at last the captain made an exasperated gesture, said, "Let them through," and turned on his heel.

Twenty minutes later they were on the moving train. The first four stations were in Poland, then at Kovno they were rolling on Russian soil. Dostoevsky could not keep still. He talked incessantly, pointing out things to the child and Anna, uncontrollably excited and moved. "Look at that muzhik with the telega. . . . And there's a little church, look. My sweet Anyechka, everything is going to be all right now. Yes, yes, I feel it."

3

It was a new life. Anna met the creditors and subdued them, quietly dealt with Pasha and the family, got together some furniture. She transformed everything. When he had finished *The Possessed*, she took up its publication in book form and triumphantly sold out the first edition. She took the children into the country to Staraya Russa, outside Petersburg, for the summer and by ruse and cleverness induced Dostoevsky to settle there with them for the winter as an economy, then all the year round. Money was short. But the books were being reprinted. Dostoevsky was famous. People wrote to him and came to see him from all over Russia.

There were more children. Dostoevsky kept up the Petersburg flat but liked the tranquillity of Staraya Russa. The fits were fewer but he had developed a bad chest complaint and was glad to escape to the fresh countryside. Nekrasov called, deferent and full of praise, asking for a novel for the *Annals of the Fatherland*, which he had acquired. Dostoevsky was overjoyed and plunged into writing *A Raw Youth*. The aristocracy of Petersburg sought after him and constantly invited him to soirees. He was presented to the Tsar. He began publishing a monthly, *Diary of a Writer,* a mixture of stories, articles, accounts of court trials, and impassioned pieces on social and religious questions. He was writing with some return of sympathy for the liberal ideals and hopes of his youth, acknowledging that the revolutionary background in *The Possessed* had been imperfect and leading on to his faith in the Russian people. The *Diary* was an enormous success. It brought in money, a huge correspondence, and gave him still greater popularity.

The life of struggle seemed past. Yet the idea of a novel to embrace everything that his life had meant to him and all the problems that had tortured him pressed him increasingly, begged to be expressed. He broke off the *Diary* to write it.

In a strange way he had little groundwork to do. He found he had been making ready to write the book all his life, since the Schiller days at school and the Engineers' Château. And now, imperceptibly and involuntarily, it had been composing itself in his mind. He planned it out on a vast scale and wrote it slowly but with the greatest intensity of love and passion. Katkov was publishing it in the *Russian Messenger;* it was called *The Brothers Karamazov.*

The novel presented the supreme contest between love and hate, between father and son, the flesh and the devil, God and Antichrist, expressing all Dostoevsky's everlasting doubts and his search for God and the terrible question of suffering: *Why does God allow it?* It had the simplest framework. The scene was provincial Russia, the world of Fyodor Pavlovich Karamazov, a small landowner, and his three sons. The old man was disputing with the eldest son, Dmitry, for Grushenka, a prostitute but not an entirely lost creature. There were blows and threats and after some scandalous scenes the father, a buffoon and lecher, was murdered. Dmitry, who had wished for his death, was convicted of the crime on circumstantial evidence, although it was Smerdyakov, the old man's illegitimate son, who had committed the murder.

The whole family, torn between spirituality, subtle mental insight, and moral awareness on one side and animal lust on the other, embodied the struggle between good and evil. Dostoevsky labored with loving care on the portrayal of the three Karamazov brothers. He believed he had caught the essence of the religious spirit with Alyosha, the handsome, fresh-faced youth who had been a novice in a monastery, a figure almost like the Idiot in his moral goodness yet sometimes greatly tempted by the world of the flesh. There was Dmitry, generous and impulsive, who finally rejected the devil and went with God and cried to his accusers when he was sentenced, "Well, gentlemen, I don't blame you. I accept the torture of accusation and my public shame. I want to suffer and by suffering I shall purify myself. I accept my punishment not because I killed him but because I meant to kill him and because I really might have killed him." And Ivan, the rationalist, the denier of God and of God's creation, repudiator of virtue and immortality, who had sought passionately for the meaning of life and come to the conclusion that "all is permitted." He was the real murderer because this "all is permitted" had pushed Smerdyakov to act. There were wonderfully exciting echoes of Mr. Golyadkin of *The Double* in Ivan's conversations with himself!

In the midst of the work Katkov came on a visit. Dostoevsky explained, "The essence of the book, Mikhail Nikiforovich, is the scene between Ivan and Alyosha. Ivan expresses the extreme blasphemy and anarchism, the idea of destruction among the present young generation in Russia that has torn itself away from reality. Father Zosima, the monk, when he is dying later on, refutes all that. Ivan's convictions are a synthesis of Russian anarchism now—the denial not of God but of the meaning of His creation. Socialism, the whole of socialism, sprang up with the denial of the meaning of historical actuality and arrived at a policy of destruction and anarchy. Do you see what I mean? The chief anarchists were sincere men, but they proclaimed revolt because the whole Christian world, its entire social order, had to be remade, all overturned, if necessary by force. It was denial of everything.

"Ivan takes a theme which I think is unassailable: the senselessness of the suffering of children—and he deduces from it the absurdity of the whole historical actuality. He is even willing to believe there is a God; but *he cannot accept God's world*. That's the point! Do you see?

"And listen, Mikhail Nikiforovich, I beg you, tell them not to change the word 'excrement' in that story Ivan tells about the child. It's true! She was five years old and because she didn't ask to be attended to at night the parents smeared her face with her own excrement and filled her mouth with it—and locked her up in the lavatory like that! It's true, it's true! I read it in the newspapers." He was trembling violently.

Katkov said, "Do you think that argument is unassailable?"

"I admit it to you. Yes, I do. Profoundly I do. There was another case—a serf boy on a general's estate threw a stone at the general's favorite dog. The general had him stripped naked, brought out before all the huntsmen, house serfs, dependents, his mother, and made him run, then set the pack of hounds on him. The hounds caught the boy and tore him to pieces." He was pale and shook all over.

"There are plenty of other aspects, Mikhail Nikiforovich, but I've only taken the children. Because if it's harmony, if it's all a question of making everybody suffer to pay for the eternal harmony, I renounce that harmony. I don't want it. No, no! It's not worth the tears of that one tortured child. It's not worth it! What does it matter if the general, if those ignoble parents are punished, if they are sent to the worst hell? If the children's sufferings go to swell the sufferings necessary to pay for the truth, then I *protest!* I PROTEST!

The truth isn't worth such a price. It's too high a price for harmony; it's beyond my means, the means of all of us. And so I give back my entrance ticket. It isn't God I don't accept, it's only that—with the greatest respect—I give Him back the ticket."

"Do you, Fyodor Mikhailovich?" Katkov said. "Or does Ivan Karamazov?"

"Wait a minute, my dear friend. There is another chapter, another confession. I make Ivan stand for the Grand Inquisitor. Christ returns to earth in Seville, at the height of the Inquisition. The crowds recognize Him and greet Him with joy. But the Grand Inquisitor has him thrown into prison and the next day comes to the cell and reproaches Christ with all the errors of his teaching and tells him he will burn him at the stake. He reproaches Christ for rejecting the Devil's temptation to turn stones into bread and thus have men 'run after him like sheep' and in its place offering the freedom to choose between good and evil—exactly the thing they feared and dreaded most. Millions of God's creatures have been created as a mockery and will never be capable of using their freedom, he says.

"He tells Christ that because of this error men will rise up against him and destroy his temple with the cry of 'Feed us first—and ask us to be virtuous afterward.' And if it's only heavenly bread that Christ promised, for which the tens of thousands will follow him, then, the Grand Inquisitor says, what becomes of the millions and thousands of millions who won't have the strength to forgo the earthly bread for the sake of the heavenly?

" 'We,' says the Grand Inquisitor, 'will endure the freedom these weak millions found so dreadful. We will give rest to all.' He reproaches Christ for rejecting the three forces able to conquer and hold the human conscience—miracle, mystery, and authority. By refusing the Devil's other temptation to cast himself down from the height, Christ had forgotten the doubts of weak humanity, its need of the sign of divinity.

" 'We,' says the Grand Inquisitor, 'we have *corrected* thy work. And men have rejoiced that they were again led like sheep. We have so loved mankind that we have lightened its burden—permitted these weak natures to sin. They are weak and helpless and they love us like children because we allow them to sin.'

"In the end, Christ, who has not spoken, kisses the Grand Inquisitor and goes away." Dostoevsky extended his hands urgently. "Listen, listen, Mikhail Nikiforovich, you understand what I am saying. It is there for the nihilists, all that. That's what the complete denier and atheist comes to— bread, the kingdom of socialism, and the overthrow of freedom of conscience. But, you see, my nihilist, Ivan Karamazov, he agrees with the Grand Inquisitor that Christ's teaching has raised man much higher than man actually stands. So the question is, 'Do you despise mankind, you, its coming saviors, or respect it?' And they do all this in the name of love of mankind, as if to say, 'Christ's law is difficult and abstract and intolerable for weak people,' and instead of the law of liberty and enlightenment, they bring the law of chains to mankind and subjection by means of bread."

There was a pause. In a moved voice Katkov said, "Just now, Fyodor Mikhailovich, were you speaking for Ivan Karamazov or yourself?"

Dostoevsky was greatly worked up. "I answer it later. Later. It comes out. It is the great problem of faith."

"Tell me, my friend. Are you for Christ or his Double?"

"What! What did you say?" Dostoevsky was staring at him. "Perhaps there is a balance, I don't know—I don't know, Mikhail Nikiforovich. I want to believe there is. Yes, yes, *I will believe.*"

"Anna," he said one morning in the green-papered breakfast room at Staraya Russa. "Look at this. They want me to go to Moscow for the Pushkin celebrations."

She took the imposing envelope and the sheaf of papers that had just arrived by post and read out: " 'The Moscow City Council, the Slavic Charitable Society, the Society of Friends of Russian Literature.' H'm, I see." She looked up at him anxiously; the writing of Karamazov was exhausting him; his chest was worse and he looked old and worn out. It was as well that the book was nearly finished.

"I shall have to go. They're unveiling a statue to him. Aksakov has been invited, everybody. They want me to speak."

She wished she could go with him; but there were the children, and money was still short. "Of course. It's a great honor. You must go." She kissed him.

The thaw passed. He arrived in Moscow late in May. Katkov, old Ivan Aksakov, and a group of Slavophiles greeted him warmly at the station. "Thank God you've come. Turgenev is here and Kovalevsky—all the Westerners, in strength. They have pretty well the whole university with them. They're out to lower Pushkin, diminish his stature as a Russian, and attack the idea of nationality in that way so as to push their views."

"The old quarrel again?" he said.

"Yes, but you've never spoken in Moscow, my dear Dostoevsky," Aksakov said. "Everybody is waiting for you."

It was true; he was received and feted everywhere. On the second evening he met Turgenev at a banquet. "*Mon cher ami,*" Turgenev said; they bowed and smiled and shook hands as if nothing untoward had ever passed between them.

Then the official proceedings began. There was a religious service at the Strastnoy Monastery, the statue was unveiled, and the writers and delegates laid their wreaths. Next day at the Faculty, Turgenev was elected honorary member of the university and loudly cheered by the students. In the evening the City Council gave a banquet at the Nobles' Club

where there were more toasts and speeches. Dostoevsky and
Turgenev were each called to read a passage from Pushkin.
Dostoevsky chose a scene with the monk Pimene; the
applause was good. Turgenev got up. He read badly.
Dostoevsky watched him. It was a duel between them;
yes, yes, they were still enemies. The whole celebration was
a struggle between the two ideas they stood for. Turgenev's
squeaky voice went on. Dostoevsky thought he noticed some
signs of impatience in the listeners. But the applause was
deafening. "Bravo! Bravo!" the guests kept shouting. Turgenev had a satisfied smile and kept running the third finger
of his hand through his dangling white locks. It was his
victory.

And at last, next day, there was the culminating session
in public in the gilded hall with the double colonnade and
the chandeliers glittering with a thousand crystal drops.
Walking onto the platform with the others, Dostoevsky
caught his breath. The hall was packed. Everything had led
up to this. There were students, *grandes dames*, modestly
dressed women, men in state uniform, more standing at the
sides and at the back. A sort of impatient clatter came from
them. The atmosphere was charged with excitement.

The officials of the Literary Society made brief introductions. Then Turgenev rose, advanced to the center of
the platform, and began to speak. Dostoevsky sat on the
uncomfortable straight chair, his nerves keyed up to an
extraordinary pitch. He couldn't help noticing that Turgenev's voice was sounding mellower. Turgenev was superbly
self-assured. He was an actor—the played-out pause, the
selected gesture, the search for a word. The audience was
attentive and still. Turgenev's phrases were fine, precise,
well turned.

Presently there were one or two coughs. Turgenev was
failing to warm them. Above all he was avoiding a conclusion
about Pushkin. He seemed puzzled, embarrassed, doubtful
whether Pushkin was a great national poet like Shakespeare,

Dante, Racine, was even inclined to despise him. It was chilling. And then with great skill he glided into a eulogy of Nekrasov, "poet of the people," and managed to wind up with applause.

There was a break. Dostoevsky felt very uncertain. He heard his name being spoken by the official in front of the platform, then the clapping. He rose and stood before them, slightly bent forward with his reddish beard, lined, sunken cheeks, and deep eyes, old, subtle, and still full of passion.

When he began to speak he was afraid, awkward, and longed for Turgenev's ease. His voice would not carry and he was sure he was looking at his notes too often. Slowly he felt steadier. He had loved Pushkin all his life and the depth of his feeling gave him its own confidence and he felt he was managing to communicate this love and admiration to the people listening. "The first of all, Pushkin showed us the two Russian types—the wandering man, torn away from the soil, and Tatyana, the Russian ideal of faithfulness and moral duty. Such a beautiful type of Russian woman as Tatyana has scarcely been repeated in our literature except perhaps Lisa in Turgenev's *Nest of Gentlefolk*" Applause; Turgenev blew him a kiss. "Pushkin's gift of universal comprehension is a Russian gift. We should listen to that voice. Pushkin the poet and his great work are the symbols of Russia's destiny." He stopped abruptly at a crash of applause; he was carrying them with him.

He went on. Russia had a world mission to understand and reconcile the rest of Europe. To be truly Russian meant being the brother of all men and humble in the universal service. His voice gained strength and rang through the hall. The audience applauded again and again. The rivalry with Turgenev, the struggle with the Westerners faded, vanished from his mind. He swept the differences away. Westerners and Slavophiles were both the instruments of Russia's future. Russia's true greatness lay in her aptitude for universal service for the sake of universal reconciliation. "To a true

Russian, Europe and the destiny of all are as dear as Russia herself; because our destiny is universality won not by the sword but by the strength of brotherhood and our fraternal aspirations, to reunite mankind. And in course of time I believe we shall, without exception, understand that to be a Russian does mean to aspire finally to reconcile the contradictions of Europe, to show the end of our European yearning in our Russian soul, all-human and all-uniting, to include within our soul by brotherly love all our brethren."

Let them unite themselves with the masses and take a new message of humility and love into the world, the message of the Russian Christ. The Russian people bore God in their midst. In them lay the solution for Europe and the world—and they could bring universal unity in the name of Christ. With meekness and humanity they could create a new golden age when all men would forgive each other and become reconciled and embrace, when they would live amid the joyous creation and worship God.

He had forgotten everything else. He spoke with all the conviction of his soul. "And at last it may be we may by brotherly love pronounce the final word of the great general harmony, of the general brotherly communion of all nations in accordance with the law and the gospel of Christ." As he proclaimed the world-wide unity of mankind, the whole hall full of people stood up in great emotion. They shouted and yelled with enthusiasm. People unknown to each other wept, sobbed, embraced each other. The session broke up. They rushed to the platform, kissed him, and wept. Others who could not get near waved handkerchiefs to him. Two old men struggled up to him and cried, "We have been enemies for twenty years and wouldn't speak to each other, but now you've reconciled us, we have embraced and made up."

Voices in the crowd were shouting out: "You are our saint!"

"Prophet!"

"Our prophet!"

He was surrounded by them all. Turgenev managed to reach him and threw himself into his arms. They embraced with tears in their eyes. Then Annenkov pressed his hand and kissed him. "You are a genius. More than a genius."

Ivan Aksakov made his way to the front of the platform and shouted out for everybody, "It's history! Fyodor Mikhailovich's speech is a historical event. From this time, brotherhood will begin and there will be no more misunderstandings."

"Yes! Yes!" they all shouted and there were more embracings and more tears. Dostoevsky managed to escape into the wings, but they all broke in after him from the hall.

"Thank you. It is a great honor," he said. "Thank you." He looked at them, shaking their outthrust hands. It was triumph.

Seven months after this tremendous scene Fyodor Mikhailovich had a hemorrhage of the lungs and died in Petersburg. For his funeral a throng of thirty thousand people gathered in the streets around his house and, singing chorals, they carried the coffin to the Alexander Nevsky Convent on their shoulders like a living stream.